Chéri

A Dual-Language Book

Colette

Edited and Translated by
STANLEY APPELBAUM

DOVER PUBLICATIONS, INC.
Mineola, New York

Bibliographical Note

This Dover edition, first published in 2001, contains the complete French text of *Chéri*, as originally published by Arthème Fayard, Paris, in 1920, together with a new English translation, a new Introduction, and footnotes in English, all by Stanley Appelbaum.

Library of Congress Cataloging-in-Publication Data

Colette, 1873–1954.
    [Chéri. English & French]
    Chéri : a dual-language book / Colette ; edited and translated by Stanley Appelbaum.
       p. cm.
    ISBN-13: 978-0-486-41599-4 (pbk.)
    ISBN-10: 0-486-41599-6 (pbk.)
    I. Appelbaum, Stanley. II. Title.

PQ2605.O28 C513 2001
843'.912—dc21

                                        00-066041

Manufactured in the United States by LSC Communications
41599608   2019
www.doverpublications.com

Contents

INTRODUCTION

The Author

Sidonie-Gabrielle Colette was born in 1873 in the Burgundian town of Saint-Sauveur (often called Saint-Sauveur-en-Puisaye). She later credited her mother Sido (Sidonie Landoy) with instilling in her a love of nature (especially animals), a nonconformist attitude, and a pagan delight in all sensory pleasures. Her father was Sido's second husband, Captain Jules Colette, who had lost a leg in Napoleon III's Italian campaign of 1859, and had settled in Saint-Sauveur as tax collector. The Captain was a bad manager of money, and—to his daughter's lasting regret—the family home was lost in 1890 (they went to live with the future author's elder half-brother). In the previous year, young Sidonie had completed her only formal education, though she continued to read widely on her own.

Her life changed totally when she married an old friend of the family in 1893. Henry Gauthier-Villars, known as Willy (1859–1931), was the well-to-do son of a major publisher, and a notorious Parisian man-about-town. He had left an illegitimate child in the care of the Colettes, and had come on frequent visits. Sidonie-Gabrielle Colette now became known as Colette Willy. She lived in Paris, where she met her husband's numerous friends in the most advanced literary and musical circles.

Some of these friends were actually wage slaves who ghost-wrote Willy's articles, reviews, and trashy novels. When he discovered his young wife's literary talents, he made her another one of his slaves, publishing her half-dozen earliest novels under his own name, though he had merely touched them up. The first of these, *Claudine à l'école* (Claudine at School), was written between 1894 and 1896, but not published until 1900, when it was an immediate success. Largely autobiographical, like practically everything Colette wrote, it was heavily influenced by Willy's commercially minded prurience, and emphasized Claudine's crush on a pretty woman teacher. Three more

Claudine books, published in 1901, 1902, and 1903, chronicled the heroine's marriage and new life in Paris society. Defenders of Colette blame Willy for the flippancy of these books, and for their occasional lapses into antisemitism and homophobia (directed against men). It was not until 1904 that a different, more personal book of Colette's appeared, the *Dialogues de bêtes* (Dialogues of Animals), the first published under the name of Colette Willy.

Meanwhile, the marriage had proved very unhappy for Colette. Her husband was not only a taskmaster, but also a flagrant womanizer. There was a formal separation in 1907, followed by a divorce in 1910. But Colette had gone her own way even earlier. In 1906, after some lessons, she went on the stage, chiefly in pantomime (in later years, she also acted in revues and in straight plays). It was also in 1906 that she fell under the spell of the divorced Marquise de Belbeuf, known as Missy, and entered a lesbian relationship that lasted until 1911. In 1910, she published the novel *L'ingénue libertine* (The Gentle Libertine), a recasting of her last two Willy-inspired works, and she serialized her first outstanding novel, *La vagabonde* (The Vagabond; book publication, 1911). In this underrated novel, she paints a vivid picture of the backstage life of a touring performer of modest means, and weighs all the pros and cons of married comfort versus an independent existence as a woman.

It was also in 1910 that she began her career in journalism, joining the literary staff of the major newspaper *Le matin* (The Morning), for which she wrote countless reportages and stories until 1923. In 1912 she married her editor-in-chief, Henry de Jouvenel (1876–1935), who was later to become an eminent politician and diplomat. This second marriage made the country girl a baroness. In the same year, her mother died. In 1913, the forty-year-old author gave birth to her only child, Colette de Jouvenel. That same year, she published *L'entrave* (The Shackle), a weak sequel to *La vagabonde*, and *L'envers du music-hall* (Music-Hall Sidelights).

There were no publications of novels during the war years. Colette's formal connection with the cinematic world began in 1915, when she worked for the magazine *Le film*. In 1919, when she became head of the literary staff at *Le matin*, she published a novel she had begun in 1917, *Mitsou; ou Comment l'esprit vient aux filles* (Mitsou; or How Girls Grow Wise). In 1920, the year of *Chéri* (see separate section below), she became a member of the Légion d'honneur (successive promotions were to follow in 1928, 1936, and 1953), and she commenced her liaison with her sixteen-year-old stepson Bertrand de

Jouvenel (this romance apparently didn't inspire *Chéri*, but was inspired by the book).

In 1922 and 1923 Colette did more stage work. Her second marriage was going badly, too. Her notable novel *Le blé en herbe* (The Ripening Seed),[1] serialized in 1922 and published in book form in 1923, was the first one signed simply "Colette." The author was separated from Henry de Jouvenel in 1923 and divorced him in 1925, the year in which she met the man who was to become her third husband. Maurice Goudeket, her junior by sixteen years, a salesman who later entered journalism, never stole any of her limelight, and proved to be devoted after they married in 1935 (he survived her). Another event of 1925 was the creation in Monte Carlo of Maurice Ravel's one-act opera *L'enfant et les sortilèges* (The Child and the Magic Spells), to a libretto Colette had written years earlier.

The later 1920s and the 1930s were years of glory for Colette. She was her own mistress, and she had "arrived" as a writer. She published novels and books of personal reminiscences; she wrote reviews of plays (from 1929 on); she traveled as a lecturer; she opened a cosmetics shop in Paris (briefly, in 1932); she wrote film scripts (particularly the charming *Lac aux dames*, directed by Marc Allégret, which premiered in 1934); she was on the maiden voyage of the *Normandie* in 1935; she was elected to the Belgian Royal Academy of French Language and Literature in 1936.

A major personal setback was the onset of arthritis in 1936, perhaps the result of a broken leg in 1931. By the early 1940s, one hip was severely affected, and she was increasingly immobilized for the rest of her life, largely confined to her apartment in the Palais-Royal. The Second World War impinged on her life: her husband, a Jew, was arrested in 1941, but released the following year. Her last work of fiction, the story *Gigi* (a return to the Belle Epoque courtesan world of *Chéri*), appeared in 1944, when she was seventy-one. Thanks to its stage and film versions, it is now probably her best-known work. (She was personally instrumental in choosing the unknown Audrey Hepburn for the title role of the 1951 Broadway adaptation.) In 1945, Colette was elected to the Académie Goncourt, an extremely prestigious literary society; she became its president in 1949, the year in

---

1. This English version of the title fails to convey the connotation of the French, which refers to a proverbial saying warning against eating one's grain stalks while they are still green ("in grass").

which her last reminiscences were published (not counting posthumous works).

In 1953 Colette was honored by Americans, receiving an award from the National Institute of Arts and Letters. When she died in 1954, she was the first woman ever to be buried in France with national honors. The funeral did not include a religious service, because she had always remained aloof from religion, and had been twice divorced.

All these honors indicate the injustice of the remark occasionally made that Colette's reputation is owed chiefly to the efforts of feminists and lesbian activists in recent decades. Not that their publicity hasn't helped, or that it has been misplaced. Colette stood for the emancipation of women, for the recognition and glorification of their specific sexuality. In her books, men are the weaker sex, more prone than women to commit suicide over disappointments in love. Irreligious, unmystical, attuned to nature, in her last years she saw herself, and others saw her, as a sort of earth mother, an archetype of femininity.

The Novel

Chéri, possibly Colette's best-known novel, is often regarded as her best, as well. A character named Chéri apparently figured in several stories she contributed to *Le matin* in 1911 and 1912. According to one report, she first conceived of the plot as we know it in 1912, but in the form of a play. She began writing the definitive novel form in 1919, and *Chéri* was originally published serially in the weekly *La vie parisienne* between the issues of January 3 and June 5, 1920; it was published in volume form shortly afterward by Arthème Fayard, Paris. As early as 1921 a stage version, by Colette and Léopold Marchand, was performed in Paris; Colette played the part of Léa at the hundredth performance, in 1922, and went on tour with the play the following year. A new Paris production was mounted in 1925, and again in 1949. A French film version was released in 1950.

In fact, as far as action and incidents go, the novel *Chéri* has no more material than would fill a short story. The book, whether first conceived as a play or not, certainly resembles one. It has lots of dialogue, not many characters, and a minimum of principal "sets," especially Léa's bedroom and Charlotte's garden room; the other locales are reminiscent of the exteriors with which a screenplay writer "opens

up" the movie version of a stage work. And the entire last chapter is one big "noble renunciation" scene that barely needs further adaptation for the footlights.

The time of the plot is 1912 and 1913, the tail end of the frivolous, frothy Belle Epoque—frivolous for those with plenty of money, like Léa, her fellow ex-courtesans, and their offspring. There is never a word about social or political problems, or the impending war that was to bring such drastic changes. Even the drug and lesbian subculture that is fleetingly introduced isn't meant as a salutary warning but just a slice of life, because Colette herself participated in it fully.[2]

All the Parisian neighborhoods and streets (and all or most of the commercial establishments) mentioned in the novel are real, and appropriate. Léa lives in Passy (the sixteenth arrondissement), more particularly in the neighborhood now called the Quartier Dauphine. (Passy is Paris's largest stretch of upmarket housing.) The eastern end of the Avenue Bugeaud is the Place Victor-Hugo; the western end is the Porte Dauphine, one of the entrances to the fashionable park known as the Bois (de Boulogne), a stylish site for coaching meets, horseback riding, carriage drives, and elegant dining. Charlotte lives on the Boulevard d'Inkermann in Neuilly (-sur-Seine); Neuilly is technically a suburb, but for all practical purposes it is a well-to-do residential part of Paris just north of the Bois. When Léa visits Charlotte, she rides through the Bois, emerging through one of the former tollhouse gates (perhaps the Porte des Sablons, which is the closest to the Boulevard d'Inkermann). When Chéri builds a new house, it is on the Avenue Henri-Martin, in the more southerly part of Passy now called Passy-La Muette; this house is still unfinished, and he and his wife are still living with his mother, when the novel ends, so that Léa indicates Neuilly when referring to his wife Edmée in the last chapter.

The Blue Dragon Restaurant, where Chéri and Desmond dine on the night that Chéri begins to "play hookey" from his wife, may possibly be a disguised name; at any rate, the nature of its clientele would preclude its being listed in a tourist guide of the time, where it might be traced today. It is located, in the novel, on or near the Rue Caumartin, in the vicinity of a cluster of Boulevard theaters (ninth arrondissement). Weber's, where the friends meet shortly after leaving the Blue Dragon, was a popular "English tavern" (a haunt of artists

---

2. The self-characterization of Chéri and Edmée as "orphans" may be an anachronism, because a fashionable feeling of *orphelinisme* was a postwar phenomenon in Paris.

and writers) not far away, on the Rue Royale, which connects the church of the Madeleine with the Place de la Concorde. From there it's just a short walk to the Rue de Rivoli, site of Desmond's hotel, the "Morris." This name is almost surely a thin disguise for the venerable Meurice, opposite the Tuileries Gardens, where Colette had stayed for several weeks after breaking up with Missy in 1911; the Meurice was to gain new notoriety during the Second World War as top Nazi headquarters in occupied Paris. Visiting Patron's gym was really a harrowing expedition for Léa: besides smelling sweat, she had to journey to the Place d'Italie in the distant thirteenth arrondissement, in a neighborhood of hospitals and technical schools. The Lewis that Léa plans to visit when she returns from her trip to the south was probably the milliner of that name located on the Rue Royale (like Weber's). The restaurant where she can't picture herself having lunch with Chéri (last chapter) is the Pavillon d'Armenonville (or just Armenonville), located in the Bois; it was popular with the horsy set at lunchtime, and very swank at dinnertime. The jeweler Schwabe, where Léa intends to buy a wedding present for Chéri, proved impossible to locate in a Cook's guide, a Baedeker, and two shopping directories of the period.

The characterizations in the novel depend largely on a repetition of the people's tics. Charlotte constantly repeats words and flaps her arms. The Baroness de la Berche is always wishing people well—out loud, only. Léa is always scolding Chéri like a child, and Chéri is always trying to save money in cheese-paring ways. But for Léa, Chéri, and Edmée the author provides a myriad of reflections, interior monologues, and descriptions of gestures which flesh out the characters and the book, turning it into the traditional French conception of a *roman psychologique*. As elsewhere, Colette introduces some improbabilities:[3] as different in nature, intelligence, and background as her characters are supposed to be, nearly each one is a past master at bitchy repartee, as if Charlotte Peloux's Sunday open house were the Algonquin Round Table! And even Edmée, the eighteen-year-old ingenue, is allowed to indulge in a complex literary metaphor.

The plot of *Chéri* is not particularly original; for instance, the subject of a young man deserting his older mistress is the chief element of *Adolphe*, the 1816 masterpiece by Benjamin Constant. It is with

---

3. A flagrant instance occurs at the very end of the novel *Mitsou*, when Mitsou, a naïve and uneducated performer in a cheap theater, writes a letter so worldly-wise and eloquent that it could have been signed by Simone de Beauvoir!

her distinctive style, made up of swift, sure, almost impressionistic touches and skillful use of leitmotifs, that Colette creates her own atmosphere and her own emotional universe.

The opening chapter of *Chéri* is outstanding in this regard. Through dialogue, gesture, and brief description—without any consecutive "history"—we are made aware of the year and of the two main characters' social standing and wealth, individual natures, and relationship to each other; and we are introduced to the main "set" of the "play": Léa's bedroom, to which we'll return again and again. Léa's constant reprimands reveal her as a "perverted mother," and Chéri's "ugly laugh" warns us about nasty undertones in his character. We first see Chéri in silhouette, as a cavorting devil (later we are repeatedly told about his devilishly sloping eyebrows); much later, when he leaves home and returns to Léa, he is a dark silhouette against her bedroom door. In the opening chapter, Léa helps Chéri get dressed; in the closing chapter, he refuses her aid (in both instances, his tie has been wrapped around a bust of Léa). The pearl necklace mentioned in the opening dialogue becomes a major motif, a symbol of Léa (explaining her past life, and indicating her own solidity as well as Chéri's childishness and vanity); later we learn that Chéri had fingered that necklace when they became lovers; we will find him comparing it to the necklaces worn by Edmée and by "Pal." Finally, the opening chapter warns Léa about Chéri's marriage, preparing the entire plot of the novel.

(Another example of a recurring leitmotif is Chéri as a hunting hound. He sighs like one when he sleeps, when he laughs, he's like a hound about to bite; and Edmée is flung to him, like a doe flung to a hound.)

The language and style of *Chéri* are a personal mixture of idioms and slang with classically correct, and even hyper-correct, fine writing (*préciosité*). Colette indulges extensively in a couple of grammatical tics: (1) connecting two words with a comma instead of *et* ("and"); and (2) using *et* instead of *mais* ("but") where the meaning is clearly adversative. She also overemploys certain favorite words, particularly the adjective *sec*, which is put to a bewildering number of uses.

Fond of sequels (*Claudine à l'école* had four, including *La retraite sentimentale*; the novel *L'entrave* was a poor sequel to *La vagabonde*), Colette belatedly supplied one to *Chéri*, as well, in 1926: *La fin de Chéri* (The Last of Chéri; begun as early as 1923, when Colette was gloomy over the failure of her second marriage). This austere, acerb, grim, humorless book (as different from *Chéri* as possible) takes place

after the First World War. Edmée has become completely emanci-
pated, thanks to wartime conditions, and Chéri's marriage is totally
meaningless. He seeks out Léa again, but she is now beyond caring,
and almost beyond everything (at sixty, or less!). With nothing left to
live for, he kills himself.

Some critics find that this ending reveals the depths of character
that were only latent in the title character of *Chéri*. Others find that
his suicide is ludicrous, both in the general circumstances and vis-à-
vis his particular self-loving nature. Certainly, the sequel reads as if
Colette had unwisely identified herself much too closely with the Léa
of *Chéri*, and was taking personal revenge on her poor character for
having deserted her some years earlier.

Chéri

"Léa! Donne-le-moi, ton collier de perles! Tu m'entends, Léa? Donne-moi ton collier!"

Aucune réponse ne vint du grand lit de fer forgé et de cuivre ciselé, qui brillait dans l'ombre comme une armure.

"Pourquoi ne me le donnerais-tu pas, ton collier? Il me va aussi bien qu'à toi, et même mieux!"

Au claquement du fermoir, les dentelles du lit s'agitèrent, deux bras nus, magnifiques, fins au poignet, élevèrent deux belles mains paresseuses.

"Laisse ça, Chéri, tu as assez joué avec ce collier.

— Je m'amuse. . . . Tu as peur que je te le vole?"

Devant les rideaux roses traversés de soleil, il dansait, tout noir, comme un gracieux diable sur fond de fournaise. Mais quand il recula vers le lit, il redevint tout blanc, du pyjama de soie aux babouches de daim.

"Je n'ai pas peur, répondit du lit la voix douce et basse. Mais tu fatigues le fil du collier. Les perles sont lourdes.

— Elles le sont, dit Chéri avec considération. Il ne s'est pas moqué de toi, celui qui t'a donné ce meuble."

Il se tenait devant un miroir long, appliqué au mur entre les deux fenêtres, et contemplait son image de très beau et très jeune homme, ni grand ni petit, le cheveu bleuté comme un plumage de merle. Il ouvrit son vêtement de nuit sur une poitrine mate et dure, bombée en bouclier, et la même étincelle rose joua sur ses dents, sur le blanc de ses yeux sombres et sur les perles du collier.

"Ote ce collier, insista la voix féminine. Tu entends ce que je te dis?"

Immobile devant son image, le jeune homme riait tout bas:

"Oui, oui, j'entends. Je sais si bien que tu as peur que je te le prenne!

— Non. Mais si je te le donnais, tu serais capable de l'accepter."

Il courut au lit, s'y jeta en boule:

2

"LÉA! Let me have this pearl necklace of yours! Are you listening, Léa? Let me have your necklace!"

No reply came from the large wrought-iron and chased-copper bed, which was gleaming in the shadows like a suit of armor.

"Why won't you let me have your necklace? It looks as good on me as it does on you, if not more so!"

When the clasp clicked, the lace on the bed stirred, and two splendid bare arms with delicate wrists extended two beautiful, slothful hands.

"Stop it, Chéri. You've played with that necklace long enough."

"I'm having fun . . . Afraid I'll steal it from you?"

In front of the sun-drenched pink curtains his dark silhouette was dancing, like a graceful devil with a furnace behind him. But when he stepped backwards toward the bed, he became all white again, from his silk pajamas to his buckskin Turkish slippers.

"I'm not afraid," replied the gentle, deep voice from the bed. "But you're wearing out the string of the necklace. The pearls are heavy."

"They are," said Chéri with respect. "The man who gave you this article sure didn't fool you."

He was standing in front of a long mirror that was attached to the wall between the two windows, and he was observing his image, that of a very handsome, very young man, not too tall and not too short, with hair of a blue sheen like a blackbird's plumage. He opened his pajama shirt to reveal a firm, mat chest as convex as a buckler, and one and the same rosy spark played on his teeth, the whites of his dark eyes, and the pearls of the necklace.

"Take off that necklace," the woman's voice insisted. "Do you hear what I'm saying to you?"

Motionless before his image, the young man said very quietly, with a laugh:

"Yes, yes, I hear. How well I know you're afraid I'll take it away from you!"

"No. But if I made you a present of it, you'd be capable of accepting it."

He ran to the bed, leaped onto it, and curled up:

3

"Et comment! Je suis au-dessus des conventions, moi. Moi je trouve idiot qu'un homme puisse accepter d'une femme une perle en épingle, ou deux pour des boutons, et se croie déshonoré si elle lui en donne cinquante. . . .

— Quarante-neuf.

— Quarante-neuf, je connais le chiffre. Dis-le donc que ça me va mal? Dis-le donc que je suis laid?"

Il penchait sur la femme couchée un rire provocant qui montrait des dents toutes petites et l'envers mouillé de ses lèvres. Léa s'assit sur le lit:

"Non, je ne le dirai pas. D'abord parce que tu ne le croirais pas. Mais tu ne peux donc pas rire sans froncer ton nez comme ça? Tu seras bien content quand tu auras trois rides dans le coin du nez, n'est-ce pas?"

Il cessa de rire immédiatement, tendit la peau de son front, ravala le dessous de son menton avec une habileté de vieille coquette. Ils se regardaient d'un air hostile; elle, accoudée parmi ses lingeries et ses dentelles, lui, assis en amazone au bord du lit. Il pensait: "Ça lui va bien de me parler des rides que j'aurai." Et elle: "Pourquoi est-il laid quand il rit, lui qui est la beauté même?" Elle réfléchit un instant et acheva tout haut sa pensée:

"C'est que tu as l'air si mauvais quand tu es gai. . . . Tu ne ris que par méchanceté ou par moquerie. Ça te rend laid. Tu es souvent laid.

— Ce n'est pas vrai!" cria Chéri, irrité.

La colère nouait ses sourcils à la racine du nez, agrandissait les yeux pleins d'une lumière insolente, armés de cils, entrouvrait l'arc dédaigneux et chaste de la bouche. Léa sourit de le voir tel qu'elle l'aimait révolté puis soumis, mal enchaîné, incapable d'être libre; — elle posa une main sur la jeune tête qui secoua impatiemment le joug. Elle murmura, comme on calme une bête:

"Là . . . là. . . . Qu'est-ce que c'est . . . qu'est-ce que c'est donc. . . ."

Il s'abattit sur la belle épaule large, poussant du front, du nez, creusant sa place familière, fermant déjà les yeux et cherchant son somme protégé des longs matins, mais Léa le repoussa:

"Pas de ça, Chéri! Tu déjeunes chez notre Harpie nationale et il est midi moins vingt.

— Non? je déjeune chez la patronne? Toi aussi?"

Léa glissa paresseusement au fond du lit.

"Pas moi, j'ai vacances. J'irai prendre le café à deux heures et demie

"I'll say I would! I'm above petty conventions. I find it ridiculous that a man can accept one pearl from a woman on a tie pin, or two on cuff-links, but has to consider himself dishonored if she gives him fifty . . ."

"Forty-nine."

"Forty-nine, I know the number. But just tell me it doesn't look good on me. Just tell me that I'm ugly!"

He leaned over the recumbent woman with a provoking laugh that showed his very small teeth and the moist inside of his lips. Léa sat up in bed:

"No, I won't say that. First of all, because you wouldn't believe it. But can't you laugh without wrinkling up your nose like that? You'll be very happy when you have three creases at the corners of your nose, won't you?"

Immediately he stopped laughing, smoothed out the skin on his forehead, and tucked in his chin with the skill of an old coquette. They looked at each other with an air of hostility, she propped up on one elbow amid her night clothes and lace, he seated on the edge of the bed in a sidesaddle position. He was thinking: "She's one to talk about the wrinkles I'll get!" And she: "Why is he, the epitome of beauty, so ugly when he laughs?" She reflected for a moment and pronounced her conclusion out loud:

"It's because you look so vicious when you're cheerful . . . You only laugh out of malice or sarcasm. That makes you ugly. You're often ugly."

"That's not so!" Chéri shouted in his irritation.

Whenever he was angry, his eyebrows got pinned to the springing of his nose, his heavily lashed eyes, filled with an insolent light, grew large, and the scornful, chaste bow of his lips opened slightly. Léa smiled to see him the way she loved him, first rebellious, then sub-missive, chained only loosely but incapable of being free. She laid one hand on the youthful head that impatiently tried to shake off its yoke. She murmured, like someone calming an animal:

"There, there . . . What's wrong? What's wrong, now? . . ."

He plunged at her beautiful broad shoulder, digging into it with his forehead and his nose, burrowing out his customary place there, al-ready shutting his eyes and seeking his sheltered late-morning sleep, but Léa repulsed him:

"None of that, Chéri! You're having lunch with our national harpy, and it's twenty minutes to noon."

"No? I'm lunching at the boss-lady's place? You, too?"

Léa slid lazily all the way back in bed.

"Not me, I'm on vacation. I'll go there for coffee at two-thirty, or tea

— ou le thé à six heures — ou une cigarette à huit heures moins le quart. . . . Ne t'inquiète pas, elle me verra toujours assez. . . . Et puis, elle ne m'a pas invitée."

Chéri, qui boudait debout, s'illumina de malice:

"Je sais, je sais pourquoi! Nous avons du monde bien! Nous avons la belle Marie-Laure et sa poison d'enfant!"

Les grands yeux bleus de Léa, qui erraient, se fixèrent:

"Ah! oui! Charmante, la petite. Moins que sa mère, mais charmante. . . . Ote donc ce collier, à la fin.

— Dommage, soupira Chéri en le dégrafant. Il ferait bien dans la corbeille."

Léa se souleva sur un coude:

"Quelle corbeille?

— La mienne, dit Chéri avec une importance bouffonne. MA corbeille de MES bijoux de MON mariage. . . ."

Il bondit, retomba sur ses pieds après un correct entrechat-six, enfonça la portière d'un coup de tête et disparut en criant:

"Mon bain, Rose! Tant que ça peut! Je déjeune chez la patronne!

— C'est ça, songea Léa. Un lac dans la salle de bain, huit serviettes à la nage, et des raclures de rasoir dans la cuvette. Si j'avais deux salles de bains. . . ."

Mais elle s'avisa, comme les autres fois, qu'il eût fallu supprimer une penderie, rogner sur le boudoir à coiffer, et conclut comme les autres fois:

"Je patienterai bien jusqu'au mariage de Chéri."

Elle se recoucha sur le dos et constata que Chéri avait jeté, la veille, ses chaussettes sur la cheminée, son petit caleçon sur le bonheur-du-jour, sa cravate au cou d'un buste de Léa. Elle sourit malgré elle à ce chaud désordre masculin et referma à demi ses grands yeux tranquilles d'un bleu jeune et qui avaient gardé tous leurs cils châtains. A quarante-neuf ans, Léonie Vallon, dite Léa de Lonval, finissait une carrière heureuse de courtisane bien rentée, et de bonne fille à qui la vie a épargné les catastrophes flatteuses et les nobles chagrins. Elle cachait la date de sa naissance; mais elle avouait volontiers, en laissant tomber sur Chéri un regard de condescendance voluptueuse, qu'elle atteignait l'âge de s'accorder quelques petites douceurs. Elle aimait l'ordre, le beau linge, les vins mûris, la cuisine réfléchie. Sa jeunesse de blonde adulée, puis sa maturité de demi-mondaine riche n'avaient accepté ni l'éclat fâcheux, ni l'équivoque, et ses amis se souvenaient

at six, or a cigarette at seven forty-five . . . Don't worry, she'll get to see enough of me . . . Besides, she didn't invite me."

Chéri, on his feet and sulking, lit up with mischievousness:

"I know, I know why! There's going to be a select society! The lovely Marie-Laure and her pesky brat are going to be there!"

Léa's big blue eyes, which had been wandering, came to a halt:

"Yes! Yes! A charming little creature. Not as much so as her mother, but charming . . . Now take off that necklace, won't you?"

"Too bad," Chéri sighed as he undid the clasp. "It would look good among the wedding presents."

Léa raised herself up on one elbow:

"What wedding presents?"

"Mine," said Chéri with comical smugness. "MY jewelry, which will be MY presents for MY wedding . . ."

He leaped into the air, landed on his feet again after a correct entrechat-six, butted the door curtains open with his head, and vanished, shouting:

"My bath, Rose! A nice big one! I'm lunching with the boss-lady!"

"There he goes," thought Léa. "A lake in the bathroom with eight towels floating in it, and whisker shavings in the washstand. If I only had two bathrooms . . ."

But, like every other time, she recalled that it would mean eliminating one clothes closet and making her dressing room smaller; and, like every other time, she concluded:

"I'll just have to be patient till Chéri gets married."

She lay down on her back again and observed that, the night before, Chéri had thrown his socks onto the mantelpiece and his drawers onto the escritoire, and had tied his cravat around the neck of a bust of Léa. She smiled despite herself at that hot masculine disorderliness, and once again half-closed her large, calm eyes, which were of a youthful blue and had retained all their chestnut-brown lashes. At forty-nine Léonie Vallon, known as Léa de Lonval, was at the end of a successful career as a well-to-do courtesan, a good-natured woman whom life had spared its flattering catastrophes and its noble sorrows. She concealed the date of her birth, but she freely confessed, whenever she glanced at Chéri with condescending amorousness, that she was reaching the age when she could indulge herself in various small ways. She was fond of orderliness, fine linens, mature wines, and skillful cooking. When a young, highly praised blond, and later as a wealthy, older demi-mondaine, she had never allowed either vexatious notoriety or any ambiguity about her status; and her friends still recalled one

d'une journée de Drags, vers 1895, où Léa répondit au secrétaire
du *Gil Blas* qui la traitait de "chère artiste":

"Artiste? Oh! vraiment, cher ami, mes amants sont bien
bavards. . . ."

Ses contemporaines jalousaient sa santé imperturbable, les jeunes
femmes, que la mode de 1912 bombait déjà du dos et du ventre, rail-
laient le poitrail avantageux de Léa, — celles-ci et celles-là lui envi-
aient également Chéri.

"Eh, mon Dieu! disait Léa, il n'y a pas de quoi. Qu'elles le pren-
nent. Je ne l'attache pas, et il sort tout seul."

En quoi elle mentait à demi, orgueilleuse d'une liaison, — elle disait quelquefois: adoption, par penchant à la sincérité — qui durait
depuis six ans.

"La corbeille . . . redit Léa. Marier Chéri. . . . Ce n'est pas possible, — ce n'est pas . . . humain. . . . Donner une jeune fille à Chéri, —
pourquoi pas jeter une biche aux chiens? Les gens ne savent pas ce
que c'est que Chéri."

Elle roulait entre ses doigts, comme un rosaire, son collier jeté sur
le lit. Elle le quittait la nuit, à présent, car Chéri, amoureux des belles
perles et qui les caressait le matin, eût remarqué trop souvent que le
cou de Léa, épaissi, perdait sa blancheur et montrait, sous la peau, des
muscles détendus. Elle l'agrafa sur sa nuque sans se lever et prit un
miroir sur la console de chevet.

"J'ai l'air d'une jardinière, jugea-t-elle sans ménagement. Une
maraîchère. Une maraîchère normande qui s'en irait aux champs de
patates avec un collier. Cela me va comme une plume d'autruche dans
le nez, — et je suis polie."

Elle haussa les épaules, sévère à tout ce qu'elle n'aimait plus en
elle: un teint vif, sain, un peu rouge, un teint de plein air, propre à en-
richir la franche couleur des prunelles bleues cerclées de bleu plus
sombre. Le nez fier trouvait grâce encore devant Léa; "le nez de
Marie-Antoinette!" affirmait la mère de Chéri, qui n'oubliait jamais
d'ajouter: ". . . et dans deux ans, cette bonne Léa aura le menton de
Louis XVI". La bouche aux dents serrées, qui n'éclatait presque jamais de rire, souriait souvent, d'accord avec les grands yeux aux clins
lents et rares, sourire cents fois loué, chanté, photographié, sourire
profond et confiant qui ne pouvait lasser.

Pour le corps, "on sait bien," disait Léa, "qu'un corps de bonne
qualité dure longtemps." Elle pouvait le montrer encore, ce grand

coaching-meet day around 1895 on which Léa had replied to the assistant editor of *Gil Blas*,[1] who was calling her "my dear artist":

"Artist? Oh, really, my friend, my lovers are such chatterboxes . . ."

Her peers were envious of her unshakable good health, while younger women, whose backs and stomachs were already being puffed out by the 1912 fashions, used to laugh at Léa's ample bosom—both groups joined in envying her for Chéri.

"Oh, Lord," Léa would say, "there's no reason to. Let them take him. I don't keep him tied up, and he goes out on his own."

In saying this she was half-lying, because she prided herself in that liaison (or adoption, as she sometimes called it, in her liking for sincerity), which had lasted six years now.

"The wedding presents . . ." Léa repeated. "To marry off Chéri . . . It's impossible . . . it's hardly human . . . To hand over a girl to Chéri— why not fling a doe to the hounds? People don't know what Chéri is really like."

She was fingering her necklace, which had been tossed onto the bed, as if it were a rosary. She took it off at night nowadays because Chéri, who loved beautiful pearls and caressed them in the morning, would have noticed too frequently that Léa's throat had thickened, was losing its whiteness, and was revealing flaccid muscles beneath its skin. She closed the clasp behind her neck without getting up, and picked up a mirror from the night table.

"I look like a woman gardener," she judged without sparing herself. "A market gardener. A market gardener from Normandy off to the potato fields wearing a necklace. It suits me the way an ostrich feather would, stuck in my . . . nose—to be polite!"

She shrugged her shoulders, a harsh judge of whatever she no longer liked about herself: her lively, healthy complexion, a little red, an outdoors complexion that tended to enrich the hearty color of her blue irises, circled with a darker blue. Her proud nose still pleased Léa, "Marie Antoinette's nose," Chéri's mother used to declare, never forgetting to add: "And in two years, good old Léa will have Louis XVI's chin." Her mouth, with its closely spaced teeth, almost never burst into laughter, but it often smiled, in harmony with her large eyes, which blinked slowly and seldom. Her smile, praised, immortalized in verse, and photographed a hundred times, was a deep, trusting smile that people couldn't tire of.

As for her body, "Everyone knows," Léa used to say, "that a body of good quality lasts a long time." She could still show that big white

---

1. One of the most popular Parisian magazines of the Belle Epoque.

corps blanc teinté de rose, doté des longues jambes, du dos plat qu'on voit aux nymphes des fontaines d'Italie; la fesse à fossette, le sein haut suspendu pouvaient tenir, disait Léa, "jusque bien après le mariage de Chéri".

Elle se leva, s'enveloppa d'un saut-de-lit et ouvrit elle-même les rideaux. Le soleil de midi entra dans la chambre rose, gaie, trop parée et d'un luxe qui datait, dentelles doubles aux fenêtres, faille feuille-de-rose aux murs, bois dorés, lumières électriques voilées de rose et de blanc, et meubles anciens tendus de soies modernes. Léa ne renonçait pas à cette chambre douillette ni à son lit, chef-d'œuvre considérable, indestructible, de cuivre, d'acier forgé, sévère à l'œil et cruel aux tibias.

"Mais non, mais non, protestait la mère de Chéri, ce n'est pas si laid que cela. Je l'aime, moi, cette chambre. C'est une époque, ça a son chic. Ça fait Païva."

Léa souriait à ce souvenir de la "Harpie nationale" tout en relevant ses cheveux épars. Elle se poudra hâtivement le visage en entendant deux portes claquer et le choc d'un pied chaussé contre un meuble délicat. Chéri revenait en pantalon et chemise, sans faux col, les oreilles blanches de talc et l'humeur agressive.

"Où est mon épingle? boîte de malheur! On barbote les bijoux à présent?

— C'est Marcel qui l'a mise à sa cravate pour aller faire le marché", dit Léa gravement.

Chéri, dénué d'humour, butait sur la plaisanterie comme une fourmi sur un morceau de charbon. Il arrêta sa promenade menaçante et ne trouva à répondre que:

"C'est charmant! . . . et mes bottines?

— Lesquelles?

— De daim!"

Léa, assise à sa coiffeuse, leva des yeux trop doux:

"Je ne te le fais pas dire, insinua-t-elle d'une voix caressante.

— Le jour où une femme m'aimera pour mon intelligence, je serai bien fichu, riposta Chéri. En attendant, je veux mon épingle et mes bottines.

body, with its rosy tint, endowed with long legs and the flat back seen on the nymphs of Italian fountains; the dimpled buttocks and the firm, high breasts could last, as Léa would say, "till long after Chéri gets married."

She got up, wrapped a dressing gown around her, and opened the curtains herself. The noonday sun entered the room: a cheerful, pink room, over-ornamented with a luxury no longer up-to-date, double lace curtains on the windows, rose-petal faille covering the walls, gilded woodwork, electric lights with pink and white shades, and antique furniture upholstered in modern silks. Léa refused to give up that cozy bedroom or her bed, a substantial, indestructible masterpiece of copper and wrought iron, harsh to the eyes and wicked on the shins.

"No, no," Chéri's mother used to protest, "it's not as ugly as all that. I like that room. It's an era in itself, it's got its own class. It's like the days of Païva."[2]

Léa was smiling as she recalled that saying of the "national harpy" while she gathered up her disheveled hair. She hastily powdered her face when she heard the slamming of two doors and the thud of a shod foot against a delicate piece of furniture. Chéri was returning, wearing shirt and trousers, but without his detachable collar. His ears were white with talcum powder, and his mood was aggressive.

"Where's my tie pin? Damn this dump! Are you pinching jewelry here now?"

"Marcel stuck it in his tie when he went out for groceries," Léa said seriously.

Chéri, who had no sense of humor, was stopped short by this joke like an ant coming across a lump of coal. He ceased his threatening pacing and could only reply:

"Lovely! And my boots?"

"Which ones?"

"The buck!"[3]

Léa, seated at her vanity table, raised her eyes, which were intentionally too gentle:

"It wasn't me who said it," she said insinuatingly in a caressing tone.

"The day when a woman loves me for my intelligence will be the end of me," was Chéri's comeback. "Meanwhile, I want my tie pin and my boots."

---

2. The highly successful Russian-born adventuress Thérèse Lachman, Marquise de Païva (1819–1884), set trends in fashion and in interior decoration in the Paris of the Second Empire. 3. He means buckskin, but it could be taken as: "the ones a buck (dandy) would wear."

— Pourquoi faire? On ne met pas d'épingle avec un veston, et tu es déjà chaussé."

Chéri frappa du pied.

"J'en ai assez, personne ne s'occupe de moi, ici! J'en ai assez!"

Léa posa son peigne.

"Eh bien! va-t'en."

Il haussa les épaules, grossier:

"On dit ça!

— Va-t'en. J'ai toujours eu horreur des invités qui bêchent la cuisine et qui collent le fromage à la crème contre les glaces. Va chez ta sainte mère, mon enfant, et restes-y."

Il ne soutint pas le regard le Léa, baissa les yeux, protesta en écolier:

"Enfin, quoi, je ne peux rien dire? Au moins, tu me prêtes l'auto pour aller à Neuilly?

— Non.

— Parce que?

— Parce que je sors à deux heures et que Philibert déjeune.

— Où vas-tu, à deux heures?

— Remplir mes devoirs religieux. Mais si tu veux trois francs pour un taxi? . . . Imbécile, reprit-elle doucement, je vais peut-être prendre le café chez Madame Mère, à deux heures. Tu n'es pas content?"

Il secouait le front comme un petit bélier.

"On me bourre, on me refuse tout, on me cache mes affaires, on me . . .

— Tu ne sauras donc jamais t'habiller tout seul?"

Elle prit des mains de Chéri le faux col qu'elle boutonna, la cravate qu'elle noua.

"Là . . . Oh! cette cravate violette. . . . Au fait, c'est bien bon pour la belle Marie-Laure et sa famille. . . . Et tu voulais encore une perle, là-dessus? Petit rasta. . . . Pourquoi pas des pendants d'oreilles? . . ."

Il se laissait faire, béat, mou, vacillant, repris d'une paresse et d'un plaisir qui lui fermaient les yeux. . . .

"Nounoune chérie . . ." murmura-t-il.

Elle lui brossa les oreilles, rectifia la raie, fine et bleuâtre, qui divisait les cheveux noirs de Chéri, lui toucha les tempes d'un doigt mouillé de parfum et baisa rapidement, parce qu'elle ne put s'en défendre, la bouche tentante qui respirait si près d'elle. Chéri ouvrit les yeux, les lèvres, tendit les mains. . . . Elle l'écarta:

"Non! une heure moins le quart! File et que je ne te revoie plus!

— Jamais?

"What for? Men don't wear a tie pin with a jacket, and you already have shoes on."

Chéri stamped his foot.

"I've had enough, no one here looks after me! I've had enough!"

Léa put down her comb.

"All right! Leave."

He shrugged his shoulders and said rudely:

"You're just saying that!"

"Leave. I've always loathed guests who grumble at the cooking and sling the cream cheese at the mirrors. Go back to your sainted mother, my child, and stay there."

He was unable to abide Léa's gaze; he lowered his eyes and protested like a schoolboy:

"What, can't I even say a word? At least lend me your car to go to Neuilly."

"No."

"Why?"

"Because I'm going out at two, and Philibert is having his lunch now."

"Where are you going at two?"

"To fulfill my religious duties. But do you want three francs for a taxi?" Then she continued gently: "Poor dope, maybe I'll drop in for coffee at your Lady Mother's at two o'clock. You're not happy about that?"

He was tossing his head like a little ram.

"I'm reprimanded, I'm refused everything, my belongings are hidden from me, I'm . . ."

"Won't you ever learn how to dress yourself?"

She took Chéri's collar out of his hands and buttoned it, she took the tie and tied it.

"There! Oh, that violet tie . . . In fact, it's good enough for lovely Marie-Laure and her family . . . And you wanted a pearl, on top of all that? Little fancy-pants . . . Why not earrings, too?"

He let her dress him. He was blissful, limp, hesitant, back in the embrace of a pleasurable sloth that made him close his eyes . . .

"Darling Nursie . . ." he murmured.

She brushed the hair over his ears, straightened the thin, bluish part in Chéri's black hair, touched his temples with a finger dipped in scent, and rapidly, because she couldn't help it, kissed the tempting mouth that was breathing so close to her. Chéri opened his eyes and lips, and held out his hands . . . She brushed him aside:

"No! It's a quarter to one! Beat it, and don't let me see you again!"

"Ever?"

— Jamais!" lui jeta-t-elle en riant avec une tendresse emportée.

Seule, elle sourit orgueilleusement, fit un soupir saccadé de convoitise matée, et écouta les pas de Chéri dans la cour de l'hôtel. Elle le vit ouvrir et refermer la grille, s'éloigner de son pas ailé, tout de suite salué par l'extase de trois trottins qui marchaient bras sur bras:

"Ah! maman! . . . c'est pas possible, il est en toc! . . . On demande à toucher?"

Mais Chéri, blasé, ne se retourna même pas.

"MON bain, Rose! La manucure peut s'en aller; il est trop tard. Le costume tailleur bleu, le nouveau, le chapeau bleu, celui qui est doublé de blanc, et les petits souliers à pattes . . . non, attends. . . ."

Léa, les jambes croisées, tâta sa cheville nue et hocha la tête:

"Non, les bottines lacées en chevreau bleu. J'ai les jambes un peu enflées aujourd'hui. C'est la chaleur."

La femme de chambre, âgée, coiffée de tulle, leva sur Léa un regard entendu:

"C'est . . . c'est la chaleur", répéta-t-elle docilement, en haussant les épaules, comme pour dire: "Nous savons. . . . Il faut bien que tout s'use. . . ."

Chéri parti, Léa redevint vive, précise, allégée. En moins d'une heure, elle fut baignée, frottée d'alcool parfumé au santal, coiffée, chaussée. Pendant que le fer à friser chauffait, elle trouva le temps d'éplucher le livre de comptes du maître d'hôtel, d'appeler le valet de chambre Émile pour lui montrer, sur un miroir, une buée bleue. Elle darda autour d'elle un œil assuré, qu'on ne trompait presque jamais, et déjeuna dans une solitude joyeuse, souriant au Vouvray sec et aux fraises de juin servies avec leurs queues sur un plat de Rubelles, vert comme une rainette mouillée. Un beau mangeur dut choisir autrefois pour cette salle à manger rectangulaire, les grandes glaces Louis XVI et les meubles anglais de la même époque, dressoirs aérés, desserte haute sur pieds, chaises maigres et solides, le tout d'un bois presque noir, à guirlandes minces. Les miroirs et de massives pièces d'argenterie recevaient le jour abondant, les reflets verts des arbres de l'avenue Bugeaud, et Léa scrutait, tout en mangeant, la poudre rouge demeurée aux ciselures d'une fourchette, fermait un œil pour mieux juger le poli des bois sombres. Le maître d'hôtel, derrière elle, redoutait ces jeux.

"Never!" She flung the word at him while laughing with passionate tenderness.

Alone again, she smiled proudly, heaved a broken sigh of suppressed longing, and listened to Chéri's footsteps in the courtyard of the town house. She saw him open the gate and shut it again, and walk away at his rapid pace, when he was suddenly greeted ecstatically by three dressmaker's errand girls who were walking arm in arm:

"Oh, my . . . it can't be true, he must be artificial! . . . Is it okay to touch?"

But Chéri, blasé, didn't even turn around.

"My bath, Rose! The manicurist can leave; it's too late. My blue jacket-and-skirt outfit, the new one; my blue hat, the one lined in white; and my low shoes with straps . . . no, wait . . ."

Her legs crossed, Léa touched her bare ankle and shook her head:

"No, the blue kid half-boots with laces. My legs are a little swollen today. It's the heat."

Léa's maid, an elderly woman with a tulle cap, looked at her understandingly:

"It's . . . it's the heat," she repeated docilely, shrugging her shoulders as if to say: "We know . . . Everything's got to wear out . . ."

Now that Chéri had gone, Léa became lively once more, precise, relieved. In less than an hour she had been bathed and rubbed down with alcohol scented with sandalwood, had done her hair and had put on her shoes. While the curling iron was heating, she found the time to examine her butler's account book and to call Emile, her footman, to show him a blue haze on a mirror. She cast all around her her practiced eyes, which were almost never deceived, and she lunched in cheerful solitude, smiling at the dry Vouvray and the June strawberries, served with their stems on a Rubelles enamel dish as green as a wet tree frog. It must have been a fine gourmet in the past who had selected for that rectangular dining room the large Louis XVI mirrors and the English furniture of the same period, the airy sideboards, the credenza on high legs, the slender but solid chairs, all of a nearly black wood with narrow garlands. The mirrors and massive silver vessels caught the abundant daylight and the green reflections of the trees on the Avenue Bugeaud, and as she ate Léa examined the red cleansing powder still visible in the chasing of a fork, and she closed one eye the better to judge the polish on the dark woodwork. The butler, standing behind her, was in dread of those maneuvers.

"Marcel, dit Léa, votre encaustique colle, depuis une huitaine.
— Madame croit?
— Elle croit. Rajoutez-y de l'essence en fondant au bain-marie,
ce n'est rien à refaire. Vous avez monté le Vouvray un peu tôt. Tirez
les persiennes dès que vous aurez desservi, nous tenons la vraie
chaleur.
— Bien, Madame. Monsieur Ch. . . . Monsieur Peloux dîne?
— Je pense. . . . Pas de crème-surprise ce soir, qu'on nous fasse
seulement des sorbets au jus de fraises. Le café au boudoir."
En se levant, grande et droite, les jambes visibles sous la jupe
plaquée aux cuisses, elle eut le loisir de lire, dans le regard con-
tenu du maître d'hôtel, le "Madame est belle" qui ne lui déplaisait
pas.
"Belle . . ." se disait Léa en montant au boudoir. Non. Plus maintenant. A présent il me faut le blanc du linge près du visage, le rose
très pâle pour les dessous et les déshabillés. Belle. . . . Peuh . . . je n'en
ai plus guère besoin. . . ."
Pourtant, elle ne s'accorda point de sieste dans le boudoir aux soies
peintes, après le café et les journaux. Et ce fut avec un visage de
bataille qu'elle commanda à son chauffeur:
"Chez Madame Peloux."

Les allées du Bois, sèches sous leur verdure neuve de juin que
le vent fane, la grille de l'octroi, Neuilly, le boulevard d'Inkermann. . . . "Combien de fois l'ai-je fait, ce trajet-là?" se demanda Léa. Elle compta, puis se lassa de compter, et épia, en retenant
ses pas sur le gravier de Mme Peloux, les bruits qui venaient de la
maison.
"Ils sont dans le hall", dit-elle.
Elle avait remis de la poudre avant d'arriver et tendu sur son menton la voilette bleue, un grillage fin comme un brouillard. Et elle
répondit au valet qui l'invitait à traverser la maison:
"Non, j'aime mieux faire le tour par le jardin."
Un vrai jardin, presque un parc, isolait, toute blanche, une vaste
villa de grande banlieue parisienne. La villa de Mme Peloux s'appelait
"une propriété à la campagne" dans le temps où Neuilly était encore
aux environs de Paris. Les écuries, devenues garages, les communs
avec leurs chenils et leurs buanderies en témoignaient, et aussi les dimensions de la salle de billard, du vestibule, de la salle à manger.
"Madame Peloux en a là pour de l'argent", redisaient dévotement
les vieilles parasites qui venaient, en échange d'un dîner et d'un verre

"Marcel," said Léa, "your wax has been sticking for a week now."

"You believe so, madame?"

"Yes, I do. Add some turpentine to it when you melt it in the double boiler, it won't take much doing over. You brought up the Vouvray a little too soon. Close the shutters as soon as you've cleared away, it's really hot outside."

"Yes, madame. Is Monsieur Ch— . . . Is Monsieur Peloux dining here tonight?"

"I believe so . . . No *crème-surprise* tonight, just have them make us some strawberry sorbet. My coffee in the boudoir."

When she stood up, tall and erect, her legs showing below the skirt that clung to her thighs, she had time enough to read in her butler's restrained glance that expression signifying "Madame is beautiful" which was far from displeasing her.

"Beautiful . . . ," Léa said to herself while going upstairs to the boudoir. No. Not anymore. Now I need to have white linen showing near my face, and a very pale pink in my underthings and boudoir wraps. Beautiful . . . Bah . . . I scarcely need to be anymore . . ."

And yet, she didn't permit herself any nap in her boudoir, with its painted silks, after her coffee and newspapers. And it was with a grimly determined expression that she instructed her chauffeur:

"To Madame Peloux's."

The avenues of the Bois, dry beneath their new June foliage faded by the wind; the tollhouse gate; Neuilly; the Boulevard d'Inkermann . . . "How many times have I made this trip?" Léa wondered. She counted, then got tired of counting; soon, treading cautiously on Madame Peloux's gravel path, she listened to the sounds coming from the house.

"They're in the garden room," she said.

She had put on more powder before arriving and had pulled the blue veil, a netting subtle as a mist, down over her chin. And she replied to the footman who invited her to walk through the house:

"No, I prefer to go around by way of the garden."

A true garden, almost a park, insulated the all-white house from its surroundings; it was a vast villa typical of a major Parisian suburb. Madame Peloux's villa was called a "country estate" in the days when Neuilly was still outside of Paris. The stables, turned into garages, the outbuildings with their kennels and washhouses, bore witness to this, as did the dimensions of the billiard room, the vestibule, and the dining room.

"Madame Peloux has her money's worth here," piously repeated the elderly female hangers-on who, in return for a dinner and a liqueur,

de fine, tenir en face d'elle les cartes du bésigue et du poker. Et elles
ajoutaient: "Mais où Madame Peloux n'a-t-elle pas d'argent?"

En marchant sous l'ombre des acacias, entre des massifs embrasés
de rhododendrons et des arceaux de roses, Léa écoutait un murmure
de voix, percé par la trompette nasillarde de Mme Peloux et l'éclat de
rire sec de Chéri.

"Il rit mal, cet enfant", songea-t-elle. Elle s'arrêta un instant, pour
entendre mieux un timbre féminin nouveau, faible, aimable, vite couvert par la trompette redoutable.

"Ça, c'est la petite", se dit Léa.

Elle fit quelques pas rapides et se trouva au seuil d'un hall vitré,
d'où Mme Peloux s'élança en criant:

"Voici notre belle amie!"

Ce tonnelet, Mme Peloux, en vérité Mlle Peloux, avait été
danseuse, de dix à seize ans. Léa cherchait parfois sur Mme
Peloux ce qui pouvait rappeler l'ancien petit Éros blond et potelé,
puis la nymphe à fossettes, et ne retrouvait que les grands yeux
implacables, le nez délicat et dur, et encore une manière coquette
de poser les pieds en "cinquième" comme les sujets du corps de
ballet.

Chéri, ressuscité du fond d'un rocking, baisa la main de Léa avec
une grâce involontaire, et gâta son geste par un:

"Flûte! tu as encore mis une voilette, j'ai horreur de ça.

— Veux-tu la laisser tranquille! intervint Mme Peloux. On ne demande pas à une femme pourquoi elle a mis une voilette! Nous n'en
ferons jamais rien", dit-elle tendrement a Léa.

Deux femmes s'étaient levées dans l'ombre blonde du store de
paille. L'une, en mauve, tendit assez froidement sa main à Léa, qui la
contempla des pieds à la tête.

"Mon Dieu, que vous êtes belle, Marie-Laure, il n'y a rien d'aussi
parfait que vous!"

Marie-Laure daigna sourire. C'était une jeune femme rousse, aux
yeux bruns, qui émerveillait sans geste et sans paroles. Elle désigna,
comme par coquetterie, l'autre jeune femme:

"Mais reconnaîtrez-vous ma fille Edmée?" dit-elle.

Léa tendit vers la jeune fille une main qu'on tarda à prendre:

"J'aurais dû vous reconnaître, mon enfant, mais une pensionnaire
change vite, et Marie-Laure ne change que pour déconcerter chaque
fois davantage. Vous voilà libre de tout pensionnat?

— Je crois bien, je crois bien, s'écria Mme Peloux. On ne peut pas

used to play bezique and poker with her. And they'd add: "But where hasn't Madame Peloux got money invested?"

While walking beneath the shade of the acacias, among glowing clumps of rhododendrons and bowers of roses, Léa was listening to a murmur of voices which was pierced by Madame Peloux's nasal, trumpet-like tones and a burst of Chéri's harsh laughter.

"That boy has a bad laugh," she thought. She stopped for a moment in order to make out more clearly a new female tone, soft and charming, which was quickly smothered by the fearful trumpet.

"That's the girl," Léa said to herself.

She took a few rapid steps and arrived at the threshold of a glass-walled garden room, from which Madame Peloux darted out, shouting: "Here's our lovely friend!"

That rolypoly, Madame Peloux (in actuality, Mademoiselle Peloux), had been a ballerina from ages ten to sixteen. At times Léa would examine Madame Peloux, looking for some reminder of the former little chubby blond Eros, or the later dimpled nymph, but all she could rediscover was the large, implacable eyes, the delicate but firm nose, and the lingering coquettish mannerism of placing her feet in the fifth position, like a member of the corps de ballet.

Chéri, rising from the seat of a rocking-chair, kissed Léa's hand with unaffected grace, but spoiled his gesture by saying:

"Darn! You've put on a veil again. I hate that."

"Oh, leave her alone!" Madame Peloux intervened. "A woman is never asked why she's put on a veil! We'll never do anything with him," she said tenderly to Léa.

Two women had gotten up in the pale yellow shade of the straw blinds. One, dressed in mauve, very coldly held out one hand to Léa, who looked her over from head to foot.

"Lord, how beautiful you are, Marie-Laure, nothing is as perfect as you!"

Marie-Laure condescended to smile. She was a redheaded young woman with brown eyes, who cast a spell without words or gestures. As if out of coquetry, she indicated the other young woman.

"But would you recognize my daughter Edmée?" she asked.

Léa held out her hand to the girl, who was slow to take it.

"I should have recognized you, child, but a schoolgirl changes quickly, and Marie-Laure changes only to disconcert people more every time. Are you all through with boarding school?"

"I think so, I think so," cried Madame Peloux. "That charm, that

laisser sous le boisseau éternellement ce charme, cette grâce, cette merveille de dix-neuf printemps!

— Dix-huit, dit suavement Marie-Laure.

— Dix-huit, dix-huit! . . . Mais oui, dix-huit! Léa, tu te souviens? Cette enfant faisait sa première communion l'année où Chéri s'est sauvé du collège, tu sais bien? Oui, mauvais garnement, tu t'étais sauvé et nous étions aussi affolées l'une que l'autre!

— Je me souviens très bien, dit Léa, et elle échangea avec Marie-Laure un petit signe de tête, — quelque chose comme le "touché" des escrimeurs loyaux.

— Il faut la marier, il faut la marier! continua Mme Peloux qui ne répétait jamais moins de deux fois une vérité première. Nous irons tous à la noce!"

Elle battit l'air de ses petits bras et la jeune fille la regarda avec une frayeur ingénue.

"C'est bien une fille pour Marie-Laure, songeait Léa très attentive. Elle a, en discret, tout ce que sa mère a d'éclatant. Des cheveux mousseux, cendrés, comme poudrés, des yeux inquiets qui se cachent, une bouche qui se retient de parler, de sourire. . . . Tout à fait ce qu'il fallait à Marie-Laure, qui doit la haïr quand même. . . ."

Mme Peloux interposa entre Léa et la jeune fille un sourire maternel:

"Ce qu'ils ont déjà camaradé dans le jardin, ces deux enfants-là!"

Elle désignait Chéri, debout devant la paroi vitrée et fumant. Il tenait son fume-cigarette entre les dents et rejetait la tête en arrière pour éviter la fumée. Les trois femmes regardèrent le jeune homme qui, le front renversé, les cils mi-clos, les pieds joints et immobiles, semblait pourtant une figure ailée, planante et dormante dans l'air. . . . Léa ne se trompa point à l'expression effarée, vaincue, des yeux de la jeune fille. Elle se donna le plaisir de la faire tressaillir en lui touchant le bras. Edmée frémit tout entière, retira son bras et dit farouchement tout bas:

"Quoi? . . .

— Rien, répondit Léa. C'est mon gant qui était tombé.

— Allons, Edmée?" ordonna Marie-Laure avec nonchalance.

La jeune fille, muette et docile, marcha vers Mme Peloux qui battit des ailerons:

"Déjà? Mais non! On va se revoir! on va se revoir!

— Il est tard, dit Marie-Laure. Et puis, vous attendez beaucoup de gens, le dimanche après-midi. Cette enfant n'a pas l'habitude du monde. . . .

grace, that marvel of nineteen springs, can't be hidden beneath a bushel forever!"

"Eighteen springs," said Marie-Laure gently.

"Eighteen, eighteen! . . . Of course, eighteen! Remember, Léa? This child was taking her First Communion the year that Chéri ran away from school, right? Yes, you bad boy, you ran away and both of us women were scared out of our wits!"

"I remember quite well," said Léa, exchanging a slight nod with Marie-Laure, something like a "touché" called out by an honest fencer.

"She must get married, she must get married," continued Madame Peloux, who never uttered a commonplace less than twice. "We'll all go to the wedding!"

She fanned the air with her short arms, and the girl looked at her in naïve dismay.

"She's the kind of daughter just right for Marie-Laure," thought Léa, studying her. "She possesses discreetly everything her mother possesses in a flashy way. Fluffy ash-blond hair, as if powdered, restless eyes that look away from you, a mouth that refrains from speaking or smiling . . . Just what Marie-Laure needed, though she must hate the girl anyway . . ."

Madame Peloux interposed a maternal smile between Léa and the girl:

"How chummy those two youngsters were in the garden before!"

She was pointing to Chéri, who was standing in front of the glass wall, smoking. His cigarette holder was clenched in his teeth, and his head was thrown back to avoid the smoke. The three women looked at the young man, who, though his head was leaning back, his eyes half-closed and his motionless feet close together, nevertheless resembled a winged figure, hovering somnolently in the air . . . Léa wasn't mistaken about the frightened, vanquished expression in the girl's eyes. She gave herself the pleasure of making her jump by touching her arm. Edmée shuddered all over, withdrew her arm, and said wildly, very low:

"What is it?"

"Nothing," Léa replied. "My glove fell."

"Shall we go, Edmée?" Marie-Laure asked commandingly, though nonchalantly.

The girl, taciturn and docile, walked up to Madame Peloux, who was flapping her pinions:

"So soon? Oh, no! Let's get together again! Let's get together again!"

"It's late," said Marie-Laure. "Besides, you must be expecting lots of people on a Sunday afternoon. My daughter isn't used to society . . ."

— Oui, oui, cria tendrement Mme Peloux, elle a vécu si enfermée, si seule!"

Marie-Laure sourit, et Léa la regarda pour dire: "A vous!"

". . . Mais nous reviendrons bientôt.

— Jeudi, jeudi! Léa, tu viens déjeuner aussi, jeudi?

— Je viens", répondit Léa.

Chéri avait rejoint Edmée au seuil du hall, où il se tenait auprès d'elle, dédaigneux de toute conversation. Il entendit la promesse de Léa et se retourna:

"C'est ça. On fera une balade, proposa-t-il.

— Oui, oui, c'est de votre âge, insista Mme Peloux attendrie. Edmée ira avec Chéri sur le devant, il nous mènera, et nous irons au fond, nous autres. Place à la jeunesse! Place à la jeunesse! Chéri, mon amour, veux-tu demander la voiture de Marie-Laure?"

Encore que ses petits pieds ronds chavirassent sur les graviers, elle emmena ses visiteuses jusqu'au tournant d'une allée, puis les abandonna à Chéri. Quand elle revint, Léa avait retiré son chapeau et allumé une cigarette.

"Ce qu'ils sont jolis, tous les deux! haleta Mme Peloux. Pas, Léa?

— Ravissants, souffla Léa avec un jet de fumée. Mais c'est cette Marie-Laure . . ."

Chéri rentrait:

"Qu'est-ce qu'elle a fait, Marie-Laure? demanda-t-il.

— Quelle beauté!

— Ah! . . . Ah! . . . approuva Mme Peloux, c'est vrai, c'est vrai . . . qu'elle a été bien jolie!"

Chéri et Léa rirent en se regardant.

"A été!" souligna Léa. Mais c'est la jeunesse même! Elle n'a pas un pli! Et elle peut porter du mauve tendre, cette sale couleur que je déteste et qui me le rend!"

Les grands yeux impitoyables et le nez mince se détournèrent d'un verre de fine:

"La jeunesse même! la jeunesse même! glapit Mme Peloux. Pardon! pardon! Marie-Laure a eu Edmée en 1895, non, 14. Elle avait à ce moment-là fichu le camp avec un professeur de chant et plaqué Khalil-Bey qui lui avait donné le fameux diamant rose que. . . . Non! non! . . . Attends! . . . C'est d'un an plus tôt! . . ."

Elle trompettait fort et faux. Léa mit une main sur son oreille et Chéri déclara, sentencieux:

"Ça serait trop beau, un après-midi comme ça, s'il n'y avait pas la voix de ma mère."

"Yes, yes," Madame Peloux shouted tenderly, "she's lived so shut up, so alone!"

Marie-Laure smiled, and Léa looked at her as if to say: "So much for you!"

". . . But we'll be back soon."

"Thursday, Thursday! Léa, will you come for lunch, too, on Thursday?"

"I will," Léa replied.

Chéri had caught up with Edmée at the entrance to the garden room, where he was standing near her, scorning to indulge in conversation. He heard Léa's promise and turned around:

"Right! We'll go out for a ride," he suggested.

"Yes, yes, that suits your age," Madame Peloux insisted in a heartfelt voice. "Edmée will sit up front with Chéri, he'll drive, and the rest of us will sit in the back. Make way for youth! Make way for youth! Chéri darling, please go ask for Marie-Laure's car."

Her little round feet floundering on the gravel, she accompanied her two guests to a bend in the walk, then consigned them to Chéri. When she returned, Léa had taken off her hat and had lit a cigarette.

"How good-looking both children are!" Madame Peloux panted. "Aren't they, Léa?"

"Ravishing," said Léa, exhaling a puff of smoke. "But that Marie-Laure!"

Coming back in, Chéri asked:

"What did Marie-Laure do?"

"How beautiful she is!"

"Oh! . . . Oh! . . ." Madame Peloux agreed, "it's true, it's true . . . she used to be very pretty!"

Chéri and Léa looked at each other and laughed.

"Used to be!" Léa said with emphasis. "But she's the embodiment of youth! She doesn't have a wrinkle! And she can wear light mauve, that vile color which I hate, and which hates me back!"

The large, merciless eyes and the thin nose turned away from her glass of brandy.

"The embodiment of youth! The embodiment of youth!" Madame Peloux yelped. "Excuse me! Excuse me! Marie-Laure had Edmée in 1895—no, '94. At the time she had run away with a singing instructor and had jilted Khalil-Bey, who had given her that much-discussed pink diamond which . . . No, no! . . . Wait! . . . That was a year earlier!"

Her trumpet was loud and off-key. Léa put one hand to an ear, and Chéri declared sententiously:

"An afternoon like this would be too beautiful, if it weren't for my mother's voice."

Elle regarda son fils sans colère, habituée à son insolence, s'assit dignement, les pieds ballants, au fond d'une bergère trop haute pour ses jambes courtes. Elle chauffait dans sa main un verre d'eau-de-vie. Léa, balancée dans un rocking, jetait de temps en temps les yeux sur Chéri, Chéri vautré sur le rotin frais, son gilet ouvert, une cigarette à demi éteinte à la lèvre, une mèche sur le sourcil, — et elle le traitait flatteusement, tout bas, de belle crapule.

Ils demeuraient côte à côte, sans effort pour plaire ni parler, paisibles et en quelque sorte heureux. Une longue habitude l'un de l'autre les rendait au silence, ramenait Chéri à la veulerie et Léa à la sérénité. A cause de la chaleur qui augmentait, Mme Peloux releva jusqu'aux genoux sa jupe étroite, montra ses petits mollets de matelot, et Chéri arracha rageusement sa cravate, geste que Léa blâma d'un: "Tt . . . tt . . ." de langue.

"Oh! laisse-le, ce petit, protesta, comme du fond d'un songe, Mme Peloux. Il fait si chaud. . . . Veux-tu un kimono, Léa?

— Non, merci. Je suis très bien."

Ces abandons de l'après-midi l'écœuraient. Jamais son jeune amant ne l'avait surprise défaite, ni le corsage ouvert, ni en pantoufles dans le jour. "Nue, si on veut", disait-elle, "mais pas dépoitraillée". Elle reprit son journal illustré et ne le lut pas. "Cette mère Peloux et son fils", songeait-elle, "mettez-les devant une table bien servie ou menez-les à la campagne, — crac: la mère ôte son corset et le fils son gilet. Des natures de bistrots en vacances." Elle leva les yeux vindicativement sur le bistrot incriminé et vit qu'il dormait, les cils rabattus sur ses joues blanches, la bouche close. L'arc délicieux de la lèvre supérieure, éclairé par en dessous, retenait à ses sommets deux points de lumière argentée, et Léa s'avoua qu'il ressemblait beaucoup plus à un dieu qu'à un marchand de vins. Sans se lever, elle cueillit délicatement entre les doigts de Chéri une cigarette fumante, et la jeta au cendrier. La main du dormeur se détendit et laissa tomber comme des fleurs lasses ses doigts fuselés, armés d'ongles cruels, main non point féminine, mais un peu plus belle qu'on ne l'eût voulu, main que Léa avait cent fois baisée sans servilité, baisée pour le plaisir, pour le parfum. . . .

Elle regarda, par-dessus son journal, du côté de Mme Peloux. "Dort-elle aussi?" Léa aimait que la sieste de la mère et du fils lui donnât, à elle bien éveillée, une heure de solitude morale parmi la chaleur, l'ombre et le soleil.

Mais Mme Peloux ne dormait point. Elle se tenait bouddhique dans

She looked at her son without anger, accustomed as she was to his insolence, and sat down in a dignified manner, her feet swinging, in an upholstered armchair that was too high off the floor for her short legs. In her hand she cradled a glass of brandy. Léa, moving back and forth in a rocking-chair, cast an occasional glance at Chéri, who was sprawling on a cool cane chair, his vest open, a half-extinguished cigarette on his lip, a lock of hair over his forehead—and very quietly, and flatteringly, she called him a good-looking scoundrel.

They remained there side by side, making no effort to be pleasant or to speak, peaceful and, in a way, happy. Their long acquaintance with one another made them silent, inducing inertia in Chéri and serenity in Léa. Because of the increasing heat, Madame Peloux raised her narrow skirt up to her knees, revealing her small calves, like those of a sailor, and Chéri angrily tore off his tie, a gesture that Léa reprimanded by clicking her tongue.

"Oh, leave the boy alone," Madame Peloux protested, as if lost in a dream. "It's so hot . . . Do you want a kimono, Léa?"

"No, thanks. I'm fine as I am."

These afternoon laxities disgusted her. Her young lover had never caught her in disarray, with her bodice open, or wearing slippers in the daytime. "Naked, if you like," she said to herself, "but not slovenly." She picked up her picture magazine again, but didn't read it. "This old lady Peloux and her son!" she thought. "Put a hearty meal in front of them, or take them to the country—bang! the mother takes off her corset and the son takes off his vest. They're like saloonkeepers on vacation." She cast a vindictive glance at the saloonkeeper in question and saw that he was asleep, his lashes touching his white cheeks, his mouth shut. At its highest points the delicious bow of his upper lip, lit from below, captured and held two dots of silvery light, and Léa confessed that he looked much more like a god than like a bar proprietor. Without getting up, she delicately removed a smoking cigarette from Chéri's fingers and tossed it into the ashtray. The sleeper's hand opened, revealing, like weary blossoms, his slender fingers tipped with cruel nails, a hand not at all feminine, but a little more beautiful than one might have wished, a hand that Léa had kissed a hundred times without servility, kissed for the pleasure of it, for its fragrance . . .

Peering over her magazine, she looked at Madame Peloux. "Is she sleeping, too?" Léa liked to have the mother and son nap, granting her a wide-awake hour of mental solitude in the heat, shade, and sun.

But Madame Peloux wasn't asleep. She was sitting in her armchair

sa bergère, regardant droit devant elle et suçant sa fine-champagne
avec une application de nourrisson alcoolique.

"Pourquoi ne dort-elle pas? se demanda Léa. C'est dimanche. Elle
a bien déjeuné. Elle attend les vieilles frappes de son jour à cinq
heures. Par conséquent, elle devrait dormir. Si elle ne dort pas, c'est
qu'elle fait quelque chose de mal."

Elles se connaissaient depuis vingt-cinq ans. Intimité ennemie de
femmes légères qu'un homme enrichit puis délaisse, qu'un autre
homme ruine, — amitié hargneuse de rivales à l'affût de la première ride et du cheveu blanc. Camaraderie de femmes positives,
habiles aux jeux financiers, mais l'une avare et l'autre sybarite. . . .
Ces liens comptent. Un autre lien plus fort venait les unir sur le
tard: Chéri.

Léa se souvenait de Chéri enfant, merveille aux longues boucles.
Tout petit, il ne s'appelait pas encore Chéri, mais seulement Fred.

Chéri, tour à tour oublié et adoré, grandit entre les femmes de
chambre décolorées et les longs valets sardoniques. Bien qu'il eût
mystérieusement apporté, en naissant, l'opulence, on ne vit nulle
miss, nulle fraulein auprès de Chéri, préservé à grands cris de "ces
goules". . . .

"Charlotte Peloux, femme d'un autre âge!" disait familièrement le
vieux, tari, expirant et indestructible baron de Berthellemy, "Charlotte
Peloux, je salue en vous la seule femme de mœurs légères qui ait osé
élever son fils en fils de grue! Femme d'un autre âge, vous ne lisez
pas, vous ne voyagez jamais, vous vous occupez de votre seul
prochain, et vous faites élever votre enfant par les domestiques.
Comme c'est pur! comme c'est About! comme c'est même Gustave
Droz! et dire que vous n'en savez rien!"

Chéri connut donc toutes les joies d'une enfance dévergondée. Il
recueillit, zézayant encore, les bas racontars de l'office. Il partagea
les soupers clandestins de la cuisine. Il eut les bains de lait d'iris dans
la baignoire de sa mère, et les débarbouillages hâtifs avec le coin
d'une serviette. Il endura l'indigestion de bonbons, et les crampes
d'inanition quand on oubliait son dîner. Il s'ennuya, demi-nu et enrhumé, aux fêtes des Fleurs où Charlotte Peloux l'exhibait, assis dans
des roses mouillées; mais il lui arriva de se divertir royalement à
douze ans, dans une salle de tripot clandestin où une dame améri-

like a Buddha, staring straight in front of her and sipping her brandy as singlemindedly as an alcoholic infant.

"Why isn't she sleeping?" Léa wondered. "It's Sunday. She's had a big lunch. She's expecting those good-for-nothing old dames who come at five on her open-house day. And so, she ought to be sleeping. Since she's not sleeping, she's up to some wickedness."

They had known each other for twenty-five years. A hostile intimacy of loose women whom a man enriches, then deserts, whom another man ruins—a peevish friendship of rivals on the lookout for the first wrinkle and gray hair. A comradeship between matter-of-fact women, skilled in financial matters, but one of whom was miserly and the other pleasure-loving . . . Such attachments mean something. A different bond, a stronger one, was to unite them later on: Chéri.

Léa could recall Chéri as a child, a beauty with long curls. When very little, he was not yet called Chéri, but just Fred.

Chéri, alternately neglected and worshiped, grew up among washed-out chambermaids and lanky, sardonic footmen. Though his birth had mysteriously brought wealth to the household, no English or German governess was to be seen around Chéri, who was clamorously kept free of "those ghouls" . . .

"Charlotte Peloux, woman of a bygone era," the old, worn-out, half-dead but indestructible Baron de Berthellemy used to say unceremoniously, "Charlotte Peloux, I salute in you the only woman of easy virtue who ever dared to bring up her son like a tart's child! Woman of a bygone era, you don't read books, you never travel, all you care about is your neighbors' business, and you let servants raise your boy. How pure that is! How very like About! In fact, it's just like Gustave Droz![4] And to think you're not even aware of it!"

And so, Chéri experienced all the joys of a shameless childhood. While still lisping, he was privy to the low gossip of the servants' quarters. He partook of the clandestine suppers in the kitchen. He took baths of milk of orris root in his mother's tub, or else had his face hastily cleaned with the corner of a towel. He suffered stomach aches from too much candy, or hunger pangs when they forgot to feed him. Half-naked, with a head cold, he underwent the boredom of the flower festivals at which Charlotte Peloux exhibited him, sitting amid damp roses. But he also had a rollicking good time at the age of

---

4. Edmond About (1828–1885) and Gustave Droz (1832–1895) were popular novelists interested in social and moral issues.

caine lui donnait pour jouer des poignées de louis et l'appelait "petite chef-d'œuvre". Vers le même temps, Mme Peloux donna à son fils un abbé précepteur qu'elle remercia au bout de dix mois "parce que", avoua-t-elle, "cette robe noire que je voyais partout traîner dans la maison, ça me faisait comme si j'avais recueilli une parente pauvre — et Dieu sait qu'il n'y a rien de plus attristant qu'une parente pauvre chez soi!"

A quatorze ans, Chéri tâta du collège. Il n'y croyait pas. Il défiait toute geôle et s'échappa. Non seulement Mme Peloux trouva l'énergie de l'incarcérer à nouveau, mais encore, devant les pleurs et les injures de son fils, elle s'enfuit, les mains sur les oreilles, en criant: "Je ne veux pas voir ça! Je ne veux pas voir ça!" Cri si sincère qu'en effet elle s'éloigna de Paris, accompagnée d'un homme jeune mais peu scrupuleux pour revenir deux ans plus tard, seule. Ce fut sa dernière faiblesse amoureuse.

Elle retrouva Chéri grandi trop vite, creux, les yeux fardés de cerne, portant des complets d'entraîneur et parlant plus gras que jamais. Elle se frappa les seins et arracha Chéri à l'internat. Il cessa tout à fait de travailler, voulut chevaux, voitures, bijoux, exigea des mensualités rondes et, au moment que sa mère se frappa les seins en poussant des appels de paonne, il l'arrêta par ses mots:

"Mame Peloux, ne vous bilez pas. Ma mère vénérée, s'il n'y a que moi pour te mettre sur la paille, tu risques fort de mourir bien au chaud sous ton couvre-pied américain. Je n'ai pas de goût pour le conseil judiciaire. Ta galette, c'est la mienne. Laisse-moi faire. Les amis, ça se rationne avec des dîners et du champagne. Quant à ces dames, vous ne voudriez pourtant pas, Mame Peloux, que fait comme vous m'avez fait, je dépasse avec elles l'hommage du bibelot artistique, — et encore!"

Il pirouetta, tandis qu'elle versait de douces larmes et se proclamait la plus heureuse des mères. Quand Chéri commença d'acheter des automobiles, elle trembla de nouveau, mais il lui recommanda: "L'œil à l'essence, s'il vous plaît, Mame Peloux!" et vendit ses chevaux. Il ne dédaignait pas d'éplucher les livres des deux chauffeurs; il calculait vite, juste, et les chiffres qu'il jetait sur le papier juraient, élancés, renflés, agiles, avec sa grosse écriture assez lente.

Il passa dix-sept ans, en tournant au petit vieux, au rentier tatillon. Toujours beau, mais maigre, le souffle raccourci. Plus d'une fois Mme

twelve, in a room in an illicit gambling house where an American lady gave him handfuls of gold coins to bet with and called him "little masterpiece."[5] Around the same time, Madame Peloux gave her son an abbé for a tutor, but dismissed him ten months later "because," she confessed, "that black robe I saw wandering all over the house made me feel as if I had taken in a female poor relation—and God knows there's nothing more depressing than a poor relation in your house!"

At fourteen Chéri had a taste of boarding school. It was not for him. Defying jails of any sort, he ran away. Not only did Madame Peloux find the energy to lock him up again: what's more, faced with her son's tears and insults, she clapped her hands to her ears and ran off, shouting: "I don't want to see this! I don't want to see this!" Her outcry was so sincere that she actually did leave Paris, in the company of a young but unscrupulous man, only to return two years later, alone. That was her last amorous weakness.

On her return she found that Chéri had grown up too fast; he was gaunt, had dark rings around his eyes, wore suits that a horse trainer might sport, and was more foul-mouthed than ever. She beat her bosom and yanked Chéri out of boarding school. He stopped working altogether, and asked for horses, carriages, and jewelry; he demanded a substantial allowance and, when his mother beat her bosom and shrieked like a peahen, he cut her short with the words:

"Ma'me Peloux, don't work yourself up! Venerated mother, if I'm the only one who can make you go broke, you have every chance of dying nice and warm under your American comforter. I have no liking for a guardianship arrangement. Your dough is mine, too. Leave things to me. Friends can be bought off cheaply with dinners and champagne. As for the ladies, Ma'me Peloux, me being the way you've made me, you surely don't expect me to go beyond a gift of an artistic trinket—if that much!"

He performed a pirouette, while she shed tears of joy and declared she was the happiest of mothers. When Chéri began buying cars, she trembled again, but he enjoined her: "See to the gesoline supply, please, Ma'me Peloux!" and he sold his horses. He wasn't too proud to pore over the two chauffeurs' accounts; he was fast and accurate with calculations, and the figures he dashed down on paper, tall, well-rounded, and agile, were in striking contrast with his clumsy and very slow handwriting.

On passing the age of seventeen, he became like a little old man, a finical coupon-clipper. Still handsome, but thin and short of breath.

---

5. The American lady's French was a little shaky, because her adjective and noun are of different genders.

Peloux le rencontra dans l'escalier de la cave, d'où il revenait de
compter les bouteilles dans les casiers.

"Crois-tu! disait Mme Peloux à Léa, c'est trop beau!

— Beaucoup trop, répondait Léa, ça finira mal. Chéri, montre ta
langue?"

Il la tirait avec une grimace irrévérencieuse; et d'autres vilaines
manières qui ne choquaient point Léa, amie trop familière, sorte de
marraine-gâteau qu'il tutoyait.

"C'est vrai, interrogeait Léa, qu'on t'a vu au bar avec la vieille Lili,
cette nuit, assis sur ses genoux?

— Ses genoux! gouaillait Chéri. Y a longtemps qu'elle n'en a plus,
de genoux! Ils sont noyés.

— C'est vrai, insistait Léa plus sévère, qu'elle t'a fait boire du gin
au poivre? Tu sais que ça fait sentir mauvais de la bouche?"

Un jour Chéri, blessé, avait répondu à l'enquête de Léa:

"Je ne sais pas pourquoi tu me demandes tout ça, tu as bien dû voir
ce que je faisais, puisque tu y étais, dans le petit cagibi du fond, avec
Patron le boxeur!

— C'est parfaitement exact, répondit Léa impassible. Il n'a rien du
petit claqué, Patron, tu sais? Il a d'autres séductions qu'une petite
gueule de quatre sous et des yeux au beurre noir."

Cette semaine-là, Chéri fit grand bruit la nuit à Montmartre et aux
Halles, avec des dames qui l'appelaient "ma gosse" et "mon vice",
mais il n'avait le feu nulle part, il souffrait de migraines et toussait de
la gorge. Et Mme Peloux, qui confiait à sa masseuse, à Mme Ribot, sa
corsetière, à la vieille Lili, à Berthellemy-le-Desséché, ses angoisses
nouvelles: "Ah! pour nous autres mères, quel calvaire, la vie!" passa
avec aisance de l'état de plus-heureuse-des-mères à celui de mère-
martyre.

Un soir de juin, qui rassemblait sous la serre de Neuilly Mme
Peloux, Léa et Chéri, changea les destins du jeune homme et de la
femme mûre. Le hasard dispersant pour un soir les "amis" de
Chéri, — un petit liquoriste en gros, le fils Boster, et le vicomte
Desmond, parasite à peine majeur, exigeant et dédaigneux, — ra-
menait Chéri à la maison maternelle où l'habitude conduisait aussi
Léa.

Vingt années, un passé fait de ternes soirées semblables, le
manque de relations, cette défiance aussi, et cette veulerie qui iso-
lent vers la fin de leur vie les femmes qui n'ont aimé que d'amour,
tenaient l'une devant l'autre, encore un soir, en attendant un autre

More than once Madame Peloux met him on the stairs to the cellar, where he had just been counting the bottles in the racks.

"Would you believe it!" Madame Peloux used to say to Léa. "It's too wonderful!"

"Much too wonderful," Léa would reply. "No good will come of it. Chéri, show me your tongue."

He would stick it out with a disrespectful grimace, and other bad manners that didn't upset Léa. She was too close a friend, a sort of child-spoiling godmother, and he addressed her with *tu*.

"Is it true," Léa would ask, "that you were seen in a bar with old Lili last night, sitting on her knees?"

"Her knees!" Chéri would quip. "She hasn't had any knees for some time. They're submerged."

"Is it true," Léa would go on, more severely, "that she gave you pepper gin to drink? Do you know it makes one's mouth smell?"

One day, Chéri was hurt and replied to Léa's interrogation:

"I don't know why you're asking me all this. You must have seen what I was doing, because you were there in the little back room with that boxer Patron!"

"That's perfectly correct," Léa replied calmly. "There's nothing of the feeble runt about Patron, see? He's got other attractions than a cheap pretty face and eyes with dark circles."

That week Chéri raised Cain every night in Montmartre and at Les Halles with women who called him "kiddie" and "cutie," but his heart wasn't in it, he had migraines and a chest cough. And Madame Peloux, who confided her new anguish to her masseuse, to Madame Ribot her corsetmaker, to old Lili, to Dried-up Berthellemy—"Oh, what suffering life is for us mothers!"—passed readily from the status of happiest of mothers to that of martyred mother.

One June evening, when Madame Peloux, Léa, and Chéri were assembled in the glass-walled garden room at Neuilly, changed the destiny of the young man and the older woman. For that evening, chance had scattered Chéri's friends—young Boster, a little wholesale liquor dealer, and Viscount Desmond, a demanding and haughty parasite who had barely attained his majority—and brought Chéri back to his mother's house, where habit also led Léa.

Twenty years, a past made up of similar lackluster evenings, the lack of social relations, and also that mistrust and inertia by which women who have loved only sensually are made lonely in their old days, kept the two women in each other's company one more evening (and just such another

soir, ces deux femmes, l'une à l'autre suspectes. Elles regardaient
toutes deux Chéri taciturne, et Mme Peloux, sans force et sans autorité pour soigner son fils, se bornait à haïr un peu Léa, chaque fois
qu'un geste penchait, près de la joue pâle, de l'oreille transparente de
Chéri, la nuque blanche et la joue sanguine de Léa. Elle eût bien
saigné ce cou robuste de femme, où les colliers de Vénus com-
mençaient de meurtrir la chair, pour teindre de rose le svelte lis
verdissant, — mais elle ne pensait pas même à conduire son bien-
aimé aux champs.

"Chéri, pourquoi bois-tu de la fine? grondait Léa.

— Pour ne pas faire affront à Mame Peloux qui boirait seule,
répondait Chéri.

— Qu'est-ce que tu fais, demain?

— Sais pas, et toi?

— Je vais partir pour la Normandie.

— Avec?

— Ça ne te regarde pas.

— Avec notre brave Spéleïeff?

— Penses-tu, il y a deux mois que c'est fini, tu retardes. Il est en
Russie, Spéleïeff.

— Mon Chéri, où as-tu la tête! soupira Mme Peloux. Tu oublies le
charmant dîner de rupture que nous a offert Léa le mois dernier. Léa,
tu ne m'as pas donné la recette des langoustines qui m'avaient tellement plu!"

Chéri se redressa, fit briller ses yeux:

"Oui, oui, des langoustines avec une sauce crémeuse, oh! j'en voudrais!

— Tu vois, reprocha Mme Peloux, lui qui a si peu d'appétit, il aurait mangé des langoustines. . . .

— La paix! commanda Chéri. Léa, tu vas sous les ombrages avec
Patron?

— Mais non, mon petit; Patron et moi, c'est de l'amitié. Je pars
seule.

— Femme riche, jeta Chéri.

— Je t'emmène, si tu veux, on ne fera que manger, boire, dormir. . . .

— C'est où, ton patelin?"

Il s'était levé et planté devant elle.

"Tu vois Honfleur? la côte de Grâce? Oui? . . . Assieds-toi, tu es
vert. Tu sais bien, sur la côte de Grâce, cette porte charretière devant
laquelle nous disions toujours en passant, ta mère et moi. . . ."

Elle se tourna du côté de Mme Peloux: Mme Peloux avait disparu.

evening would follow . . .), even though they were so wary of each other. Both of them were looking at the silent Chéri, and Madame Peloux, who had neither the strength nor the authority to look after her son properly, contented herself with hating Léa a little every time a gesture brought Léa's white neck and ruddy cheek close to Chéri's pale cheek and translucent ear. She would gladly have cut that robust feminine throat, on which wrinkles were beginning to mortify the flesh, in order to dye with red his slender greenish-white face—but it never even entered her mind that she could take her beloved son to the country for his health.

"Chéri, why do you drink brandy?" Léa was scolding.

"So as not to make Ma'me Peloux feel bad for drinking alone," Chéri replied.

"What are you doing tomorrow?"

"Dunno. What about you?"

"I'm taking a trip to Normandy."

"Who with?"

"That's none of your business."

"With good old Speleyev?"

"No, no, that's been over with for two months now. You're behind the times. Speleyev is in Russia."

"Chéri, you have no memory!" Madame Peloux sighed. "You've forgotten that charming end-of-the-affair dinner that Léa gave us last month. Léa, you still haven't given me the recipe for those langoustines that I liked so much!"

Chéri sat up straight, his eyes flashing:

"Yes, yes, langoustines in a cream sauce. How I'd like some!"

"You see," said Madame Peloux reproachfully, "he has almost no appetite, but he'd eat langoustines . . ."

"Quiet!" Chéri ordered. "Léa, is it Patron you're going to the sticks with?"

"Of course not, child. Patron and I are just friends. I'm going alone."

"Rich woman!" Chéri exclaimed.

"I'll take you along if you like; we'll do nothing but eat, drink, sleep . . ."

"Where is this little burg of yours?"

"You know Honfleur? The Côte de Grâce? Do you? . . . Sit down, you look green. You know, on the Côte de Grâce, that carriage gate in front of which your mother and I always used to say when we passed by . . ."

She turned to face Madame Peloux: Madame Peloux had vanished.

Ce genre de fuite discrète, cet évanouissement étaient si peu en accord avec les coutumes de Charlotte Peloux, que Léa et Chéri se regardèrent en riant de surprise. Chéri s'assit contre Léa.

"Je suis fatigué, dit-il.

— Tu t'abîmes", dit Léa.

Il se redressa, vaniteux:

"Oh! tu sais, je suis encore assez bien.

— Assez bien ... peut-être pour d'autres ... mais pas ... pas pour moi, par exemple.

— Trop vert?

— Juste le mot que je cherchais. Viens-tu à la campagne, en tout bien tout honneur? Des bonnes fraises, de la crème fraîche, des tartes, des petits poulets grillés. ... Voilà un bon régime, et pas de femmes!"

Il se laissa glisser sur l'épaule de Léa et ferma les yeux.

"Pas de femmes. ... Chouette. ... Léa, dis, es-tu un frère? Oui? Eh bien, partons, les femmes ... j'en suis revenu. ... Les femmes ... je les ai vues."

Il disait ces choses basses d'une voix assoupie, dont Léa écoutait le son plein et doux et recevait le souffle tiède sur son oreille. Il avait saisi le long collier de Léa et roulait les grosses perles entre ses doigts. Elle passa son bras sous la tête de Chéri et le rapprocha d'elle, sans arrière-pensée, confiante dans l'habitude qu'elle avait de cet enfant, et elle le berça.

"Je suis bien, soupira-t-il. T'es un frère, je suis bien. ...."

Elle sourit comme sous une louange très précieuse. Chéri semblait s'endormir. Elle regardait de tout près les cils brillants, comme mouillés, rabattus sur la joue, et cette joue amaigrie qui portait les traces d'une fatigue sans bonheur. La lèvre supérieure, rasée du matin, bleuissait déjà, et les lampes roses rendaient un sang factice à la bouche. ...

"Pas de femmes! déclara Chéri comme en songe. Donc ... embrasse-moi!"

Surprise, Léa ne bougea pas.

"Embrasse-moi, je te dis!"

Il ordonnait, les sourcils joints, et l'éclat de ses yeux soudain rouverts gêna Léa comme une lumière brusquement rallumée. Elle haussa les épaules et mit un baiser sur le front tout proche. Il noua ses bras au cou de Léa et la courba vers lui.

Elle secoua la tête, mais seulement jusqu'à l'instant où leurs bouches se touchèrent; alors, elle demeura tout à fait immobile et retenant son souffle comme quelqu'un qui écoute. Quand il la lâcha,

That sort of discreet escape, that disappearance, were so unlike Charlotte Peloux's ways that Léa and Chéri looked at each other and laughed in surprise. Chéri sat down next to Léa.

"I'm tired," he said.

"You're wearing yourself out," Léa said.

He straightened up, feeling vain:

"Oh, I'm still in good enough shape, you know."

"Good enough . . . maybe for others . . . but not . . . not for me, for example."

"Too green?"

"Exactly the word I was looking for. Will you come to the country, with strictly honorable intentions? Good strawberries, fresh cream, pies, little grilled chickens . . . That's a good diet, and no women!"

He let himself slide down onto Léa's shoulder, and he closed his eyes.

"No women . . . Terrific . . . Léa, tell me, are you a brother to me? Are you? All right, good-bye, women . . . I've gotten over them . . . Women . . . I've seen them."

He made those coarse remarks in a calm voice. Léa listened to his rich, soft tones and felt his warm breath on her ear. He had grasped Léa's long necklace and was rolling the large pearls in his fingers. She put her arm under Chéri's head, pulled him near her—with no ulterior motive, trusting in her long acquaintance with this child—and rocked him.

"I feel good," he sighed. "You're a brother, I feel good . . ."

She smiled as if she had been given rare praise. Chéri seemed to be falling asleep. At close range she looked at his lashes, which, gleaming as if wet, had fallen onto his cheeks, and at those emaciated cheeks, which bore the marks of a strain that had brought no happiness. His upper lip, which had been shaved that morning, was already turning blue, and the pink lamps gave his mouth a ruddiness it didn't really possess . . .

"No women!" Chéri declared, as if in a dream. "And so . . . kiss me!"

Léa was surprised and didn't move.

"Kiss me, I say!"

He gave the order with knitted brows, and the flash of his suddenly reopened eyes dazzled Léa like a light hastily turned on. She shrugged her shoulders and planted a kiss on his forehead, which was so close. He threw his arms around Léa's neck and drew her toward him.

She shook her head, but only at the moment when their lips met; after that, she remained completely motionless, holding her breath like a person listening attentively. When he released his grip, she

elle le détacha d'elle, se leva, respira profondément et arrangea sa coiffure qui n'était pas défaite. Puis elle se retourna un peu pâle et les yeux assombris, et sur un ton de plaisanterie:
"C'est intelligent!" dit-elle.

Il gisait au fond d'un rocking et se taisait en la couvant d'un regard actif, si plein de défi et d'interrogations qu'elle dit, après un moment:
"Quoi?
— Rien, dit Chéri, je sais ce que je voulais savoir."

Elle rougit, humiliée, et se défendit adroitement:
"Tu sais quoi? que ta bouche me plaît? Mon pauvre petit, j'en ai embrassé de plus vilaines. Qu'est-ce que ça te prouve? Tu crois que je vais tomber à tes pieds et crier: prends-moi! Mais tu n'as donc connu que des jeunes filles? Penser que je vais perdre la tête pour un baiser! . . ."

Elle s'était calmée en parlant et voulait montrer son sang-froid.

"Dis, petit, insista-t-elle en se penchant sur lui, crois-tu que ce soit quelque chose de rare dans mes souvenirs, une bonne bouche?"

Elle lui souriait de haut, sûre d'elle, mais elle ne savait pas que quelque chose demeurait sur son visage, une sorte de palpitation très faible, de douleur attrayante, et que son sourire ressemblait à celui qui vient après une crise de larmes.

"Je suis bien tranquille, continua-t-elle. Quand même je te rembrasserais, quand même nous. . . ."

Elle s'arrêta et fit une moue de mépris.

"Non, décidément, je ne vous vois pas dans cette attitude-là.
— Tu ne nous voyais pas non plus dans celle de tout à l'heure, dit Chéri sans se presser. Et pourtant, tu l'as gardée un bon bout de temps. Tu y penses donc, à l'autre? Moi, je ne t'en ai rien dit."

Ils se mesurèrent en ennemis. Elle craignit de montrer un désir qu'elle n'avait pas eu le temps de nourrir ni de dissimuler, elle en voulut à cet enfant, refroidi en un moment et peut-être moqueur.

"Tu as raison, concéda-t-elle légèrement. N'y pensons pas. Je t'offre, nous disions donc, un pré pour t'y mettre au vert, et une table. . . . La mienne, c'est tout dire.
— On peut voir, répondit Chéri. J'amènerais la Renouhard découverte?
— Naturellement, tu ne la laisserais pas à Charlotte.
— Je paierai l'essence, mais tu nourriras le chauffeur."

Léa éclata de rire.

pushed him away from her, got up, took a deep breath, and straightened her hair, which hadn't been mussed. Then she turned around, a little pale and her eyes darkened, and said in a joking tone:

"That was clever!"

He was slumped in a rocking-chair, silent as he leveled a lively gaze at her, a gaze so full of challenge and inquiry that she said, after a moment: "What is it?"

"Nothing," said Chéri, "I now know what I wanted to know."

She blushed with humiliation and defended herself adroitly:

"What is it that you know? That I like your lips? Poor boy, I've kissed uglier ones. What does that prove to you? You think I'm going to fall at your feet and shout: 'Take me!' But is it only young girls that you've known? To imagine that I'm going to lose my head over a kiss! . . ."

While speaking she had calmed down, and wanted to show how cool and collected she was.

"Tell me, sonny," she continued, leaning over him, "do you think that a good pair of lips is something rare among my memories?"

She was smiling at him in a superior way, sure of herself, but she was unaware that her face retained some trace of the experience, a sort of very weak palpitation and attractive sorrow, and that her smile resembled the smile that follows a crying jag.

"I'm perfectly calm," she went on. "Even if I were to kiss you again, even if we . . ."

She stopped and made a contemptuous face.

"No, definitely, I don't see you in that position."

"You didn't see us in the position we were in a few minutes ago, either," said Chéri unhurriedly. "And yet you kept it up for quite some time. And so, you're thinking about the other thing? I never mentioned it to you myself."

They studied each other like enemies. She was afraid to manifest a desire that she hadn't had time either to foster or to hide. She was cross with that child, who had cooled down in an instant and was possibly making fun of her.

"You're right," she admitted offhandedly. "Let's not think about it. Well, as we were saying, I'm offering you a place where you can put yourself out to pasture, and I'm offering good cooking—*my* kind of cooking, and that says it all."

"It's a possibility," Chéri replied. "Could I take the open Renouhard?"

"Naturally. You wouldn't leave that for Charlotte."

"I'll pay for the gasoline, but you'll give the chauffeur his meals."

Léa burst out laughing.

"Je nourrirai le chauffeur! Ah! ah! fils de Madame Peloux, va! Tu
n'oublies rien. ... Je ne suis pas curieuse, mais je voudrais entendre
ce que ça peut être entre une femme et toi, une conversation
amoureuse!"

Elle tomba assise et s'éventa. Un sphinx, de grands moustiques à
longues pattes tournaient autour des lampes, et l'odeur du jardin, à
cause de la nuit venue, devenait une odeur de campagne. Une bouffée d'acacia entra, si distincte, si active, qu'ils se retournèrent tous
deux comme pour la voir marcher.

"C'est l'acacia à grappes rosées, dit Léa à demi-voix.

— Oui, dit Chéri. Mais comme il en a bu, ce soir, de la fleur
d'oranger!"

Elle le contempla, admirant vaguement qu'il eût trouvé cela. Il respirait le parfum en victime heureuse, et elle se détourna, craignant
soudain qu'il ne l'appelât; mais il l'appela quand même, et elle vint.

Elle vint à lui pour l'embrasser, avec un élan de rancune et d'é-
goïsme et des pensées de châtiment: "Attends, va. ... C'est joliment
vrai que tu as une bonne bouche, cette fois-ci, je vais en prendre mon
content, parce que j'en ai envie, et je te laisserai, tant pis, je m'en
moque, je viens. ..."

Elle l'embrassa si bien qu'ils se délièrent ivres, assourdis, essoufflés,
tremblant comme s'ils venaient de se battre. ... Elle se remit debout
devant lui qui n'avait pas bougé, qui gisait toujours au fond du fauteuil
et elle le défiait tout bas: "Hein? ... Hein? ..." et elle s'attendait à
être insultée. Mais il lui tendit les bras, ouvrit ses belles mains incer-
taines, renversa une tête blessée et montra entre ses cils l'étincelle
double de deux larmes, tandis qu'il murmurait des paroles, des
plaintes, tout un chant animal et amoureux où elle distinguait son
nom, des "chérie ..." des "viens ..." des "plus te quitter ..." un chant
qu'elle écoutait penchée et pleine d'anxiété, comme si elle lui eût, par
mégarde, fait très mal.

QUAND Léa se souvenait du premier été en Normandie, elle con-
statait avec équité: "Des nourrissons méchants, j'en ai eu de plus
drôles que Chéri. De plus aimables aussi et de plus intelligents. Mais
tout de même, je n'en ai pas eu comme celui-là."

"C'est rigolo, confiait-elle, à la fin de cet été de 1906, à
Berthellemy-le-Desséché, il y a des moments où je crois que je
couche avec un nègre ou un chinois.

"I'll give the chauffeur his meals! Ha! Ha! You're really Madame
Peloux's son! You don't overlook a thing . . . I'm not curious, but I'd
like to hear what a lovers' conversation between a woman and you
would be like!"

She dropped onto a chair and fanned herself. A hawkmoth and big,
long-legged mosquitos were circling the lamps; and, because night had
fallen, the fragrance of the garden was becoming a countryside fragrance. A whiff of acacia scent came in, so distinct and forceful that
they both turned around as if to watch it proceeding through the room.

"It's the acacia with pink clusters," said Léa softly.

"Yes," said Chéri. "But all the orange blossom it's imbibed this
evening!"

She gazed at him, vaguely admiring him for coming up with that. He
was inhaling the scent like a willing victim, and she turned away, suddenly
afraid he might call her; but he called her all the same, and she came.

She came to him to kiss him, with a spurt of resentment and self-
ishness, and with thoughts of punishing him: "Just wait . . . Yes, it's
true you have fine lips. For now, I'll take my fill of them, because I
feel like it, then I'll leave you flat. Too bad about it, I don't give a
damn, here I come . . ."

She kissed him so hard that when they pulled apart they were intoxi-
cated, deafened, breathless, trembling as if they had just been fighting . . .
She stood up again in front of him; he hadn't budged, but was still slumped
deep in his armchair, while she was challenging him in a whisper: "Well?
Well?" And she expected him to revile her. Instead, he held out his arms,
opened his lovely, hesitant hands, threw back his head as if it had been
wounded, and revealed between his lashes the double gleam of two tears,
while he kept murmuring words, laments, a long animal chant of love, in
which she could make out her name, "darling," "come to me," "never leave
you"—a chant that she listened to while bending over him, filled with anxiety, as if she had inadvertently wounded him very severely.

WHENEVER Léa recalled that first summer in Normandy, she would
note very honestly: "I've had more amusing nasty infants than Chéri
is. Also, more likable ones and more intelligent ones. But, all the
same, I've never had another one like him."

"It's funny," she confided to Dried-up Berthellemy at the end of
that summer of 1906, "there are moments when I think I'm sleeping
with an African or a Chinese."

— Tu as déjà eu un chinois et un nègre?

— Jamais.

— Alors?

— Je ne sais pas. Je ne peux pas t'expliquer. C'est une impression."

Une impression qui lui était venue lentement, en même temps qu'un étonnement qu'elle n'avait pas toujours su cacher. Les premiers souvenirs de leur idylle n'abondaient qu'en images de mangeaille fine, de fruits choisis, en soucis de fermière gourmette. Elle revoyait, plus pâle au grand soleil, un Chéri exténué qui se traînait sous les charmilles normandes, s'endormait sur les margelles chaudes des pièces d'eau. Léa le réveillait pour le gaver de fraises, de crème, de lait mousseux et de poulets de grain. Comme assommé, il suivait d'un grand œil vide, à dîner, le vol des éphémères autour de la corbeille de roses, regardait sur son poignet l'heure d'aller dormir, tandis que Léa, déçue et sans rancune, songeait aux promesses que n'avait pas tenues le baiser de Neuilly et patientait bonnement:

"Jusqu'à fin août, si on veut, je le garde à l'épinette. Et puis, à Paris, ouf! je le rends à ses chères études...."

Elle se couchait miséricordieusement de bonne heure pour que Chéri, réfugié contre elle, poussant du front et du nez, creusant égoïstement la bonne place de son sommeil, s'endormît. Parfois, la lampe éteinte, elle suivait une flaque de lune miroitante sur le parquet. Elle écoutait, mêlés au clapotis du tremble et aux grillons qui ne s'éteignent ni nuit ni jour, les grands soupirs de chien de chasse qui soulevaient la poitrine de Chéri.

"Qu'est-ce que j'ai donc que je ne dors pas? se demandait-elle vaguement. Ce n'est pas la tête de ce petit sur mon épaule, j'en ai porté de plus lourdes.... Comme il fait beau.... Pour demain matin, je lui ai commandé une bonne bouillie. On lui sent déjà moins les côtes. Qu'est-ce que j'ai donc que je ne dors pas? Ah! oui, je me rappelle, je vais faire venir Patron le boxeur, pour entraîner ce petit. Nous avons le temps, Patron d'un côté, moi de l'autre, de bien épater Madame Peloux...."

Elle s'endormait, longue dans les draps frais, bien à plat sur le dos, la tête noire du nourrisson méchant couchée sur son sein gauche. Elle s'endormait, réveillée quelquefois — mais si peu! — par une exigence de Chéri, vers le petit jour.

"Have you already had a Chinese and an African?"

"Never."

"Well, then?"

"I don't know. I can't explain it to you. It's just an impression I have."

An impression that had come to her gradually, at the same time as a feeling of surprise that she hadn't always been able to conceal. The earliest memories of their idyll were filled exclusively with images of good meals and select fruit, and with her own solicitousness, like that of a farmwife who was also a gourmet. She recalled Chéri, a physical wreck looking even paler in the country sunlight, dragging himself forward beneath the Normandy hedgerows and falling asleep on the warm paved banks of ponds. Léa would awaken him to stuff him with strawberries, cream, foaming milk, and grain-fed chickens. As if stunned, he would watch the mayflies hovering around the basket of roses at dinnertime, and he'd look at his wristwatch to see if it was time to go to sleep, while Léa, disappointed but not angry, thought about the broken promises of that kiss in Neuilly, though she remained good-naturedly patient: "I'll keep him in the fattening cage till the end of August, if need be. Then, back to Paris—whew!—and I'll let him revert to his old habits . . ."

Charitably, she would go to bed early so that Chéri, snuggling against her and selfishly burrowing out a comfortable resting place with his forehead and his nose, could more readily fall asleep. At times, after the lamp was out, she would watch a patch of moonlight shining on the parquet. She would listen, as they mingled with the rustling of the aspen and the cricket chirps that never ceased night or day, to the deep hunting-dog sighs that stirred Chéri's chest.

"What's wrong with me that's preventing me from sleeping?" she wondered vaguely. "It's not this boy's head on my shoulder; I've carried heavier ones . . . How nice the weather is! . . . For tomorrow morning I've ordered some good porridge for him. By now his ribs aren't sticking out so much. So, why can't I sleep? Oh, yes, I remember, I'll have Patron the boxer come to train the boy. With Patron on one side and me on the other, there's still time to prepare a terrific surprise for Madame Peloux . . ."

She would fall asleep, stretched out in the cool sheets, flat on her back, the dark head of the nasty infant lying on her left breast. She'd fall asleep, only to be awakened sometimes—but so seldom!—by an urgent demand from Chéri, toward daybreak.

Le deuxième mois de retraite avait en effet amené Patron, sa grande valise, ses petites haltères d'une livre et demie et ses trousses noires, ses gants de quatre onces, ses brodequins de cuir lacés sur les doigts de pieds; — Patron à la voix de jeune fille, aux longs cils, couvert d'un si beau cuir bruni, comme sa valise, qu'il n'avait pas l'air nu quand il retirait sa chemise. Et Chéri, tour à tour hargneux, veule, ou jaloux de la puissance sereine de Patron, commençait l'ingrate et fructueuse gymnastique des mouvements lents et réitérés.

"Un . . . sss . . . deux . . . sss. . . . je vous entends pas respirer . . . trois . . . sss . . . Je le vois, votre genou qui trich . . . sss. . . ."

Le couvert de tilleuls tamisait le soleil d'août. Un tapis rouge épais, jeté sur le gravier, fardait de reflets violets les deux corps nus du moniteur et de l'élève. Léa suivait des yeux la leçon, très attentive. Pendant les quinze minutes de boxe, Chéri, grisé de ses forces neuves, s'emballait, risquait des coups traîtres et rougissait de colère. Patron recevait les swings comme un mur et laissait tomber sur Chéri, du haut de sa gloire olympique, des oracles plus pesants que son poing célèbre.

"Heu là! que vous avez l'œil gauche curieux. Si je ne l'aurais pas empêché, il venait voir comment qu'il est cousu, mon gant gauche.

— J'ai glissé, rageait Chéri.

— Ça ne provient pas de l'équilibre, poursuivait Patron. Ça provient du moral. Vous ne ferez jamais un boxeur.

— Ma mère s'y oppose, quelle tristesse!

— Même si votre mère ne s'y opposerait pas, vous ne feriez pas un boxeur, parce que vous êtes méchant. La méchanceté, ça ne va pas avec la boxe. Est-ce pas, madame Léa?"

Léa souriait et goûtait le plaisir d'avoir chaud, de demeurer immobile et d'assister aux jeux des deux hommes nus, jeunes, qu'elle comparait en silence: "Est-il beau, ce Patron! Il est beau comme un immeuble. Le petit se fait joliment. Des genoux comme les siens, ça ne court pas les rues, et je m'y connais. Les reins aussi sont . . . non, seront merveilleux. . . . Où diable la mère Peloux a-t-elle pêché. . . . Et l'attache du cou! une vraie statue. Ce qu'il est mauvais! Il rit, on jurerait un lévrier qui va mordre. . . ." Elle se sentait heureuse et maternelle, et baignée d'une tranquille vertu. "Je le changerais bien pour un autre", se disait-elle devant Chéri nu l'après-midi sous les tilleuls, ou Chéri nu le matin sur la couverture d'hermine, ou Chéri nu le soir au bord du bassin d'eau tiède. "Oui, tout beau qu'il est, je le changerais bien, s'il n'y avait pas une question de conscience." Elle confiait son indifférence à Patron.

And in fact the second month of their retreat had brought Patron, with his big valise, his little pound-and-a-half dumbbells and his black tights, his four-ounce gloves, and his leather boots laced over the toes—Patron, with his girlish voice and long lashes, and his hide so beautifully tanned, like his valise, that he didn't look naked when he took off his shirt. And Chéri, now peevish, now sluggish, now envious of Patron's serene strength, began the frustrating but profitable course of training with slow, repeated movements.

"One . . . er . . . two . . . er . . . I don't hear you breathing . . . three . . . er . . . I can see you're not keeping your knees straight . . . er . . ."

The canopy of lindens filtered the August sun. A thick red rug thrown onto the gravel tinged the two bare bodies of the instructor and the pupil with violet reflections. Léa watched the lesson very attentively. During the fifteen minutes of boxing, Chéri, drunk with his new strength, became wild, ventured some unethical blows, and got red with anger. Patron received his swings like a brick wall and, from the height of his Olympian glory, showered Chéri with comments that were more damaging than his celebrated fists.

"Hey, there, your left eye is very inquisitive! If I hadn't prevented it, it would have found out exactly how my left glove is stitched."

"My foot slipped," said Chéri in a rage.

"It's not a matter of your balance," Patron continued. "It's a question of your character. You'll never make a good boxer."

"My mother is against it, isn't that a pity?"

"Even if your mother weren't against it, you wouldn't make a good boxer, because you're mean. Meanness doesn't go with boxing. Right, Madame Léa?"

Léa smiled and enjoyed the pleasure of being warm, sitting still, and watching the maneuvers of the two stripped young men, whom she was silently comparing: "How good-looking Patron is! He's as beautiful as a building. The little one is turning out quite well. You don't see knees like his all over the place, and I'm an expert. And his back, also, is . . . no, *will be* marvelous . . . How the hell did old lady Peloux produce anything like him? . . . And the springing of his neck! A real statue! How malevolent he is! When he laughs he's just like a greyhound that's going to bite . . ." She felt happy and maternal, suffused with tranquil virtue. "I'd readily exchange him for another man," she said to herself when she saw Chéri naked under the lindens in the afternoon, or Chéri naked on the ermine bedspread in the morning, or Chéri naked beside the pool of lukewarm water in the evening. "Yes, handsome as he is, I'd readily exchange him, if it weren't a matter of conscience." She used to confide her feeling of indifference to Patron.

"Pourtant, objectait Patron, il est d'un bon modèle. Vous lui voyez déjà des muscles comme à des types qui ne sont pas d'ici, des types de couleur, malgré qu'il n'y a pas plus blanc. Des petits muscles qui ne font pas d'épate. Vous ne lui verrez jamais des biceps comme des cantaloups.

— Je l'espère bien, Patron! Mais je ne l'ai pas engagé pour la boxe, moi!

— Évidemment, acquiesçait Patron en abaissant ses longs cils. Il faut compter avec le sentiment."

Il supportait avec gêne les allusions voluptueuses non voilées et le sourire de Léa, cet insistant sourire des yeux qu'elle appuyait sur lui quand elle parlait de l'amour.

"Évidemment, reprenait Patron, s'il ne vous donne pas toutes satisfactions. . . ."

Léa riait:

"Toutes, non . . . mais je puise ma récompense aux plus belles sources du désintéressement, comme vous, Patron.

— Oh! moi. . . ."

Il craignait et souhaitait la question qui ne manquait pas de suivre:

"Toujours de même, Patron? Vous vous obstinez?

— Je m'obstine, madame Léa, j'ai encore eu une lettre de Liane, au courrier de midi. Elle dit qu'elle est seule, que je n'ai pas de raisons de m'obstiner, que ses deux amis sont éloignés.

— Alors?

— Alors, je pense que ce n'est pas vrai. . . . Je m'obstine parce qu'elle s'obstine. Elle a honte, qu'elle dit, d'un homme qui a un métier, surtout un métier qui oblige de se lever à bon matin, de faire son entraînement tous les jours, de donner des leçons de boxe et de gymnastique raisonnée. Pas plus tôt qu'on se retrouve, pas plus tôt que c'est la scène. "On croirait vraiment, qu'elle crie, que je ne suis pas capable de nourrir l'homme que j'aime!" C'est d'un beau sentiment, je ne contredis pas, mais ce n'est pas dans mes idées. Chacun a ses bizarreries. Comme vous dites si bien, madame Léa: c'est une affaire de conscience."

Ils causaient à demi-voix sous les arbres; lui pudique et nu, elle vêtue de blanc, les joues colorées d'un rose vigoureux. Ils savouraient leur amitié réciproque, née d'une inclination pareille vers la simplicité, vers la santé, vers une sorte de gentilhommerie du monde bas. Pourtant Léa ne se fût point choquée que Patron reçût, d'une belle Liane haut cotée, des cadeaux de poids. "Donnant, donnant." Et elle essayait de corrompre, avec des arguments d'une équité antique, la "bizarrerie" de Patron. Leurs causeries lentes, qui réveillaient un peu chaque fois les deux mêmes dieux, — l'amour, l'argent, — s'écartaient de l'argent et de

"And yet," Patron objected, "he's got a good build. He's already showing muscles like those on guys not from these parts, colored men—though no one could be whiter than he is. Little muscles that aren't conspicuous. He'll never have biceps big as cantaloupes."

"I hope not, Patron! But it wasn't boxing that *I* signed him up for!"

"Of course," Patron agreed, lowering his long lashes. "You have to take personal feelings into account."

He was embarrassed by Léa's undisguised allusions to lovemaking and by her smile, that insistent smile from her eyes that she rested on him when speaking of love.

"Of course," Patron continued, "if he doesn't satisfy you in every way . . ."

Léa laughed:

"No, not in every way . . . But I derive my reward from a wonderful feeling of unselfishness, just as you do, Patron."

"Oh, as for me . . ."

He both feared and hoped for the question that never failed to follow:

"Still the same, Patron? Are you still being stubborn?"

"I'm still being stubborn, Madame Léa. I had another letter from Liane, in the noon mail. She says she's alone, that I have no reason to be obstinate, that her two friends have gone away."

"And so?"

"And so, I tell myself it's not true . . . I act obstinate because she does. She says she's ashamed of a man who has a job, especially a job that forces him to get up early, train every day, and give lessons in boxing and gymnastics. The moment we get together, we quarrel. 'People would really think,' she yells, 'that I'm unable to support the man I love!' It's a fine sentiment, I don't deny it, but I don't agree with it. Everyone has his eccentricities. As you put it so well, Madame Léa: it's a matter of conscience."

They were chatting in low tones beneath the trees, he modest in his seminudity, she dressed in white, her cheeks tinged with a vigorous pink. They were enjoying their mutual friendship, which sprang from an identical leaning toward simplicity and good health, toward a sort of chivalry among the lower orders of society. And yet Léa wouldn't have been shocked if Patron received expensive presents from beautiful Liane, highly placed as she was. "One hand washes the other." And she'd try to overcome Patron's "eccentricity" with arguments based on traditional fairmindedness. Their slow-paced conversations, each of which appealed to some extent to the same two gods, love and money, would move away

l'amour pour revenir à Chéri, à sa blâmable éducation, à sa beauté
"inoffensive au fond", disait Léa; à son caractère "qui n'en est pas
un", disait Léa. Causeries où se satisfaisaient leur besoin de confiance et leur répugnance pour des mots nouveaux ou des idées nouvelles, causeries troublées par l'apparition saugrenue de Chéri
qu'ils croyaient endormi ou roulant sur une route chaude, Chéri qui
surgissait, demi-nu mais armé d'un livre de comptes et le stylo derrière l'oreille.

"Voyez accolade! admirait Patron. Il a tout du caissier.

— Qu'est-ce que je vois? s'écriait de loin Chéri, trois cent vingt
francs d'essence? On la boit! nous sommes sortis quatre fois depuis
quinze jours! et soixante-dix-sept francs d'huile!

— L'auto va au marché tous les jours, répondait Léa. A propos ton
chauffeur a repris trois fois du gigot à déjeuner, il paraît. Tu ne trouves pas que ça excède un peu nos conventions? . . . Quand tu ne
digères pas une addition, tu ressembles à ta mère."

A court de riposte, il demeurait un moment incertain, oscillant sur
ses pieds fins, balancé par cette grâce volante de petit Mercure qui
faisait pâmer et glapir Mme Peloux: "Moi à dix-huit ans! Des pieds
ailés, des pieds ailés!" Il cherchait une insolence et frémissait de tout
son visage, la bouche entrouverte, le front en avant, dans une attitude
tendue qui rendait évidente et singulière l'inflexion satanique des
sourcils relevés sur la tempe.

"Ne cherche pas, va, disait bonnement Léa. Oui, tu me hais. Viens
m'embrasser. Beau démon. Ange maudit. Petit serin. . . ."

Il venait, vaincu par le son de la voix et offensé par les paroles.
Patron, devant le couple, laissait de nouveau fleurir la vérité sur ses
lèvres pures:

"Pour un physique avantageux, vous avez un physique avantageux.
Mais moi, quand je vous regarde, monsieur Chéri, il me semble que
si j'étais une femme, je me dirais: "Je repasserai dans une dizaine
d'années."

— Tu entends, Léa, il dit dans une dizaine d'années, insinuait Chéri
en écartant de lui la tête penchée de sa maîtresse. Qu'est-ce que tu en
penses?"

Mais elle ne daignait pas entendre et tapotait, de la main, le
jeune corps qui lui devait sa vigueur renaissante, n'importe où, sur
la joue, sur la jambe, sur la fesse, avec un plaisir irrévérencieux de
nourrice.

from money and love and come back to Chéri, to his faulty upbringing; to his good looks, which were "basically harmless," as Léa put it; to his character, which was "a lack of character," Léa would say. Conversations that satisfied their need to confide in someone and their dislike for novel terminology and new ideas, conversations that were interrupted by the preposterous arrival of Chéri, who they had thought was asleep or else driving down some hot road, but who would appear half-naked and yet carrying an account book and wearing a fountain pen behind his ear.

"There's a hello for you!" Patron said admiringly. "He looks just like a cashier."

"What's this I see?" Chéri shouted from the distance, "three hundred twenty francs for gasoline? We must be drinking it! We went out only four times in the last two weeks! And seventy-seven francs for oil!"

"The car travels to the market every day," Léa replied. "And, by the way, your chauffeur took three helpings of leg of lamb at lunch, it seems. Don't you think that goes a little beyond our agreement? . . . When you find fault with an account, you look just like your mother."

At a loss for a retort, he remained hesitant for a moment, rocking back and forth on his well-shaped feet, swayed by that winged gracefulness—like that of a little Mercury—which always made Madame Peloux yelp ecstatically: "Just like me when I was eighteen! Wings on his feet, wings on his feet!" He was trying to come up with some fresh remark, and his whole face was trembling, his mouth half-open, his forehead jutting forward, in a strained attitude that made the satanic curve of his highly raised eyebrows both evident and unusual.

"Don't try so hard," Léa said good-naturedly. "Yes, you hate me. Come give me a kiss. Handsome demon. Fallen angel. Little ninny . . ."

He did come, vanquished by the sound of her voice, though insulted by the words themselves. Patron, looking at the pair, allowed the truth to reappear on his honest lips:

"There's no question about your having a good body. But when I look at you, Monsieur Chéri, it seems to me that, if I were a woman, I'd say to myself: 'I'll be back ten years from now.'"

"You hear, Léa, he says ten years from now," Chéri said insinuatingly, pushing away his mistress' head, which had been leaning over him. "What do *you* say to that?"

But she didn't deign to hear him; instead she tapped with her hand on the young body that owed its new lease on life to her, touching it anywhere, on the cheek, on the leg, on the buttock, with the irreverent pleasure that a nursemaid would feel.

"Quel contentement ça vous donne, d'être méchant?" demandait
alors Patron à Chéri.

Chéri enveloppait l'hercule lentement, tout entier, d'un regard barbare, impénétrable, avant de répondre:

"Ça me console. Tu ne peux pas comprendre."

A la vérité, Léa n'avait, au bout de trois mois d'intimité, rien compris à Chéri. Si elle parlait encore, à Patron qui ne venait plus que le
dimanche, à Berthellemy-le-Desséché qui arrivait sans qu'elle l'invitât
mais s'en allait deux heures après, de "rendre Chéri à ses chères
études", c'était par une sorte de tradition, et comme pour s'excuser de
l'avoir gardé si longtemps. Elle se fixait des délais, chaque fois dé-
passés. Elle attendait.

"Le temps est si beau . . . et puis sa fugue à Paris l'a fatigué, la semaine dernière. . . . Et puis, il vaut mieux que je me donne une bonne
indigestion de lui. . . ."

Elle attendait en vain, pour la première fois de sa vie, ce qui ne lui
avait jamais manqué: la confiance, la détente, les aveux, la sincérité,
l'indiscrète expansion d'un jeune amant, — ces heures de nuit totale
où la gratitude quasi filiale d'un adolescent verse sans retenue des
larmes, des confidences, des rancunes, au sein chaleureux d'une mûre
et sûre amie.

"Je les ai tous eus, songeait-elle obstinée, j'ai toujours su ce qu'ils
valaient, ce qu'ils pensaient et ce qu'ils voulaient. Et ce gosse-là, ce
gosse-là. . . . Ce serait un peu fort."

Robuste à présent, fier de ses dix-neuf ans, gai à table, impatient au
lit, il ne livrait rien de lui que lui-même, et restait mystérieux comme
une courtisane. Tendre? oui, si la tendresse peut percer dans le cri involontaire, le geste des bras refermés. Mais la "méchanceté" lui revenait avec la parole, et la vigilance à se dérober. Combien de fois, vers
l'aube, Léa tenant dans ses bras son amant contenté, assagi, l'œil mi-
fermé avec un regard, une bouche, où la vie revenait comme si
chaque matin et chaque étreinte le recréaient plus beau que la veille,
combien de fois, vaincue elle-même à cette heure-là par l'envie de
conquérir et la volupté de confesser, avait-elle appuyé son front contre le front de Chéri:

"Dis . . . parle . . . dis-moi. . . ."

Mais nul aveu ne montait de la bouche arquée, et guère d'autres
paroles que des apostrophes boudeuses ou enivrées, avec ce nom de
"Nounoune" qu'il lui avait donné quand il était petit et qu'aujourd'hui
il lui jetait du fond de son plaisir, comme un appel au secours.

"Oui, je t'assure, un chinois ou un nègre", avouait-elle à Anthime de

"What enjoyment do you get out of being nasty?" Patron then asked Chéri.

Chéri then slowly looked the bruiser up and down with a barbarous, inscrutable gaze, before replying:

"It consoles me. You wouldn't understand."

To tell the truth, after three months of intimacy, Léa still hadn't understood anything about Chéri. If she still spoke about "letting Chéri revert to his old habits" in her talks with Patron, who now came out only on Sundays, or with Dried-up Berthellemy, who would arrive uninvited but would be gone two hours later, it was only to keep up a sort of tradition, and as if to excuse herself for having kept him so long. She set deadlines for herself, but always let them go by. She was waiting.

"The weather is so fine . . . and, besides, his foray to Paris last week tired him out . . . . And, besides, it's better for me to have a real surfeit of him . . ."

She was waiting in vain, for the first time in her life, for something that had never been lacking in her relationships: confidentiality, a relaxed atmosphere, avowals, sincerity, the indiscreet expansiveness of a young lover—those hours of the deepest night in which the almost filial gratitude of an adolescent pours out without control its tears, confidences, and resentments onto the warm bosom of a mature, safe mistress.

"I've had them all," she would think obstinately, "I've always known what they were worth, what they thought, and what they wanted. But this boy, this boy . . . That would be a bit too much!"

Robust now, proud of his nineteen years, merry at mealtimes, impatient in bed, he surrendered nothing of himself but his person, and remained as mysterious as a courtesan. Was he loving? Yes, if lovingness can be detected in an involuntary cry, in the gesture of his arms closing around her. But his "nastiness" came back whenever he spoke, and was apparent in his care to isolate himself. How many times, toward dawn, when Léa held in her arms her satisfied, sobered lover, his eyes half-closed, his gaze and his lips filled with new life, as if each morning and each embrace restored him and left him more handsome than the day before—how many times, she too overcome at that hour by the desire to conquer and the bliss of avowal, she had rested her forehead on Chéri's forehead:

"Say something . . . speak . . . talk to me . . ."

But no avowal of love issued from his shapely lips, and hardly any other words than sulky or impassioned calls, and that name "Nursie" he had bestowed on her when he was a child and that he now cast at her from the depths of his sensual pleasure, like a cry for help.

"Yes, I assure you, a Chinese or an African," she would admit to

Berthellemy; et elle ajoutait: "je ne peux pas t'expliquer", nonchalante et malhabile à définir l'impression, confuse et forte, que Chéri et elle ne parlaient pas la même langue.

Septembre finissait quand ils revinrent à Paris. Chéri retournait à Neuilly pour "épater", dès le premier soir, Mme Peloux. Il brandissait des chaises, cassait des noix d'un coup de poing, sautait sur le billard et jouait au cow-boy dans le jardin, aux trousses des chiens de garde épouvantés.

"Ouf, soupirait Léa en rentrant seule dans sa maison de l'avenue Bugeaud. Que c'est bon, un lit vide!"

Mais le lendemain soir, pendant qu'elle savourait son café de dix heures en se défendant de trouver la soirée longue et la salle à manger vaste, l'apparition soudaine de Chéri, debout dans le cadre de la porte, Chéri venu sur ses pieds ailés et muets, lui arrachait un cri nerveux. Ni aimable, ni loquace, il accourait à elle.

"Tu n'es pas fou?"

Il haussait les épaules, il dédaignait de se faire comprendre: il accourait à elle. Il ne la questionnait pas: "Tu m'aimes? Tu m'oubliais déjà?" Il accourait à elle.

Un moment après, ils gisaient au creux du grand lit de Léa, tout forgé d'acier et de cuivre. Chéri feignait le sommeil, la langueur, pour pouvoir mieux serrer les dents et fermer les yeux, en proie à une fureur de mutisme. Mais elle l'écoutait quand même, couchée contre lui, elle écoutait avec délices la vibration légère, le tumulte lointain et comme captif dont résonne un corps qui nie son angoisse, sa gratitude et son amour.

"Pourquoi ta mère ne me l'a-t-elle pas appris elle-même hier soir en dînant?

— Elle trouve plus convenable que ce soit moi.

— Non?

— Qu'elle dit.

— Et toi?

— Et moi, quoi?

— Tu trouves ça aussi plus convenable?"

Chéri leva sur Léa un regard indécis.

"Oui."

Il parut penser et répéta:

"Oui, c'est mieux, voyons."

Anthime de Berthellemy; and she'd add: "I can't explain it to you," saying this nonchalantly, unable to make more precise her confused but strong impression that Chéri and she didn't speak the same language.

It was late September when they returned to Paris. On the very first evening, Chéri went back to Neuilly to "astonish" Madame Peloux. He brandished chairs, broke walnuts with his fist, leaped onto the billiard table, and played cowboys in the garden, chasing the frightened watchdogs.

"Whew!" Léa sighed as she returned alone to her house on the Avenue Bugeaud. "How good it is to have an empty bed!"

But on the evening of the next day, while she was sipping her ten-o'clock coffee and forcing herself not to find the night long and the dining room too spacious, the sudden appearance of Chéri standing in the door frame, Chéri who had arrived on his silent, winged feet, elicited a nervous cry from her. Neither friendly nor talkative, he was nevertheless running to her for help.

"Are you crazy?" she said.

He shrugged his shoulders, not deigning to explain his actions: he had come running to her. He asked her no questions: "Do you love me? Were you already forgetting about me?" He had come running to her.

A moment later, they were lying in the bosom of Léa's big wrought-iron and copper bed. Chéri pretended to be sleeping in exhaustion, so that he could grit his teeth and shut his eyes all the harder, in a veritable fit of taciturnity. But, lying next to him, she could hear him all the same; in delight she listened to that slight vibration, that distant and almost captive uproar which is audible in a body that denies its anguish, its gratitude, and its love.

"Why didn't your mother tell me about it last night at dinner?"

"She thinks it's more proper for me to do it."

"Really?"

"That's what she says."

"And you?"

"What about me?"

"Do *you* think it's more proper, too?"

Chéri gave Léa an undecided look.

"Yes."

He seemed to think about it, then repeated:

"Yes, it's better, come on now."

Pour ne le point gêner, Léa détourna les yeux vers la fenêtre. Une pluie chaude noircissait ce matin d'août et tombait droite sur les trois platanes, déjà roussis, de la cour plantée. "On croirait l'automne", remarqua Léa, et elle soupira.

"Qu'est-ce que tu as?" demanda Chéri.

Elle le regarda, étonnée:

"Mais je n'ai rien, je n'aime pas cette pluie.

— Ah! bon, je croyais. . . .

— Tu croyais?

— Je croyais que tu avais de la peine."

Elle ne put s'empêcher de rire franchement.

"Que j'avais de la peine parce que tu vas te marier? Non, écoute . . . tu es . . . tu es drôle. . . ."

Elle éclatait rarement de rire, et sa gaieté vexa Chéri. Il haussa les épaules et alluma une cigarette avec sa grimace habituelle, le menton trop tendu, la lèvre inférieure avancée.

"Tu as tort de fumer avant le déjeuner", dit Léa.

Il répliqua quelque chose d'impertinent qu'elle n'entendit pas, occupée qu'elle était tout à coup d'écouter le son de sa propre voix et l'écho de son conseil quotidien, machinal, répercuté jusqu'au fond de cinq années écoulées. . . . "Ça me fait comme la perspective dans les glaces", songea-t-elle. Puis elle remonta d'un petit effort vers la réalité et la bonne humeur.

"Une chance que je passe bientôt la consigne à une autre, pour le tabac à jeun! dit-elle à Chéri.

— Celle-là, elle n'a pas voix au chapitre, déclara Chéri. Je l'épouse, n'est-ce pas? Qu'elle baise la trace de mes pieds divins, et qu'elle bénisse sa destinée. Et ça va comme ça."

Il exagéra la saillie de son menton, serra les dents sur son fume-cigarette, écarta les lèvres et ne réussit à ressembler ainsi, dans son pyjama de soie immaculé, qu'à un prince asiatique, pâli dans l'ombre impénétrable des palais.

Léa, nonchalante dans son saut-de-lit rose, d'un rose qu'elle nommait "obligatoire", remuait des pensées qui la fatiguaient et qu'elle se décida à jeter, une à une, contre le calme feint de Chéri:

"Enfin, cette petite, pourquoi l'épouses-tu?"

Il s'accouda des deux bras à une table, imita inconsciemment le visage composé de Mme Peloux:

"Tu comprends, ma chère. . . .

— Appelle-moi Madame, ou Léa. Je ne suis ni ta femme de chambre, ni un copain de ton âge."

To avoid embarrassing him, Léa turned away her eyes and looked at the window. A warm rain was darkening that August morning, falling straight down onto the three plane trees, their leaves already red, planted in the courtyard. "You'd think it was fall," Léa remarked, and she sighed.

"What's the matter with you?" Chéri asked.

She looked at him in surprise:

"Nothing's the matter with me, I just don't like this rain."

"Good! Because I thought . . ."

"You thought . . . ?"

"I thought that you were hurt."

She couldn't keep from laughing out loud.

"That I was hurt because you're getting married? No, listen . . . you're . . . you're comical . . ."

She rarely burst out laughing, and her merriment annoyed Chéri. He shrugged his shoulders and lit a cigarette with his usual grimace, his chin thrust out too far and his lower lip protruding.

"You really shouldn't smoke before lunch," said Léa.

His comeback was some bit of impertinence that she didn't hear because she was suddenly too busy listening to the sound of her own voice and the echo of her daily admonition, now mechanical, and re-verberating all the way back through the previous five years. . . . "It's like a pair of mirrors reflecting to infinity," she thought. Then, making a small effort, she resurfaced into reality and a good mood.

"Lucky for me that I can soon transmit the watchword about smoking on an empty stomach to some other woman!" she said to Chéri.

"Oh, her! She's got nothing to say about it," Chéri declared. "I'm marrying her, aren't I? She can just kiss the print of my divine feet and bless her destiny. And that's that."

He stuck out his chin even more, clamped his teeth down on his cigarette holder, and opened his mouth, but even so, in his immaculate silk pajamas, he only succeeded in looking like an Asiatic prince who had grown pale in the impenetrable shadows of his palaces.

Léa, nonchalant in her pink boudoir wrap, whose shade of pink she called "compulsory," was struggling with thoughts that fatigued her, and which she decided to fling one by one at Chéri's feigned calmness.

"Well, why are you marrying this girl?"

He leaned both elbows on a table, unknowingly imitating Madame Peloux's impassive face:

"You understand, my dear . . ."

"Call me 'madame' or 'Léa.' I'm neither your chambermaid nor a pal of your own age."

Elle parlait sec, redressée dans son fauteuil, sans élever la voix. Il voulut riposter, brava la belle figure un peu meurtrie sous la poudre, et les yeux qui le couvraient d'une lumière si bleue et si franche, puis il mollit et céda d'une manière qui ne lui était pas habituelle:

"Nounoune, tu me demandes de t'expliquer. . . . N'est-ce pas, il faut faire une fin. Et puis, il y a de gros intérêts en jeu.

— Lesquels?

— Les miens, dit-il sans sourire. La petite a une fortune personnelle.

— De son père?"

Il bascula, les pieds en l'air.

"Ah! je ne sais pas. T'en as des questions! Je pense. La belle Marie-Laure ne prélève pas quinze cents billets sur sa cassette particulière, hein? Quinze cents billets, et des bijoux de monde bien.

— Et toi?

— Moi, j'ai plus, dit-il avec orgueil.

— Alors, tu n'as pas besoin d'argent."

Il hocha sa tête lisse où le jour courut en moires bleues.

"Besoin, besoin . . . tu sais bien que nous ne comprenons pas l'argent de la même façon. C'est une chose sur laquelle nous ne nous entendons pas.

— Je te rends cette justice que tu m'as épargné ce sujet de conversation pendant cinq ans."

Elle se pencha, mit une main sur le genou de Chéri:

"Dis-moi, petit, qu'est-ce que tu as économisé sur tes revenus, depuis cinq ans?"

Il bouffonna, rit, roula aux pieds de Léa, mais elle l'écarta du pied.

"Sincèrement, dis. . . . Cinquante mille par an, ou soixante? Dis-le donc, soixante? soixante-dix?"

Il s'assit sur le tapis, renversa sa tête sur les genoux de Léa.

"Je ne les vaux donc pas?"

Il s'étalait en plein jour, tournait la nuque, ouvrait tout grands ses yeux qui semblaient noirs, mais dont Léa connaissait la sombre couleur brune et rousse. Elle toucha de l'index, comme pour désigner et choisir ce qu'il y avait de plus rare dans tant de beauté, les sourcils, les paupières, les coins de la bouche. Par moments, la forme de cet amant qu'elle méprisait un peu lui inspirait une sorte de respect. "Etre beau à ce point-là, c'est une noblesse", pensait-elle.

"Dis-moi, petit. . . . Et la jeune personne, dans tout ça? Comment est-elle avec toi?

Sitting up straight in her armchair, she spoke dryly, not raising her voice. He intended to make a clever retort; he defied her beautiful face, which was a little battered-looking beneath its powder, and her eyes, which were bathing him in such a sincere blue light; then he gave way and yielded in a manner that wasn't customary with him:

"Nursie, you're asking me to explain it to you. Don't you think we should wrap things up? Besides, there are major interests at stake."

"What interests?"

"Mine," he said without smiling. "The girl has a fortune of her own."

"From her father?"

He rocked back and forth, his feet in the air.

"Oh, I don't know. The questions you come up with! I think so. The lovely Marie-Laure isn't about to pay out a million and a half francs from her own moneybox, is she? A million and a half francs, plus some serious jewelry."

"And you?"

"Oh, me, I've got more," he said with pride.

"In that case you don't need any money."

He shook his smooth hair, in which the daylight created bluish ripples.

"Need, need . . . You know very well that we don't share the same conception of money. It's a thing we don't agree on."

"I'll say this much for you: you've spared me that topic of conversation for five years."

She leaned over and put a hand on Chéri's knee:

"Tell me, boy, how much have you saved from your income the last five years?"

He played the clown, laughing and rolling on the floor at Léa's feet, but she pushed him away with one foot.

"Tell me honestly . . . Fifty thousand a year, or sixty? Come on and tell me: sixty? Seventy?"

He sat down on the rug, leaning his head back on Léa's knees.

"Am I not worth that much?"

He stretched himself out in full daylight, turning his neck and opening wide those eyes which looked black, but whose dark brown and russet color Léa knew so well. With her index finger, as if to choose and point out the rarest features of all that beauty, she touched his eyebrows, his eyelids, and the corners of his mouth. At moments the physique of that lover, for whom she had a touch of contempt, inspired a kind of respect in her. "To be that handsome is a sort of nobility in itself," she thought.

"Tell me, boy . . . Where does the girl come in, in all this? How does she act with you?"

— Elle m'aime. Elle m'admire. Elle ne dit rien.

— Et toi, comment es-tu avec elle?

— Je ne suis pas, répondit-il avec simplicité.

— Jolis duos d'amour", dit Léa rêveuse.

Il se releva à demi, s'assit en tailleur:

"Je trouve que tu t'occupes beaucoup d'elle, dit-il sévèrement. Tu ne penses donc pas à toi, dans ce cataclysme?"

Elle regarda Chéri avec un étonnement qui la rajeunissait, les sourcils hauts et la bouche entrouverte.

"Oui, toi, Léa. Toi, la victime. Toi, le personnage sympathique dans la chose, puisque je te plaque."

Il avait un peu pâli et semblait, en rudoyant Léa, se blesser lui-même. Léa sourit:

"Mais, mon chéri, je n'ai pas l'intention de rien changer à mon existence. Pendant une huitaine, je retrouverai de temps en temps dans mes tiroirs une paire de chaussettes, une cravate, un mouchoir. . . . Et quand je dis une huitaine . . . ils sont très bien rangés, tu sais, mes tiroirs. Ah! et puis je ferai remettre à neuf la salle de bains. J'ai une idée de pâte de verre. . . ."

Elle se tut et prit une mine gourmande, en dessinant du doigt dans l'air un plan vague. Chéri ne désarmait pas son regard vindicatif.

"Tu n'es pas content? Qu'est-ce que tu voudrais? Que je retourne en Normandie cacher ma douleur? Que je maigrisse? Que je ne me teigne plus les cheveux? Que madame Peloux accoure à mon chevet?"

Elle imita la trompette de Mme Peloux en battant des avant-bras:

"L'ombre d'elle-même! l'ombre d'elle-même! La malheureuse a vieilli de cent ans! de cent ans!" C'est ça que tu voudrais?"

Il l'avait écoutée avec un sourire brusque et un frémissement des narines qui était peut-être de l'émotion:

"Oui", cria-t-il.

Léa posa sur les épaules de Chéri ses bras polis, nus et lourds:

"Mon pauvre gosse! Mais j'aurais dû déjà mourir quatre ou cinq fois, à ce compte-là! Perdre un petit amant . . . Changer un nourrisson méchant. . . ."

Elle ajouta plus bas, légère:

"J'ai l'habitude.

— On le sait, dit-il âprement. Et je m'en fous! Ça, oui, je m'en fous bien, de ne pas avoir été ton premier amant! Ce que j'aurais voulu, ou plutôt ce qui aurait été . . . convenable . . . propre . . . c'est que je sois le dernier."

Il fit tomber, d'un tour d'épaules, les bras superbes.

"Au fond, ce que j'en dis, n'est-ce pas, c'est pour toi.

"She loves me. She admires me. She says nothing."

"And how are you with her?"

"I'm not there at all," he answered simply.

"Fine love duets!" said Léa thoughtfully.

He straightened himself somewhat and assumed a cross-legged position.

"It seems to me you're worrying about her a lot," he said severely. "Aren't you thinking about yourself in this catastrophe?"

She stared at Chéri with an astonishment that made her look younger, her eyebrows raised and her mouth slightly open.

"Yes, you, Léa. You, the victim. You, the sympathetic character in the affair, since I'm jilting you."

He had turned a little pale and, by bullying Léa, seemed to be striking at himself. Léa smiled:

"But, darling, I have no intention of making any changes in my way of life. For a week or so, I'll occasionally find a pair of socks in my dresser drawers, or a necktie, or a handkerchief . . . And when I say a week . . . You know, my dresser drawers are in very good order. Oh! And then I'll remodel my bathroom. I'm thinking about a glass-composition facing . . ."

She fell silent and assumed a greedy expression, drawing a vague sketch in the air with her finger. Chéri didn't let up his vindictive gaze.

"You're not satisfied? What would you like me to do? Go back to Normandy to hide my grief? Get thin? Give up dyeing my hair? Have Madame Peloux hasten to my bedside?"

She imitated Madame Peloux's trumpet tones, flapping her forearms:

"'A ghost of herself! A ghost of herself! The poor thing has grown a hundred years older! A hundred years older!' Is that what you'd like?"

He had listened to her with a sudden smile and a quivering of his nostrils that perhaps betokened some emotion.

"Yes!" he cried.

Léa placed her smooth, bare, heavy arms on Chéri's shoulders:

"Poor kid! But, at that rate, I would have already died four or five times! To lose a young lover . . . To exchange a nasty infant . . ."

She added more quietly, lightly:

"I'm used to it."

"I know," he said harshly. "And I don't give a damn! Yes, you heard me, I don't give a damn that I wasn't your first lover! What I would have liked, or, rather, what would have been fitting . . . proper . . . is to have been your last."

With a twist of his shoulders he shook off her magnificent arms.

"After all, what I'm saying is for your sake, isn't it?"

— Je comprends parfaitement. Toi, tu t'occupes de moi, moi je m'occupe de ta fiancée, tout ça, c'est très bien, très naturel. On voit que ça se passe entre grands cœurs."

Elle se leva, attendant qu'il répondît quelque goujaterie, mais il se tut et elle souffrit de voir pour la première fois, sur le visage de Chéri, une sorte de découragement.

Elle se pencha, mit ses mains sous les aisselles de Chéri:

"Allons, viens, habille-toi. Je n'ai que ma robe à mettre, je suis prête en dessous, qu'est-ce que tu veux qu'on fasse par un temps pareil, sinon aller chez Schwabe te choisir une perle? Il faut bien que je te fasse un cadeau de noces."

Il bondit, avec un visage étincelant:

"Chouette! Oh, chic, une perle pour la chemise! une un peu rosée, je sais laquelle!

— Jamais de la vie, une blanche, quelque chose de mâle, voyons! Moi aussi, je sais laquelle. Encore la ruine! Ce que je vais en faire, des économies, sans toi!"

Chéri reprit son air réticent:

"Ça, ça dépend de mon successeur."

Léa se retourna au seuil du boudoir et montra son plus gai sourire, ses fortes dents de gourmande, le bleu frais de ses yeux habilement bistrés:

"Ton successeur? Quarante sous et un paquet de tabac! Et un verre de cassis le dimanche, c'est tout ce que ça vaut! Et je doterai tes gosses!"

Ils devinrent tous deux très gais, pendant les semaines qui suivirent. Les fiançailles officielles de Chéri les séparaient chaque jour quelques heures, parfois une ou deux nuits. "Il faut donner confiance", affirmait Chéri. Léa, que Mme Peloux écartait de Neuilly, cédait à la curiosité et posait cent questions à Chéri important, lourd de secrets qu'il répandait dès le seuil, et qui jouait à l'escapade chaque fois qu'il retrouvait Léa:

"Mes amis! criait-il un jour en coiffant de son chapeau le buste de Léa. Mes amis, qu'est-ce qu'on voit au Peloux's Palace depuis hier!

— Ote ton chapeau de là, d'abord. Et puis n'invoque pas ta vermine d'amis ici. Qu'est-ce qu'il y a encore?"

Elle grondait, en riant d'avance.

"I understand perfectly. You're worried about me, I'm worried about your fiancée. All that is very good, very natural. Obviously nothing but the noblest hearts are at work here."

She got up, expecting him to make some churlish reply, but he remained silent, and she was pained to see a sort of discouragement on Chéri's face for the first time.

She leaned over and put her hands under Chéri's arms:

"All right, come on, get dressed. I only need to put my dress on, I'm all set underneath. What would you like us to do, with the weather the way it is, except to go to Schwabe's and pick out a pearl for you? I must give you a wedding present."

He jumped up, his face shining:

"Terrific! Oh, swell, a pearl for my shirt! One with a slight pink tinge, I know the one!"

"Not on your life! A white one, something masculine, come on now. I know the one, also. Wiped out again! All the money I'm going to save when you're gone!"

Chéri resumed his reticent air:

"That depends on who my successor is."

Léa turned around on the threshold to her boudoir and flashed her brightest smile, showing her strong, voracious teeth and the clear blue of her skillfully shadowed eyes:

"Your successor? Two francs and a pack of cigarettes! And a glass of cassis on Sundays, he won't be worth more than that! And I'll give dowries to your children!"

BOTH of them became very cheerful during the weeks that followed. Chéri's official status as an engaged man kept them apart for a few hours every day, and occasionally for a night or two. "I must make her trust me," Chéri would declare. Léa, whom Madame Peloux kept away from Neuilly, was succumbing to curiosity and plying Chéri with a hundred questions. He was self-important, chock-full of secrets that he divulged the second he arrived, and feeling like a truant each time he rejoined Léa:

"My friends!" he cried one day, putting his hat on Léa's sculptured bust. "My friends, what doings in Peloux's Palace since yesterday!"

"First of all, take your hat off there. Second, don't mention your filthy friends here. What's going on now?"

She was scolding him, but already laughing.

"Y a le feu, Nounoune! Le feu parmi ces dames! Marie-Laure et Mame Peloux qui se peignent au-dessus de mon contrat!

— Non?

— Si! c'est un spectacle magnifique. (Gare les hors-d'œuvre que je te fasse les bras de Mame Peloux. . . .) "Le régime dotal! le régime dotal! Pourquoi pas le conseil judiciaire? C'est une insulte personnelle! personnelle! La situation de fortune de mon fils! . . . Apprenez, Madame. . . ."

— Elle l'appelait Madame?

— Large comme un parapluie. "Apprenez, Madame, que mon fils n'a pas un sou de dettes depuis sa majorité, et la liste des valeurs achetées depuis mil neuf cent dix représente. . . ." Représente ci, représente ça, représente mon nez, représente mon derrière. . . . Enfin, Catherine de Médicis en plus diplomate, quoi!"

Les yeux bleus de Léa brillaient de larmes de rire.

"Ah! Chéri! tu n'as jamais été si drôle depuis que je te connais. Et l'autre, la belle Marie-Laure?

— Elle, oh! terrible, Nounoune. Cette femme-là doit avoir un quarteron de cadavres derrière elle. Toute en vert jade, ses cheveux roux, sa peau . . . enfin, dix-huit ans, et le sourire. La trompette de ma mère vénérée ne lui a pas fait bouger un cil. Elle a attendu la fin de la charge pour répondre: "Il vaudrait peut-être mieux, chère Madame, ne pas mentionner trop haut les économies réalisées par votre fils pendant les années mil neuf cent dix et suivantes. . . ."

— Pan, dans l'œil! . . . dans le tien. Où étais-tu, pendant ce temps-là?

— Moi? Dans la grande bergère.

— Tu étais là?"

Elle cessa de rire et de manger.

"Tu étais là? et qu'est-ce que tu as fait?

— Un mot spirituel . . . naturellement. Mame Peloux empoignait déjà un objet de prix pour venger mon honneur, je l'ai arrêtée, sans me lever: "Mère adorée, de la douceur. Imite-moi, imite ma charmante belle-mère, qui est tout miel . . . et tout sucre." C'est là-dessus que j'ai eu la communauté réduite aux acquêts.

— Je ne comprends pas.

"It's war, Nursie! War between the two mothers. Marie-Laure and Ma'me Peloux are scrapping over my marriage contract!"

"Really?"

"Yes! It's a magnificent spectacle. (Woe to the hors-d'œuvres if I imitate Ma'me Peloux's arm gestures for you!) 'Protection for her money! Protection for her money![6] Why not appoint a legal guardian for him?! It's a personal insult! Personal! My son's financial situation! . . . Let me inform you, madame . . .'"

"She called her 'madame'?"

"Right to her face. 'Let me inform you, madame, that my son hasn't incurred one cent of debt since he's been of age, and the stock portfolio acquired since 1910 amounts to . . .' Amounts to this, amounts to that, amounts to my nose, amounts to my ass . . . In short, she's a Catherine de Médicis, but more diplomatic!"

Léa's blue eyes were gleaming with tears of laughter.

"Oh, Chéri, you haven't ever been this funny since I've known you. And the other one, the lovely Marie-Laure?"

"She? Oh, a terror, Nursie. That woman must have left two dozen corpses in her wake. All dressed in jade green, with her red hair, her complexion . . . well, like an eighteen-year-old's, and that smile. My revered mother's trumpet didn't make her bat an eyelash. She waited until the attack was over, then replied: 'Dear madame, it might be better not to speak too loudly about how much money your son saved during 1910 and the years following . . .'"

"Pow, right in the eye! . . . *Your* eye. Where were you all that time?"

"I? In the big easy chair."

"You were right there?"

She stopped laughing and eating.

"You were right there? And what did you do?"

"Said something witty . . . naturally. Ma'me Peloux was already taking hold of some objet d'art in order to avenge my honor, but, without getting up, I stopped her. 'Gently, mother dear, gently! Follow my example, follow the example of my charming mother-in-law, who is all honey . . . and all *sugar.*' Thereby I regained community property of all wealth acquired after the wedding."

"I don't understand."

---

6. To be more precise, a *régime dotal* was a legal arrangement by which a husband could avail himself only of so much of his wife's money as she brought him in her dowry.

— Les fameuses plantations de canne que le pauvre petit prince Ceste a laissées par testament à Marie-Laure. . . .

— Oui. . . .

— Faux testament. Famille Ceste très excitée! Procès possible! Tu saisis?"

Il jubilait.

"Je saisis, mais comment connais-tu cette histoire?

— Ah! voilà. La vieille Lili vient de s'abattre de tout son poids sur le cadet Ceste, qui a dix-sept ans et des sentiments pieux. . . .

— La vieille Lili? quelle horreur!

— . . . et le cadet Ceste lui a murmuré cette idylle, parmi des baisers. . . .

— Chéri! j'ai mal au cœur!

— . . . et la vieille Lili m'a repassé le tuyau au jour de maman, dimanche dernier. Elle m'adore, la vieille Lili! Elle est pleine de considération pour moi, parce que je n'ai jamais voulu coucher avec elle!

— Je l'espère bien, soupira Léa. C'est égal. . . ."

Elle réfléchissait et Chéri trouva qu'elle manquait d'enthousiasme.

"Hein, dis, je suis épatant? Dis?"

Il se penchait au-dessus de la table et la nappe blanche, la vaisselle où jouait le soleil l'éclairaient comme une rampe.

"Oui. . . ."

"C'est égal", songeait-elle, "cette empoisonneuse de Marie-Laure l'a proprement traité de barbeau . . .".

"Il y a du fromage à la crème, Nounoune?

— Oui. . . ."

". . . et il n'a pas plus sauté en l'air que si elle lui jetait une fleur. . . ."

"Nounoune, tu me donneras l'adresse? l'adresse des cœurs à la crème, pour mon nouveau cuisinier que j'ai engagé pour octobre?

— Penses-tu! on les fait ici. Un cuisinier, voyez sauce aux moules et vol-au-vent!"

". . . il est vrai que depuis cinq ans, j'entretiens à peu près cet enfant. . . . Mais il a tout de même trois cent mille francs de rente. Voilà. Est-on un barbeau quand on a trois cent mille francs de rente? Ça ne dépend pas du chiffre, ça dépend de la mentalité. . . . Il y a des types à qui j'aurais pu donner un demi-million et qui ne seraient pas pour cela des barbeaux. . . . Mais Chéri? et pourtant, je ne lui ai jamais donné d'argent. . . . Tout de même. . . ."

"Tout de même, éclata-t-elle . . . elle t'a traité de maquereau!

— Qui ça?

"'Those much talked-about sugar-cane plantations that the late little Prince Ceste left Marie-Laure in his will . . .'"

"Yes . . ."

"Forged will. Ceste family very upset! Possible lawsuit! Get it?" He was jubilant.

"I get it, but how did you find out about all this?"

"Oh. Like this: Old Lili has just fallen with all her weight for junior Ceste, who's seventeen and has religious leanings . . ."

"Old Lili? How horrible!"

"And junior Ceste whispered that love story to her in between kisses . . ."

"Chéri! I'm feeling faint!"

"And old Lili tipped me off about it on Mother's open-house day, last Sunday. Old Lili just adores me! She respects me no end, because I never wanted to sleep with her!"

"I should hope not," Léa sighed. "All the same . . ."

She was reflecting, and it seemed to Chéri that she wasn't sufficiently enthusiastic.

"Well, say it, am I wonderful, or am I? Say it!"

He was leaning over the table and the white cloth; the chinaware, on which the sun was playing, illuminated him like footlights.

"Yes . . ."

"All the same," she was thinking, "that murderess Marie-Laure came out and called him a pimp . . ."

"Is there any cream cheese, Nursie?"

"Yes . . ."

"And he didn't get any more riled up than if she had thrown a flower at him . . ."

"Nursie, please give me the address—the place where you get these heart-shaped cream cheeses—for the new cook I've hired for October."

"What an idea! They're made right in the house. Without a cook, would I have mussel sauce or vol-au-vent?"

"It's true that for five years I've practically been supporting this boy . . . But he does have a yearly income of three hundred thousand francs. So there! Is someone a pimp when he has an income of three hundred thousand francs? It doesn't depend on the amount, it depends on his frame of mind . . . There are men whom I might have given a half-million, but that still wouldn't have made them pimps . . . But Chéri? And yet I never gave him money . . . But all the same . . ."

"All the same," she suddenly said out loud, "she called you a procurer!"

"Who did?"

— Marie-Laure!"

Il s'épanouit et eut l'air d'un enfant:

"N'est-ce pas? n'est-ce pas, Nounoune, c'est bien ça qu'elle a voulu dire?

— Il me semble!"

Chéri leva son verre empli d'un vin de Château-Chalon, coloré comme de l'eau-de-vie:

"Vive Marie-Laure! Quel compliment, hein! Et qu'on m'en dise autant quand j'aurai ton âge, je n'en demande pas plus!

— Si ça suffit à ton bonheur. . . ."

Elle l'écouta distraitement jusqu'à la fin du déjeuner. Habitué aux demi-silences de sa sage amie, il se contenta des apostrophes maternelles et quotidiennes: "Prends le pain le plus cuit. . . . Ne mange pas tant de mie fraîche. . . . Tu n'as jamais su choisir un fruit . . ." tandis que, maussade en secret, elle se gourmandait: "Il faudrait pourtant que je sache ce que je veux! Qu'est-ce que j'aurais voulu? Qu'il se dresse en pied: "Madame, vous m'insultez! Madame, je ne suis pas ce que vous croyez!" Au fond, je suis responsable. Je l'ai élevé à la coque, je l'ai gavé de tout. . . . A qui l'idée serait-elle venue qu'il aurait un jour l'envie de jouer au père de famille? Elle ne m'est pas venue, à moi! En admettant qu'elle me soit venue, comme dit Patron: "le sang, c'est le sang!" Même s'il avait accepté les propositions de Liane, il n'aurait fait qu'un tour, le sang de Patron, si on avait parlé de marée à portée de ses oreilles. Mais Chéri, il a du sang de Chéri, lui. Il a. . . ."

"Qu'est-ce que tu disais, petit? s'interrompit-elle, je n'écoutais pas.

— Je disais que jamais, tu m'entends, jamais rien ne m'aura fait rigoler comme mon histoire avec Marie-Laure!"

"Voilà, acheva Léa en elle-même, lui, ça le fait rigoler."

Elle se leva d'un mouvement las. Chéri passa un bras sous sa taille, mais elle l'écarta.

"C'est quel jour, ton mariage, déjà?

— Lundi en huit."

Il semblait si innocent et si détaché qu'elle s'effara:

"C'est fantastique!

— Pourquoi fantastique, Nounoune?

— Tu n'as réellement pas l'air d'y songer!

— Je n'y songe pas, dit-il d'une voix tranquille. Tout est réglé. Cérémonie à deux heures, comme ça on ne s'affole pas pour le grand déjeuner. Five o'clock chez Charlotte Peloux. Et puis les sleepings, l'Italie, les lacs. . . .

"Marie-Laure!"

He beamed and looked like a child:

"She did, didn't she? Didn't she, Nursie? Is that what she meant?"

"I believe so!"

Chéri raised his glass of Château-Chalon wine, which was deep-colored as brandy:

"Here's to Marie-Laure! Say, what a compliment! Let people call me that when I'm as old as you, that's all I ask!"

"If that's enough to make you happy . . ."

She listened to him only absentmindedly till lunch was over. He, accustomed to the intermittent silences of his sagacious friend, was contented with her usual brief maternal admonitions: "Take the crust of the bread . . . Don't eat so much of the soft part . . . You've never learned how to pick out a fruit." Meanwhile, secretly grumpy, she was reprimanding herself: "I've just got to decide what I really want! What would I have liked him to do? To stand up to her: 'Madame, you're insulting me! Madame, I'm not what you think!' After all, I'm responsible. I pampered him with the best of everything, I filled his tummy . . . Who would ever have thought that one day he'd feel like playing the role of father figure? I never did, anyway! And even if I had had the idea, it's as Patron says: 'It depends on what's in your blood!' Even if Patron had accepted Liane's propositions, he would have boiled over with anger if anyone had mentioned pimps or gigolos in his hearing. But Chéri has the blood of Chéri. He has . . ."

"What were you saying, little one?" she interrupted her thoughts. "I wasn't listening."

"I was saying that nothing—you hear—nothing will ever tickle me like that business with Marie-Laure!"

"There you go!" Léa concluded her train of thought. "It merely tickles him."

She got up wearily. Chéri put an arm around her waist, but she brushed it away.

"Tell me again, what day are you getting married?"

"A week from Monday."

He seemed so innocent and carefree that she got frightened:

"It's amazing!"

"Why amazing, Nursie?"

"You really look as if it's not on your mind!"

"It isn't on my mind," he said calmly. "Everything's arranged. Ceremony at two; that way, there's no flurry over a big luncheon. Five-o'clock tea at Charlotte Peloux's. And then the sleeping cars, Italy, the lakes . . ."

— Ça se reporte donc, les lacs?

— Ça se reporte. Des villas, des hôtels, des autos, des restaurants
. . . Monte-Carlo, quoi!

— Mais elle! il y a elle. . . .

— Bien sûr, il y a elle. Il n'y a pas beaucoup elle, mais il y a elle.

— Et il n'y a plus moi."

Chéri n'attendait pas la petite phrase et le laissa voir. Un
tournoiement maladif des prunelles, une décoloration soudaine de la
bouche le défigurèrent. Il reprit haleine avec précaution pour qu'elle
ne l'entendît pas respirer et redevint pareil à lui-même:

"Nounoune, il y aura toujours toi.

— Monsieur me comble.

— Il y aura toujours toi, Nounoune . . . — il rit maladroitement —
dès que j'aurai besoin que tu me rendes un service."

Elle ne répondit rien. Elle se pencha pour ramasser une fourche
d'écaille tombée et l'enfonça dans ses cheveux en chantonnant. Elle
prolongea sa chanson avec complaisance devant un miroir, fière de se
dompter si aisément, d'escamoter la seule minute émue de leur sépa-
ration, fière d'avoir retenu les mots qu'il ne faut pas dire: "Parle . . .
mendie, exige, suspends-toi . . . tu viens de me rendre heureuse. . . ."

MME Peloux avait dû parler beaucoup et longtemps, avant l'entrée
de Léa. Le feu de ses pommettes ajoutait à l'éclat de ses grands yeux
qui n'exprimaient jamais que le guet, l'attention indiscrète et impénétrable. Elle portait ce dimanche-là une robe d'après-midi noire à jupe
très étroite, et personne ne pouvait ignorer que ses pieds étaient très
petits ni qu'elle avait le ventre remonté dans l'estomac. Elle s'arrêta
de parler, but une gorgée dans le calice mince qui tiédissait dans sa
paume et pencha la tête vers Léa avec une langueur heureuse.

"Crois-tu qu'il fait beau? Ce temps! ce temps! Dirait-on qu'on est
en octobre?

— Ah! non? . . . Pour sûr que non!" répondirent deux voix serviles.

Un fleuve de sauges rouges tournait mollement le long de l'allée,
entre des rives d'asters d'un mauve presque gris. Des papillons souci
volaient comme en été, mais l'odeur des chrysanthèmes chauffés au
soleil entrait dans le hall ouvert. Un bouleau jaune tremblait au vent,
au-dessus d'une roseraie de bengale qui retenait les dernières
abeilles.

"Et qu'est-ce que c'est, clama Mme Peloux soudain lyrique, qu'est-

"So a lake honeymoon is back in style?"

"Yes, it is. Villas, hotels, cars, restaurants . . . like Monte Carlo!"

"But what about *her*? *She's* a part of all that . . ."

"Of course, she's a part of it. Not a very big part, but she is a part."

"But I'm no longer any part of it."

Chéri wasn't expecting that little utterance, and he showed it. A sickly turning up of his eyes and a sudden lack of color on his lips made him look ugly. He caught his breath again carefully, so she wouldn't hear him breathe, and then he became himself once more:

"Nursie, there'll always be you."

"You're much too good to me."

"There'll always be you, Nursie . . .," he laughed clumsily, "as soon as I need you to do me a favor."

She made no reply. She stooped down to pick up a tortoise-shell comb that had fallen, and she put it back in her hair, humming. She kept up her song in self-satisfaction in front of her mirror, proud that she had regained her self-control so easily, proud of disguising the only emotional moment of their separation, proud of having kept back the words that mustn't be spoken: "Speak . . . beg, make demands, cling to me . . . you've just made me happy."

MADAME Peloux must have been speaking a lot, for a long time, before Léa came in. The flush on her cheeks added to the gleam of her large eyes, which never expressed anything but watchfulness, indiscreet and inscrutable attention. That Sunday she was wearing a black afternoon gown with a very tight skirt, and no one could fail to notice that her feet were very small and her belly was pulled in. She stopped speaking, took a sip from the thin glass she was warming in the palm of her hand, and leaned her head toward Léa in blissful languor.

"Do you believe how nice it is out? What weather! What weather! Would anyone think it was October?"

"Oh, no . . . Definitely not!" replied two servile voices.

A river of red salvia gently flowed down the garden path between banks of asters of an almost gray mauve. Orange-red sulphur butterflies flitted about as if it were summer, and the fragrance of the sun-baked chrysanthemums entered the open garden room. A yellow birch was quaking in the breeze above a clump of China roses that was detaining the last bees.

"But how does it compare?" exclaimed Madame Peloux, who was

ce que c'est que ce temps, à côté de celui qu'*ils* doivent avoir en
Italie!

— Le fait est. . . . Vous pensez! . . ." répondirent les voix serviles.

Léa tourna la tête vers les voix en fronçant les sourcils:

"Si au moins elles ne parlaient pas", murmura-t-elle.

Assises à une table de jeu, la baronne de la Berche et Mme Aldonza
jouaient au piquet. Mme Aldonza, une très vieille danseuse, aux
jambes emmaillotées, souffrait de rhumatisme déformant, et portait
de travers sa perruque d'un noir laqué. En face d'elle et la dominant
d'une tête et demie, la baronne de la Berche carrait d'inflexibles
épaules de curé paysan, un grand visage que la vieillesse virilisait à
faire peur. Elle n'était que poils dans les oreilles, buissons dans le nez
et sur la lèvre, phalanges velues. . . .

"Baronne, vous ne coupez pas à mon quatre-vingt-dix, chevrota
Mme Aldonza.

— Marquez, marquez, ma bonne amie. Ce que je veux, moi, c'est
que tout le monde soit content."

Elle bénissait sans trêve et cachait une cruauté sauvage. Léa la considéra comme pour la première fois, avec dégoût, et ramena son regard vers Mme Peloux.

"Au moins, Charlotte a une apparence humaine, elle. . . ."

"Qu'est-ce que tu as, ma Léa? Tu n'as pas l'air dans ton assiette?"
interrogea tendrement Mme Peloux.

Léa cambra sa belle taille et répondit:

"Mais si, ma Lolotte. . . . Il fait si bon chez toi que je me laisse vivre
. . ." tout en songeant: "Attention . . . la férocité est là aussi . . ." et elle
mit sur son visage une impression de bien-être complaisant, de
rêverie repue, qu'elle souligna en soupirant:

"J'ai trop mangé . . . je veux maigrir, là! Demain, je commence un
régime."

Mme Peloux battit l'air et minauda:

"Le chagrin ne te suffit donc pas?

— Ah! Ah! Ah! s'esclaffèrent Mme Aldonza et la baronne de la
Berche. Ah! Ah! Ah!"

Léa se leva, grande dans sa robe d'automne d'un vert sourd, belle
sous son chapeau de satin bordé de loutre, jeune parmi ces décom-
bres qu'elle parcourut d'un œil doux:

"Ah! là là, mes enfants . . . donnez-m'en douze, de ces chagrins-là,
que je perde un kilo!

— T'es épatante, Léa, lui jeta la baronne dans une bouffée de
fumée.

suddenly lyrical. "How does this weather compare to the weather *they* must be having in Italy?"

"Yes, indeed . . . Just imagine!" replied the servile voices.

Léa turned her head in the direction of the voices, knitting her brow: "If only they didn't speak, at least," she murmured.

Seated at a card table, the Baroness de la Berche and Madame Aldonza were playing piquet. Madame Aldonza, a very old ballerina with swathed legs, suffered from crippling rheumatism; her lacquer-black wig was on crooked. Opposite her, and towering a head and a half over her, the Baroness de la Berche had inflexible square shoulders like those of a peasant priest, and a large face that her age made frighteningly masculine. She was all hair in the ears, tufts in the nose and over the lips, furry fingers . . .

"Baroness, you're not going to get away from my ninety points," Madame Aldonza bleated shakily.

"Mark it down, mark it down, dear friend. All *I* want is for everyone to be happy."

She was constantly showering blessings, but underneath it she was savagely cruel. Léa observed her as if for the first time and felt disgusted; then she brought her eyes back to Madame Peloux.

"At least Charlotte looks like a human being . . ."

"What's wrong, Léa? You don't seem altogether yourself," said Madame Peloux warmly.

Léa thrust out her beautiful bosom and replied:

"I'm all right, Lolotte . . . It's so comfortable here at your place that I'm just letting myself drift . . ." But at the same time she was thinking: "Watch out! There's something savage behind *her* remarks, too." And her face took on an expression of self-contented peace of mind, a well-fed dreaminess, which she emphasized by sighing:

"I ate too much . . . I want to get thinner, that's what it is! Tomorrow I'll go on a diet."

Madame Peloux flapped her arms and said mincingly:

"Isn't your heartbreak enough for you?"

"Ha! Ha! Ha!" Madame Aldonza and the Baroness de la Berche guffawed. "Ha! Ha! Ha!"

Léa stood up, tall in her dull-green fall dress, beautiful in her otter-trimmed satin hat, young in the midst of that detritus which she ran her calm eyes over:

"Oh, ho, children . . . give me twelve such heartbreaks, so I can lose a couple of pounds!"

"You're remarkable, Léa," said the baroness through a puff of smoke.

— Madame Léa, après vous ce chapeau-là, quand vous le jetterez? mendia la vieille Aldonza. Madame Charlotte, vous vous souvenez, votre bleu? Il m'a fait deux ans. Baronne, quand vous aurez fini de faire de l'œil à Madame Léa, vous me donnerez des cartes?

— Voilà, ma mignonne, en vous les souhaitant heureuses!"

Léa se tint un moment sur le seuil du hall, puis descendit dans le jardin. Elle cueillit une rose de Bengale qui s'effeuilla, écouta le vent dans le bouleau, les tramways de l'avenue, le sifflet d'un train de Ceinture. Le banc où elle s'assit était tiède et elle ferma les yeux, laissant le soleil lui chauffer les épaules. Quand elle rouvrit les yeux, elle tourna la tête précipitamment vers la maison, avec la certitude qu'elle allait voir Chéri debout sur le seuil du hall, appuyé de l'épaule à la porte. . . .

"Qu'est-ce que j'ai?" se demanda-t-elle.

Des éclats de rire aigus, un petit brouhaha d'accueil dans le hall, la mirent debout, un peu tremblante.

"Est-ce que je deviendrais nerveuse?"

"Ah! les voilà, les voilà", trompettait Mme Peloux.

Et la forte voix de basse de la baronne scandait:

"Le p'tit ménage! Le p'tit ménage!"

Léa frémit, courut au seuil et s'arrêta: elle avait, devant elle, la vieille Lili et son amant adolescent, le prince Ceste, qui venaient d'arriver.

Peut-être soixante-dix ans, un embonpoint d'eunuque corseté, — on avait coutume de dire de la vieille Lili qu' "elle passait les bornes" sans préciser de quelles bornes il s'agissait. Une éternelle gaieté enfantine éclairait son visage, rond, rose, fardé, où les gros yeux et la très petite bouche, fine et rentrée, coquetaient sans honte. La vieille Lili suivait la mode, scandaleusement. Une jupe à raies, bleu révolution et blanc, contenait le bas de son corps, un petit spencer bleu béait sur un poitrail nu, à peau gaufrée de dindon coriace; un renard argenté ne cachait pas le cou nu, en pot de fleurs, un cou large comme un ventre et qui avait aspiré le menton. . . .

"C'est effroyable", pensa Léa. Elle ne pouvait détacher son regard de quelque détail particulièrement sinistre, le "breton" de feutre blanc, par exemple, gaminement posé en arrière sur la perruque de cheveux courts châtain rosé, ou bien le collier de perles, tantôt visible et tantôt enseveli dans une profonde ravine qui s'était autrefois nommée "collier de Vénus". . . .

"Léa, Léa, ma petite copine!" s'écria la vieille Lili en se hâtant vers Léa. Elle marchait difficilement sur des pieds tout ronds et enflés,

"Madame Léa, could I have that hat when you're done with it? When are you getting rid of it?" old Aldonza cadged. "Madame Charlotte, remember your blue one? It lasted me two years. Baroness, whenever you're finished giving Madame Léa the glad eye, would you deal me some cards?"

"There you are, darling, and I hope they're lucky for you!"

Léa remained a moment on the threshold to the garden room, then stepped down into the garden. She picked a China rose, which lost its petals, and listened to the breeze in the birch, the trolleys on the avenue, and the whistle of a suburban train. The bench on which she sat was warm, and she shut her eyes, letting the sun bake her shoulders. When she opened her eyes again, she suddenly turned her head toward the house in the certainty that she'd see Chéri standing at the entrance to the garden room, his shoulder leaning against the door . . .

"What's wrong with me?" she wondered.

High-pitched laughs and a slight hubbub of welcoming in the garden room made her stand up, trembling slightly.

"Am I becoming a nervous wreck?"

"Ah, there they are, there they are!" Madame Peloux was trumpeting.

And the baroness' loud bass voice recited rhythmically:

"The lov-ing pair! The lov-ing pair!"

Léa shuddered, ran to the threshold, and stopped short: in front of her were old Lili and her teenage lover, Prince Ceste, who had just arrived.

Seventy years old maybe, as fat as a eunuch in her corset—Lili was generally said to "be beyond all bounds," though the particular bounds weren't specified. An eternal childish jolliness lit up her round, pink, made-up face, in which her big eyes and very small mouth, thin and puckered, flirted shamelessly. Lili followed the fashions, scandalously. A striped skirt, white and "Revolution" blue, held in her lower body; a little blue spencer gaped wide on her bare upper chest, its skin as wrinkled as a tough turkey's; a silver fox failed to conceal her bare neck—like a flowerpot—a neck as wide as a belly, which had absorbed her chin . . . .

"It's frightful," Léa thought. She couldn't tear her eyes away from certain especially grim details, such as the white felt "Brittany" hat girlishly pushed back on the pinkish-brown short-haired wig, or the pearl necklace, one moment visible and the next moment buried in a deep ravine that had once been called a "lovely fold in her neck."

"Léa, Léa, my little buddy!" exclaimed old Lili, rushing over to Léa. She walked with difficulty on feet that were all round and swollen, and

ligotés de cothurnes et de barrettes à boucles de pierreries, et s'en congratula la première:

"Je marche comme un petit canard! c'est un genre bien à moi! Guido, ma folie, tu reconnais Mme de Lonval? Ne la reconnais pas trop, ou je te saute aux yeux. . . ."

Un enfant mince à figure italienne, vastes yeux vides, menton effacé et faible, baisa vite la main de Léa et rentra dans l'ombre, sans mot dire. Lili le happa au passage et lui plaqua la tête contre son poitrail grenu, en prenant l'assistance à témoin.

"Savez-vous ce que c'est, Madame, savez-vous ce que c'est? C'est mon grand amour, ça, Mesdames!

— Tiens-toi, Lili, conseilla la voix mâle de Mme de la Berche.

— Pourquoi donc? Pourquoi donc? dit Charlotte Peloux.

— Par propreté, dit la baronne.

— Baronne, tu n'es pas aimable! Sont-ils gentils, tous les deux! Ah! soupira-t-elle, ils me rappellent mes enfants.

— J'y pensais, dit Lili avec un rire ravi. C'est notre lune de miel aussi, à nous deux Guido! On vient pour savoir des nouvelles de l'autre jeune ménage! On vient pour se faire raconter tout."

Mme Peloux devint sévère:

"Lili, tu ne comptes pas sur moi pour te raconter des grivoiseries, n'est-ce pas?

— Si, si, si, s'écria Lili en battant des mains. Elle essaya de sautiller, mais parvint seulement à soulever un peu ses épaules et ses hanches. C'est comme ça qu'on m'a, c'est comme ça qu'on me prend! Le péché de l'oreille! On ne me corrigera pas. Cette petite canaille-là en sait quelque chose!"

L'adolescent muet, mis en cause, n'ouvrit pas les lèvres. Ses prunelles noires allaient et venaient sur le blanc de ses yeux comme des insectes effarés. Léa, figée, regardait.

"Madame Charlotte nous a raconté la cérémonie, bêla Mme Aldonza. Sous la fleur d'oranger la jeune dame Peloux était un rêve.

— Une madone! Une madone! rectifia Charlotte Peloux de tous ses poumons, soulevée par un saint délire. Jamais, jamais on n'avait vu un spectacle pareil! Mon fils marchait sur des nuées! Sur des nuées! . . . Quel couple! Quel couple!

— Sous la fleur d'oranger . . . tu entends, ma folie? murmura Lili. . . . Dis donc, Charlotte, et notre belle-mère? Marie-Laure?"

L'œil impitoyable de Mme Peloux étincela.

"Oh! elle. . . . Déplacée, absolument déplacée. . . . Tout en noir col-

enclosed in boots with jeweled buckles on their straps, and she was the first to appreciate herself:

"I walk like a little duck! It's my own way of doing it! Guido, my passion, do you know Madame de Lonval? Don't let me see that you know her too well, or I'll scratch your eyes out . . ."

A thin boy with an Italian face, huge, expressionless eyes, and a weak, receding chin rapidly kissed Léa's hand and withdrew into the shadows again without saying a word. Lili seized him as he went, and flattened his head against her grainy chest, calling everyone present to witness.

"Do you know who this is, madame, do you know who this is? This is my great love, ladies!"

"Control yourself, Lili," advised Madame de la Berche's masculine voice.

"What for? What for?" asked Charlotte Peloux.

"Out of decency," said the baroness.

"Baroness, you're mean! How nice they are together! Ah!" she sighed, "they remind me of *my* little ones."

"I was thinking about that," said Lili with a happy laugh. "It's our honeymoon, too, Guido's and mine! We've come to hear news about the other young couple! We've come to have you tell us everything."

Madame Peloux became stern.

"Lili, you're not expecting me to tell you dirty stories, are you?"

"Oh, yes, I am," shouted Lili, clapping her hands. She tried to give a hop, but merely managed to raise her shoulders and hips a little. "That's how I am, that's how you've got to take me! The sins of the ear! I'm incorrigible. This little scoundrel here knows what I'm talking about!"

The silent adolescent, thus thrown into the limelight, didn't open his mouth. His dark pupils moved to and fro over the whites of his eyes like frightened insects. Léa stood rooted to the spot, watching.

"Madame Charlotte told us about the ceremony," Madame Aldonza bleated. "Wearing her orange blossoms, young Madame Peloux was a dream."

"A madonna! A madonna!" Charlotte Peloux corrected her at the top of her lungs, exalted by a holy delirium. "Never, never has such a sight been seen! My son was walking in the clouds! In the clouds! . . . What a pair! What a pair!"

"Wearing her orange blossoms . . . Hear that, my passion?" murmured Lili. "Tell us, Charlotte, what about our mother-in-law? What about Marie-Laure?"

Madame Peloux's merciless eyes glistened.

"Oh, her . . . Unsuitable, completely unsuitable . . . Wearing a form-

lant, comme une anguille qui sort de l'eau; les seins, le ventre, on lui
voyait tout! tout!

— Mâtin! grommela la baronne de la Berche avec une furie mili-
taire.

— Et cet air de se moquer du monde, cet air d'avoir tout le temps
du cyanure dans sa poche et un demi-setier de chloroforme dans son
réticule! Enfin, déplacée, voilà le mot! Elle a donné l'impression de
n'avoir que cinq minutes à elle — à peine la bouche essuyée: "Au
revoir, Edmée, au revoir, Fred" et la voilà partie!"

La vieille Lili haletait, assise sur le bord d'un fauteuil, sa petite
bouche d'aïeule, aux coins plissés, entrouverte:

"Et les conseils? jeta-t-elle.

— Quels conseils?

— Les conseils, — ô ma folie, tiens-moi la main! — les conseils à la
jeune mariée? Qui les lui a donnés?"

Charlotte Peloux la toisa d'un air offensé.

"Ça se faisait peut-être de ton temps, mais c'est un usage tombé."

Gaillarde, la vieille se mit les poings sur les hanches:

"Tombé? tombé ou non, qu'est-ce que t'en peux savoir, ma pauvre
Charlotte? On se marie si peu, dans ta famille!

— Ah! Ah! Ah!" s'esclaffèrent imprudemment les deux ilotes. . . .

Mais un seul regard de Mme Peloux les consterna.

"La paix, la paix, mes petits anges! Vous avez chacune votre paradis
sur la terre, que voulez-vous de plus?"

Et Mme de la Berche étendit une forte main de gendarme pacifi-
cateur entre les têtes congestionnées de ces dames. Mais Charlotte
Peloux flairait la bataille comme un cheval de sang:

"Tu me cherches, Lili, tu n'auras pas de mal à me trouver! Je te dois
le respect et pour cause, sans quoi. . . ."

Lili tremblait de rire du menton aux cuisses:

"Sans quoi, tu te marierais rien que pour me donner un démenti?
C'est pas difficile de se marier, va! Moi, j'épouserais bien Guido, s'il
était majeur!

— Non? fit Charlotte qui en oublia sa colère.

— Mais! . . . Princesse Ceste, ma chère! la *piccola principessa!*
Piccola principessa! c'est comme ça qu'il m'appelle, mon petit
prince!"

Elle pinçait sa jupe et tournait, découvrant une gourmette d'or à la
place probable de sa cheville.

"Seulement, poursuivit-elle mystérieusement, son père. . . ."

fitting black dress, like an eel coming out of the water. You could see her breasts, her stomach, everything! Everything!"

"Fancy that!" the Baroness de la Berche growled with soldierlike fury.

"And that air of caring nothing for the others, that air of having cyanide in her pocket the whole time, and a half-gallon of chloroform in her reticule. In short: unsuitable, there's no other word for it! She gave the impression that she had only five minutes to spare—the moment she wiped her mouth: 'So long, Edmée! So long, Fred!' and she was off like a shot!"

Old Lili was panting as she sat on the edge of an armchair, holding open her little ancient mouth, with its wrinkled corners:

"And the advice?" she blurted out.

"What advice?"

"The advice—oh, my passion, hold my hand!—the advice to the young bride? Who gave it to her?"

Charlotte seemed offended as she looked her up and down.

"Maybe that was done in your day, but it's an obsolete practice."

The ribald old woman put her fists on her hips:

"Obsolete? How would you possibly know whether it's obsolete or not, poor Charlotte? There are so few marriages in your family!"

"Ha! Ha! Ha!" the two lowly slaves guffawed imprudently . . .

But one look from Madame Peloux alarmed them.

"Calm down, calm down, my little angels! Each of you has her earthly paradise, what more do you want?"

And Madame de la Berche stretched out her strong hand, like that of a policeman breaking up a fight, between the angrily flushed faces of the two women. But Charlotte Peloux smelled battle like a thoroughbred warhorse:

"You're asking for it, Lili, and I'm not afraid to let you have it! I owe you respect, and for a good reason. Otherwise . . ."

Lili was shaking with laughter from her chin to her thighs:

"Otherwise, you'd get married just to prove I'm a liar? It's not hard to get married, anyhow! *I* would gladly marry Guido if he were of age!"

"No!?" said Charlotte, forgetting to be angry when she heard that.

"Oh, yes! . . . Princess Ceste, my dear! The *piccola principessa! Piccola principessa!* That's what my little prince calls me!"

She lifted her skirt and turned around, revealing a gold chain at the probable location of her ankle.

"Only," she continued with an air of mystery, "his father . . ."

Elle s'essoufflait, et appela du geste l'enfant muet qui parla bas et précipitamment, comme s'il récitait:

"Mon père, le duc de Parese, veut me mettre au couvent si j'épouse Lili. . . .

— Au couvent! glapit Charlotte Peloux. Au couvent, un homme!

— Un homme au couvent! hennit en basse profonde Mme de la Berche. Sacrebleu, que c'est excitant!

— C'est des sauvages", lamenta Aldonza en joignant ses mains informes.

Léa se leva si brusquement qu'elle fit tomber un verre plein.

"C'est du verre blanc, constata Mme Peloux avec satisfaction. Tu vas porter bonheur à mon jeune ménage. Où cours-tu? il y a le feu chez toi?"

Léa eut la force d'esquisser un petit rire cachotier:

"Le feu, peut-être. . . . Chut! pas de questions! mystère. . . .

— Non? du nouveau? pas possible!"

Charlotte Peloux piaulait de convoitise:

"Aussi, je te trouvais un drôle d'air. . . .

— Oui, oui! dites tout!" jappèrent les trois vieilles.

Les paumes à bourrelets de Lili, les moignons déformés de la mère Aldonza, les doigts durs de Charlotte Peloux avaient saisi ses mains, ses manches, son sac de mailles d'or. Elle s'arracha à toutes ces pattes et réussit à rire encore avec un air taquin:

"Non, c'est trop tôt, ça gâterait tout! c'est mon secret! . . ."

Et elle s'élança dans le vestibule. Mais la porte s'ouvrit devant elle et un ancêtre desséché, une sorte de momie badine la prit dans ses bras:

"Léa, ma belle, embrasse ton petit Berthellemy, ou tu ne passeras pas!"

Elle cria de peur et d'impatience, souffleta les os gantés qui la tenaient, et s'enfuit.

Ni dans les avenues de Neuilly, ni dans les allées du Bois, bleues sous un rapide crépuscule, elle ne s'accorda le loisir de penser. Elle grelottait légèrement et remonta la glace de l'automobile. La vue de sa maison nette, de sa chambre rose et de son boudoir, trop meublé et fleuri, la réconfortèrent:

"Vite, Rose, une flambée dans ma chambre!

— Le calo est pourtant à soixante-dix comme en hiver: Madame a eu tort de ne prendre qu'une bête de cou. Les soirées sont traîtres.

— La boule dans le lit tout de suite, et pour dîner une grande tasse

She ran out of breath and signaled to the silent boy, whose words came out quietly and in a rush, as if he were reciting:

"My father, the Duke of Parese, says he'll put me in a monastery if I marry Lili . . ."

"In a monastery!" yelped Charlotte Peloux. "Cloistering a man, the way girls are locked up in a convent!"

"Cloistering a man!" Madame de la Berche neighed in her basso profondo. "Damn, but that's one for the books!"

"They're savages," Aldonza lamented, clasping her shapeless hands.

Léa stood up so brusquely that she knocked over a full glass.

"It's clear glass," Madame Peloux noted with satisfaction. "You'll bring luck to my young couple. Where are you dashing off to? Is your house on fire?"

Léa had the strength to utter a little secretive laugh:

"On fire, maybe . . . Sh! No questions! It's a mystery . . ."

"No!? Again? Impossible!"

Charlotte Peloux was whimpering with prurience:

"I thought you had a peculiar way about you . . ."

"Yes! Yes! Tell us everything," yapped the three old women.

Lili's palms, with their rolls of fat, old lady Aldonza's misshapen stumps, and Charlotte Peloux's hard fingers had grasped her hands, her sleeves, and her gold-mesh bag. She tore herself loose from all those claws, and managed to laugh again in a teasing way:

"No, it's too soon, it would spoil everything! It's my secret! . . ."

And she darted into the vestibule. But the door opened in front of her, and a dried-up ancient, a sort of playful mummy, caught her in his arms:

"Léa, my beauty, kiss your little Berthellemy, or you won't get by!"

She gave a cry of fear and impatience, slapped the gloved bones that were holding her, and escaped.

Neither in the wide streets of Neuilly nor in the avenues of the Bois, blue in the swiftly descending dusk, did she allow herself time to think. She was shivering slightly, and she rolled up the car window. The sight of her neat house, her pink bedroom, and her boudoir, which was overfurnished and had too many flowers, comforted her:

"Quick, Rose, a nice big fire in my room!"

"But the thermostat is at seventy, just as in wintertime: Madame was wrong to take only a fur collar. The evenings can get so cold unexpectedly."

"A hot-water bottle in my bed at once, and for dinner a big cup of

de chocolat bien réduit, un jaune d'œuf battu dedans, et des rôties, du raisin. . . . Vite, mon petit, je gèle. J'ai pris froid dans ce bazar de Neuilly. . . ."

Couchée, elle serra les dents et les empêcha de claquer. La chaleur du lit détendit ses muscles contractés, mais elle ne s'abandonna point encore et le livre de comptes du chauffeur Philibert l'occupa jusqu'au chocolat, qu'elle but bouillant et mousseux. Elle choisit un à un les grains de chasselas en balançant la grappe attachée à son bois, une longue grappe d'ambre vert devant la lumière. . . .

Puis, elle éteignit sa lampe de chevet, s'étendit à sa mode favorite, bien à plat sur le dos, et se laissa aller.

"Qu'est-ce que j'ai?"

Elle fut reprise d'anxiété, de grelottement. L'image d'une porte vide l'obsédait: la porte du hall flanquée de deux touffes de sauges rouges.

"C'est maladif, se dit-elle, on ne se met pas dans cet état-là pour une porte."

Elle revit aussi les trois vieilles, le cou de Lili, la couverture beige que Mme Aldonza traînait partout avec elle depuis vingt ans.

"A laquelle des trois me faudra-t-il ressembler, dans dix ans?"

Mais cette perspective ne l'épouvanta pas. Pourtant, son anxiété augmentait. Elle erra d'image en image, de souvenir en souvenir, cherchant à s'écarter de la porte vide encadrée de sauges rouges. Elle s'ennuyait dans son lit et tremblait légèrement. Soudain un malaise, si vif qu'elle le crut d'abord physique, la souleva, lui tordit la bouche, et lui arracha, avec une respiration rauque, un sanglot et un nom:

"Chéri!"

Des larmes suivirent, qu'elle ne put maîtriser tout de suite. Dès qu'elle reprit de l'empire sur elle-même, elle s'assit, s'essuya le visage, ralluma la lampe.

"Ah! bon, fit-elle. Je vois."

Elle prit dans la console de chevet un thermomètre, le logea sous son aisselle.

"Trente-sept. Donc, ce n'est pas physique. Je vois. C'est que je souffre. Il va falloir s'arranger."

Elle but, se leva, lava ses yeux enflammés, se poudra, tisonna les bûches, se recoucha. Elle se sentait circonspecte, pleine de défiance contre un ennemi qu'elle ne connaissait pas: la douleur. Trente ans de vie facile, aimable, souvent amoureuse, parfois cupide, venaient de se

very thick hot chocolate with an egg yolk beaten into it, some toast, and grapes . . . Quick, my dear, I'm freezing. I caught a chill at that barn in Neuilly . . ."

Once in bed, she gritted her teeth to keep them from chattering. The warmth of the bed eased her tensed muscles, but she didn't let herself relax completely just yet; she went over her chauffeur Philibert's account book until the arrival of the chocolate, which she drank while it still steamed and foamed. She chose the Chasselas grapes one by one, while swinging the whole cluster by its stem; it was a long cluster, greenish amber in the light . . .

Then she turned off the night-table lamp, stretched out in her favorite way, flat on her back, and let herself drift.

"What's wrong with me?"

She had another attack of anxiety and shivering. She was obsessed with the image of an empty doorway: the garden-room doorway flanked by two tufts of red salvia.

"It's morbid," she told herself, "a person doesn't get into this state on account of a door."

She also had fresh visions of the three old women, Lili's neck, and the beige lap rug that Madame Aldonza had been dragging around with her for twenty years.

"Which of those three am I fated to look like ten years from now?"

But that prospect didn't frighten her. Yet her anxiety was getting worse. She wandered from image to image, from memory to memory, trying to get away from that empty doorway framed by the red salvia. She was getting bored lying in bed, and was trembling slightly. Suddenly a feeling of discomfort, so strong that she thought at first it was physical, stirred her, twisted her mouth, and, in a hoarse breath, made her utter a sigh and a name:

"Chéri!"

Tears followed, tears she couldn't immediately keep back. When she had regained control over herself, she sat up, wiped her face, and turned on the lamp again.

"Good!" she said. "I see."

She took a thermometer from the night table and put it in her armpit.

"Ninety-eight. So it isn't physical. I see. It's because I'm suffering. I have to take steps about this."

She drank some water, got up, washed her reddened eyes, powdered her face, poked up the logs in the fire, and lay down again. She felt circumspect, full of caution in the face of an unfamiliar enemy: sorrow. Thirty years of easy living, of a life that had been pleasant, often occu-

détacher d'elle et de la laisser, à près de cinquante ans, jeune et comme nue. Elle se moqua d'elle-même, ne perçut plus sa douleur et sourit:

"Je crois que j'étais folle, tout à l'heure. Je n'ai plus rien."

Mais un mouvement de son bras gauche, involontairement ouvert et arrondi pour recevoir et abriter une tête endormie, lui rendit tout son mal et elle s'assit d'un saut.

"Eh bien! ça va être joli", dit-elle à voix haute, sévèrement.

Elle regarda l'heure et vit qu'il était à peine onze heures. Au-dessus d'elle, le pas feutré de la vieille Rose passa, gagna l'escalier de l'étage mansardé, s'éteignit. Léa résista à l'envie d'appeler à son aide cette vieille fille déférente.

"Ah! non, pas d'histoires à l'office, n'est-ce pas?"

Elle se releva, se vêtit chaudement d'une robe de soie ouatée, se chauffa les pieds. Puis elle entrouvrit une fenêtre, tendit l'oreille pour écouter elle ne savait quoi. Un vent humide et plus doux avait amené des nuages, et le Bois tout proche, encore feuillu, murmurait par bouffées. Léa referma la fenêtre, prit un journal dont elle lut la date:

"Vingt-six octobre. Il y a un mois juste que Chéri est marié."

Elle ne disait jamais "qu'Edmée est mariée".

Elle imitait Chéri et n'avait pas encore compté pour vivante cette jeune ombre de femme. Des yeux châtains, des cheveux cendrés, très beaux, un peu crépus, — le reste fondait dans le souvenir comme les contours d'un visage qu'on a vu en songe.

"Ils font l'amour en Italie, à cette heure-ci, sans doute. Et ça, ce que ça m'est égal. . . ."

Elle ne fanfaronnait pas. L'image qu'elle se fit du jeune couple, les attitudes familières qu'elle évoqua, le visage même de Chéri, évanoui pour une minute, la ligne blanche de la lumière entre ses paupières sans force, tout cela n'agitait en elle ni curiosité, ni jalousie. En revanche, la convulsion animale la reprit, la courba, devant une encoche de la boiserie gris perle, la marque d'une brutalité de Chéri. . . .

"La belle main qui a laissé ici sa trace s'est détournée de toi à jamais. . . ."

"Ce que je parle bien! Vous allez voir que le chagrin va me rendre poétique!"

Elle se promena, s'assit, se recoucha, attendit le jour. Rose, à huit heures, la trouva assise à son bureau et écrivant, spectacle qui inquiéta la vieille femme de chambre.

pied by love and sometimes by greed, had just fallen away from her, leaving her young and, as it were, naked, though she was nearly fifty. She laughed at herself, no longing feeling her sorrow, and she smiled: "I think I was crazy a while ago. Nothing's wrong with me anymore."

But a movement of her left arm, which had involuntarily opened and bent to receive and shelter the head of a sleeper, brought back all her pain, and she sat up with a start.

"Well, well! This is going to be nice!" she said aloud, and sternly.

She looked at the time and saw that it was scarcely eleven. Over her head, old Rose's light tread could be heard; it reached the stairs to the attic story and became inaudible. Léa resisted her urge to call for help from that deferential old maid.

"No, no, no gossip in the servants' quarters, right?"

She got up again, dressed warmly in a quilted silk robe, and chafed her feet. Then she opened a window part-way and put her ear to it, though she didn't know what she wanted to listen to. A moist, gentler wind had brought clouds with it, and the nearby Bois, which still retained its foliage, transmitted gusts of rustling. Léa shut the window again and picked up a newspaper, reading its date:

"October twenty-sixth. Exactly a month since Chéri got married."

She never said "since Edmée got married."

Imitating Chéri, she had never counted that shadowy young woman as a living being. Brown eyes, ash-blond hair that was very beautiful and a little curly—all the rest melted away in her memory like the outlines of a face seen in a dream.

"They're making love in Italy at this very hour, no doubt. And how little I care . . ."

She wasn't boasting. Her mental picture of the young couple; the familiar gestures that she recalled; even Chéri's face, which had vanished for a moment, the white line that the light threw between his weak eyelids—none of that aroused her curiosity or jealousy. On the other hand, a purely animal seizure came over her again, bending her double, at the sight of a nick in the pearl-gray woodwork, the trace of one of Chéri's rages . . .

"The lovely hand that left its trace here has turned away from you for all time . . ."

"How eloquent I am! Wait and see, my broken heart will make a poet of me!"

She walked to and fro, sat down, went back to bed, and waited for daylight. At eight Rose found her seated at her desk writing, a sight that worried the old chambermaid.

"Madame est malade?

— Couci, couça, Rose. L'âge, tu sais. . . . Vidal veut que je change d'air. Tu viens avec moi? L'hiver s'annonce mauvais, ici, on va aller manger un peu de cuisine à l'huile, au soleil.

— Où ça donc?

— Tu es trop curieuse. Fais seulement sortir les malles. Tape-moi bien mes couvertures de fourrure. . . .

— Madame emmène l'auto?

— Je crois. Je suis même sûre. Je veux toutes mes commodités, Rose. Songe donc, je pars toute seule: c'est un voyage d'agrément."

Pendant cinq jours, Léa courut Paris, écrivit, télégraphia, reçut des dépêches et des lettres méridionales. Et elle quitta Paris, laissant à Mme Peloux une courte lettre qu'elle avait pourtant recommencée trois fois:

"*Ma chére Charlotte,*

"*Tu ne m'en voudras pas si je pars sans te dire au revoir, et en gardant mon petit secret. Je ne suis qu'une grande folle! . . . Bah! la vie est courte, au moins qu'elle soit bonne.*

"*Je t'embrasse bien affectueusement. Tu feras mes amitiés au petit quand il reviendra.*

"*Ton incorrigible,*
"*Léa.*

"*P. S. — Ne te dérange pas pour venir interviewer mon maître d'hôtel ou le concierge, personne ne sait rien chez moi.*"

"Sais-tu bien, mon trésor aimé, que je ne trouve pas que tu aies très bonne mine?

— C'est la nuit en chemin de fer", répondit brièvement Chéri.

Mme Peloux n'osait pas dire toute sa pensée. Elle trouvait son fils changé.

"Il est . . . oui, il est fatal", décréta-t-elle; et elle acheva tout haut avec enthousiasme:

"C'est l'Italie!

— Si tu veux", concéda Chéri.

La mère et le fils venaient de prendre ensemble leur petit déjeuner et Chéri avait daigné saluer de quelques blasphèmes flatteurs son "café au lait de concierge", un café au lait gras, blond et sucré que l'on

"Is madame ill?"

"So-so, Rose. My age, you know . . . Vidal wants me to get away for awhile. Will you come with me? It looks like a bad winter here, so we'll go eat some dishes cooked in oil, in the sunshine."

"Where?"

"You're too inquisitive. Just have the trunks brought out. Give a good beating to my fur lap rugs . . ."

"Madame is taking the car?"

"I think so. In fact, I'm sure. I want all my comforts, Rose. Just think, I'm traveling all by myself: it'll be a pleasure trip."

For five days Léa ran all over Paris, wrote letters, sent telegrams, and received cables and letters from the South. And she left Paris, leaving Madame Peloux a short letter, but one that she had started three times over:

"Dear Charlotte,

"I hope you won't be annoyed with me for leaving without saying good-bye in person, and for keeping my little secret. I'm just a big fool! . . . Bah! Life is short, so why not make it sweet?

"Love and kisses. When your boy comes back, give him my best regards.

"Your incorrigible
"Léa

"P.S.: Don't take the trouble to interrogate my butler or the concierge. No one at my place knows where I've gone."

"YOU know, darling, I don't find you looking too well."

"It's the night I spent on the train," Chéri replied succinctly.

Madame Peloux didn't have the courage to say all that she was thinking. She found her son changed.

"He's . . . yes, he's grim," she decided. And she finished her thought out loud, declaring enthusiastically:

"It was Italy!"

"If you like," Chéri concurred.

Mother and son had just had breakfast together, and Chéri had deigned to bestow some blasphemous compliments on her "concierge-style" café au lait, a thick, yellowish, sweet café au lait that was put back for a second time over a gentle charcoal flame after

confiait une seconde fois à un feu doux de braise, après y avoir rompu
des tartines grillées et beurrées qui recuisaient à loisir et masquaient
le café d'une croûte succulente.

Il avait froid dans son pyjama de laine blanche et serrait ses genoux
dans ses bras. Charlotte Peloux, coquette pour son fils, inaugurait un
saut-de-lit souci et un bonnet du matin, serré aux tempes, qui donnait
à la nudité de son visage une importance sinistre.

Comme son fils la regardait, elle minauda:

"Tu vois, j'adopte le genre aïeule! Bientôt la poudre. Ce bonnet-là,
tu l'aimes? Il fait dix-huitième, pas? Dubarry ou Pompadour? De quoi
ai-je l'air?

— Vous avez l'air d'un vieux forçat, lui assena Chéri. C'est pas des
choses à faire, ou bien on prévient."

Elle gémit, puis s'esclaffa:

"Ah! ah! tu l'as, la dent dure!"

Mais il ne riait pas et regardait dans le jardin la neige mince,
tombée la nuit sur les gazons. Le gonflement spasmodique, presque
insensible, de ses muscles maxillaires trahissait seul sa nervosité.
Mme Peloux intimidée imita son silence. Un trille étouffé de sonnette
résonna.

"C'est Edmée qui sonne pour son petit déjeuner", dit Mme Peloux.

Chéri ne répondit pas.

"Qu'est-ce qu'il a donc, le calorifère? il fait froid, ici, dit-il au bout
d'un moment.

— C'est l'Italie, répéta Mme Peloux avec lyrisme. Tu reviens ici
avec du soleil plein les yeux, plein le cœur! Tu tombes dans le
pôle! dans le pôle! Les dahlias n'ont pas fleuri huit jours! Mais sois
tranquille, mon amour adoré. Ton nid s'avance. Si l'architecte
n'avait pas eu une paratyphoïde, ce serait fini. Je l'avais prévenu;
si je ne lui ai pas dit vingt fois, je ne lui ai pas dit une: "Monsieur
Savaron. . . . "

Chéri qui était allé à la fenêtre se retourna brusquement:

"Elle est datée de quand, cette lettre?"

Mme Peloux ouvrit de grands yeux de petit enfant:

"Quelle lettre?

— Cette lettre de Léa que tu m'as montrée tout à l'heure.

— Elle n'est pas datée, mon amour, mais je l'ai reçue la veille de
mon dernier dimanche d'octobre.

— Bon. Et vous ne savez pas qui c'est? . . .

— Qui c'est, ma merveille?

— Oui, enfin, le type avec qui elle est partie?"

crumbling into it bits of buttered toast that slowly boiled in it and coated the coffee with a tasty crust.

He was cold in his white wool pajamas, and he was hugging his knees. Charlotte Peloux, coquettish for her son, was wearing for the first time a marigold-colored boudoir wrap and a morning cap that was tight at the temples, making her bare face stand out in a sinister way.

While her son was watching her, she said mincingly:

"You see, I'm adopting old-folks' styles. Pretty soon, powder. Do you like this cap? It's eighteenth-century, isn't it? Dubarry or Pompadour? What do I look like?"

"You look like an old galley slave," Chéri flung at her. "People don't do such things, or at least they give you some warning."

She groaned, then guffawed:

"Ha! Ha! You really are sharp-tongued!"

But he wasn't laughing; he was looking at the light snow in the garden; it had fallen on the lawns during the night. The spasmodic bulging of his jaw muscles, all but imperceptible, was the only thing that revealed his nervous state. Madame Peloux, intimidated, remained as silent as he was. A muffled ringing was heard.

"It's Edmée ringing for her breakfast," Madame Peloux said.

Chéri didn't reply.

"What's wrong with the heating system? It's cold in here," he said after awhile.

"It was Italy," Madame Peloux repeated lyrically. "You've come back here with your eyes and your heart full of sunshine, and you find yourself at the North Pole! The North Pole! The dahlia blooms didn't last a week! But relax, darling! Your love nest is making progress. If the architect hadn't caught paratyphoid fever, it would be finished. I had warned him. If I didn't tell him twenty times, I didn't tell him once: 'Monsieur Savaron . . .'"

Chéri, who had gone over to the window, turned around brusquely.

"What's the date on that letter?"

Madame Peloux opened eyes as wide as a little child's:

"What letter?"

"The letter from Léa you showed me awhile ago."

"It isn't dated, dear, but I got it the day before my last Sunday open-house in October."

"Good. And you don't know who it is? . . ."

"Who who is, darling?"

"You know, the guy she went off with."

Le visage nu de Mme Peloux se fit malicieux:

"Non, figure-toi! Personne ne sait! La vieille Lili est en Sicile et aucune de ces dames n'a eu vent de la chose! Un mystère, un mystère
angoissant! Pourtant, tu me connais, j'ai bien recueilli ici et là
quelques petits renseignements. . . ."

La prunelle noire de Chéri bougea sur le blanc de son œil.

"Quels potins?

— Il s'agirait d'un jeune homme . . . chuchota Mme Peloux. Un
jeune homme . . . peu recommandable tu m'entends! . . . Très bien de
sa personne, par exemple!"

Elle mentait, choisissant la conjecture la plus basse. Chéri haussa
les épaules:

"Ah! là là . . . très bien de sa personne! Cette pauvre Léa, je vois ça
d'ici, un petit costaud de l'école à Patron, avec du poil noir sur les
poignets et les mains humides. . . . Tiens, je me recouche, tu me
donnes sommeil."

Traînant ses babouches, il regagna sa chambre, en s'attardant aux
longs corridors et aux paliers larges de la maison qu'il lui semblait dé-
couvrir. Il buta contre une armoire ventrue et s'étonna:

"Du diable, si je me souvenais qu'il y avait une armoire là. . . . Ah!
si, je me rappelle vaguement. . . . Et ce type-là, qui ça peut-il être?"

Il interrogeait un agrandissement photographique, pendu funèbre
dans son cadre de bois noir, auprès d'une faïence polychrome que
Chéri ne reconnaissait pas non plus.

Mme Peloux n'avait pas déménagé depuis vingt-cinq ans et
maintenait en leur place toutes les erreurs successives de son goût
saugrenu et thésaurisateur. "Ta maison, c'est la maison d'une
fourmi qui serait dingo", lui reprochait la vieille Lili, gourmande
de tableaux et surtout de peintres avancés. A quoi Mme Peloux
répliquait:

"Pourquoi toucher à ce qui est bien?"

Un corridor vert d'eau, — vert couloir d'hôpital, disait Léa, — s'é-
caillait-il? Charlotte Peloux le faisait repeindre en vert, et cherchait
jalousement, pour changer le velours grenat d'une chaise longue, le
même velours grenat. . . .

Chéri s'arrêta sur le seuil d'un cabinet de toilette ouvert. Le marbre rouge d'une table-lavabo encastrait des cuvettes blanches à ini-
tiales, et deux appliques électriques soutenaient des lis en perles.
Chéri remonta ses épaules jusqu'à ses oreilles comme s'il souffrait
d'un courant d'air:

"Bon Dieu, c'est laid, ce bazar!"

Madame Peloux's stark face turned malicious:

"No, just imagine! Nobody knows! Old Lili is in Sicily, and none of the women had any news of the business! It's a mystery, a painful mystery! But you know me, I managed to pick up some bits of information here and there . . ."

Chéri's black pupils twitched in the whites of his eyes.

"What rumors?"

"They say a young man is involved," whispered Madame Peloux. "A young man . . . of dubious standing, follow me? . . . Very good-looking, to be sure!"

She was lying, choosing the most unworthy conjecture. Chéri shrugged his shoulders:

"Oh, ho . . . very good-looking! Poor Léa, I can see the whole thing, a beefy little guy from Patron's gym, with black hairs on his wrists and damp hands . . . Well, I'm going back to bed, you make me sleepy."

Shuffling his slippers, he returned in the direction of his room, lingering in the long corridors and on the wide landings of that house, which seemed unfamiliar to him. He bumped into a convex armoire and was surprised:

"Damn me if I remembered there was an armoire here! . . . Oh, yes, I recall vaguely . . . And who can this guy be?"

His question pertained to an enlarged photo that was hanging gloomily in its frame of black wood near a piece of polychrome faience that Chéri no longer recognized, either.

Madame Peloux hadn't moved in twenty-five years, and she kept in their places all the successive errors in her foolish, packrat-like taste. "Your house is like a crazy ant's," was the constant reproach of old Lili, who was wild about paintings, especially by avant-garde artists. To which Madame Peloux would reply:

"Why change something when there's nothing wrong with it?"

If a sea-green corridor (hospital-corridor green, Léa called it) started to peel, Charlotte Peloux would have it repainted green, and to change the garnet velvet on a chaise longue, she would avidly hunt for the same garnet velvet . . .

Chéri came to a halt on the threshold of a lavatory whose door was open. The red marble of the washstand framed white, monogrammed basins, and two electric fixtures supported pearl fleur-de-lis shades. Chéri raised his shoulders up to his ears as if he were standing in a draft:

"God, but this flea market is ugly!"

Il repartit à grands pas. La fenêtre, au bout du corridor qu'il arpentait, se parait d'une bordure de petits vitraux rouges et jaunes.

"Il me fallait encore ça", grommela-t-il. Il tourna à gauche et ouvrit une porte — la porte de son ancienne chambre — d'une main rude, sans frapper. Un petit cri jaillit du lit où Edmée achevait de déjeuner.

Chéri referma la porte et contempla sa jeune femme sans s'approcher du lit.

"Bonjour, lui dit-elle en souriant. Comme tu as l'air étonné de me voir!"

Le reflet de la neige l'éclairait d'une lumière bleue et égale. Elle portait défaits ses cheveux crépelés, d'un châtain cendré, qui ne couvraient pas tout à fait ses épaules basses et élégantes. Avec ses joues blanches et rosées comme son vêtement de nuit, sa bouche d'un rose que la fatigue pâlissait, elle était un tableau frais, inachevé et un peu lointain.

"Dis-moi bonjour, Fred?" insista-t-elle.

Il s'assit auprès de sa femme et la prit dans ses bras. Elle se renversa doucement, entraînant Chéri. Il s'accouda pour regarder de tout près, au-dessous de lui, cette créature si neuve que la lassitude ne défleurissait pas. La paupière inférieure, renflée et pleine, sans un coup d'ongle, semblait l'émerveiller, et aussi la suavité argentée de la joue.

"Quel âge as-tu?" demanda-t-il soudain.

Edmée ouvrit ses yeux qu'elle avait tendrement fermés. Chéri vit la couleur noisette des prunelles, les petites dents carrées que le rire découvrait:

"Oh! voyons . . . j'aurai dix-neuf ans le cinq janvier, tâche d'y penser! . . ."

Il retira son bras avec brusquerie et la jeune femme glissa au creux du lit comme une écharpe détachée.

"Dix-neuf ans, c'est prodigieux! Sais-tu que j'en ai plus de vingt-cinq?

— Mais oui, je le sais, Fred. . . ."

Il prit sur la table de chevet un miroir d'écaille blonde et s'y mira:

"Vingt-cinq ans!"

Vingt cinq ans, un visage de marbre blanc et qui semblait invincible. Vingt-cinq ans, mais au coin externe de l'œil, puis au-dessous de l'œil, doublant finement le dessin à l'antique de la paupière, deux lignes, visibles seulement en pleine lumière, deux incisions, faites d'une main si redoutable et si légère. . . . Il posa le miroir:

"Tu es plus jeune que moi, dit-il à Edmée, ça me choque.

He walked away with big strides. The window at the end of the corridor he was pacing was adorned with a border of little red and yellow panes of stained glass.

"That's all I needed," he grumbled. He turned left and opened a door—the door to his old room—with a rough shove, and without knocking. A little cry issued from the bed, where Edmée was finishing her breakfast.

Chéri shut the door behind him and looked at his young wife without approaching the bed.

"Good morning," she said with a smile. "You look so surprised to see me!"

The reflection off the snow lit her with a uniform blue light. Her wavy ash-blond hair, which didn't completely cover her elegant, low shoulders, was undone. With her cheeks as white and pink as her nightgown, and her mouth of a pink that her fatigue made pale, she was like a newly painted picture, not quite completed and a little indistinct.

"Won't you say good morning, Fred?" she said insistently.

He sat down beside his wife and took her in his arms. She let herself fall backward gently, pulling Chéri along with her. He propped himself on his elbows to take a close look under him at that brand-new being, whose bloom wasn't diminished by weariness. Her lower eyelids, fully rounded and without the most minute wrinkle, seemed to amaze him, as did the silvery smoothness of her cheeks.

"How old are you?" he suddenly asked.

Edmée opened the eyes she had amorously shut. Chéri saw the hazel color of her irises and the little square teeth that her laughter revealed:

"Oh, let's see . . . I'll be nineteen on January fifth, and try to keep it in mind! . . ."

He brusquely pulled away his arm, and the young woman slid into the hollow of the bed like an untied sash.

"Nineteen, it's miraculous! Do you know I'm over twenty-five?"

"Of course I know, Fred . . ."

He picked up a light-yellow tortoiseshell mirror from the night table and looked into it:

"Twenty-five!"

Twenty-five, with a white marble face that seemed invincible. Twenty-five, but at the outer corners of his eyes, and also below his eyes, subtly following the Greco-Roman contours of his eyelids, there were two lines, visible only in strong light, two incisions made by a hand that was so delicate but so dreadful . . . He put down the mirror.

"You're younger than I am," he said to Edmée. "I'm shocked."

— Pas moi!"

Elle avait répondu d'une voix mordante et pleine de sous-entendus. Il ne s'y arrêta point.

"Tu sais pourquoi j'ai de beaux yeux? lui demanda-t-il avec un grand sérieux.

— Non, dit Edmée. Peut-être parce que je les aime?

— Poésie, dit Chéri qui haussa les épaules. C'est parce que j'ai l'œil fait comme une sole.

— Comme une. . . .

— Comme une sole."

Il s'assit près d'elle pour la démonstration.

"Tiens, ici, le coin qui est près du nez, c'est la tête de la sole. Et puis ça remonte en haut, c'est le dos de la sole, tandis qu'en dessous ça continue plus droit: le ventre de la sole. Et puis le coin de l'œil bien allongé vers la tempe, c'est la queue de la sole.

— Ah?

— Oui, si j'avais l'œil en forme de limande, c'est-à-dire aussi ouvert en bas qu'en haut, j'aurais l'air bête. Voilà. Toi qui es bachelière, tu savais ça, toi?

— Non; j'avoue. . . ."

Elle se tut et demeura interdite, car il avait parlé sentencieusement, avec une force superflue, comme certains extravagants.

"Il y a des moments, pensait-elle, où il ressemble à un sauvage. Un être de la jungle? Mais il ne connaît ni les plantes ni les animaux, et il a parfois l'air de ne pas même connaître l'humanité. . . ."

Chéri, assis contre elle, la tenait d'un bras par les épaules et maniait de sa main libre les perles petites, très belles, très rondes, toutes égales, du collier d'Edmée. Elle respirait le parfum dont Chéri usait avec excès et fléchissait, enivrée, comme une rose dans une chambre chaude.

"Fred. . . . Viens dormir . . . on est fatigués. . . ."

Il ne parut pas entendre. Il fixait sur les perles du collier un regard obstiné et anxieux.

"Fred. . . ."

Il tressaillit, se leva, quitta furieusement son pyjama et se jeta tout nu dans le lit, cherchant la place de sa tête sur une jeune épaule où la clavicule fine pointait encore. Edmée obéissait de tout son corps, creusait son flanc, ouvrait son bras. Chéri ferma les yeux et devint immobile. Elle se tenait éveillée avec précaution, un peu essoufflée sous le poids, et le croyait endormi. Mais au bout d'un instant il se retourna d'un saut en imitant le grogne-

"I'm not!"

She had replied in a tone that was biting and full of unspoken meanings. He didn't heed it.

"Do you know why my eyes are beautiful?" he asked her in all seriousness.

"No," Edmée said. "Maybe because I love them?"

"That's just poetry," said Chéri, shrugging his shoulders. "It's because my eyes are shaped like a sole."

"Like a . . ."

"Like a sole."

He sat down near her in order to demonstrate.

"Look over here. The corner next to my nose is the head of the sole. Then the top of the eye rises; that's the back of the sole. But the bottom of the eye continues in a straighter line: the belly of the sole. Then, the corner of my eye next to my temple stretches out; that's the tail of the sole."

"Oh?"

"Yes. Now, if my eyes were shaped like a flounder—that is, if they were as open at the bottom as at the top—I'd look stupid. There you go. You graduated from school, but did you know that?"

"No, I admit I didn't . . ."

She fell silent, feeling disconcerted, because he had spoken sententiously, with unnecessary emphasis, the way some cranks do.

"There are times," she was thinking, "when he's like a savage. A jungle creature? But he's not familiar with either plants or animals, and sometimes he even seems unfamiliar with human beings . . ."

Chéri was sitting next to her, holding her by the shoulders with one arm, and with his free hand he was fingering the small, very beautiful, very round, evenly matched pearls in Edmée's necklace. She was inhaling the scent that Chéri put on too much of, and she was wilting, in her intoxication, like a rose in a hot room.

"Fred . . . come to bed . . . we're both tired . . ."

He didn't seem to hear. His obstinate, anxious gaze was fixed on the pearls in the necklace.

"Fred . . ."

He started, stood up, furiously ripped off his pajamas, and leaped into bed naked, seeking a place for his head on her young shoulder, on which the delicate collarbone was still prominent. Edmée yielded with her whole body, drawing in her side and opening her arm. Chéri shut his eyes and became motionless. She carefully kept awake, a little out of breath beneath his weight, and she thought he had fallen asleep. But a moment later, he turned around with a jump, imitating

ment d'un dormeur inconscient, et se roula dans le drap à l'autre bord du lit.

"C'est son habitude", constata Edmée.

Elle devait s'éveiller tout l'hiver dans cette chambre carrée à quatre fenêtres. Le mauvais temps retardait l'achèvement d'un hôtel neuf, avenue Henri-Martin, et aussi les caprices de Chéri qui voulut une salle de bains noire, un salon chinois, un sous-sol aménagé en piscine et un gymnase. Aux objections de l'architecte, il répondait: "Je m'en fous. Je paye, je veux être servi. Je ne regarde pas au prix." Mais, parfois, il épluchait âprement un devis, affirmant qu' "on ne faisait pas le poil au fils Peloux". De fait, il discourait prix de séries, fibro-ciment, et stuc coloré avec une aisance inattendue, une mémoire précise des chiffres qui forçaient la considération des entrepreneurs.

Il consultait peu sa jeune femme, bien qu'il fît parade, pour elle, de son autorité et qu'il prît soin de masquer, à l'occasion, son incertitude par des ordres brefs. Elle découvrit que s'il savait d'instinct jouer avec les couleurs, il méprisait les belles formes et les caractéristiques des styles.

"Tu t'embarrasses d'un tas d'histoires, toi, chose . . . heu . . . Edmée. Une décision pour le fumoir? Tiens, en v'là une: bleu pour les murs, un bleu qui n'a peur de rien. Un tapis violet, d'un violet qui fout le camp devant le bleu des murs. Et puis, là-dedans, ne crains pas le noir, ni l'or pour les meubles et les bibelots.

— Oui, tu as raison, Fred. Mais ce sera un peu impitoyable, ces belles couleurs. Il va manquer la grâce, la note claire, le vase blanc ou la statue. . . .

— Que non, interrompait-il assez roidement. Le vase blanc, ce sera moi tout nu. Et n'oublions pas un coussin, un machin, un fourbi quelconque rouge potiron, pour quand je me baladerai tout nu dans le fumoir."

Elle caressait, secrètement séduite et révoltée, de telles images qui transformaient leur demeure future en une sorte de palais équivoque, de temple à la gloire de Chéri. Mais elle ne luttait pas, quémandait avec douceur "un petit coin", pour un mobilier minuscule et précieux, au point sur fond blanc, cadeau de Marie-Laure.

Cette douceur qui cachait une volonté si jeune et déjà si bien exercée lui valut de camper quatre mois chez sa belle-mère, et de déjouer, quatre mois durant, l'affût constant, les pièges tendus quo-

the groan of a man obliviously asleep, and rolled himself up in the sheet on the other side of the bed.

"It's his habit," Edmée noted.

She was to wake up in that square, four-windowed room all winter long. The completion of their new town house on the Avenue Henri-Martin was delayed by bad weather, but also by the caprices of Chéri, who insisted on a black bathroom, a Chinese parlor, and a basement with built-in swimming pool and gym. Whenever the architect objected, he'd reply: "I don't give a damn. I'm paying, and I want my wishes carried out. The price doesn't concern me." But at times he pored harshly over an estimate, declaring that "young Peloux wasn't one to let himself get fleeced." As a matter of fact, he would talk about standard costs, fibrocement, and painted stucco with unexpected fluency and a precise recollection of figures that elicited the contractors' respect.

He rarely consulted his young wife, though he showed off his authority in front of her and was careful to hide his occasional uncertainty by giving concise orders. She discovered that, though he might have an instinct for playing with colors, he had contempt for the beauty of form and the features of various styles.

"You're filling your head with a lot of nonsense, what's-your-name . . . er . . . Edmée. A decision about the smoking room? Here's one for you: blue for the walls, a blue that will stand up to anything. A violet rug, of a violet that shrinks away from the blue on the walls. And in a room like that, don't be afraid of black or gold for the furniture and accessories."

"Yes, you're right, Fred. But those beautiful colors will be a bit merciless. A touch of grace will be missing, a bright accent, a white vase or a statue . . ."

"No, no!" he interrupted quite rigidly. "The white vase will be me with nothing on. And let's not forget a pumpkin-colored cushion, thingamabob, or what-do-you-call-it, for the times that I march around naked in the smoking room."

Secretly both charmed and repelled, she lingered over similar visions that were transforming their future home into a sort of palace of dubious reputation, a temple to the glory of Chéri. But she didn't fight him, she merely begged gently for "a little nook" for a tiny but valuable set of furniture, upholstered in needlework on a white background, that was a gift from Marie-Laure.

That gentleness, which concealed a will power so young but already so well trained, stood her in good stead while camping out for four months in her mother-in-law's house, spending those entire four months

tidiennement à sa sérénité, à sa gaieté encore frileuse, à sa diplomatie; Charlotte Peloux, exaltée par la proximité d'une victime si tendre, perdait un peu la tête et gaspillait les flèches, mordait à tort et à travers. . . .

"Du sang-froid, madame Peloux, jetait de temps en temps Chéri. Qui boufferez-vous l'hiver prochain, si je ne vous arrête pas?"

Edmée levait sur son mari des yeux où la peur et la gratitude tremblaient ensemble et essayait de ne pas trop penser, de ne pas trop regarder Mme Peloux. Un soir, Charlotte lança à trois reprises et comme à l'étourdie, par-dessus les chrysanthèmes du surtout, le nom de Léa au lieu de celui d'Edmée. Chéri baissa ses sourcils sataniques:

"Madame Peloux, je crois que vous avez des troubles de mémoire. Une cure d'isolement vous paraît-elle nécessaire?"

Charlotte Peloux se tut pendant une semaine, mais jamais Edmée n'osa demander à son mari: "C'est à cause de moi, que tu t'es fâché? C'est bien moi que tu défendais? Ce n'est pas l'autre femme, celle d'avant moi?"

Son enfance, son adolescence lui avaient appris la patience, l'espoir, le silence, le maniement aisé des armes et des vertus des prisonniers. La belle Marie-Laure n'avait jamais grondé sa fille: elle se bornait à la punir. Jamais une parole dure, jamais une parole tendre. La solitude, puis l'internat, puis encore la solitude de quelques vacances, la relégation fréquente dans une chambre parée; enfin la menace du mariage, de n'importe quel mariage, dès que l'œil de la mère trop belle discerna sur la fille l'aube d'une autre beauté, beauté timide, comme opprimée, d'autant plus touchante. . . . Au prix de cette mère d'ivoire et d'or insensibles, la ronde méchanceté de Charlotte Peloux n'était que roses. . . .

"Tu as peur de ma mère vénérée?" lui demanda un soir Chéri.

Edmée sourit, fit une moue d'insouciance.

"Peur? non. On tressaute pour une porte qui claque, mais on n'a pas peur. On a peur du serpent qui passe dessous. . . .

— Fameux serpent, Marie-Laure, hein?

— Fameux."

Il attendit une confidence qui ne vint pas et serra d'un bras les minces épaules de sa femme, en camarade:

"On est quelque chose comme orphelins, nous, pas?

— Oui, on est orphelins! On est si gentils!"

Elle se colla contre lui. Ils étaient seuls dans le hall. Mme Peloux, comme disait Chéri, préparait en haut ses poisons du lendemain.

eluding the eternal watchfulness and the daily traps laid for her peace of mind, her still sensitive cheerfulness, and her diplomacy. Charlotte Peloux, stimulated by the presence of such a tender victim, was growing a little wild, wasting her arrows and biting recklessly on all sides . . .

"Stay cool-headed, Madame Peloux," Chéri would interject from time to time. "Who will you have left to gobble up next winter if I don't stop you?"

Edmée would look at her husband with eyes in which fear and gratitude trembled jointly, and she tried not to think too much or look at Madame Peloux too often. One evening, as if absentmindedly, three times Charlotte flung Léa's name in place of Edmée's across the chrysanthemums in the centerpiece. Chéri lowered his devilish eyebrows:

"Madame Peloux, I think you're having trouble with your memory. Do you think a stay in an isolation ward is called for?"

Charlotte Peloux kept quiet for a week, but Edmée never dared to ask her husband: "Are you angry on my account? Was it me you were protecting? Or was it the other woman, the one before me?"

Her childhood and adolescence had taught her to be patient, hopeful, and silent, and how to handle easily the arms and virtues available to prisoners. The lovely Marie-Laure had never scolded her daughter: she had merely punished her. Never a hard word, never a loving word. Solitude, then boarding school, then the further solitude of several vacations, and frequent relegation to a well-decorated bedroom; finally the threat of marriage, marriage to anyone at all, the moment that the overly beautiful mother's eyes discerned that a different kind of beauty was dawning on her daughter, a shy beauty that seemed oppressed but was all the more touching for that . . . Compared with that mother of unfeeling ivory and gold, the unvarnished malice of Charlotte Peloux was a bed of roses . . .

"Are you afraid of my revered mother?" Chéri asked her one evening.

Edmée smiled and gave a pout indicating that she wasn't concerned.

"Afraid? No. You jump when a door slams, but that doesn't mean you're afraid. What you're really afraid of is the snake that slithers under it . . ."

"Marie-Laure is quite a snake, isn't she?"

"Quite a snake!"

He waited for an unburdening that didn't come, and with one arm he clutched his wife's thin shoulders, in a comradely gesture:

"We're orphans, in a way, aren't we?"

"Yes, we're orphans! And such nice ones!"

She clung to him. They were alone in the garden room. Madame Peloux, as Chéri would say, was upstairs preparing her next day's poi-

La nuit encore froide derrière les vitres mirait les meubles et les
lampes comme un étang. Edmée se sentait tiède et protégée, confiante aux bras de cet inconnu. Elle leva la tête et cria de saisisse-
ment, car il renversait vers le lustre un visage magnifique et
désespéré, en fermant les yeux sur deux larmes, retenues et scin-
tillantes entre ses cils. . . .

"Chéri, Chéri! Qu'est-ce que tu as?"

Malgré elle, elle lui avait donné ce petit nom trop caressant, qu'elle
ne voulait jamais prononcer. Il obéit à l'appel avec égarement, et ramena son regard sur elle.

"Chéri! mon Dieu, j'ai peur. . . . Qu'est-ce que tu as? . . ."

Il l'écarta un peu, la tint par les bras en face de lui.

"Ah! ah! cette petite . . . cette petite. . . . De quoi donc as-tu peur?"

Il lui livrait ses yeux de velours, plus beaux pour une larme, paisibles, grands ouverts, indéchiffrables. Edmée allait le supplier de se
taire quand il parla:

"Ce qu'on est bêtes! . . . C'est cette idée qu'on est orphelins. . . .
C'est idiot. C'est tellement vrai. . . ."

Il reprit son air d'importance comique et elle respira, assurée qu'il
ne parlerait pas davantage. En commençant d'éteindre soigneuse-
ment les candélabres, il se tourna vers Edmée, avec une vanité très
naïve, ou très retorse:

"Tiens, pourquoi est-ce que je n'aurais pas un cœur, moi aussi?"

"QU'EST-CE que tu fais là?"

Bien qu'il l'eût interpellée presque bas, le son de la voix de Chéri
atteignit Edmée au point qu'elle plia en avant comme s'il l'eût
poussée. Debout, près d'un bureau grand ouvert, elle posait les deux
mains sur des papiers épars.

"Je range . . ." dit-elle d'une voix molle. Elle leva une main qui s'arrêta en l'air comme engourdie. Puis elle sembla s'éveiller et cessa de
mentir:

"Voilà, Fred. . . . Tu m'avais dit que pour notre emménagement
prochain, tu avais horreur de t'occuper toi-même de ce que tu veux
emporter: cette chambre, ces meubles. . . . J'ai voulu, de bonne foi,
ranger, trier . . . et puis, le poison est venu, la tentation, les mauvaises
pensées — la mauvaise pensée. . . . Je te demande pardon. J'ai touché
à des choses qui ne m'appartiennent pas."

Elle tremblait bravement et attendait. Il se tenait le front penché,

son. The night, still cold behind the window panes, reflected the furniture and the lamps like a pool. Edmée felt warm and protected, as she trusted herself to that stranger's arms. She raised her head and cried out in shock, because he had thrown back his magnificent, despairing face so that it looked toward the chandelier. His eyes were closed over two tears that were caught, glistening, on his lashes . . .

"Chéri! Chéri! What's the matter?"

In spite of herself she had called him by that overly fond pet name which she had never wanted to utter. He obeyed the call dazedly, bringing his eyes back to her.

"Chéri! My God, I'm afraid . . . What's wrong with you?"

He held her at a little distance, by her arms, facing him.

"Ha! Ha! Little girl . . . little girl . . . What are you afraid of?"

He surrendered to her his velvety eyes, more beautiful for the tears in them, peaceful, wide-open, indecipherable. Edmée was about to beseech him to keep silent when he spoke:

"How silly we are! . . . It's that notion about being orphans . . . How foolish! It's so true . . ."

He resumed his comically self-important manner, and she was relieved, certain that he wouldn't go on speaking. While he began to turn off the torchère lamps carefully, he turned to Edmée with a vanity that was either very naïve or very sly:

"Tell me, why shouldn't I be warm-hearted like other people?"

"WHAT are you doing there?"

Though he had addressed her almost in a whisper, Edmée was so affected by the sound of Chéri's voice that she slumped forward as if he had pushed her. Standing by a wide-open desk, she was resting her hands on some scattered papers.

"I'm tidying up . . ." she said in a weak voice. She raised one hand, which stopped short in the air as if it had gone to sleep. Then she seemed to rouse herself, and she stopped lying:

"It's like this, Fred . . . You had told me that, when we move into our house soon, you hated bothering yourself with what to take away from here: the items in this room, this furniture. In all good faith, I intended to tidy up and sort out things . . . then the poison came over me, temptation, evil thoughts—*the* evil thought . . . Please forgive me. I've touched things that don't belong to me."

She was trembling violently and waiting. He was standing with his

les mains fermées, dans une attitude menaçante, mais il ne paraissait pas voir sa femme. Il avait le regard si voilé qu'elle garda, de cette heure-là, le souvenir d'un colloque avec un homme aux yeux pâles. . . .

"Ah! oui, dit-il enfin. Tu cherchais. . . . Tu cherchais des lettres d'amour."

Elle ne nia pas.

"Tu cherchais mes lettres d'amour!"

Il rit, de son rire maladroit et contraint. Edmée rougit, blessée:

"Tu me trouves bête, évidemment. Tu n'es pas homme à ne pas les avoir mises en sûreté ou brûlées. Et puis, enfin, cela ne me regardait pas. Je n'ai que ce que je mérite. Tu ne m'en garderas pas trop rancune, Fred?"

Elle priait avec un peu d'effort et se faisait jolie exprès, les lèvres tendues, le haut du visage dissimulé dans l'ombre des cheveux mousseux. Mais Chéri ne changeait pas d'attitude et elle remarqua, pour la première fois, que son beau teint sans nuance prenait la transparence d'une rose blanche d'hiver, et que l'ovale des joues avait maigri.

"Des lettres d'amour . . . répéta-t-il. C'est crevant."

Il fit un pas et prit à poignée des papiers qu'il effeuilla. Cartes postales, factures de restaurants, lettres de fournisseurs, télégrammes des petites copines rencontrées une nuit, pneumatiques d'amis pique-assiette, trois lignes, cinq lignes; — quelques pages étroites, sabrées de l'écriture coupante de Mme Peloux. . . .

Chéri se retourna vers sa femme:

"Je n'ai pas de lettres d'amour.

— Oh! protesta-t-elle, pourquoi veux-tu. . . .

— Je n'en ai pas, interrompit-il. Tu ne peux pas comprendre. Je ne m'en étais pas aperçu. Je ne peux pas avoir de lettres d'amour, puisque. . . ."

Il s'arrêta.

"Ah! attends, attends. Il y a pourtant une fois, je me souviens, je n'avais pas voulu aller à la Bourboule, et alors. . . . Attends, attends. . . ."

Il ouvrait des tiroirs, jetait fébrilement des papiers sur le tapis.

"Trop fort! Qu'est-ce que j'en ai fait? J'aurais juré que c'était dans le haut à gauche. . . . Non. . . ."

Il referma rudement les tiroirs vides et fixa sur Edmée un regard pesant:

head down and his hands closed, in a menacing attitude, but he didn't seem to see his wife. His eyes were so dimmed that, from that time on, she retained the memory of a conversation with a pale-eyed man . . .

"Ah, yes," he finally said. "You were looking for . . . You were looking for love letters."

She didn't deny it.

"You were looking for my love letters!"

He laughed one of his clumsy, forced laughs. Edmée was hurt, and blushed:

"Obviously you think me stupid. You're not the kind of man who wouldn't have stashed them away safely or burnt them. Besides, it was none of my business, after all. I'm getting nothing more than I deserve. You won't be too sore with me about it, Fred?"

She was making a slight effort in asking this, and she was intentionally trying to look pretty, with her lips thrust out and the top of her face hidden in the shadow of her fluffy hair. But Chéri didn't change his stance, and for the first time she noticed that his fine, uniform complexion was taking on the translucency of a white winter rose, and that the oval of his cheeks had become thinner.

"Love letters . . ." he repeated. "That's hilarious."

He took a step forward, seizing a handful of papers and leafing through them. Postcards, restaurant bills, letters from tradesmen, telegrams from casual girls he had gone with for one night, express letters from friends who wanted to cadge a meal, three lines, five lines—and a few narrow pages stabbed with Madame Peloux's slashing handwriting . . .

Chéri turned to his wife again:

"I have no love letters."

"Oh!" she protested. "Why do you want . . ."

"I don't have any," he interrupted. "You can't understand. I didn't notice it myself. I can't have any love letters because . . ."

He stopped.

"Oh, wait, wait. There *was* one once, I remember. I had refused to go to La Bourboule,[7] and then . . . Wait, wait . . ."

He was opening drawers and feverishly throwing papers onto the rug.

"This beats all! What did I do with it? I'd have sworn it was at the top left . . . No . . ."

He shut the empty drawers again roughly and stared firmly at Edmée:

---

7. A spa near Clermont-Ferrand in the Auvergne.

"Tu n'as rien trouvé? Tu n'aurais pas pris une lettre qui commençait: "Mais non, je ne m'ennuie pas. On devrait toujours se quitter huit jours par mois", et puis, ça continuait par je ne sais plus quoi, à propos d'un chèvrefeuille qui grimpait à la fenêtre. . . ."

Il ne se tut que parce que sa mémoire le trahissait, et esquissa un geste d'impatience. Edmée, raidie et mince, devant lui, ne faiblissait pas:

"Non, non, je n'ai rien *pris,* appuya-t-elle avec une irritation sèche. Depuis quand suis-je capable de *prendre?* Une lettre qui t'est si précieuse, tu l'as donc laissée traîner? Une lettre pareille, je n'ai pas besoin de demander si elle était de Léa!"

Il tressaillit faiblement, mais non pas comme Edmée l'attendait. Un demi-sourire errant passa sur le beau visage fermé, et la tête inclinée de côté, les yeux attentifs, l'arc délicieux de la bouche détendu, il écouta peut-être l'écho d'un nom. . . . Toute la jeune force amoureuse et mal disciplinée d'Edmée creva en cris, en larmes, en gestes des mains tordues ou ouvertes pour griffer:

"Va-t'en! je te déteste! Tu ne m'as jamais aimée! Tu ne te soucies pas plus de moi que si je n'existais pas! Tu me blesses, tu me méprises, tu es grossier, tu es . . . tu es. . . . Tu ne penses qu'à cette vieille femme! Tu as des goûts de malade, de dégénéré, de . . . de. . . . Tu ne m'aimes pas! Pourquoi, je me demande, pourquoi m'as-tu épousée? . . . Tu es. . . . Tu es. . . ."

Elle secouait la tête comme une bête prise par le cou, et quand elle renversait la nuque pour aspirer l'air en suffoquant, on voyait luire les laiteuses petites perles égales de son collier. Chéri contemplait avec stupeur les gestes désordonnés de ce cou charmant et onduleux, l'appel des mains nouées l'une à l'autre, et surtout ces larmes, ces larmes. . . . Il n'avait jamais vu tant de larmes. . . . Qui donc avait pleuré devant lui, pour lui? Personne. . . . Mme Peloux? "Mais, songea-t-il, les larmes de Mme Peloux, ça ne compte pas. . . ." Léa? . . . non. Il consulta, au fond de son souvenir le plus caché, deux yeux d'un bleu sincère, qui n'avaient brillé que de plaisir, de malice et de tendresse un peu moqueuse. . . . Que de larmes sur cette jeune femme qui se débat devant lui! Que fait-on pour tant de larmes? Il ne savait pas. Tout de même, il étendit le bras, et comme Edmée reculait, craignant peut-être une brutalité, il lui posa sur la tête sa belle main douce, imprégnée de parfums, et il flatta cette tête désordonnée, en essayant d'imiter une voix et des mots dont il connut le pouvoir:

"You didn't find anything? Didn't you by chance take a letter that began: 'Oh, no, I'm not bored. We ought to get away from each other for one week out of every month,' and then went on to say something or other about a honeysuckle vine that was climbing by the window? . . ."

He stopped talking only because his memory was failing him. He made a slight gesture of impatience. Edmée, slender and rigid before him, didn't lose heart:

"No, no, I didn't *take* anything," she emphasized with curt irritation. "Since when have I been capable of *taking* things? So, you allowed a letter that's so precious to you to just lie around somewhere? I don't need to ask whether a letter like that was from Léa!"

He gave a slight start, but not in the way Edmée expected. A transitory half-smile passed over his handsome, expressionless face, and, with his head leaning to one side, his eyes watchful, and the delectable bow of his lips relaxed, he might have been listening to the echo of a name . . . With all of her young strength, loving but not yet under control, Edmée burst out into shouts, tears, and gestures of her hands, either contorted or open as if to scratch:

"Go away! I hate you! You've never loved me! You care no more about me than if I didn't exist! You hurt me, you have contempt for me, you're rude, you're . . . you're . . . All you think about is that old woman! Your desires are those of a sick man, a degenerate, a . . . a . . . You don't love me! Why, I wonder, why did you marry me? . . . You're . . . You're . . ."

She was tossing her head like an animal that has been grasped by the neck, and when she threw her head back to gasp for air in a choking fit, he could see the gleam of the small, milky, evenly matched pearls of her necklace. Chéri was stupefied as he observed the unruly motions of that charming, swelling throat, the supplication in those tightly clasped hands, and, above all, those tears, those tears . . . He had never seen so many tears . . . Who had ever wept in his presence, on his account? Nobody . . . Madame Peloux? "But," he thought, "Madame Peloux's tears don't count . . ." Léa? No. In the depths of his most profoundly hidden memories he recalled two eyes of a frank blue which had never glistened except with pleasure, mischievousness, and a somewhat mocking tenderness . . . So many tears on the face of that young woman thrashing about in front of him! What can be done for all those tears? He didn't know. All the same, he held out an arm and, when Edmée recoiled, perhaps fearing some rough treatment, he placed on her head his beautiful, soft, scent-steeped hand, and he caressed that disheveled head, trying to imitate a voice and words whose power he knew:

"Là . . . là. . . . Qu'est-ce que c'est. . . . Qu'est-ce que c'est donc . . . là. . . ."

Edmée fondit brusquement et tomba sur un siège où elle se ramassa toute, et elle se mit à sangloter avec passion, avec une frénésie qui ressemblait à un rire houleux et aux saccades de la joie. Son gracieux corps courbé bondissait, soulevé par le chagrin, l'amour jaloux, la colère, la servilité qui s'ignore, et cependant, comme le lutteur en plein combat, comme le nageur au sein de la vague, elle se sentait baignée dans un élément nouveau, naturel et amer.

Elle pleura longtemps et se remit lentement, par accalmies traversées de grandes secousses, de hoquets tremblés. Chéri s'était assis près d'elle et continuait de lui caresser les cheveux. Il avait dépassé le moment cuisant de sa propre émotion, et s'ennuyait. Il parcourait du regard Edmée, jetée de biais sur le canapé sec, et il n'aimait pas que ce corps étendu, avec sa robe relevée, son écharpe déroulée, aggravât le désordre de la pièce.

Si bas qu'il eût soupiré d'ennui, elle l'entendit et se redressa.

"Oui, dit-elle, je t'excède. . . . Ah! il vaudrait mieux. . . ."

Il l'interrompit, redoutant un flot de paroles:

"Ce n'est pas ça, mais je ne sais pas ce que tu veux.

— Comment, ce que je veux. . . . Comment, ce que je. . . ."

Elle montrait son visage enrhumé par les larmes.

"Suis-moi bien."

Il lui prit les mains. Elle voulut se dégager.

"Non, non, je connais cette voix-là! Tu vas me tenir encore un raisonnement de l'autre monde! Quand tu prends cette voix et cette figure-là, je sais que tu vas me démontrer que tu as l'œil fait comme un surmulet et la bouche en forme de chiffre trois couché sur le dos! Non, non, je ne veux pas!"

Elle récriminait puérilement, et Chéri se détendit à sentir qu'ils étaient tous les deux très jeunes. Il secoua les mains chaudes qu'il retenait:

"Mais, écoute-moi donc! Bon Dieu, je voudrais savoir ce que tu me reproches! Est-ce que je sors le soir sans toi? Non! Est-ce que je te quitte souvent dans la journée? Est-ce que j'ai une correspondance clandestine?

— Je ne sais pas. . . . Je ne crois pas. . . ."

Il la faisait virer de côté et d'autre, comme une poupée.

"Est-ce que j'ai une chambre à part? Est-ce que je ne te fais pas bien l'amour?"

"There, there . . . What's wrong? . . . What's wrong, now? . . . There . . ."

Edmée melted all at once and dropped onto a seat, on which she curled up and started to sob passionately, with a frenzy that resembled tempestuous laughter and the upheavals of joy. Her graceful bent body was shaking up and down, agitated by sorrow, jealous love, anger, and an unconscious feeling of inferiority; nevertheless, like a wrestler in the midst of a match, like a swimmer in the heart of a wave, she felt herself enveloped in a new element, one that was natural and bitter.

She wept for a long time, coming out of it only slowly, through periods of calm that were interrupted by violent shudders and irregular hiccups. Chéri had sat down beside her, and was continuing to caress her hair. He had passed the most painful moment of his own emotion, and he was already bored. He cast his eyes over Edmée, who had flung herself diagonally across the hard sofa-bed. He didn't like seeing that outstretched body, with its pulled-up dress and unrolled sash, increasing the disorder of the room.

Though his sigh of boredom was very low, she heard it and sat up.

"Yes," she said, "I'm trying your patience . . . Oh, it would be better . . ."

He interrupted her, fearing a flood of words:

"It's not that, but I don't know what you want."

"What do you mean, what I want? . . . What do you mean, what I . . ."

She showed her face, which was red and wet with tears.

"Follow me."

He took her hands. She wanted to pull away.

"No, no, I know that tone in your voice! You're going to make me another absolutely incredible speech! When you take on that tone and put that expression on your face, I know that you're going to show me that your eyes are shaped like mullets, and your mouth looks like a figure 3 lying on its side! No, no, I won't listen!"

Her recriminations were childish, and Chéri grew calmer when he realized how young they both were. He shook the two hot hands he was holding:

"But just listen! My God, I'd like to know what you're blaming me for! Do I go out at night without you? No! Do I leave you alone frequently during the day? Am I carrying on a secret correspondence?"

"I don't know . . . I don't think so . . ."

He was turning her this way and that, like a doll.

"Do I have a separate bedroom? Don't I make love to you properly?"

Elle hésita, sourit avec une finesse soupçonneuse.

"Tu appelles cela l'amour, Fred. . . .

— Il y a d'autres mots, mais tu ne les apprécies pas.

— Ce que tu appelles l'amour . . . est-ce que cela ne peut pas être, justement, une . . . une espèce . . . d'alibi?"

Elle ajouta précipitamment:

"Je généralise, Fred, tu comprends. . . . Je dis, cela *peut* être, dans certains cas. . . . "

Il lâcha les mains d'Edmée:

"Ça, dit-il froidement, c'est la gaffe.

— Pourquoi?" demanda-t-elle d'une voix faible.

Il siffla, le menton en l'air, en s'éloignant de quelques pas. Puis, il revint sur sa femme, la toisa en étrangère. Une bête terrible n'a pas besoin de bondir pour effrayer, — Edmée vit qu'il avait les narines gonflées et le bout du nez blanc.

"Peuh! . . ." souffla-t-il, en regardant sa femme. Il haussa les épaules et fit demi-tour. Au bout de la chambre, il revint.

"Peuh! . . . répéta-t-il. Ça parle.

— Comment?

— Ça parle et pour dire quoi? Ça se permet, ma parole. . . . "

Elle se leva avec rage:

"Fred, cria-t-elle, tu ne me parleras pas deux fois sur ce ton-là! Pour qui me prends-tu?

— Mais pour une gaffeuse, est-ce que je ne viens pas d'avoir l'honneur de te le dire?"

Il lui toucha l'épaule d'un index dur, elle en souffrit comme d'une meurtrissure grave.

"Toi qui es bachelière, est-ce qu'il n'y a pas quelque part un . . . une sentence, qui dit: "Ne touchez pas au couteau, au poignard", au truc, enfin?

— A la hache, dit-elle machinalement.

— C'est ça. Eh bien, mon petit, il ne faut pas toucher à la hache. C'est-à-dire blesser un homme . . . dans ses faveurs, si j'ose m'exprimer ainsi. Tu m'as blessé dans les dons que je te fais. . . . Tu m'as blessé dans mes faveurs.

— Tu . . . tu parles comme une cocotte!" bégaya-t-elle.

Elle rougissait, perdait sa force et son sang-froid. Elle le haïssait de demeurer pâle, de garder une supériorité dont tout le secret tenait dans le port de tête, l'aplomb des jambes, la désinvolture des épaules et des bras. . . .

L'index dur plia de nouveau l'épaule d'Edmée.

She hesitated, then smiled with a subtlety that had an element of suspicion in it.

"You call that love, Fred . . ."

"There are other words for it, but you don't care for them."

"What you call love . . . Might that not be really a . . . a kind of . . . alibi?"

She added hastily:

"I'm speaking in general terms, Fred, you understand . . . I mean, in certain cases, it *could* be . . ."

He let go of Edmée's hands.

"That," he said coldly, "was a foolish blunder."

"Why?" she asked in a weak voice.

He started to whistle with his chin in the air, walking away a few steps. Then he returned to his wife and looked her up and down as if she were a stranger. A wild animal doesn't have to leap at you to frighten you— Edmée saw that his nostrils were flaring and the tip of his nose was pale.

"Bah!" he puffed, looking at his wife. He shrugged his shoulders and did an about-face. When he reached the end of the room, he returned.

"Bah!" he repeated. "It speaks."

"How's that?"

"It speaks, and what does it say? My word, it takes the liberty . . ."

She stood up, furious:

"Fred," she shouted, "I won't have you talk to me like that again! Who do you take me for?"

"For a blunderer, that's what. Haven't I just had the honor of telling you so?"

He prodded her shoulder with a hard index finger, and it hurt her like a heavy bruise.

"You graduated from school. Isn't there some . . . some maxim somewhere that says: 'Don't lay hands on the knife,' or 'on the dagger,' or on some such thing?"

"On the axe," she said mechanically.

"Right! Well, my girl, you shouldn't lay hands on the axe—that is, wound a man . . . where his 'favors' are concerned, if I may express it that way. You have wounded me with regard to the gifts that I give you . . . You've wounded me with regard to my favors."

"You . . . you speak just like a cocotte!" she stammered.

She was blushing and losing her strength and her equanimity. She hated him for remaining pale and retaining a superiority, the whole secret of which consisted of the way he held his head, the steadiness of his legs, and the nonchalant posture of his shoulders and arms . . .

His hard index finger made a new dent in Edmée's shoulder.

"Pardon, pardon. Je vous épaterais bien en affirmant qu'au contraire c'est vous qui pensez comme une grue. En fait d'estimation, on ne trompe pas le fils Peloux. Je m'y connais en "cocottes", comme vous dites. Je m'y connais un peu. Une "cocotte", c'est une dame qui s'arrange généralement pour recevoir plus qu'elle ne donne. Vous m'entendez?"

Elle entendait surtout qu'il ne la tutoyait plus.

"Dix-neuf ans, la peau blanche, les cheveux qui sentent la vanille; et puis, au lit, les yeux fermés et les bras ballants. Tout ça, c'est très joli, mais est-ce que c'est bien rare? Croyez-vous que c'est bien rare?"

Elle tressaillait à chaque mot et chaque piqûre l'éveillait pour le duel de femelle à mâle.

"Possible que ce soit rare, dit-elle d'une voix ferme, mais comment pourrais-tu le savoir?"

Il ne répondit pas et elle se hâta de marquer un avantage:

"Moi, dit-elle, j'ai vu en Italie des hommes plus beaux que toi. Ça court les rues. Mes dix-neuf ans valent ceux de la voisine, un joli garçon vaut un autre joli garçon, va, va, tout peut s'arranger. . . . Un mariage, à présent, c'est une mesure pour rien. Au lieu de nous aigrir à des scènes ridicules. . . ."

Il l'arrêta d'un hochement de tête presque miséricordieux:

"Ah! pauvre gosse . . . ce n'est pas si simple. . . .

— Pourquoi? Il y a des divorces rapides, en y mettant le prix."

Elle parlait d'un air tranchant de pensionnaire évadée, qui faisait peine. Ses cheveux soulevés audessus de son front, le contour doux et enveloppé de sa joue rendaient plus sombres ses yeux anxieux et intelligents, ses yeux de femme malheureuse, ses yeux achevés et définitifs dans un visage indécis.

"Ça n'arrangerait rien, dit Chéri.

— Parce que?

— Parce que. . . ."

Il pencha son front où les sourcils s'effilaient en ailes pointues, ferma les yeux et les rouvrit comme s'il venait d'avaler une amère gorgée:

"Parce que tu m'aimes. . . ."

Elle ne prit garde qu'au tutoiement revenu, et surtout au son de la voix, plein, un peu étouffé, la voix des meilleures heures. Elle acquiesça au fond d'elle-même: "C'est vrai, je l'aime; il n'y a pas, en ce moment, de remède."

La cloche du dîner sonna dans le jardin, une cloche trop petite qui

"Excuse me, excuse me. You'd probably be astonished if I told you that, on the contrary, you're the one who's thinking like a tart. When it comes to evaluating such things, no one fools young Peloux here. I know my way around 'cocottes,' as you call them. I think I know my way around them. A 'cocotte' is a lady who generally arranges to get more than she gives. Understand?"

What she heard more than anything else was that he had stopped addressing her as *tu*.

"Nineteen years old, white skin, hair that smells of vanilla—then, in bed, eyes closed and dangling arms. All that is very pretty, but is it very unusual? Do you think it's very unusual?"

She winced at every word, and every sting aroused her for the duel between female and male.

"Maybe it *is* unusual," she said in a firm tone, "but how would *you* know?"

He didn't answer, and she hastened to mark up a point against him:

"As for me," she said, "in Italy I saw men who were handsomer than you. The streets are full of them. I, at nineteen, am as good as the next girl of that age; one good-looking boy is as good as the next; come now, everything can be arranged . . . A marriage nowadays is a meaningless ceremony. Instead of embittering ourselves by making ridiculous scenes . . ."

He stopped her with an almost pitying shake of his head:

"Oh, poor kid . . . it's not that simple . . ."

"Why not? There are quick divorces, you just have to pay enough."

She was speaking in a peremptory fashion, like a runaway boarding-school girl, and it was painful to hear her. Her hair, raised above her forehead, and the gentle, plump outline of her cheeks made her anxious, intelligent eyes darker—those eyes of an unhappy woman, eyes that were complete and definitive in a face that was still undetermined.

"That wouldn't settle anything," Chéri said.

"Why not?"

"Because . . ."

He leaned his head forward—that forehead on which the eyebrows narrowed into pointed wings—shut his eyes, and opened them again as if he had just swallowed a bitter mouthful:

"Because you love me . . ."

All she paid attention to was the fact that he was addressing her as *tu* again, and especially the sound of his voice, full and slightly muffled, the tone he used when he was at his best. Deep in her heart she concurred: "It's true, I love him; there's no help for it at the moment."

The dinner bell rang in the garden, a too-small bell that had been

datait d'avant Mme Peloux, une cloche d'orphelinat de province, triste et limpide. Edmée frissonna:

"Oh! je n'aime pas cette cloche. . . .

— Oui? dit Chéri distraitement.

— Chez nous, on annoncera les repas au lieu de les sonner. Chez nous, on n'aura pas ces façons de pension de famille; tu verras, chez nous. . . ."

Elle parlait en suivant le corridor vert hôpital sans se retourner et ne voyait pas, derrière elle, l'attention sauvage que Chéri donnait à ses dernières paroles, ni son demi-rire muet.

IL marchait légèrement, stimulé par un printemps sourd que l'on goûtait seulement dans le vent humide, inégal, dans le parfum exalté de la terre des squares et des jardinets. Une glace lui rappelait de temps en temps, au passage, qu'il portait un chapeau de feutre seyant, rabattu sur l'œil droit, un ample pardessus léger, de gros gants clairs, une cravate couleur de terre cuite. L'hommage silencieux des femmes le suivit, les plus candides lui dédiaient cette stupeur passagère qu'elles ne peuvent ni feindre, ni dissimuler. Mais Chéri ne regardait jamais les femmes dans la rue. Il quittait l'hôtel de l'avenue Henri-Martin, laissant aux tapissiers quelques ordres, contradictoires mais jetés sur un ton de maître.

Au bout de l'avenue, il respira longuement l'odeur végétale qui venait du Bois sur l'aile lourde et mouillée du vent d'Ouest, et pressa le pas vers la porte Dauphine. En quelques minutes, il atteignit le bas de l'avenue Bugeaud et s'arrêta net. Pour la première fois depuis six mois, ses pieds foulaient le chemin familier. Il ouvrit son pardessus.

"J'ai marché trop vite", se dit-il. Il repartit puis s'arrêta encore et, cette fois, son regard visa un point précis: à cinquante mètres, tête nue, la peau de chamois à la main, le concierge Ernest, le concierge de Léa "faisait" les cuivres de la grille, devant l'hôtel de Léa. Chéri se mit à fredonner en marchant, mais il s'aperçut au son de sa voix qu'il ne fredonnait jamais, et il se tut.

"Ça va, Ernest, toujours à l'ouvrage?"

Le concierge s'épanouit avec réserve.

"Monsieur Peloux! Je suis ravi de voir monsieur, monsieur n'a pas changé.

— Vous non plus, Ernest. Madame va bien?"

there since before Madame Peloux's occupancy, a bell like one in a provincial orphanage, sad and clear. Edmée shuddered:

"Oh, how I dislike that bell . . ."

"Yes?" said Chéri absentmindedly.

"At *our* place, meals will be announced, not rung for. At our place, we won't have these boardinghouse ways; you'll see, at our place . . ."

She was saying this while walking down the hospital-green corridor without looking back, so she didn't see how, behind her, Chéri was listening fiercely to her last words and giving a silent half-smile.

HE was walking with light steps, inspirited by a surreptitious springtime that could only be detected in the irregular moist breeze and in the heady fragrance of the ground in the planted squares and little gardens. As he went, a mirror occasionally reminded him that he was wearing a becoming felt hat, pulled down over his right eye, a capacious light overcoat, large light-colored gloves, and a terra-cotta tie. The unspoken admiration of female passers-by accompanied him; he inspired in the more candid among them that transitory awe which they're unable either to feign or to conceal. But Chéri never looked at women in the street. He had just stepped out of his Avenue Henri-Martin town house, having left the paperhangers with some orders that were self-contradictory but imperiously issued.

At the end of the avenue, he inhaled for some time the fragrance of plant life that arrived from the Bois on the heavy, moist wings of the west wind, then he hastened onward toward the Porte Dauphine. A few minutes later he reached the lower end of the Avenue Bugeaud, and stopped short. For the first time in six months his feet were treading that familiar path. He opened his overcoat.

"I've been walking too fast," he said to himself. He set out again, then stopped again, and this time his eyes focused on a precise spot: fifty meters away Ernest the concierge, Léa's concierge, bareheaded and his chamois cloth in hand, was "doing" the brass mountings of the gate in front of Léa's house. Chéri began humming as he walked, but the sound of his own voice reminded him that he never hummed, and he fell silent.

"How are things, Ernest, still at work?"

The concierge beamed, but in moderation.

"Monsieur Peloux! I'm delighted to see you sir; you haven't changed."

"Neither have you, Ernest. Is madame all right?"

Il parlait de profil, attentif aux persiennes fermées du premier
étage.

"Je pense, monsieur, nous n'avons eu que quelques cartes postales.

— D'où ça? de Biarritz, je crois?

— Je ne crois pas, monsieur.

— Où est madame?

— Je serais embarrassé de le dire à monsieur: nous transmettons le
courrier de madame, — trois fois rien, — au notaire de madame."

Chéri tira son portefeuille en regardant Ernest d'un air câlin.

"Oh, monsieur Peloux, de l'argent entre nous? Vous ne voudriez
pas. Mille francs ne feraient pas parler un homme qui en ignore. Si
monsieur veut l'adresse du notaire de madame?

— Non, merci, sans façons. Et elle revient quand?"

Ernest écarta les bras:

"Voilà encore une question qui n'est pas de ma compétence! Peut-
être demain, peut-être dans un mois. . . . J'entretiens, vous voyez.
Avec madame, il faut se méfier. Vous me diriez: "la voilà qui tourne au
coin de l'avenue", je n'en serais pas plus surpris."

Chéri se retourna et regarda le coin de l'avenue.

"Monsieur Peloux ne désire rien d'autre? Monsieur passait en se
promenant? C'est une belle journée. . . .

— Non, merci, Ernest. Au revoir, Ernest.

— Toujours dévoué à monsieur Peloux."

Chéri monta jusqu'à la place Victor-Hugo, en faisant tournoyer
sa canne. Il buta deux fois et faillit choir, comme les gens qui se
croient âprement regardés dans le dos. Parvenu à la balustrade du
métro, il s'accouda, penché sur l'ombre noire et rose du souter-
rain, et se sentit écrasé de fatigue. Quand il se redressa, il vit
qu'on allumait le gaz de la place et que la nuit bleuissait toutes
choses.

"Non, ce n'est pas possible? . . . Je suis malade!"

Il avait touché le fond d'une sombre rêverie et se ranimait péniblement. Les mots nécessaires lui vinrent enfin.

"Allons, allons, bon Dieu. . . . Fils Peloux, vous déraillez, mon bon
ami? Vous ne vous doutez pas qu'il est l'heure de rentrer?"

Ce dernier mot rappela la vision qu'une heure avait suffi à bannir:
une chambre carrée, la grande chambre d'enfant de Chéri, une jeune
femme anxieuse, debout contre la vitre, et Charlotte Peloux adoucie
par un Martini apéritif. . . .

He presented his profile as he spoke, while he looked hard at the closed shutters on the second story.

"I believe, sir, that we've had only a few postcards from her."

"Where from? Biarritz, I believe?"

"I don't believe so, sir."

"Where is madame?"

"I'd find it hard to tell you, sir: we forward madame's mail—which hardly amounts to anything—to madame's lawyer."

Chéri pulled out his wallet and looked at Ernest with an expression of shrewdness.

"Oh, Monsieur Peloux, money between us? You can't really mean it. A thousand francs couldn't make a man talk if he had no information. Would you like the address of madame's lawyer, sir?"

"No, thanks, don't bother. And when is she returning?"

Ernest flung out his arms:

"That's another question that's beyond me! Maybe tomorrow, maybe a month from now . . . As you see, I'm keeping things in shape. With madame, you have to be on your guard. If you were to say, 'There she is now, turning the corner of the avenue,' I wouldn't be at all surprised."

Chéri turned around and looked at the corner of the avenue.

"Do you desire anything further, Monsieur Peloux? Were you taking a stroll and just passing by? It's a lovely day . . ."

"No. Thank you, Ernest. I'll be seeing you, Ernest."

"Always ready to oblige you, Monsieur Peloux."

Chéri walked up as far as the Place Victor-Hugo, spinning his walking-stick. He stumbled twice, nearly falling, as people do when they think someone's behind them, staring at them hard. When he reached the railing of the Métro station, he leaned his elbows on it, looking down into the black-and-pink shadows of the underground passage, and he felt overwhelmed with fatigue. When he straightened up again, he saw that the gas lamps on the square were being lit, and that night was turning everything blue.

"No, it can't be possible . . . I'm ill!"

He had reached the depths of his gloomy musing, and it was hard to shake himself out of it. Finally the words he wanted came to him.

"Come on, come on, my God . . . Young Peloux, my good friend, are you losing your head? Don't you realize it's time to go home?"

The last word summoned back the vision which one hour had been enough to dispel: a square bedroom, the big room that had been Chéri's nursery; a worried young woman standing by the window; and Charlotte Peloux mollified by a Martini aperitif . . .

"Ah! non, dit-il tout haut. Non. . . . Ça, c'est fini."

Au geste de sa canne levée, un taxi s'arrêta.

"Au restaurant . . . euh . . . au restaurant du *Dragon Bleu*."

Il traversa le grill-room au son des violons, baigné d'une électricité atroce qu'il trouva tonifiante. Un maître d'hôtel le reconnut, et Chéri lui serra la main. Devant lui, un grand jeune homme creux se leva et Chéri soupira tendrement:

"Ah! Desmond! moi qui avais si envie de te voir! Comme tu tombes!"

La table où ils s'assirent était fleurie d'œillets roses. Une petite main, une grande aigrette s'agitaient vers Chéri, à une table voisine:

"C'est la Loupiote", avertit le vicomte Desmond. . . .

Chéri ne se souvenait pas de la Loupiote, mais il sourit à la grande aigrette, toucha la petite main sans se lever, du bout d'un éventail-réclame. Puis il toisa, de son air le plus grave de conquérant, un couple inconnu, parce que la femme oubliait de manger depuis que Chéri s'était assis non loin d'elle.

"Il a une tête de cocu, pas, le type?"

Pour murmurer ces mots-là, il se penchait à l'oreille de son ami et la joie dans son regard étincelait comme la crue des pleurs.

"Tu bois quoi, depuis que tu es marié? demanda Desmond. De la camomille?

— Du Pommery, dit Chéri.

— Avant le Pommery?

— Du Pommery, avant et après!"

Et il humait dans son souvenir, en ouvrant les narines, le pétillement à odeur de roses d'un vieux champagne de mil huit cent quatre-vingt-neuf que Léa gardait pour lui seul. . . .

Il commanda un dîner de modiste émancipée, du poisson froid au porto, des oiseaux rôtis, un soufflé brûlant dont le ventre cachait une glace acide et rouge. . . .

"Hé ha, criait la Loupiote, en agitant vers Chéri un œillet rose.

— Hé ha", répondit Chéri, en levant son verre.

Le timbre d'un cartel anglais, au mur, sonna huit heures.

"Oh! flûte, grommela Chéri. Desmond, fais-moi une commission au téléphone."

Les yeux pâles de Desmond espérèrent des révélations:

"Va demander Wagram 17-08, qu'on te donne ma mère et dis-lui, que nous dînons ensemble.

"Oh, no," he said out loud. "No . . . *That's* over with."

At the summons of his raised walking-stick a taxi stopped.

"To the . . . er . . . to the Blue Dragon restaurant."

He crossed the grill room to the sound of violins. It was drenched in a hideous electric glare which he found bracing. He was recognized by a maitre d', whose hand Chéri shook. In front of him, a thin young man got up; Chéri sighed warmly:

"Oh! Desmond! I so much wanted to see you! How lucky it is that you're here!"

The table at which they sat down bore a vase of pink carnations. At an adjacent table, a small hand and a large aigrette bobbed in Chéri's direction.

"It's Girlie," Viscount Desmond warned him . . .

Chéri didn't recall Girlie, but he smiled to the large aigrette and, without getting up, touched the small hand with the tip of an advertisement-bearing fan. Then, with his most serious heartbreaker manner, he gazed at a couple he didn't know, because the woman had been forgetting to eat ever since Chéri had sat down not far from her.

"The guy looks like a cuckold, doesn't he?"

To murmur those words, he was leaning over toward his friend's ear, and the joy in his eyes glistened like a surge of tears.

"What do you drink now that you're married?" Desmond asked. "Camomile tea?"

"Pommery," said Chéri.

"But before the Pommery?"

"Pommery, before and after!"

And in his memory, he opened his nostrils wide and sniffed the rose-scented bubbles of an old champagne from 1889 that Léa used to keep for him alone . . .

He ordered a dinner that a milliner with liberal ideas might order: cold fish with port wine, roast chicken, and a piping hot soufflé that hid a tart, red ice inside it . . .

"Hey there!" Girlie called, waving a red carnation at Chéri.

"Hey there!" Chéri replied, raising his glass.

An English clock hanging on the wall struck eight.

"Oh, damn," Chéri grumbled. "Desmond, do me a favor and make a call for me."

Desmond's pale eyes hoped for revelations.

"Go call Wagram 17-08, ask for my mother, and tell her we're having dinner together."

— Et si c'est Mme Peloux jeune qui vient à l'appareil?

— La même chose. Je suis très libre, tu vois. Je l'ai dressée."

Il but et mangea beaucoup, très occupé de paraître sérieux et blasé. Mais le moindre éclat de rire, un bris de verre, une valse vaseuse exaltaient son plaisir. Le bleu dur des boiseries miroitantes le ramenait à des souvenirs de la Riviera, aux heures où la mer trop bleue noircit à midi autour d'une plaque de soleil fondu. Il oublia sa froideur rituelle d'homme très beau et se mit à balayer la dame brune, en face, de regards professionnels dont elle frémissait toute.

"Et Léa?" demanda soudain Desmond.

Chéri ne tressaillit pas, il pensait à Léa.

"Léa? elle est dans le Midi.

— C'est fini, avec elle?"

Chéri mit un pouce dans l'entournure de son gilet.

"Oh! naturellement, tu comprends. On s'est quittés très chic, très bons amis. Ça ne pouvait pas durer toute la vie. Quelle femme charmante, intelligente, mon vieux. . . . D'ailleurs, tu l'as connue! Une largeur d'idées. . . . Très remarquable. Mon cher, je l'avoue, s'il n'y avait pas eu la question d'âge. . . . Mais il y avait la question d'âge, et n'est-ce pas. . . .

— Evidemment", interrompit Desmond.

Ce jeune homme aux yeux décolorés, qui connaissait à fond son dur et difficile métier de parasite, venait de céder à la curiosité et se le reprochait comme une imprudence. Mais Chéri, tout ensemble circonspect et grisé, ne cessa pas de parler de Léa. Il dit des choses raisonnables, imprégnées d'un bon sens conjugal. Il vanta le mariage, mais en rendant justice aux vertus de Léa. Il chanta la douceur soumise de sa jeune femme, pour trouver l'occasion de critiquer le caractère résolu de Léa: "Ah! la bougresse, je te garantis qu'elle avait ses idées, celle-là!" Il poussa plus loin les confidences, il alla, à l'egard de Léa, jusqu'à la sévérité, jusqu'à l'impertinence. Et pendant qu'il parlait, abrité derrière les paroles imbéciles que lui soufflait une défiance d'amant persécuté, il goûtait le bonheur subtil de parler d'elle sans danger. Un peu plus, il l'eût salie, en célébrant dans son cœur le souvenir qu'il avait d'elle, son nom doux et facile dont il s'était privé depuis six mois, toute l'image miséricordieuse de Léa, penchée sur lui, barrée de deux ou trois grandes rides graves, irréparables, belle, perdue pour lui, mais — bah! — si présente. . . .

Vers onze heures, ils se levèrent pour partir, refroidis par le restau-

"What if it's young Madame Peloux who comes to the phone?"

"Same message. I'm a free man, as you see. I've got her trained."

He ate and drank a lot, intent on seeming serious and blasé. But the slightest burst of laughter, a broken glass, a shabby waltz, heightened his pleasure. The harsh blue of the shiny woodwork evoked memories of the Riviera, on the days when the sea, all too blue, becomes black at noon around a sheet of molten sunshine. He forgot the ritual coldness proper to a very handsome man, and began to look the dark-haired woman opposite him up and down with a professional gaze that made her shudder all over.

"And Léa?" Desmond asked all of a sudden.

Chéri didn't jump, because he had been thinking of Léa.

"Léa? She's in the south."

"Is it all over with her?"

Chéri stuck one thumb in the armhole of his vest.

"Oh, naturally, you understand. We broke up in the nicest way, as very good friends. It couldn't last a lifetime. What a charming, intelligent woman, my friend . . . Anyway, you've met her! Broadminded . . . Very remarkable. My friend, I confess, if it hadn't been for the difference in our ages . . . But there *was* a difference in our ages, and don't you think . . ."

"Of course," Desmond interrupted.

That young man with colorless eyes, who knew thoroughly his tough, difficult trade as a hanger-on, had just succumbed to curiosity, and he was reproaching himself for it, fearing he'd been incautious. But Chéri, who was simultaneously circumspect and tipsy, didn't stop talking about Léa. He was speaking rationally, making remarks that were imbued with a husband's good sense. He praised married life, but still did justice to Léa's good points. He lauded his young wife's gentle submissiveness in order to find an opportunity to criticize Léa's determined character: "Oh, that tough customer, *she* had a mind of her own, I can assure you!" He became even more confiding, and even became severe and impertinent with regard to Léa. And while he was talking, sheltering behind the foolish words that were suggested to him by a persecuted lover's mistrust, he was tasting the subtle pleasure of being able to speak about her without danger. A little longer, and he would have besmirched her, all the while extolling in his heart his precious memories of her; her soft, easy-to-say name that he had deprived himself of for six months; the entire merciful image of Léa bending over him, her face lined with two or three large, deep, irreparable wrinkles—a beautiful face, lost to him, but oh, so present . . .

Around eleven, they got up to leave, their good humor cooled by

rant presque vide. Pourtant, à la table voisine, la Loupiote s'appliquait à sa correspondance, et réclamait des petits bleus. Elle leva vers les deux amis son visage inoffensif de mouton blond, quand ils passèrent:

"Eh bien, on ne dit pas bonsoir?

— Bonsoir", concéda Chéri.

La Loupiote appela, pour admirer Chéri, le témoignage de son amie:

"Crois-tu, hein! et penser qu'il a tant de galette! Il y a des types qui ont tout."

Mais Chéri ne lui offrit que son étui à cigarettes ouvert; et elle devint acerbe.

"Ils ont tout, excepté la manière de s'en servir. . . . Rentre chez ta mère, mon chou! . . .

— Justement, dit Chéri à Desmond, quand ils atteignirent la rue. Justement, je voulais te demander, Desmond. . . . Attends qu'on soit hors de ce boyau où on est foulé. . . ."

La soirée douce et humide attardait les promeneurs, mais le boulevard, après la rue Caumartin, attendait encore la sortie des théâtres. Chéri prit le bras de son ami:

"Voilà, Desmond . . . je voudrais que tu retournes au téléphone."

Desmond s'arrêta.

"Encore?

— Tu appelleras le Wagram. . . .

— 17-08. . . .

— Je t'adore. Tu diras que je me suis trouvé souffrant chez toi. . . . Où demeures-tu?

— A l'Hôtel Morris.

— Parfait. . . . Que je rentrerai demain matin, que tu me fais de la menthe. . . . Va, vieux. Tiens, tu donneras ça au petit gosse du téléphone, ou bien tu le garderas. . . . Reviens vite. Je t'attends à la terrasse de Weber."

Le long jeune homme serviable et rogue partit en froissant des billets dans sa poche et sans se permettre une observation. Il retrouva Chéri penché sur une orangeade intacte, dans laquelle il semblait lire sa destinée.

"Desmond! . . . Qui t'a répondu?

— Une dame, dit laconiquement le messager.

— Laquelle?

— Je ne sais pas.

— Qu'est-ce qu'elle a dit?

— Que c'était bien.

the near-emptiness of the restaurant. But at the adjacent table Girlie was busy with her correspondence and was asking for express-letter forms. She raised her innocuous face, like that of a blond sheep, to the two friends when they passed by:

"Well, don't you say good night?"

"Good night," Chéri said obediently.

To admire Chéri, Girlie called her girl friend to witness:

"Would you believe it! And to think he's got so much dough! Some guys have everything."

But Chéri offered her only his open cigarette case, and she became vinegary.

"They've got everything, except the brains to know how to use it . . . Go home to mother, honey! . . ."

"That's it!" Chéri said to Desmond when they were out in the street. "That's it: I wanted to ask you, Desmond . . . Wait till we're out of this tight spot where people walk all over you . . ."

The mild, moist night was attracting strollers, but the boulevard, beyond the Rue Caumartin, was not yet filled with people leaving the theaters. Chéri took his friend's arm:

"It's like this, Desmond . . . I'd like you to make another call."

Desmond stopped walking.

"Again?"

"You'll call Wagram . . ."

"17-08."

"You're terrific. Say that I'm at your place and that I'm feeling ill . . . Where do you live?"

"At the Hotel Morris."

"Fine . . . Say that I'll be home tomorrow morning, that you're making mint tea for me . . . Go on, buddy. Here, give this to the kid at the phone desk, or else keep it yourself . . . Come right back. I'll be waiting for you at an outside table at Weber's."

The tall, obliging, haughty young man set out, crumpling the banknotes in his pocket, and not daring to make a remark. He found Chéri bent over an orangeade that he hadn't touched; he seemed to be reading his future in it.

"Desmond! . . . Who answered?"

"A lady," the messenger said laconically.

"What lady?"

"I don't know."

"What did she say?"

"That it was all right."

— Sur quel ton?

— Celui sur lequel je te le répète.

— Ah! bon; merci."

"C'était Edmée", pensa Chéri. Ils marchaient vers la place de la Concorde et Chéri avait repris le bras de Desmond. Il n'osait pas avouer qu'il se sentait très las.

"Où veux-tu aller? demanda Desmond.

— Ah! mon vieux, soupira Chéri avec gratitude, au Morris, et tout de suite. Je suis claqué."

Desmond oublia son impassibilité:

"Comment, c'est vrai? On va au Morris? Qu'est-ce que tu veux faire? Pas de blagues, hé? Tu veux. . . .

— Dormir, répondit Chéri. Et il ferma les yeux comme prêt à tomber, puis les rouvrit. Dormir, dormir, c'est compris?"

Il serrait trop fort le bras de son ami.

"Allons-y", dit Desmond.

En dix minutes, ils furent au Morris. Le bleu ciel et l'ivoire d'une chambre à coucher, le faux empire d'un petit salon sourirent à Chéri comme de vieux amis. Il se baigna, emprunta à Desmond une chemise de soie trop étroite, se coucha et, calé entre deux gros oreillers mous, sombra dans un bonheur sans rêves, dans un sommeil noir et épais qui le défendait de toutes parts. . . .

IL coula des jours honteux, qu'il comptait. "Seize . . . dix-sept. . . . Les trois semaines sonnées, je rentre à Neuilly." Il ne rentrait pas. Il mesurait lucidement une situation à laquelle il n'avait plus la force de remédier. La nuit, ou le matin, parfois, il se flattait que sa lâcheté fini-rait dans quelques heures. "Plus la force? Pardon, pardon. . . . Pas en-core la force. Mais ça revient. A midi tapant, qu'est-ce que je parie que je suis dans la salle à manger du boulevard d'Inkermann? Une, deux et. . . ." Midi tapant le trouvait au bain, ou menant son auto-mobile à côté de Desmond.

L'heure des repas lui accordait un moment d'optimisme conju-gal, ponctuel comme une attaque fiévreuse. En s'asseyant à une table de célibataire, en face de Desmond, il voyait apparaître Edmée et songeait en silence à la déférence inconcevable de sa jeune femme: "Elle est trop gentille, aussi, cette petite! A-t-on ja-mais vu un amour de femme comme celle-là? Pas un mot, pas une plainte! Je vais lui coller un de ces bracelets, quand je rentrerai. . . .

"In what tone of voice?"

"The same tone I'm using now."

"Oh, good! Thanks."

"It was Edmée," Chéri thought. They were walking toward the Place de la Concorde, and Chéri had taken Desmond's arm again. He didn't dare confess that he was feeling very weary.

"Where do you want to go?" Desmond asked.

"Oh, my friend," Chéri sighed with gratitude, "to the Morris, and right away. I'm bushed."

Desmond forgot his cool-and-collected manner:

"What, really? We're going to the Morris? What do you want to do? No kidding around, right? You want . . ."

"To sleep," Chéri answered. And he closed his eyes as if he were ready to drop; then he opened them again. "To sleep, sleep, understand?"

He was squeezing his friend's arm too hard.

"Let's go," said Desmond.

Ten minutes later they were at the Morris. The sky-blue and ivory of a bedroom, and the imitation Empire style of a little sitting-room, greeted Chéri like old friends. He took a bath, borrowed from Desmond a silk nightshirt that was too small for him, lay down, and, wedged between two big soft pillows, drifted off into a dreamless happiness, into a thick, pitch-dark slumber that protected him on all sides . . .

HE spent shame-laden days, counting them one by one. "Sixteen . . . seventeen . . . When three weeks are over, I'll go back to Neuilly." But he wasn't going home yet. He lucidly observed a situation that he no longer had the strength to remedy. At times, at night or in the morning, he made himself believe that his cowardly absence would be over in a few hours. "No more strength? Excuse me, excuse me . . . No strength *yet*. But it's coming back. What do you bet that, at the stroke of noon, I'll be in the dining room on the Boulevard d'Inkermann? One, two, . . ." And the stroke of noon would find him in his bath, or driving his car with Desmond beside him.

Mealtimes would grant him a moment of optimism with regard to his marriage, a moment as punctual as an attack of recurring fever. Sitting down to a bachelor table opposite Desmond, he would see Edmée appear, and he would silently think about his young wife's unbelievable respectfulness: "She's just too nice, that girl! Have you ever seen such a darling of a woman as she is? Not one word, not one complaint! I'm

Ah! l'éducation . . . parlez-moi de Marie-Laure pour élever une jeune fille!" Mais un jour, dans le grill-room du Morris, l'apparition d'une robe verte à col de chinchilla, qui ressemblait à une robe d'Edmée, avait peint sur le visage de Chéri toutes les marques d'une basse terreur.

Desmond trouvait la vie belle et engraissait un peu. Il ne gardait son arrogance que pour les heures où Chéri, sollicité de visiter une "anglaise prodigieuse, noire de vices" ou "un prince indien dans son palais d'opium", refusait en termes concis ou consentait avec un mépris non voilé. Desmond ne comprenait plus rien à Chéri, mais Chéri payait, et mieux qu'au meilleur temps de leur adolescence. Une nuit, ils retrouvèrent la blonde Loupiote, chez son amie dont on oubliait toujours le nom terne: "Chose . . . vous savez bien . . . la copine de la Loupiote. . . ."

La Copine fumait et donnait à fumer. Son entresol modeste fleurait, dès l'entrée, le gaz mal clos et la drogue refroidie, et elle conquérait par une cordialité larmoyante, une constante provocation à la tristesse qui n'étaient point inoffensives. Desmond fut traité, chez elle, de "grand gosse désespéré" et Chéri de "beauté qui a tout et qui n'en est que plus malheureux". Mais il ne fuma point, regarda la boîte de cocaïne avec une répugnance de chat qu'on veut purger, et se tint presque toute la nuit assis sur la natte, le dos au capiton bas du mur, entre Desmond endormi et la Copine qui ne cessait de fumer. Presque toute la nuit, il aspira, sage et défiant, l'odeur qui contente la faim et la soif et il sembla parfaitement heureux, sauf qu'il regarda souvent, avec une fixité pénible et interrogatrice, le cou fané de la Copine, un cou rougi et grenu où luisait un collier de perles fausses.

Un moment, Chéri tendit la main, caressa du bout des doigts les cheveux teints au henné sur la nuque de la Copine; il soupesa les grosses perles creuses et légères, puis il retira sa main avec le frémissement nerveux de quelqu'un qui s'est accroché les ongles à une soie éraillée. Peu après, il se leva et partit.

"Tu n'en as pas assez, demanda Desmond à Chéri, de ces boîtes où on mange, où on boit, où tu ne consommes pas de femmes, et de cet hôtel où on claque les portes? Et des boîtes où on va le soir, et de tourner dans ta soixante chevaux de Paris à Rouen, de Paris à Compiègne, de Paris à Ville-d'Avray. . . . Parle-moi de la Riviera! Ce n'est pas décembre ni janvier, la saison chic là-bas, c'est mars, c'est avril, c'est. . . .

going to treat her to a good bracelet when I get home . . . Ah, upbringing . . . It's Marie-Laure for me when it comes to raising a girl!" But one day, in the grill room of the Morris, the sudden appearance of a green dress with a chinchilla collar, resembling one of Edmée's dresses, had painted all the traces of a base terror on Chéri's face.

Desmond was finding life beautiful, and was putting on a little weight. He saved his arrogance for the times when Chéri, urged to visit "an amazing Englishwoman, a hotbed of vice" or "a Hindu prince in his opium palace," either flatly refused or else agreed with undisguised contempt. Desmond couldn't understand Chéri at all anymore, but Chéri kept paying, and more liberally than in the headiest days of their adolescence. One night they met blond Girlie again, at the home of her girl friend, whose dull name they could never remember: "What's-her-name . . . you know who . . . Girlie's pal . . ."

The Pal used to smoke and hand out smokes. As soon as you stepped into her humble mezzanine-floor rooms, you could smell leaking gas and drugs that had grown cold. She would subdue you with a tearful cordiality and a constant inducement to sadness that were far from being harmless. At her place Desmond was called "the big, despairing kid," and Chéri was called "the beauty who has everything, though it only makes him more unhappy." But he never smoked; he looked at the box of cocaine with the repugnance of a cat about to be purged, and kept sitting nearly all night long on the mat, his back against the base of the wall, in between the sleeping Desmond and Pal, who never stopped smoking. Nearly all night, wellbehaved but suspicious, he inhaled the aroma that quiets hunger and thirst, and he seemed perfectly happy, except that often, with a questioning gaze of painful rigidity, he looked at Pal's faded neck, a reddened, grainy neck on which a necklace of imitation pearls gleamed.

At one moment, Chéri reached out a hand and, with his fingertips, caressed the henna-dyed hair on the back of Pal's neck; he weighed the big, light, hollow pearls in his fingers, then withdrew his hand with the nervous shudder of a person who has caught his fingernails in frayed silk. A little later, he got up and left.

"Haven't you had enough," Desmond asked Chéri, "of those joints where we eat and drink, where you make no use of the women, or of this hotel where some door is always slamming? Or of the night spots we go to? Or of riding around in your sixty-horsepower car from Paris to Rouen, from Paris to Compiègne, from Paris to Ville-d'Avray . . . ? It's the Riviera for me! The high season down there isn't December or January, it's March, April, it's . . ."

— Non, dit Chéri.

— Alors?

— Alors, rien."

Il s'adoucit sans sincérité et prit ce que Léa nommait autrefois sa "gueule d'amateur éclairé".

"Mon cher . . . tu ne comprends pas la beauté de Paris en cette saison. . . . Ce . . . cette indécision, ce printemps qui ne peut pas se dérider, cette lumière douce . . . tandis que la banalité de la Riviera. . . . Non, vois-tu, je me plais ici."

Desmond faillit perdre sa patience de valet:

"Oui, et puis peut-être que le divorce Peloux fils. . . ."

Les narines sensibles de Chéri blanchirent.

"Si tu as une combine avec un avocat, décourage-le tout de suite. Il n'y a pas de divorce Peloux fils.

— Mon cher! . . . protesta Desmond qui tâcha de paraître blessé. Tu as une singulière façon de répondre à une amitié d'enfance, qui en toute occasion. . . ."

Chéri n'écoutait pas. Il dirigeait du côté de Desmond un menton aminci, une bouche qu'il pinçait en bouche d'avare. Pour la première fois, il venait d'entendre un étranger disposer de son bien.

Il réfléchissait. Le divorce Peloux fils? Il y avait songé à mainte heure du jour et de la nuit, et ces mots-là représentaient alors la liberté, une sorte d'enfance recouvrée, peut-être mieux encore. . . . Mais la voix, nasillarde exprès, du vicomte Desmond venait de susciter l'image nécessaire: Edmée quittant la maison de Neuilly, résolue sous son petit chapeau d'auto et son long voile, et s'en allant vers une maison inconnue, où vivait un homme inconnu. "Évidemment, ça arrangerait tout", convint Chéri le bohème. Mais, dans le même temps, un autre Chéri singulièrement timoré regimbait: "Ce n'est pas des choses à faire!" L'image se précisa, gagna en couleurs et en mouvement. Chéri entendit le son grave et harmonieux de la grille et vit, de l'autre côté de la grille, sur une main nue, une perle grise, un diamant blanc. . . .

"Adieu . . ." disait la petite main.

Chéri se leva en repoussant son siège.

"C'est à moi, tout ça! La femme, la maison, les bagues, c'est à moi!"

Il n'avait pas parlé haut, mais son visage avouait une si barbare violence que Desmond crut venue la dernière heure de sa prospérité. Chéri s'apitoya sans bonté:

"Pauvre mimi, t'as les foies? Ah! cette vieille noblesse d'épée!

"No," said Chéri.

"What then?"

"Nothing then."

He became gentler without really meaning it, and his face assumed what Léa used to call his "expression like an enlightened amateur's":

"My friend . . . you don't understand how beautiful Paris is at this time of the year . . . This . . . this undecidedness, this springtime that's unable to brighten up, this soft light . . . whereas the banality of the Riviera . . . No, don't you see, I like being here."

Desmond almost lost his valet-like patience:

"Yes, and besides, maybe young Peloux's divorce . . ."

Chéri's sensitive nostrils turned white.

"If you've made some deal with a lawyer, talk him out of it right away. There isn't any young Peloux's divorce."

"My friend! . . ." Desmond protested, trying to look hurt. "You have a strange way of acknowledging a friendship that goes back to our childhood, one that through thick and thin . . ."

Chéri wasn't listening. He was thrusting in Desmond's direction a pointy chin, a mouth that he was screwing up like a miser's. For the first time, he had just heard an outsider trying to dictate the way he should dispose of his property.

He reflected. Young Peloux's divorce? He had thought about it at many an hour of day and night. At such times those words stood for freedom, a sort of childhood regained, perhaps something better yet . . . But Viscount Desmond's intentionally nasal voice had just evoked the necessary image: Edmée leaving the Neuilly house, looking resolute in her little driving hat and her long veil, heading for some unknown house occupied by some unknown man. "Obviously, that would settle everything," the bohemian in Chéri agreed. But, at the same time, another Chéri, oddly timorous, was balking: "People don't do such things!" The image became sharper, taking on color and movement. Chéri heard the deep, harmonious sound of the opened gate, and saw on the other side of the gate a gray pearl and a white diamond on a bare hand . . .

"Good-bye . . . ," the little hand was saying.

Chéri stood up, shoving back his chair.

"All of that belongs to me! The woman, the house, the rings, they're mine!"

He hadn't said it out loud, but his face bespoke such barbaric violence that Desmond thought the last hour of his prosperity had arrived. Chéri took pity on him, but not kindly:

"Poor baby, did it get scared? Oh, these old knightly families!

Viens, je vais te payer des caleçons pareils à mes chemises, et des chemises pareilles à tes caleçons. Desmond, nous sommes le dix-sept?

— Oui, pourquoi?

— Le dix-sept mars. Autant dire le printemps. Desmond, les gens chic, mais là, les gens véritablement élégants, femmes ou hommes, ils ne peuvent pas attendre plus longtemps avant de s'habiller pour la saison prochaine?

— Difficilement....

— Le dix-sept, Desmond! . . . Viens, tout va bien. On va acheter un gros bracelet pour ma femme, un énorme fume-cigarette pour Mame Peloux, et une toute petite épingle pour toi!"

Il eut ainsi, à deux ou trois reprises, le pressentiment foudroyant que Léa allait revenir, qu'elle venait de rentrer, que les persiennes du premier étage, ouvertes, laissaient apercevoir le rose floral des brise-bise, le réseau des grands rideaux d'application, l'or des miroirs. . . . Le 15 avril passa et Léa ne revenait pas. Des événements agaçants rayaient le cours morne de la vie de Chéri. Il y eut la visite de Mme Peloux, qui pensa perdre la vie devant Chéri plat comme un lévrier, la bouche close et l'œil mobile. Il y eut la lettre d'Edmée, une lettre tout unie, surprenante, où elle expliquait qu'elle demeurerait à Neuilly "jusqu'à nouvel ordre", et se chargeait pour Chéri des "meilleurs compliments de Mme de la Berche. . . ." Il se crut moqué, ne sut répondre et finit par jeter cette lettre incompréhensible; mais il n'alla pas à Neuilly. A mesure qu'avril, vert et froid, fleuri de pawlonias, de tulipes, de jacinthes en bottes et de cytises en grappes, embaumait Paris, Chéri s'enfonçait, seul, dans une ombre austère. Desmond maltraité, harcelé, mécontent, mais bien payé, avait mission tantôt de défendre Chéri contre des jeunes femmes familières et des jeunes hommes indiscrets, tantôt de recruter les uns et les autres pour former une bande qui mangeait, buvait et criaillait entre Montmartre, les restaurants du Bois et les cabarets de la rive gauche.

Une nuit, la Copine, qui fumait seule et pleurait ce soir-là une infidélité grave de son amie la Loupiote, vit entrer chez elle ce jeune homme aux sourcils démoniaques qui s'effilaient sur la tempe. Il réclama "de l'eau bien froide" pour sa belle bouche altérée qu'une secrète ardeur séchait. Il ne témoigna pas du moindre intérêt pour les malheurs de la Copine, lorsqu'elle les narra en poussant vers Chéri le plateau de laque et la pipe. Il n'accepta que sa part de natte, de si-

Come, I'll buy you some drawers that are like my shirts, and some shirts that are like your drawers. Desmond, is today the seventeenth?"

"Yes. Why?"

"The seventeenth of March. Practically springtime. Desmond, stylish people, I mean truly elegant people, women or men, can't wait any longer before buying a wardrobe for the coming season, can they?"

"Hardly . . ."

"The seventeenth, Desmond! . . . Come, everything's all right. We'll buy a big bracelet for my wife, an enormous cigarette holder for Ma'me Peloux, and a very small tie-pin for you!"

In that way, two or three more times, he had the dazzling presentiment that Léa was on her way back, that she had just come home, that the second-story shutters were open, revealing the flowery pink of the half-curtains, the lacework of the full window curtains, the gold of the mirrors . . . April 15 went by, but Léa wasn't back. Irritating events clawed their way into Chéri's dreary existence. There was the visit from Madame Peloux, who thought she'd die when she saw Chéri thin as a greyhound, his mouth closed and his eyes wandering. There was the letter from Edmée, a letter uniform in tone, a surprising letter in which she explained that she'd stay in Neuilly "till she received new instructions," and that she was sending Chéri "best regards from Madame de la Berche . . ." He thought she was making fun of him, he didn't know how to reply, and finally he threw away that incomprehensible letter; but he didn't go to Neuilly. While April, green and cold, a-blossom with pawlonias, tulips, heaps of hyacinths, and clusters of laburnum, made Paris fragrant, Chéri buried himself, alone, in austere shadows. Desmond—mistreated, harassed, unhappy, but well paid—was given a variety of duties. Sometimes he had to protect Chéri against overly familiar young women and indiscreet young men. At other times he had to recruit just such people to form a group that went around eating, drinking, and raising hell between Montmartre, the restaurants in the Bois, and the cabarets on the Left Bank.

One night, Pal, who was smoking alone and bewailing a serious infidelity on the part of her friend Girlie, saw that young man, with his devilish eyebrows tapering toward his temples, enter her home. He asked for "some really cold water" for his beautiful, thirsty mouth, which was parched with a secret desire. He showed not the slightest interest in Pal's misfortunes when she told them to him, pushing the lacquer tray and the pipe in Chéri's direction. He merely accepted his share of the mat, of the

lence et de demi-obscurité, et demeura là jusqu'au jour, économe de ses mouvements comme quelqu'un qui craint, s'il bouge, de réveiller une blessure. Au jour levant, il demanda à la Copine: "Pourquoi n'avais-tu pas aujourd'hui ton collier de perles, tu sais, ton gros collier?" et partit courtoisement.

Il prenait l'habitude inconsciente de marcher la nuit, sans compagnon. Rapide, allongé, son pas le menait vers un but distinct et inaccessible. Il échappait, passé minuit, à Desmond qui le retrouvait, vers l'aube, sur son lit d'hôtel, endormi à plat ventre et la tête entre ses bras pliés, dans l'attitude d'un enfant chagrin.

"Ah! bon, il est là, disait Desmond avec soulagement. Un coco pareil, on ne sait jamais. . . ."

Une nuit que Chéri marchait ainsi les yeux grands ouverts dans l'ombre, il remonta l'avenue Bugeaud, car il n'avait pas obéi, de tout le jour écoulé, au fétichisme qui l'y ramenait de quarante-huit heures en quarante-huit heures. Comme les maniaques qui ne peuvent s'endormir sans avoir touché trois fois le bouton d'une porte, il frôlait la grille, posait l'index sur le bouton de la sonnette, appelait tout bas, d'un ton farceur: "Hé ha! . . ." et s'en allait.

Mais une nuit, cette nuit-là, devant la grille, il sentit dans sa gorge un grand coup que frappait son cœur: le globe électrique de la cour luisait comme une lune mauve au-dessus du perron, la porte de l'entrée de service, béante, éclairait le pavé et, au premier étage, les persiennes filtrant la lumière intérieure dessinaient un peigne d'or. Chéri s'adossa à l'arbre le plus proche et baissa la tête.

"Ce n'est pas vrai, dit-il. Je vais relever les yeux et tout sera noir."

Il se redressa au son de la voix d'Ernest, le concierge, qui criait dans le corridor:

"Sur les neuf heures, demain matin, je monterai la grande malle noire avec Marcel, Madame!"

Chéri se détourna précipitamment et courut jusqu'à l'avenue du Bois où il s'assit. Le globe électrique qu'il avait regardé dansait devant lui, pourpre sombre cerné d'or, sur le noir des massifs encore maigres. Il appuya la main sur son cœur et respira profondément. La nuit sentait les lilas entrouverts. Il jeta son chapeau, ouvrit son manteau, se laissa aller contre le dossier du banc, étendit les jambes et ses mains ouvertes tombèrent mollement. Un poids écrasant et suave venait de descendre sur lui.

"Ah! dit-il tout bas, c'est le bonheur? . . . je ne savais pas. . . ."

Il eut le temps de se prendre en pitié et en mépris, pour tout ce

silence and semi-darkness, remaining there till daylight, as sparing in his movements as a man afraid of reopening a wound by moving around. At daybreak he asked Pal: "Why weren't you wearing your pearl necklace tonight, you know, your big necklace?" Then he left politely.

He was acquiring the unconscious habit of walking at night without a companion. His long, swift steps would lead him toward a distinct but inaccessible goal. After midnight he would elude Desmond, who found him again around dawn on his hotel bed, asleep on his stomach, his head resting on his folded arms, looking like an unhappy child.

"Good, he's there," Desmond would say, feeling relieved. "With a fellow like that, one never knows . . ."

One night while Chéri was walking that way, his eyes wide open in the dark, he went up the Avenue Bugeaud; for, all during the past day, he hadn't yielded to the fetishistic ritual that took him back there every forty-eight hours. Like those obsessive people who can't fall asleep unless they've touched a doorknob three times, he would brush up against the gate, rest his index finger on the bell, and call quietly, in a joking tone: "Hey there!" Then he'd go away.

But one night—that night—in front of the gate he felt in his throat a strong beat that came from his heart: the electric globe in the court-yard was shining above the front steps like a mauve moon; the wide-open door of the service entrance was illuminating the pavement; and, on the second floor, the shutters were filtering the light from inside in such a way that they resembled a golden comb. Chéri leaned his back against the nearest tree and lowered his head.

"It isn't true," he said. "When I raise my eyes again, everything will be dark."

He straightened up when he heard the voice of Ernest, the concierge, shouting in the corridor:

"At nine in the morning Marcel and I will bring up the big black trunk, madame!"

Chéri departed in haste and ran all the way to the Avenue du Bois, where he sat down. The electric globe he had been looking at was dancing in front of him, dark purple with a gold ring around it, against the blackness of the not yet filled-out clumps of bushes. He rested his hand on his heart and breathed deeply. The night was redolent of just-opening lilacs. He pulled off his hat, unbuttoned his coat, and slumped against the back of the bench; he stretched out his legs, and his open hands dropped limply. A crushing but pleasant weight had just fallen upon him.

"Oh!" he said very quietly, "Is this happiness? . . . I didn't know . . ."

He had the time to pity himself and to sneer at himself, thinking of

qu'il n'avait pas savouré pendant sa vie misérable de jeune homme riche au petit cœur, puis il cessa de penser pendant un instant ou pendant une heure. Il put croire, après, qu'il ne désirait plus rien au monde, pas même d'aller chez Léa.

Quand il frissonna de froid et qu'il entendit les merles annoncer l'aurore, il se leva, trébuchant et léger, et reprit le chemin de l'Hôtel Morris, sans passer par l'avenue Bugeaud. Il s'étirait, élargissait ses poumons et débordait d'une mansuétude universelle:

"Maintenant, soupirait-il exorcisé, maintenant. . . . Ah! maintenant, je vais être tellement gentil pour la petite. . . ."

Levé à huit heures, rasé, chaussé, fébrile, Chéri secoua Desmond qui dormait livide, affreux à voir et gonflé dans le sommeil comme un noyé:

"Desmond! hep! Desmond! . . . Assez! T'es trop vilain quand tu dors!"

Le dormeur s'assit et arrêta sur son ami le regard de ses yeux couleur d'eau trouble. Il feignit l'abrutissement pour prolonger un examen attentif de Chéri, Chéri vêtu de bleu, pathétique et superbe, pâle sous un velours de poudre habilement essuyé. . . . Il y avait encore des heures où Desmond souffrait, dans sa laideur apprêtée, de la beauté de Chéri. Il bâilla exprès, longuement: "Qu'est-ce qu'il y a encore?" se demandait-il en bâillant; "cet imbécile est plus beau qu'hier. Ces cils surtout, ces cils qu'il a. . . ." Il regardait les cils de Chéri, lustrés et vigoureux, et l'ombre qu'ils versaient à la sombre prunelle et au blanc bleu de l'œil. Desmond remarqua aussi que la dédaigneuse bouche arquée s'ouvrait, ce matin-là, humide, ravivée, un peu haletante, comme après une volupté hâtive.

Puis il relégua sa jalousie au plan lointain de ses soucis sentimentaux et questionna Chéri sur un ton de condescendance lassée:

"Peut-on savoir si tu sors à cette heure, ou si tu rentres?

— Je sors, dit Chéri. Ne t'occupe pas de moi. Je vais faire des courses. Je vais chez la fleuriste. Chez le bijoutier, chez ma mère, chez ma femme, chez. . . .

— N'oublie pas le nonce, dit Desmond.

— Je sais vivre, répliqua Chéri. Je lui porterai des boutons de chemise en titre-fixe et une gerbe d'orchidées."

Chéri répondait rarement à une plaisanterie et l'accueillait toujours froidement. L'importance de cette terne riposte éclaira Desmond sur l'état insolite de son ami. Il considéra l'image de Chéri dans la glace,

all that he had never experienced during his wretched life, that of a wealthy but heartless young man. Then he stopped thinking, for a minute or for an hour. After that, it seemed to him that he had no desire remaining in the world, not even to go to Léa's.

When he shivered with cold and heard the blackbirds heralding dawn, he got up, stumbling but feeling light, and made his way back to the Hotel Morris, not going by way of the Avenue Bugeaud. He was stretching, expanding his lungs, and overflowing with universal gentleness.

"Now," he sighed, as if exorcised, "now . . . Oh, now I'll be so nice to the girl . . ."

Chéri got up at eight, shaved, put his shoes on, then feverishly shook Desmond, who was sleeping, livid, a fright to see, bloated in his sleep like a drowned man:

"Desmond! Hup! Desmond! . . . Enough! You're too ugly when you're asleep!"

The sleeper sat up and looked at his friend with his eyes that were the color of muddied water. He pretended to be still half-asleep so that he could examine Chéri carefully. Chéri, dressed in blue, was pathetic and superb, pale beneath a velvety layer of skillfully applied powder . . . There were still times when Desmond, in his stiff ugliness, suffered from Chéri's good looks. He intentionally gave a long yawn. "What is it this time?" he wondered as he yawned. "This fool is handsomer than he was yesterday. Those lashes, especially, those lashes of his . . ." He was looking at Chéri's shiny, vigorous eyelashes and the shadow they cast on his dark pupils and on the bluish whites of his eyes. Desmond also noticed that the scornful bow of his mouth was opening that morning, moist, refreshed, panting slightly, as if in the aftermath of a hasty sex act.

Then he relegated his envy to the far-off region of his concerns about love life, and he questioned Chéri in a tone of condescending weariness:

"May I ask whether you're going out or coming in at this time of day?"

"Going out," said Chéri. "Don't worry about me. I've got some errands to run. I'm going to the florist's. To the jeweler's, to my mother's, home to my wife, to . . ."

"Don't forget the papal nuncio," said Desmond.

"I possess all the social graces," Chéri retorted. "I'll bring him some gold-alloy shirt studs and a bouquet of orchids."

Chéri seldom returned a joke, and always received one coldly. The significance of that dull repartee enlightened Desmond as to his friend's unusual state of mind. He observed Chéri's reflection in the

nota la blancheur des narines dilatées, la mobilité errante du regard, et risqua la plus discrète des questions:

"Tu rentres déjeuner? . . . Hep, Chéri, je te cause. Nous déjeunons ensemble?"

Chéri fit: "Non" de la tête. Il sifflotait en carrant son reflet dans le miroir oblong, juste à sa taille comme celui de la chambre de Léa, entre les deux fenêtres. Tout à l'heure, dans l'autre miroir, un cadre d'or lourd sertirait, sur un fond rose ensoleillé, son image nue ou drapée d'une soierie lâche, sa fastueuse image de beau jeune homme aimé, heureux, choyé, qui joue avec les colliers et les bagues de sa maîtresse. . . . "Elle y est peut-être déjà, dans le miroir de Léa, l'image du jeune homme? . . ." Cette pensée traversa son exaltation avec une telle virulence qu'il crut, hébété, l'avoir entendue.

"Tu dis? demanda-t-il à Desmond.

— Je ne dis rien, répondit le docile ami gourmé. C'est dans la cour qu'on parle."

Chéri quitta la chambre de Desmond, claqua la porte et retourna dans son appartement. La rue de Rivoli, éveillée, l'emplissait d'un tumulte doux, continu, et Chéri pouvait apercevoir, par la fenêtre ouverte, les feuilles printanières, raides et transparentes comme des lames de jade sous le soleil. Il ferma la fenêtre et s'assit sur un petit siège inutile qui occupait un coin triste contre le mur, entre le lit et la porte de la salle de bains.

"Comment cela se fait-il? . . ." commença-t-il à voix basse. Puis il se tut. Il ne comprenait pas pourquoi, en l'espace de six mois et demi, il n'avait presque jamais pensé à l'amant de Léa.

Je ne suis qu'une grande folle", disait la lettre de Léa pieusement conservée par Charlotte Peloux.

"Une grande folle?" Chéri secoua la tête. "C'est drôle, je ne la vois pas comme ça. Qu'est-ce qu'elle peut aimer, comme homme? Un genre Patron? Plutôt qu'un genre Desmond, naturellement. . . . Un petit argentin bien ciré? encore. . . . Mais tout de même. . . ."

Il sourit avec naïveté: "En dehors de moi, qu'est-ce qui peut bien lui plaire?"

Un nuage passa sur le soleil de mars et la chambre fut noire. Chéri appuya sa tête contre le mur. "Ma Nounoune. . . . Ma Nounoune . . . tu m'as trompé? Tu m'as salement trompé? . . . Tu m'as fait ça?"

Il fouettait son mal avec des mots et avec des images qu'il construisait péniblement, étonné et sans fureur. Il tâchait d'évoquer les jeux du matin, chez Léa, certains après-midi de plaisir long et parfaitement

mirror, noting the paleness of his flaring nostrils and the wandering restlessness of his gaze, and he risked the discreetest of questions:

"Will you be back here for lunch? . . . Say, Chéri, I'm talking to you. Are we having lunch together?"

Chéri said no with his head. He was whistling as he squared his shoulders, looking at himself in the tall mirror, which was just his height, like the one between the two windows in Léa's bedroom. In a little while, in that other mirror, the heavy gold frame would set off against a sunny pink background his reflection, naked or draped in loosely fitting silk, his splendid image of a handsome young man who was loved, happy, pampered, and who played with his mistress's necklaces and rings . . . "Is the image of that young man already there, in Léa's mirror? . . ." That thought cut through his excitement so violently that, dazed as he was, he imagined he had heard it spoken aloud.

"What did you say?" he asked Desmond.

"I didn't say anything," replied his docile, stuck-up friend. "People are talking down in the courtyard."

Chéri left Desmond's bedroom, slammed the door, and returned to his own rooms. The Rue de Rivoli, awakened, was filling them with a gentle, sustained hum, and through the open window Chéri could observe the spring foliage, as stiff and translucent as blades of jade in the sunlight. He shut the window and sat down on a little useless chair that occupied a dismal corner against the wall, between the bed and the bathroom door.

"How does a thing like this happen? . . . ," he began in a low voice. Then he was silent. He couldn't understand why, for six and a half months now, he had almost never thought about Léa's new lover.

"I'm just a big fool," said Léa's letter, which Charlotte Peloux had piously preserved.

"A big fool?" Chéri shook his head. "It's funny, I don't see her that way. What sort of man can she like? Someone like Patron? Him rather than a type like Desmond, of course . . . A little Argentine with a waxed mustache? Maybe . . . But, all the same . . ."

He smiled naïvely: "Besides me, what can she really like?"

A cloud passed over the March sun, and the room was plunged into darkness. Chéri leaned his head against the wall. "My Nursie . . . My Nursie . . . have you cheated on me? Have you been a low-down cheat? . . . Have you done that to me?"

He was exasperating his unhappiness with words and images that he put together painfully; he was surprised but not angry. He tried to recall the morning frolics at Léa's, certain afternoons of prolonged and

silencieux, chez Léa, — le sommeil délicieux de l'hiver dans le lit chaud et la chambre fraîche, chez Léa. . . . Mais il ne voyait toujours aux bras de Léa, dans le jour couleur de cerise qui flambait derrière les rideaux de Léa, l'après-midi, qu'un seul amant: Chéri. Il se leva comme ressuscité dans un mouvement de foi spontanée:

"C'est bien simple! Si je n'arrive pas à en voir un autre que moi auprès d'elle, c'est qu'il n'y en a pas d'autre!"

Il saisit le téléphone, faillit appeler, puis raccrocha le récepteur doucement.

"Pas de blagues. . . ."

Il sortit, très droit, effaçant les épaules. Sa voiture découverte l'emmena chez le joaillier où il s'attendrit sur un petit bandeau fin, des saphirs d'un bleu brûlant dans une monture d'acier bleu invisible, "tout à fait une coiffure pour Edmée", qu'il emporta. Il acheta des fleurs un peu bêtes et cérémonieuses. Comme onze heures sonnaient à peine, il usa encore une demi-heure çà et là, dans une Société de crédit où il prit de l'argent, près d'un kiosque où il feuilleta des illustrés anglais, dans un dépôt de tabacs orientaux, chez son parfumeur. Enfin, il remonta en voiture, s'assit entre sa gerbe et ses paquets noués de rubans.

"A la maison."

Le chauffeur se retourna dans son baquet:

"Monsieur? . . . Monsieur m'a dit? . . .

— J'ai dit: à la maison, boulevard d'Inkermann. Il vous faut un plan de Paris?"

La voiture s'élança vers les Champs-Elysées. Le chauffeur faisait du zèle et son dos plein de pensées semblait se pencher, inquiet, sur l'abîme qui séparait le jeune homme veule du mois passé, le jeune homme aux "si vous voulez" et aux "un glass, Antonin?" de monsieur Peloux le fils, exigeant avec le personnel et attentif à l'essence.

"Monsieur Peloux le fils", adossé au maroquin et le chapeau sur les genoux, buvait le vent et tendait toute sa volonté à ne pas penser. Il ferma lâchement les yeux, entre l'avenue Malakoff et la porte Dauphine, pour ne pas voir passer l'avenue Bugeaud, et se félicita: "J'en ai du courage!"

Le chauffeur corna, boulevard d'Inkermann, pour demander la porte qui chanta sur ses gonds avec une longue note grave et harmonieuse. Le concierge en casquette s'empressait, la voix des chiens de garde saluait l'odeur reconnue de celui qui arrivait. Très à l'aise, respirant le vert arôme des gazons tondus, Chéri entra dans la maison

completely silent pleasure at Léa's, a delectable winter sleep in the warm bed and fresh-smelling bedroom at Léa's . . . But, in all this, he could see in Léa's arms, in the cherry-colored daylight blazing behind Léa's curtains in the afternoon, only a single lover: Chéri. He stood up, as if recalled to life, in a spurt of spontaneous faith:

"It's so simple! If I can't manage to see anyone else but me with her, it's because there isn't anyone else!"

He grabbed the phone, almost put through the call, then hung up the receiver gently.

"Don't do anything foolish . . ."

He walked out, very erect, throwing back his shoulders. His open car took him to the jeweler's, where he gushed over an elegant little bandeau, sapphires of a burning blue set in a mount of "invisible" blue steel, "exactly right for Edmée's hair." He bought it. He then purchased flowers that were somewhat silly and formal. Since it was still barely eleven, he killed another half-hour here and there, withdrawing money from a bank, leafing through English picture magazines at a newsstand, visiting a store that sold Near Eastern tobacco, and stopping in at his perfume dealer's. Finally he got back in the car and sat down between the bunch of flowers and the packages tied with ribbons.

"To the house."

The chauffeur turned around in his bucket seat:

"Sir? . . . What did you say, sir? . . ."

"I said 'to the house,' Boulevard d'Inkermann. Do you need a map of Paris?"

The car sped off toward the Champs-Elysées. The chauffeur was making a show of zeal, and his thoughtful back seemed to be reflecting nervously on the gulf that separated the indolent young man of the past month, that young man who'd say "if you feel like it" and "a drink, Antonin?," from young Monsieur Peloux, strict with his employees and keeping tabs on the gasoline consumption.

"Young Monsieur Peloux," leaning back on the morocco leather, his hat on his knees, was inhaling the breeze and making every effort of his will to keep from thinking. He closed his eyes like a coward between the Avenue Malakoff and the Porte Dauphine, so he wouldn't see the Avenue Bugeaud going by, and he congratulated himself: "What courage I have!"

The chauffeur honked on the Boulevard d'Inkermann to have the gate opened. It sang on its hinges with a prolonged, deep, harmonious note. The concierge, in his peaked cap, hurried over, and the barking of the watchdogs greeted the familiar scent of the homecomer. Very much at his ease, inhaling the green smell of the mown lawns, Chéri entered the

et monta d'un pas de maître vers la jeune femme qu'il avait quittée, trois mois auparavant, comme un marin d'Europe délaisse, de l'autre côté du monde, une petite épouse sauvage.

LÉA rejeta loin d'elle, sur le bureau ouvert, les photographies qu'elle avait tirées de la dernière malle: "Que les gens sont vilains, mon Dieu! Et elles ont osé me donner ça. Et elles pensent que je vais les mettre en effigie sur ma cheminée, dans un cadre nickelé, peut-être, ou dans un petit portefeuille-paravent? Dans la corbeille aux papiers, oui, et en quatre morceaux! . . ."

Elle alla reprendre les photographies, et avant de les déchirer elle y jeta le plus dur regard dont fussent capables ses yeux bleus. Sur un fond noir de carte postale, une forte dame à corset droit voilait ses cheveux, et le bas de ses joues, d'un tulle soulevé par la brise. "*A ma chère Léa, en souvenir des heures exquises de Guéthary: Anita.*" Au centre d'un carton rugueux comme du torchis, une autre photographie groupait une famille, nombreuse et morne, une sorte de colonie pénitentiaire gouvernée par une aïeule basse sur pattes, fardée, qui élevait en l'air un tambourin de cotillon et posait un pied sur le genou tendu d'une sorte de jeune boucher robuste et sournois.

"Ça ne mérite pas de vivre", décida Léa en cassant le carton-torchis.

Une épreuve non collée qu'elle déroula remit devant elle ce couple âgé de demoiselles provinciales, excentriques, criardes, batailleuses, assises tous les matins sur un banc de promenade méridional, tous les soirs entre un verre de cassis et le carré de soie où elles brodaient un chat noir, un crapaud, une araignée: "*A notre jolie fée! ses petites camarades du Trayas, Miquette et Riquette.*"

Léa détruisit ces souvenirs de voyage et passa la main sur son front:

"C'est horrible. Et après celles-là, comme avant celles-là, d'autres, — d'autres qui ressembleront à celles-là. Il n'y a rien à y faire. C'est comme ça. Peut-être que, partout où il y a une Léa, sortent de terre des espèces de Charlotte Peloux, de La Berche,

house and, with a proprietary tread, went up the stairs to the young woman he had abandoned there three months earlier the way that a European sailor deserts a little savage bride at the other end of the world.

LÉA tossed onto the open desk, far from her, the photos she had taken out of the last trunk: "God, how ugly people are! And they had the nerve to give me this! And they think I'm going to set them up as effigies on my mantelpiece, maybe in a nickel-plated frame, or in a little folding cardboard frame. Yes, into the wastebasket, and in pieces! . . ."

She made a move to pick up the photos, but before tearing them she cast on them the most severe gaze that her blue eyes could muster up. Against a black postcard background a heavy woman in a straight corset was covering her hair and the lower part of her cheeks with a tulle veil that was being raised by the breeze. "To my dear Léa, in remembrance of the delightful times at Guéthary:[8] Anita." In the center of a sheet of cardboard rough as a mud wall, another photo showed a group shot of a family, numerous and dreary, a sort of penal colony directed by a short-legged, made-up grandma who was raising in the air a paper Provençal drum, a party favor, and resting one foot on the knee of a sort of young butcher, robust and shifty-eyed.

"It doesn't deserve to live," Léa decided, crushing the mud wall-like cardboard.

She unrolled a print that wasn't pasted down, and found before her once again the elderly pair of spinsters from the provinces, eccentric, noisy, and quarrelsome, who used to sit every morning on a bench on that southern promenade, and every evening between a glass of cassis and the square of silk on which they'd embroider a black cat, a toad, or a spider: "To our lovely fairy princess, from her little comrades at Trayas,[9] Miquette and Riquette."

Léa destroyed those travel souvenirs and wiped her forehead with her hand:

"How awful! And after those two, just as before those two, there will be others—others just like them. Nothing can be done about it. That's how it is. It may well be that, wherever there's a Léa, some kind of Charlotte Peloux, La Berche, or Aldonza comes crawling out of the

---

8. Seaside resort near Biarritz.   9. Another resort in the south of France.

d'Aldonzas, des vieux affreux qui ont été des jeunes beaux, des gens, enfin, des gens impossibles, impossibles, impossibles. . . ."

Elle entendit, dans son souvenir récent, des voix qui l'avaient hélée sur des perrons d'hôtel, qui avaient crié vers elle, de loin: "hou-hou!" sur des plages blondes, et elle baissa le front, d'un mouvement taurin et hostile.

Elle revenait, après six mois, un peu maigrie et amollie, moins sereine. Un tic bougon abaissait parfois son menton sur son col, et des teintures de rencontre avaient allumé dans ses cheveux une flamme trop rouge. Mais son teint, ambré, fouetté par le soleil et la mer, fleurissait comme celui d'une belle fermière et eût pu se passer de fard. Encore fallait-il draper prudemment, sinon cacher tout à fait le cou flétri, circlé de grands plis où le hâle n'avait pu pénétrer.

Assise, elle s'attardait à des rangements menus et cherchait autour d'elle, comme elle eût cherché un meuble disparu, son ancienne activité, sa promptitude à parcourir son douillet domaine.

"Ah! ce voyage, soupira-t-elle. Comment ai-je pu? . . . Que c'est fatigant!"

Elle fronça les sourcils et fit sa nouvelle moue bougonne, en constatant qu'on avait brisé la vitre d'un petit tableau de Chaplin, une tête de jeune fille, rose et argentée, que Léa trouvait ravissante.

"Et un accroc large comme les deux mains dans le rideau d'application. . . . Et je n'ai encore vu que ça . . . Où avais-je la tête de m'en aller si longtemps? Et en l'honneur de qui? . . . Comme si je n'aurais pas pu passer mon chagrin ici, bien tranquillement."

Elle se leva pour aller sonner, rassembla les mousselines de son peignoir en s'apostrophant crûment:

"Vieux trottin, va. . . ."

La femme de chambre entra, chargée de lingeries et de bas de soie:

"Onze heures, Rose. Et ma figure qui n'est pas faite! Je suis en retard. . . .

— Madame n'a rien qui la presse. Madame n'a plus ces demoiselles Mégret pour traîner madame en excursion et venir dès le matin pour cueillir toutes les roses de la maison. Ce n'est plus monsieur Roland qui fera endêver madame en lui jetant des petits graviers dans sa chambre. . . .

— Rose, il y a de quoi nous occuper dans la maison. Je ne sais

ground, hideous old people who were once good-looking young people: in short, impossible people, impossible, impossible . . ."

Among her recent memories she heard voices that had hailed her on hotel steps, that had called "yoo-hoo" to her from the distance on yellow beaches; and she lowered her forehead, in a hostile movement like a bull's.

After six months she was back home, a little thinner and more flaccid, less serene. At times a grumpy tic would bring her chin down onto her neck, and makeshift dye jobs had kindled a flame in her hair that was too red. But her skin, tanned, whipped by sun and sea, was as fresh-looking as that of a pretty farmer's wife, and could have done without make-up. But she had to arrange her clothing carefully around her withered neck, or else conceal it altogether, because it was ringed by deep creases inaccessible to suntan.

Sitting there, she lingered over her little bits of tidying up, and was looking all around her—as she might have looked for a missing piece of furniture—searching for her former activeness, for her readiness to walk all around her comfortable domain.

"Oh, this trip!" she sighed. "Why did I ever do it? . . . How exhausting it is!"

She knitted her brows and pouted in her new grumpy way, as she observed that the glass had been broken on a little painting by Chaplin,[10] a head of a girl, pink and silvery, which Léa found charming.

"And there's a rip as big as my two hands in the full-length curtains . . . And I haven't looked at everything yet . . . What was I thinking of to go away for so long? And in whose honor? . . . As if I couldn't have gotten over my hurt feelings here, in peace and quiet."

She stood up to ring the bell, gathering the muslin of her wrap around her and addressing herself bluntly:

"Old errand girl that you are! . . ."

The chambermaid came in, laden with lingerie and silk stockings:

"Eleven o'clock, Rose. And my face isn't done yet! I'm running late . . ."

"You have no need to hurry, madam. You no longer have those Mégret sisters to drag you on an excursion or come first thing in the morning to pick all the roses in your garden. You no longer have Monsieur Roland to drive you crazy by throwing pebbles into your bedroom . . ."

"Rose, there's plenty in the house for us to look after. I don't know

---

10. Charles Josuah Chaplin (1825–1891), who specialized in portraits of elegant Parisiennes and in decorative female nudes.

pas si trois déménagements valent un incendie, mais je suis sûre que six mois d'absence valent une inondation. Tu as vu le rideau de dentelle?

— C'est rien. . . . Madame n'a pas vu la lingerie: des crottes de souris partout et le parquet mangé. Et c'est tout de même bien curieux que je laisse à Émérancie vingt-huit essuie-verres et que j'en retrouve vingt-deux.

— Non?

— C'est comme je dis à madame."

Elles se regardèrent avec une indignation égale, attachées toutes deux à cette maison confortable, assourdie de tapis et de soieries, à ses armoires pleines et à ses sous-sols ripolinés. Léa se claqua le genou de sa forte main:

"Ça va changer, mon petit! Si Ernest et Émérancie ne veulent pas leurs huit jours, ils retrouveront les six essuie-verres. Et ce grand idiot de Marcel, tu lui avais bien écrit de revenir?

— Il est là, madame."

Prompte à se vêtir, Léa ouvrit les fenêtres et s'accouda pour contempler complaisamment son avenue aux arbres renaissants. Plus de vieilles filles flatteuses et plus de monsieur Roland, ce lourd et athlétique jeune homme de Cambo. . . .

"Ah! l'imbécile! . . ." soupira-t-elle.

Mais elle pardonnait à ce passant sa niaiserie, et ne lui faisait grief que d'avoir déplu. Dans sa mémoire de femme saine au corps oublieux, monsieur Roland n'était plus qu'une forte bête un peu ridicule, et qui s'était montrée si maladroite. . . . Léa eût nié, à présent, qu'un flot aveuglant de larmes, — certain soir de pluie où l'averse roulait parfumée sur des géraniums-rosats, — lui avait caché monsieur Roland, un instant, derrière l'image de Chéri. . . .

La brève recontre ne laissait à Léa ni regrets, ni gêne. L'"imbécile" et sa vieille follette de mère auraient trouvé chez elle, après comme avant, dans la villa louée à Cambo, les goûters bien servis, les rockings sur le balcon de bois, le confort aimable que savait dispenser Léa et dont elle tirait fierté. Mais l'imbécile, blessé, s'en était allé, laissant Léa aux soins d'un raide et bel officier grisonnant qui prétendait épouser "Mme de Lonval".

"Nos âges, nos fortunes, nos goûts d'indépendance et de mondanité, tout ne nous destine-t-il pas l'un à l'autre?" disait à Léa le colonel resté mince.

whether moving three times is as bad as a fire, but I'm sure that being away six months is as bad as a flood. Have you seen the lace curtain?"

"That's nothing . . . You haven't seen the linen closet yet, madame: mouse droppings everywhere and the parquet nibbled up. And I find it really curious that I left Emérancie with twenty-eight glass cloths and I find only twenty-two."

"Really?"

"It's as I say, madame."

They looked at each other with the same indignation, attached as they both were to that comfortable house, with its noise-absorbing carpets and silk hangings, its filled armoires, and its enamel-painted basement spaces. Léa slapped her knee with her strong hand.

"Things are going to change, my dear! If Ernest and Emérancie don't want their week's notice, they'll find those six glass cloths. And that big ninny Marcel, did you write him telling him to be back?"

"He's here, madame."

Dressing quickly, Léa opened the windows and rested her elbows on the sill, so she could cozily observe her avenue, with the new foliage on its trees. No more flattering old maids, and no more Monsieur Roland, that heavy-set, athletic young man at Cambo[11] . . .

"Oh, that fool! . . ." she sighed.

But she forgave that transitory lover for his stupidity; all that she held against him was that he hadn't satisfied her. In her memory, that of a healthy woman with a body that quickly forgets, Monsieur Roland was by this time merely a strong, somewhat ridiculous animal who had proved to be so clumsy . . . At present, Léa would have denied the fact that, one rainy evening when a scent-laden shower was soaking the rose geraniums, a blinding flow of tears had for a moment replaced Monsieur Roland with the image of Chéri . . .

The brief encounter had left Léa with neither regrets nor embarrassment. The "fool" and his giddy old mother would still have found, if they visited her in the rented villa at Cambo, those well-served meals, the rocking-chairs on the wooden balcony, the loving comfort that Léa was so good at dispensing and that she was so proud of. But the fool's feelings had been hurt, and he had gone away, leaving Léa in the care of a handsome, starched, gray-haired officer who wanted to marry "Madame de Lonval."

"Do not our ages, our fortunes, our tastes for independence and worldliness, do not all things destine us for each other?" the colonel, who had remained thin, would say to Léa.

---

11. Cambo-les-Bains, a spa in the Pyrenees near Bayonne.

Elle riait, elle prenait du plaisir à la compagnie de cet homme assez sec qui mangeait bien et buvait sans se griser. Il s'y trompa, lut dans les beaux yeux bleus, dans le sourire confiant et prolongé de son hôtesse, le consentement qu'elle tardait à donner.... Un geste précis marqua la fin de leur amitié commençante, que Léa regretta en s'accusant honnêtement dans son for intérieur.

"C'est ma faute! On ne traite pas un colonel Ypoustègue, d'une vieille famille basque, comme un monsieur Roland. Pour l'avoir remisé, je l'ai ce qui s'appelle remisé.... Il aurait agi en homme chic et en homme d'esprit s'il était revenu le lendemain, dans son break, fumer un cigare chez moi et lutiner mes vieilles filles...."

Elle ne s'avisait pas qu'un homme mûr accepte un congé, mais non pas certains coups d'œil qui le jaugent physiquement, qui le comparent clairement à un autre, à l'inconnu, à l'invisible....

Léa, embrassée à l'improviste, n'avait pas retenu ce terrible et long regard de la femme qui sait à quelles places l'âge impose à l'homme sa flétrissure: des mains sèches et soignées, sillonnées de tendons et de veines, ses yeux remontèrent au menton détendu, au front barré de rides, revinrent cruellement à la bouche prise entre des guillemets de rides.... Et toute la distinction de la "baronne de Lonval" creva dans un: "Ah! là! là!..." si outrageant, si explicite et populacier, que le beau colonel Ypoustègue passa le seuil pour la dernière fois.

"Mes dernières idylles", songeait Léa accoudée à la fenêtre. Mais le beau temps parisien, l'aspect de la cour propre et sonore et des lauriers en boules rondes dans leurs caisses vertes, la bouffée tiède et odorante qui s'évadait de la chambre en caressant sa nuque, la remplissaient peu à peu de malice et de bonne humeur. Des silhouettes de femmes passaient, descendant vers le Bois. "Voilà encore les jupes qui changent", constata Léa, "et les chapeaux qui montent". Elle projeta des visites chez le couturier, chez Lewis, une brusque envie d'être belle la redressa.

"Belle? Pour qui? Tiens, pour moi. Et puis, pour vexer la mère Peloux."

Léa n'ignorait pas la fuite de Chéri, mais elle ne savait que sa fuite. Tout en blâmant les procédés de police de Mme Peloux, elle tolérait qu'une jeune vendeuse de modes, qu'elle gâtait, épanchât sa gratitude adroite en potins versés dans l'oreille de Léa pendant l'essayage, ou consignés avec "mille mercis pour les exquis chocolats" en travers d'une grande feuille à en-tête commercial. Une carte postale de la

She'd laugh and find pleasure in the company of that quite slender man who ate heartily and drank without becoming tipsy. He interpreted this the wrong way, reading in his hostess's beautiful blue eyes and prolonged, confiding smile the consent which she was slow to give . . . A specific incident spelled finis to their budding friendship, an incident that Léa regretted, blaming herself for it in her mind.

"It was my fault. A woman doesn't treat a Colonel Ypoustègue, of an old Basque family, the way she treats a Monsieur Roland. I sure enough gave him the gate . . . He would have behaved like a clever man and a man of the world if he had come back the next day in his break to smoke a cigar at my place and tease my old maids . . ."

She didn't realize that a middle-aged man might accept a refusal, but not certain glances that size him up physically, clearly comparing him with another man, unknown, unseen . . .

When she was unexpectedly kissed, Léa hadn't held back that terrible long look which a woman gives when she knows in what places age withers up a man: from the dry, carefully tended hands, furrowed with tendons and veins, her eyes had climbed to the slack chin, the forehead lined with wrinkles, then had returned cruelly to the mouth enclosed by wrinkles as if by quotation marks . . . And all the distinguished bearing of the "Baroness de Lonval" had exploded in a cry of "No way!" that was so insulting, so explicit and plebeian, that the handsome Colonel Ypoustègue had crossed her threshold for the last time.

"My final romances," Léa thought as she leaned on the window sill. But the fine weather in Paris; the sight of her clean, resonant courtyard and the laurels trimmed into spheres in their green planters; the warm, fragrant gust that issued from her bedroom and caressed the back of her neck: all this gradually filled her with mischievousness and good humor. Women's silhouettes were passing by on their way down to the Bois. "Skirts are changing again," Léa noted, "and hats are getting taller." She planned visits to the dressmaker and to Lewis's; a sudden wish to be beautiful lifted her spirits.

"Beautiful? For whose sake? Why, for mine! And then, to irritate old lady Peloux."

Léa was not unaware of Chéri's escapade, but all she knew was that he had run away. Though she criticized Madame Peloux's detective tactics, she would permit a young milliner, whom she spoiled, to display her skillful gratitude in the form of gossip, either poured into Léa's ears during fittings or sent, along with "a thousand thanks for the delicious chocolates," scrawled across a large sheet of business letterhead paper. A postcard from

vieille Lili avait rejoint Léa à Cambo, carte postale où la folle aïeule, sans points ni virgules et d'une écriture tremblée, contait une incompréhensible histoire d'amour, d'évasion, de jeune épouse séquestrée à Neuilly. . . .

"Il faisait un temps pareil, se rappela Léa, le matin où je lisais la carte postale de la vieille Lili, dans mon bain, à Cambo. . . ."

Elle revoyait la salle de bains jaune, le soleil dansant sur l'eau et au plafond. Elle entendait les échos de la villa mince et sonore rejeter un grand éclat de rire assez féroce et pas très spontané, le sien, puis les appels qui l'avaient suivi: "Rose! . . . Rose! . . ."

Les épaules et les seins hors de l'eau, ressemblant plus que jamais — ruisselante et robuste et son bras magnifique étendu, — à une figure de fontaine, elle agitait au bout de ses doigts le carton humide:

"Rose, Rose! Chéri. . . . Monsieur Peloux a fichu le camp! Il a laissé sa femme!

— Madame ne m'en voit pas surprise, disait Rose; le divorce sera plus gai que le mariage, où ils portaient tous le diable en terre. . . ."

Cette journée-là, une hilarité incommode accompagna Léa:

"Ah! mon poison d'enfant! Ah! le mauvais gosse! Voyez-vous! . . ."

Et elle secouait la tête en riant tout bas, comme fait une mère dont le fils a découché pour la première fois. . . .

Un phaéton verni fila devant la grille, étincela et disparut, presque silencieux sur ses roues caoutchoutées et les pieds fins de ses trotteurs.

"Tiens, Spéleïeff, constata Léa. Brave type. Et voilà Merguilier sur son cheval pie: onze heures. Berthellemy-le-Desséché va suivre et aller dégeler ses os au Sentier de la vertu. . . . C'est curieux ce que les gens peuvent faire la même chose toute la vie. On croirait que je n'ai pas quitté Paris si Chéri était là. Mon pauvre Chéri, c'est fini de lui, à présent. La noce, les femmes, manger à n'importe quelle heure, boire trop. . . . C'est dommage. Qui sait s'il n'aurait pas fait un brave homme, s'il avait seulement eu une bonne petite gueule rose de charcutier et les pieds plats? . . ."

Elle quitta la fenêtre en frottant ses coudes engourdis, haussa les épaules: "On sauve Chéri une fois, mais pas deux". Elle polit ses ongles, souffla: "ha" sur une bague ternie, mira de près le rouge mal réussi de ses cheveux et leurs racines blanchissantes, nota quelques lignes sur un carnet. Elle agissait très vite et moins posément que

old Lili had reached Léa in Cambo, a postcard in which the eccentric old girl, in a shaky hand and using no periods or commas, narrated an incomprehensible story of love, of escape, of a young wife interned at Neuilly . . .

"The weather was like this," Léa recalled, "the morning I read that postcard from old Lili, in my bathtub at Cambo . . ."

She saw once again the yellow bathroom, the sunlight dancing on the bath water and on the ceiling. She heard the echoes in the thin-walled, resonant villa reverberating a loud burst of laughter, quite ferocious and not too spontaneous, her own laughter, then the calls that had followed it: "Rose! . . . Rose! . . ."

Her shoulders and breasts out of the water, dripping, robust, her magnificent arm outstretched, looking more than ever like a fountain sculpture, she was waving the damp card with her fingertips:

"Rose, Rose! Chéri . . . Monsieur Peloux has taken a powder! He's left his wife!"

"I can't say it surprises me, madame," Rose said. "His divorce will be more cheerful than his wedding, where everyone seemed as sad as at a funeral . . ."

That day, a troubling hilarity had never deserted Léa:

"Oh, that devil of a boy! Oh, that naughty kid! Just look! . . ."

And she'd shake her head while laughing very quietly, just as a mother does when her son spends the night away from home with a woman for the first time . . .

A polished phaeton pulled up in front of the gate, gleamed, and then vanished almost noiselessly on its rubber-tired wheels, to the soft pacing of its trotting horses.

"What do you know! Speleyev," Léa noted. "A swell guy. And there's Merguilier on his piebald horse: eleven o'clock. Dried-up Berthellemy will come next, on his way to thaw out his bones on the Path of Virtue . . . Strange how people can keep doing the same thing all of their life. You'd think I'd never left Paris, except that Chéri's not here. Poor Chéri, it's all up with him at the moment. Carousing, women, eating at all hours, drinking too much . . . It's a shame. He might have become a solid citizen if he'd only had a nice little red face like a butcher and flat feet . . ."

She left the window, rubbing her elbows, which had grown numb, and she shrugged her shoulders. "Chéri can be rescued once, but not twice." She polished her nails, blew "ha!" on a tarnished ring, studied up close the unsuccessful red dye on her hair with its gray roots, and wrote a few lines in a notebook. She was moving very quickly and less calmly than

d'habitude, pour lutter contre une atteinte sournoise d'anxiété qu'elle connaissait bien et qu'elle nommait — niant jusqu'au souvenir de son chagrin — son mal de cœur moral. Elle eut envie, en peu d'instants et par saccades, d'une victoria bien suspendue, attelée d'un cheval de douairière, puis d'une automobile extrêmement rapide, puis d'un mobilier de salon directoire. Elle songea même à modifier sa coiffure qu'elle portait haute depuis vingt ans et dégageant la nuque. "Un petit rouleau bas, comme Lavallière? . . . Ça me permettrait d'aborder les robes à ceinture lâche de cette année. En somme, avec un régime et mon henné bien refait, je peux prétendre encore à dix, — non, mettons cinq ans, de. . . ."

Un effort la remit en plein bon sens, en plein orgueil lucide.

"Une femme comme moi n'aurait pas le courage de finir? Allons, allons, nous en avons eu, ma belle, pour notre grade." Elle toisait la grande Léa debout, les mains aux hanches et qui lui souriait.

"Une femme comme ça ne fait pas une fin dans les bras d'un vieux. Une femme comme ça, qui a eu la chance de ne jamais salir ses mains ni sa bouche sur une créature flétrie! . . . Oui, la voilà, la "goule" qui ne veut que de la chair fraîche. . . ."

Elle appela dans son souvenir les passants et les amants de sa jeunesse préservée des vieillards, et se trouva pure, fière, dévouée depuis trente années à des jouvenceaux rayonnants ou à des adolescents fragiles.

"Et c'est à moi qu'elle doit beaucoup, cette chair fraîche! Combien sont-ils à me devoir leur santé, leur beauté, des chagrins bien sains et des laits de poule pour leurs rhumes, et l'habitude de faire l'amour sans négligence et sans monotonie? . . . Et j'irais maintenant me pourvoir, pour ne manquer de rien dans mon lit, d'un vieux monsieur de . . . de. . . ."

Elle chercha et décida avec une inconscience majestueuse:

"Un vieux monsieur de quarante ans?"

Elle essuya l'une contre l'autre ses longues mains bien faites et se détourna dans une volte dégoûtée:

"Pouah! Adieu tout, c'est plus propre. Allons acheter des cartes à jouer, du bon vin, des marques de bridge, des aiguilles à tricoter, tous les bibelots qu'il faut pour boucher un grand trou, tout ce qu'il faut pour déguiser le monstre — la vieille femme. . . ."

En fait d'aiguilles à tricoter, elle eut maintes robes, et des saut-de-

usual, fighting against an underhanded anxiety attack that she knew all too well, and that she called her mental heartburn, denying even the recollection of her disappointment in love. Within a few moments, by fits and starts, she wished for a victoria with good springs and with a dowager's placid horse harnessed to it, then for an extremely fast car, then for a Directoire drawing-room ensemble. She even thought about changing the style of her hair, which she had been wearing upswept for twenty years, leaving the back of her neck free. "A little roll of hair down low, like Lavallière?[12] That would allow me to try this year's dresses with their loose belts. All in all, if I go on a diet and dye my hair properly, I can still look forward to ten—no, let's say, five years of . . ."

Just one effort restored all of her good sense and clear-sighted pride.

"Shouldn't a woman like me have the courage to call it quits? Come now, admit it, dear, we've had all that we could ask." She ran her eyes over that tall Léa, standing with hands on hips and smiling back at her.

"A woman like this doesn't finish her career in the arms of an old man. A woman like this who's had the luck never to dirty her hands or lips on a soiled creature! . . . Yes, here she is, the 'ghoul' who insists on young flesh . . ."

She recalled to mind the transitory and the more permanent lovers of her younger days, which had been kept safe from old men, and she found herself pure, proud, a woman who had devoted herself for thirty years to glorious young men or vulnerable adolescents.

"And that young flesh owes a lot to *me*! How many men owe me their good health and good looks, their healthy heartaches and egg nogs for their colds, and their training in making love skillfully and avoiding monotony? . . . And am I now, just to keep from having an empty bed, to saddle myself with some old gent who's . . . who's . . ."

She thought for a moment, then declared with a majestic lack of self-recognition:

"Some old gent who's forty years old?"

She rubbed her long hands together and turned around sharply in disgust:

"Bah! Good-bye to everything, it's cleaner that way. Let's buy playing cards, good wine, scoring cards for bridge, knitting needles, all the trinkets that are needed to plug up a big gap, all that it takes to disguise that monster—an old woman . . ."

As far as knitting needles go: what she bought was a lot of dresses,

---

12. Probably refers to the noted actress Eve Lavallière (1866–1929).

lit comme des nuées à l'aurore. Le pédicure chinois vint une fois la semaine; la manucure deux fois et la masseuse tous les jours. On vit Léa au théâtre, et avant le théâtre dans des restaurants qu'elle ne fréquentait pas du temps de Chéri.

Elle accepta que des jeunes femmes et leurs amis, que Kühn, son ancien tailleur retiré des affaires, l'invitassent dans leur loge ou à leur table. Mais les jeunes femmes lui témoignèrent une déférence qu'elle ne requérait pas et Kühn l'appela "ma chère amie", à quoi elle lui répondit dès la première agape:

"Kühn, décidément, ça ne vous va pas d'être client."

Elle rejoignit, comme on se réfugie, Patron, arbitre et directeur d'une entreprise de boxe. Mais Patron était marié à une jeune tenancière de bar, petite, terrible et jalouse autant qu'un ratier. Jusqu'à la place d'Italie Léa risqua, pour retrouver le sensible athlète, sa robe couleur de saphir sombre alourdie d'or, ses paradis, ses bijoux imposants, ses cheveux d'acajou neuf. Elle respira l'odeur de sueur, de vinaigre et de térébenthine qu'exhalaient les "espoirs" entraînés par Patron et s'en alla, sûre de ne jamais revoir la salle vaste et basse où sifflait le gaz vert.

Ces essais qu'elle fit pour rentrer dans la vie remuante des désœuvrés lui coûtèrent une fatigue qu'elle ne comprenait pas.

"Qu'est-ce que j'ai donc?"

Elle tâtait ses chevilles un peu gonflées le soir, mirait ses fortes dents à peine menacées de déchaussement, tâtait du poing, comme on percute un tonneau, ses poumons logés au large, son estomac joyeux. Quelque chose d'indicible, en elle, penchait, privé d'un étai absent, et l'entraînait tout entière. La baronne de la Berche, rencontrée dans un "zinc" où elle arrosait, d'un vin blanc de cochers, deux douzaines d'escargots, apprit enfin à Léa le retour de l'enfant prodigue au bercail, et l'aube d'un nouvel astre de miel sur le boulevard d'Inkermann. Léa écouta cette histoire morale avec indifférence. Mais elle pâlit d'une émotion pénible, le jour d'après, en reconnaissant une limousine bleue devant sa grille et Charlotte Peloux qui traversait la cour.

"Enfin! Enfin! Je te retrouve! Ma Léa! ma grande! Plus belle que jamais! Plus mince que l'an dernier! Attention, ma Léa, pas trop maigrir à nos âges! Comme ça, mais pas plus! Et même. . . . Mais quel plaisir de te revoir!"

Jamais la voix blessante n'avait paru si douce à Léa. Elle laissait parler Madame Peloux, rendait grâce à ce flot acide qui lui donnait du temps. Elle avait assis Charlotte Peloux dans un fauteuil bas sur

and boudoir wraps that were like dawn mists. Her male Chinese pedi-
curist came once a week, her female manicurist twice a week, and her
masseuse every day. Léa was seen at the theater and, before the theater, at restaurants she hadn't gone to in Chéri's day.

She permitted young women and their escorts, and Kühn, her former
tailor, now retired, to invite her to their box or to their table. But the young
women showed her a deference that she didn't ask for, and Kühn called
her "my dear friend," to which she replied at their very first get-together:

"I assure you, Kühn, you don't make a very good customer."

As if taking refuge, she looked up Patron again. He was now a ref-
eree and had his own "stable" of boxers. But Patron was married to a
young bar owner, a small, frightening woman who was as jealous as a
rat-catching dog. To meet the sensitive athlete, Léa risked going all
the way to the Place d'Italie, in her dark-sapphire-colored dress with
heavy gold trim, her birds of paradise, her showy jewelry, and her hair
that resembled brand-new mahogany. She inhaled the smell of sweat,
vinegar, and turpentine that issued from the "hopefuls" whom Patron
was training, then left in the certainty that she'd never return to that
huge, low-ceilinged room in which the green gas was hissing.

These attempts she made to get back to the bustling existence of
the idle rich fatigued her in a way that she didn't understand.

"What's wrong with me, anyhow?"

She would feel her ankles, which were a little swollen in the evening;
she'd look in the mirror at her strong teeth, which were hardly likely to
become loose; she'd thump her lungs, which had plenty of breathing
space, and her happy stomach, like someone striking a cask to hear
how full it was. Something unnamable inside her had lost one of its
props, was leaning at a slant, and was dragging her down with it. The
Baroness de la Berche, whom she ran across in a bar washing down two
dozen snails with a white wine only fit for coachmen, finally informed
Léa of the prodigal son's return to the fold, and the dawn of a new honeymoon on the Boulevard d'Inkermann. Léa listened to that edifying
story with indifference. But she turned pale with a painful emotion the
following day, when she recognized the blue limousine outside her
gate and saw Charlotte Peloux crossing her courtyard.

"Finally! Finally! Here you are again! My Léa! My old friend! More
beautiful than ever! Thinner than last year! Watch out, Léa, we
mustn't get too thin at our age! Stay just like that, but don't lose more!
In fact . . . But what a joy it is to see you again!"

That jarring voice had never seemed so sweet to Léa. She let
Madame Peloux go on talking, grateful for the flow of acid comments

pattes, sous la douce lumière du petit salon aux murs de soieries peintes, comme autrefois. Elle-même venait de reprendre machinalement la chaise à dossier raide qui l'obligeait à effacer les épaules et à relever le menton, comme autrefois. Entre elles, la table nappée d'une rugueuse broderie ancienne portait, comme autrefois, la grosse carafe taillée à demi pleine de vieille eau-de-vie, les verres en calices vibrants, minces comme une feuille de mica, l'eau glacée et les biscuits sablés. . . .

"Ma grande! On va pouvoir se revoir tranquillement, tranquillement, pleurait Charlotte. Tu connais ma devise: fichez la paix à vos amis quand vous êtes dans les ennuis, ne leur faites part que de votre bonheur. Tout le temps que Chéri a fait l'école buissonnière, c'est exprès que je ne t'ai pas donné signe de vie, tu m'entends! A présent que tout va bien, que mes enfants sont heureux, je te le crie, je me jette dans tes bras, et nous recommençons notre bonne vie. . . ."

Elle s'interrompit, alluma une cigarette, habile à ce genre de suspension autant qu'une actrice:

". . . sans Chéri, naturellement.

— Naturellement", acquiesça Léa en souriant.

Elle contemplait, écoutait sa vieille ennemie avec une satisfaction ébahie. Ces grands yeux inhumains, cette bouche bavarde, ce bref corps replet et remuant, tout cela, en face d'elle, n'était venu que pour mettre sa fermeté à l'épreuve, l'humilier comme autrefois, toujours comme autrefois. Mais comme autrefois Léa saurait répondre, mépriser, sourire, se redresser. Déjà ce poids triste qui la chargeait hier et les jours d'avant semblait fondre. Une lumière normale, connue, baignait le salon et jouait dans les rideaux.

"Voilà, songea Léa allégrement. Deux femmes un peu plus vieilles que l'an passé, la méchanceté habituelle et les propos routiniers, la méfiance bonasse, les repas en commun; des journaux financiers le matin, des potins scandaleux l'après-midi, — il faut bien recommencer tout ça puisque c'est la vie, puisque c'est ma vie. Des Aldonzas et des La Berche, et des Lili et quelques vieux Messieurs sans foyer, tout le lot serré autour d'une table à jeu, où le verre de fine et le jeu de cartes vont voisiner, peut-être, avec une paire de petits chaussons, commencés pour un enfant qui vivra bientôt . . . Recommençons, puisque c'est dans l'ombre. Allons-y gaiement, puisque j'y retombe à l'aise comme dans l'empreinte d'une chute ancienne. . . ."

that gave her time to collect herself. She had seated Charlotte Peloux in an armchair with short legs, in the mild light of the small parlor hung with painted silk, as in the past. She herself had just automatically sat down on the stiff-backed chair that forced her to square her shoulders and lift her chin, as in the past. Between them, the table, covered with an old piece of heavy embroidery, bore, as in the past, the big cut-glass carafe half-filled with old brandy; the vibrant chalice-shaped glasses, thin as a sheet of mica; the ice water and the shortbread biscuits . . .

"My old friend! We'll be able to visit each other again in peace and quiet, peace and quiet," Charlotte was saying weepily. "You know my motto: leave your friends alone when you've got troubles, and share only your happiness with them. The whole time that Chéri was playing hookey, I intentionally gave you no sign of life, you understand! Now that everything's all right and my children are happy, I shout it to you, I throw myself into your arms, and we can take up our comfortable life again . . ."

She cut her speech short and lit a cigarette (she was as skillful as an actress at that kind of pregnant pause):

"Without Chéri, of course."

"Of course," Léa smilingly agreed.

She was observing and listening to her old enemy with a stunned satisfaction. Those large, merciless eyes, that chattering mouth, that short body, stout but restless, all of that, now sitting opposite her, had come for no other purpose than to test her firmness, to humiliate her as in the past, exactly as in the past. But, as in the past, Léa would be able to reply, to feel contempt, to smile, to bounce back. That heavy burden which had weighed her down the day before, and the days before that, seemed to be melting away already. A normal, familiar light bathed the parlor and played on the curtains.

"Here we are," Léa thought cheerfully. "Two women a little older than they were last year, the same habitual malice and the routine conversation, easy-going mistrust, meals taken together; financial newspapers in the morning, gossip about scandals in the afternoon— I've got to get back to all that, because that's life, because that's my life. Women like Aldonza, La Berche, and Lili, and a few old gents without a real home, the whole bunch crowded around a card table on which the glass of brandy and the deck of cards will perhaps be standing next to a pair of booties being knitted for a soon-to-be-born baby . . . Let's get back to it, because it's in the comfortable shade. Let's go back merrily, because I can fall back into it as easily as into the rut of an old wagon track . . ."

Et elle s'installa, les yeux clairs et la bouche détendue, pour écouter Charlotte Peloux qui parlait avidement de sa belle-fille.

"Tu le sais, toi, ma Léa, si l'ambition de toute ma vie a été la paix et la tranquillité? Eh bien, je les ai maintenant. La fugue de Chéri, en somme, c'est une gourme qu'il a jetée. Loin de moi l'idée de te le reprocher, ma Léa, mais reconnais que de dix-neuf à vingt-cinq ans, il n'a guère eu le temps de mener la vie de garçon? Eh bien, il l'a menée trois mois, quoi, la vie de garçon! La belle affaire!

— Ça vaut même mieux, dit Léa sans perdre son sérieux. C'est une assurance qu'il donne à sa jeune femme.

— Juste, juste le mot que je cherchais! glapit Mme Peloux, radieuse. Une assurance! Depuis ce jour-là, le rêve! Et tu sais, quand un Peloux rentre dans sa maison après avoir fait la bombe, il n'en ressort plus!

— C'est une tradition de famille?" demanda Léa.

Mais Charlotte ne voulut rien entendre.

"D'ailleurs, il y a été bien reçu, dans sa maison. Sa petite femme, ah! en voilà une, Léa. . . . Tu sais si j'en ai vu, des petites femmes, eh bien, je n'en ai pas vu une qui dame le pion à Edmée.

— Sa mère est si remarquable, dit Léa.

— Songe, songe, ma grande, que Chéri venait de me la laisser sur les bras pendant près de trois mois, — entre parenthèses, elle a eu de la chance que je sois là!

— C'est précisément ce que je pensais, dit Léa.

— Eh bien, ma chère, pas une plainte, pas une scène, pas une démarche maladroite, rien, rien! La patience même, la douceur, un visage de sainte, de sainte!

— C'est effrayant, dit Léa.

— Et tu crois que quand notre brigand d'enfant s'est amené un matin, tout souriant, comme s'il venait de faire un tour au Bois, tu crois qu'elle se serait permis une remarque? Rien! Pas ça! Aussi lui qui, au fond, devait se sentir un peu gêné. . . .

— Oh! pourquoi? dit Léa.

— Tout de même, voyons. . . . Il a trouvé l'accueil charmant, et l'accord s'est fait dans leur chambre à coucher, pan, comme ça et sans attendre. Ah! je t'assure, il n'y a pas eu dans le monde, pendant cette heure-là, une femme plus heureuse que moi!

— Sauf Edmée, peut-être", suggéra Léa.

Mais Mme Peloux était toute âme et eut un superbe mouvement d'ailerons:

"A quoi vas-tu penser? Moi, je ne pensais qu'au foyer reconstruit."

And, with bright eyes and lips no longer tense, she sat back, listening to Charlotte Peloux talk eagerly about her daughter-in-law.

"You're well aware, Léa dear, that all my life my ambition has been to have peace and quiet. Well, I have it now. In short, Chéri's escapade was like sowing wild oats. It's far from me to blame you for it, Léa dear, but you must admit that from the age of nineteen to twenty-five, he barely had the time to lead a bachelor's life. Well, he led it for three months, that bachelor's life! A nice thing!"

"It's all for the good," Léa said, keeping serious. "It's a sort of pledge of fidelity that he brings to his young wife."

"Exactly, exactly the phrase I was looking for!" Madame Peloux yelped radiantly. "A pledge of fidelity! Ever since that day, it's been a dream! And you know, when a Peloux comes back home after painting the town red, he never leaves again!"

"It's a family tradition?" Léa asked.

But Charlotte pretended she hadn't heard that.

"Besides, he was well received at home. That little wife of his, oh, there's one for you, Léa . . . God knows how many young wives I've seen—well, I've never seen one to top Edmée."

"Her mother is so remarkable," Léa said.

"Just think, just think, my friend, that Chéri had just left her on my hands for nearly three months—by the way, she was lucky I was there!"

"Precisely what I was thinking," Léa said.

"Well, dear, not one complaint, not one scene, not one false step, none, none! Patience itself, sweetness, a face like a saint, a saint!"

"It's scary," Léa said.

"And do you think that when our bad boy came in one morning, all smiles, as if he had just taken a drive around the Bois, do you think she even made a remark? Nothing! Nothing in the slightest! And he, who deep down must have felt a little embarrassed . . ."

"Oh, why?" Léa said.

"Come now—after all! . . . . He was greeted charmingly, and they made up in their bedroom, bang, like that, without wasting a minute. Oh, I assure you, in that hour there wasn't a happier woman in the world than me!"

"Except Edmée, maybe," Léa suggested.

But Madame Peloux was all soul, and replied with a superb fluttering of her wing stumps:

"What are you thinking of? As for me, I was only thinking about their home that was coming together again."

Elle changea de ton, plissa l'œil et la lèvre:

"D'ailleurs, je ne la vois pas bien, cette petite, dans le grand délire, et poussant le cri de l'extase. Vingt ans et des salières, peuh . . . à cet âge-là on bégaie. Et puis, entre nous, je crois sa mère froide.

— Ta religion de la famille t'égare", dit Léa.

Charlotte Peloux montra candidement le fond de ses grands yeux où on ne lisait rien.

"Non pas, non pas! l'hérédité, l'hérédité! J'y crois. Ainsi mon fils qui est la fantaisie même. . . . Comment, tu ne sais pas qu'il est la fantaisie même?

— J'aurai oublié, s'excusa Léa.

— Eh bien, je crois en l'avenir de mon fils. Il aimera son intérieur comme je l'aime, il gérera sa fortune, il aimera ses enfants comme je l'ai aimé. . . .

— Ne prévois donc pas tant de choses tristes! pria Léa. Comment est-il, leur intérieur, à ces jeunes gens?

— Sinistre, piaula Mme Peloux. Sinistre! Des tapis violets! Violets! Une salle de bains noire et or. Un salon sans meubles, plein de vases chinois gros comme moi! Aussi, qu'est-ce qui arrive: ils ne quittent plus Neuilly. D'ailleurs, sans fatuité, la petite m'adore.

— Elle n'a pas eu de troubles nerveux?" demanda Léa avec sollicitude.

L'œil de Charlotte Peloux étincela:

"Elle? pas de danger, nous avons affaire à forte partie.

— Qui ça, nous?

— Pardon, ma grande, l'habitude. . . . Nous sommes en présence de ce que j'appellerai un cerveau, un véritable cerveau. Elle a une manière de donner des ordres sans élever la voix, d'accepter les boutades de Chéri, d'avaler les couleuvres comme si c'était du lait sucré. . . . Je me demande vraiment, je me demande s'il n'y a pas là, dans l'avenir, un danger pour mon fils. Je crains, ma Léa, je crains qu'elle n'arrive à éteindre trop cette nature si originale, si. . . .

— Quoi? il file doux? interrompit Léa. Reprends de ma fine, Charlotte, c'est de celle de Spéleïeff, elle a soixante-quatorze ans, on la donnerait à des bébés. . . .

— Filer doux n'est pas le mot, mais il est . . . inter . . . impertur. . . .

— Imperturbable?

— Tu l'as dit. Ainsi, quand il a su que je venais te voir. . . .

— Comment, il le sait?"

Un sang impétueux bondit aux joues de Léa, et elle maudit son

She changed her tone, screwing up her eyes and pursing her lips:

"Anyway, I can't picture that girl in the throes of delirium or uttering cries of ecstasy. Twenty years old, with collarbones that stick out, bah . . . At that age, girls stammer. Besides, between you and me, I think her mother is frigid."

"Your devotion to family is making you talk wildly," Léa said.

Charlotte Peloux candidly displayed the depths of her big eyes, in which nothing was to be read.

"No, no! Heredity, heredity! I believe in it. Take my son, who's the soul of imagination . . . What, don't you know he's the soul of imagination?"

"I must have forgotten," Léa apologized.

"Well, I believe in my son's future. He'll love his home as much as I love mine, he'll manage his money, he'll love his children the way I loved him . . ."

"Don't make so many sad predictions!" Léa urged her. "What does that young couple's home look like?"

"Hideous," Madame Peloux whimpered. "Hideous! Violet rugs! Violet! A black and gold bathroom. A parlor without furniture, filled with Chinese vases as big as I am! And so, what's the result? They never leave Neuilly anymore. Besides, and I say this without conceit, the girl adores me."

"She didn't have any nervous problems?" Léa asked solicitously.

Charlotte Peloux's eyes sparkled:

"Her? No danger, we're dealing with a tough customer."

"Who do you mean by 'we'?"

"Excuse me, dear, it's force of habit . . . We're faced here with what I'd call a brain, a real brain. She has a way of giving orders without raising her voice, accepting Chéri's smart remarks calmly, and laughing off insults as if they were sugar water . . . I really wonder, I wonder whether there's some danger in it for my son in the future. Léa dear, I'm afraid she might end up by stifling his character, which is so original, so . . ."

"What? He's toeing the line?" Léa interrupted. "Take some more of my brandy, Charlotte. It's the one Speleyev gave me. It's seventy-four years old, you could give it to a baby . . ."

"Toeing the line isn't the right expression, but he's . . . inter- . . . impertur- . . ."

"Imperturbable?"

"That's it. And so, when he heard I was coming to see you . . ."

"What? He knows?"

Léa's cheeks were suddenly flushed, and she cursed both the

émotion fougueuse et le jour clair du petit salon. Mme Peloux, l'œil suave, se repaissait du trouble de Léa.

"Mais bien sûr, il le sait. Faut pas rougir pour ça, ma grande! Es-tu enfant!

— D'abord, comment as-tu su que j'étais revenue?

— Oh, voyons, Léa, ne pose pas des questions pareilles. On t'a vue partout. . . .

— Oui, mais Chéri, tu le lui as dit, alors, que j'étais revenue?

— Non, ma grande, c'est lui qui me l'a appris.

— Ah, c'est lui qui. . . . C'est drôle."

Elle entendait son cœur battre dans sa voix et ne risquait pas de phrases longues.

"Il a même ajouté: "Madame Peloux, vous me ferez plaisir en allant prendre des nouvelles de Nounoune." Il t'a gardé une telle affection, cet enfant!

— C'est gentil!"

Mme Peloux, vermeille, semblait s'abandonner aux suggestions de la vieille eau-de-vie et parlait comme en songe, en balançant la tête. Mais son œil mordoré demeurait ferme, acéré, et guettait Léa qui, droite, cuirassée contre elle-même, attendait, elle ne savait quel coup. . . .

"C'est gentil, mais c'est bien naturel. Un homme n'oublie pas une femme comme toi, ma Léa. Et . . . veux-tu tout mon sentiment? tu n'aurais qu'un signe à faire pour que. . . ."

Léa posa une main sur le bras de Charlotte Peloux:

"Je ne veux pas tout ton sentiment", dit-elle avec douceur.

Mme Peloux laissa tomber les coins de sa bouche:

"Oh! je te comprends, je t'approuve, soupira-t-elle d'une voix morne. Quand on a arrangé comme toi sa vie autrement. . . . Je ne t'ai même pas parlé de' toi!

— Mais il m'a bien semblé que si. . . .

— Heureuse?

— Heureuse.

— Grand amour? Beau voyage? . . . *Il* est gentil? Où est sa photo? . . .

Léa, rassurée, aiguisait son sourire et hochait la tête:

"Non, non, tu ne sauras rien! Cherche! . . . Tu n'as donc plus de police, Charlotte?

— Je ne me fie à aucune police, répliqua Charlotte. Ce n'est pas parce que celui-ci et celle-là m'auront raconté . . . que tu as éprouvé

violence of her emotions and the strong light in the small parlor. Madame Peloux, her eyes bland, was battening on Léa's agitation.

"But of course he knows. That's no reason to blush, dear! How childish you are!"

"First of all, how did you find out I was back?"

"Oh, come now, Léa, don't ask such questions. You've been seen all over . . ."

"Yes, but Chéri, you told him, then, that I was back?"

"No, dear, *he* told *me*."

"Oh, it was he that . . . It's funny."

She could hear her heartbeat in her voice, and didn't venture to speak in long sentences.

"He even added: 'Madame Peloux, I'd appreciate it if you went and found out how Nursie is doing.' He still has such an affection for you, that boy!"

"How nice!"

Madame Peloux's face was flushed, and she seemed to be yielding to the promptings of the old brandy. She was speaking as if in a dream, her head nodding. But her tawny eyes remained firm and steely, watching Léa, who, erect in her chair and on her guard against her own emotions, didn't know what blow to expect next . . .

"It's nice, but it's quite natural. A man doesn't forget a woman like you, Léa. And . . . do you want to know exactly what I feel? You'd only have to lift a finger to . . ."

Léa placed a hand on Charlotte Peloux's arm:

"I don't want to know exactly what you feel," she said gently.

Madame Peloux let the corners of her mouth sag:

"Oh! I understand you, and I approve," she sighed in a dreary tone. "When a woman has made different arrangements in her life, the way you have . . . I haven't even asked you about yourself!"

"Oh, I had the strong feeling that you did . . ."

"Happy?"

"Happy."

"A real love affair? A nice trip? . . . Is *he* nice? Do you have a photo of him? . . ."

Léa, reassured, firmed up her smile and shook her head:

"No, no, I won't tell you a thing! Ferret it out . . . Don't you have any more detectives, Charlotte?"

"I don't rely on any detectives," Charlotte retorted. "It's not because this person or that has told me . . . that you've had another disap-

une nouvelle déception . . . que tu as eu de gros ennuis, même d'argent. . . . Non! non, moi, les ragots, tu sais ce que j'en fais!

— Personne ne le sait mieux que moi. Ma Lolotte, pars sans inquiétude. Dissipe celles de nos amis. Et souhaite-leur d'avoir réalisé la moitié du sac que j'ai fait sur les pétroles, de décembre à février."

Le nuage alcoolique qui adoucissait les traits de Mme Peloux s'envola; elle montra un visage net, sec, réveillé.

"Tu étais sur les pétroles! J'aurais dû m'en douter! Et tu ne me l'as pas dit!

— Tu ne me l'as pas demandé. . . . Tu ne pensais qu'à ta famille, c'est bien naturel. . . .

— Je pensais aussi aux Briquettes comprimées, heureusement, flûta la trompette étouffée.

— Ah! tu ne me l'as pas dit non plus.

— Troubler un rêve d'amour? jamais! Ma Léa, je m'en vais, mais je reviendrai.

— Tu reviendras le jeudi, parce qu'à présent, ma Lolotte, tes dimanches de Neuilly . . . finis pour moi. Veux-tu qu'on fasse des petits jeudis ici? Rien que des bonnes amies, la mère Aldonza, notre Révérend-Père-la-Baronne, — ton poker, enfin, et mon tricot. . . .

— Tu tricotes?

— Pas encore, mais ça va venir. Hein?

— J'en saute de joie! Regarde-moi si je saute! Et tu sais, je n'en ouvre la bouche à personne, à la maison: le petit serait capable de venir te demander un verre de porto, le jeudi! Une bise encore, ma grande. . . . Dieu, que tu sens bon! Tu as remarqué que lorsqu'on arrive à avoir la peau moins tendue, le parfum y pénètre mieux? C'est bien agréable."

"Va, va. . . ." Léa frémissante suivait du regard Mme Peloux qui traversait la cour. "Va vers tes méchants projets! Rien ne t'en empêchera. Tu te tords le pied? Oui, mais tu ne tomberas pas. Ton chauffeur qui est prudent ne dérapera pas, et ne jettera pas ta voiture contre un arbre. Tu arriveras à Neuilly, et tu choisiras ton moment, — aujourd'hui, demain, la semaine prochaine, — pour dire les paroles que tu ne devrais jamais prononcer. Tu essaieras de troubler ceux qui sont peut-être en repos. Le moins que tu puisses commettre, c'est de les faire un peu trembler, comme moi, passagèrement. . . ."

Elle tremblait des jambes comme un cheval après la côte, mais elle ne souffrait pas. Le soin qu'elle avait pris d'elle-même et de ses

pointment . . . that you've had serious troubles, including money troubles . . . No, you know how little stock I put in rumors!"

"No one knows that better than I do. My Lolotte, you can go home without worries. Tell our friends not to worry, either. And tell them I wish they had made only half the killing that I made in petroleum shares between December and February."

The alcoholic cloud that had been softening Madame Peloux's features vanished; her face was now clear, wiry, and alert.

"You were investing in petroleum! I should have known! And you never told me!"

"You never asked . . . All you were thinking about was your family, which is quite natural . . ."

"Fortunately I was also thinking about brick-fuel shares," said the muted trumpet in flute-like tones.

"Oh! Well, you didn't tell me about that, either."

"And disturb a dream of love? Never! Léa dear, I'm going now, but I'll be back."

"You'll be back on Thursday, because from now on, Lolotte dear, your Sundays in Neuilly . . . are over for me. Would you like us to have little Thursdays here? Only good friends: old lady Aldonza, our Reverend Father the Baroness—in short, your poker and my knitting . . ."

"You knit?"

"Not yet, but it'll come to that. Well?"

"It makes me jump for joy! Look and see if I'm not jumping! And, you know, I won't mention it to a soul at home: I wouldn't put it past the boy to come and ask you for a glass of port on Thursdays! One more kiss, dear . . . My, how good you smell! You must have noticed that when a woman's skin finally gets looser, her perfume works into it better? It's very pleasant."

"Go, go . . ." Léa was quivering as she watched Madame Peloux cross her courtyard. "Go carry out your malicious plans! Nothing will stand in your way. You've twisted your foot? Yes, but you won't fall. Your chauffeur is careful, and he won't skid or ram your car into a tree. You'll get back to Neuilly, and you'll choose your moment—today, tomorrow, next week—to speak the words you should never utter. You'll try to upset people whose life is perhaps calm. The least damage you can do is to make them tremble, like me, temporarily . . ."

Her legs were trembling like a horse's after going uphill, but she wasn't suffering. The care she had taken with herself and with her

répliques la réjouissait. Une vivacité agréable demeurait à son teint, à son regard, et elle pétrissait son mouchoir parce qu'il lui restait de la force à dépenser. Elle ne pouvait détacher sa pensée de Charlotte Peloux.

"Nous nous sommes retrouvées", se dit-elle, "comme deux chiens retrouvent la pantoufle qu'ils ont l'habitude de déchirer. Comme c'est bizarre! Cette femme est mon ennemie et c'est d'elle que me vient le réconfort. Comme nous sommes liées. . . ."

Elle rêva longtemps, craignant tour à tour et acceptant son sort. La détente de ses nerfs lui donna un sommeil bref. Assise et la joue appuyée, elle pénétra en songe dans sa vieillesse toute proche, imagina ses jours l'un à l'autre pareils, se vit en face de Charlotte Peloux et préservée longtemps, par une rivalité vivace qui raccourcissait les heures, de la nonchalance dégradante qui conduit les femmes mûres à négliger d'abord le corset, les teintures ensuite, enfin les lingeries fines. Elle goûta par avance les plaisirs scélérats du vieillard qui ne sont que lutte secrète, souhaits homicides, espoirs vifs et sans cesse reverdissants en des catastrophes qui n'épargneraient qu'un seul être, un seul point du monde, — et s'éveilla, étonnée, dans la lumière d'un crépuscule rose et pareil à l'aube.

"Ah! Chéri . . ." soupira-t-elle.

Mais ce n'était plus l'appel rauque et affamé de l'autre année, ni les larmes, ni cette révolte de tout le corps, qui souffre et se soulève quand un mal de l'esprit le veut détruire. . . . Léa se leva, frotta sa joue gaufrée par la broderie du coussin. . . .

"Mon pauvre Chéri. . . . Est-ce drôle de penser qu'en perdant, toi ta vieille maîtresse usée, moi mon scandaleux jeune amant, nous avons perdu ce que nous possédions de plus honorable sur la terre. . . ."

Deux jours passèrent après la visite de Charlotte Peloux. Deux jours gris qui furent longs à Léa et qu'elle supporta patiemment, avec une âme d'apprentie. "Puisqu'il faudra vivre ainsi", se disait-elle, "commençons". Mais elle y mettait de la maladresse et une sorte d'application superflue bien propre à décourager son noviciat. Le second jour elle avait voulu sortir, aller à pied jusqu'aux Lacs, vers onze heures du matin.

"J'achèterai un chien, projeta-t-elle. Il me tiendra compagnie et m'obligera à marcher." Et Rose avait dû chercher, au fond des placards d'été, une paire de bottines jaunes à semelles fortes, un costume un peu bourru qui sentait l'alpe et la forêt. Léa sortit, avec l'allure

replies made her feel good. There was still a pleasant liveliness in her complexion and in her eyes, and she was crumpling her handkerchief because she still had strength to spare. She couldn't get her mind off Charlotte Peloux.

"We got together again," she said to herself, "the way two dogs rediscover the slipper they're accustomed to chew up. How odd it is! That woman is my enemy, and it's from her that my solace comes. What a bond there is between us . . ."

She mused for some time, now fearing her destiny, now accepting it. Her nerves had relaxed and allowed her a brief slumber. Seated, with one hand to her cheek, in her reverie she entered into her imminent old age, she pictured the unchanging sameness of her life, she saw herself sitting opposite Charlotte Peloux; their active rivalry, which made the time go by more quickly, would save her from that degrading apathy which makes older women neglect themselves, giving up first their corset, then their hair dye, and finally their elegant lingerie. She had a foretaste of the wicked pleasures of the aged: a secret struggle, murderous wishes, keen and ever-renewed hopes for catastrophes that would spare only a single being, a single spot in the whole world—and she woke up, surprised, in the light of a pink twilight that was like a dawn.

"Oh, Chéri . . . ," she sighed.

But it was no longer the hoarse, hungry cry of the year before; it wasn't the weeping or that rebellion of the whole body, which suffers and revolts when mental suffering tries to destroy it . . . Léa stood up and rubbed her cheek, on which the embroidery of the cushion had left its imprint . . .

"Poor Chéri . . . How funny it is to reflect that when you lost your old, worn-out mistress and I lost my scandalous young lover, we both lost the most honorable thing we owned on earth . . ."

Two days passed after Charlotte Peloux's visit, two gray days that were long for Léa and that she endured patiently, in the spirit of an apprentice. "Since I'm going to have to live this way," she repeated to herself, "let's begin." But she did so with an awkwardness and a kind of excessive effort that tended to discourage her in her first steps. On the second day, she had decided to go out, to walk to the lakes in the Bois, around eleven in the morning.

"I'll buy a dog," was her plan. "He'll keep me company, and he'll force me to take walks." And Rose had had to search in the back of the summer closets for a pair of strong-soled yellow half-boots and for a somewhat countrified jacket-and-skirt outfit redolent of mountains

résolue qu'imposent, à ceux qui les portent, certaines chaussures et certains vêtements d'étoffe rude.

"Il y a dix ans, j'aurais risqué une canne", se dit-elle. Encore tout près de sa maison, elle entendit derrière elle un pas léger et rapide qu'elle crut reconnaître. Une crainte stupéfiante, qu'elle n'eut pas le temps de chasser, l'engourdit presque et ce fut malgré elle qu'elle se laissa rejoindre, puis distancer, par un inconnu jeune et pressé qui ne la regarda pas.

Elle respira, soulagée:

"Je suis trop bête!"

Elle acheta un œillet sombre pour sa jaquette et repartit. Mais devant elle, à trente pas, plantée droite dans la brume diaphane qui couvrait les gazons de l'avenue, une silhouette masculine attendait.

"Pour le coup, je connais cette coupe de veston et la façon de faire tournoyer la canne. . . . Ah! non merci, je ne veux pas qu'il me revoie chaussée comme un facteur et avec une jaquette qui me grossit. A tant faire que de le rencontrer, j'aime mieux qu'il me voie autrement, lui qui n'a jamais pu supporter le marron, d'abord. . . . Non, non, je rentre, je. . . ."

A ce moment l'homme qui attendait héla un taxi vide, y monta et passa devant Léa; c'était un jeune homme blond qui portait une petite moustache courte. Mais Léa ne sourit pas et n'eut plus de soupir d'aise, elle tourna les talons et rentra chez elle.

"Une de ces flemmes, Rose. . . . Donne-moi mon tea-gown fleur-de-pêcher, le nouveau, et la grande chape brodée sans manches. J'étouffe dans tous ces lainages."

"Ce n'est pas la peine d'insister, songeait Léa. Deux fois de suite, ce n'était pas Chéri; la troisième fois ç'aurait été lui. Je connais ces petites embûches-là. Il n'y a rien à faire contre, et aujourd'hui je ne me sens pas d'attaque, je suis molle."

Elle se remit, toute la journée, à ses patients essais de solitude. Cigarettes et journaux l'amusèrent, après le déjeuner, et elle accueillit avec une courte joie un coup de téléphone de la baronne de la Berche, puis un autre de Spéleïeff, son ancien amant, le beau maquignon, qui l'avait vue passer la veille et offrit de lui vendre une paire de chevaux.

Il y eut ensuite une longue heure de silence total à faire peur.

"Voyons, voyons. . . ."

Elle marchait, les mains aux hanches, suivie par la traîne magnifique d'une grande chape brodée d'or et de roses qui laissait ses bras nus.

and forests. Léa went out, with that resolute gait which some shoes and some clothes of a rugged material force upon those who wear them.

"Ten years ago, I would have risked a walking-stick," she said to herself. While not far from her house, she heard a light, swift step behind her that she thought she recognized. A numbing fear, which she hadn't enough time to dispel, nearly froze her to the spot. It was unwillingly that she allowed herself to be overtaken, then left behind, by a hurried young man whom she didn't know and who didn't even look at her.

She sighed with relief:

"I'm really dumb!"

She bought a dark carnation for her jacket and set out again. But thirty paces ahead of her, erect in the transparent mist that coated the lawns on the avenue, the silhouette of a man stood waiting for her.

"This time I recognize the cut of his jacket and the way he twirls his stick . . . Oh, no, thank you, I don't want him to see me again for the first time with a postman's shoes and in a jacket that makes me look heavier. If I've got to meet him, I prefer him to see me looking different; to begin with, he was never able to abide brown . . . No, no, I'm going back home, I'm . . ."

At that moment the man who had been waiting hailed an empty taxi, got in, and passed in front of Léa; he was a young blond man with a small, short mustache. But Léa didn't smile, and this time she didn't sigh with relief; she turned on her heels and walked back home.

"One of those fits of laziness, Rose . . . Give me my peach-blossom tea gown, the new one, and the big embroidered sleeveless cape. I'm smothering in all these woolens."

"It doesn't pay to dwell on it," Léa was thinking. "Twice in a row, it wasn't Chéri; the third time, it would have been. I know those little traps. There's no way of helping yourself, and I don't feel up to it today, I'm flabby."

She devoted the rest of the day to her patient lessons in solitude. After lunch her mind was diverted by cigarettes and papers, and brief periods of joy were provided by a phone call from the Baroness de la Berche and another from her former lover Speleyev, the handsome horse trader, who had seen her pass by the day before and now offered her a pair of horses for sale.

After that there was a long hour of silence so complete that it was frightening.

"Come on now, come on . . ."

She was walking, hands on hips, followed by the magnificent train of a large cape, embroidered with gold and roses, that left her arms bare.

"Voyons, voyons . . . tâchons de nous rendre compte. Ce n'est pas au moment où ce gosse ne me tient plus au cœur que je vais me laisser démoraliser. Il y a six mois que je vis seule. Dans le Midi, je m'en tirais très bien. D'abord, je changeais de place. Et ces relations de Riviera ou des Pyrénées avaient du bon, leur départ me laissait une telle impression de fraîcheur. . . . Des cataplasmes d'amidon sur une brûlure: ça ne guérit pas, mais ça soulage à condition de les renouveler tout le temps. Mes six mois de déplacements, c'est l'histoire de l'horrible Sarah Cohen, qui a épousé un monstre: "Chaque fois que je le regarde, dit-elle, je crois que je suis jolie.""

"Mais avant ces six mois-là, je savais ce que c'était que de vivre seule. Comment est-ce que j'ai vécu, après que j'ai quitté Spéleïeff, par exemple? Ah oui, on s'est baladés ferme dans des bars et des bistrots avec Patron, et tout de suite j'ai eu Chéri. Mais avant Spéleïeff, le petit Lequellec m'a été arraché par sa famille qui le mariait . . . pauvre petit, ses beaux yeux pleins de larmes. . . . Après lui, je suis restée seule quatre mois, je me rappelle. Le premier mois, j'ai bien pleuré! Ah! non, c'est pour Bacciocchi que j'ai tant pleuré. Mais quand j'ai eu fini de pleurer, on ne pouvait plus me tenir tant j'étais contente d'être seule. Oui! Mais à l'époque de Bacciocchi j'avais vingt-huit ans, et trente après Lequellec, et entre eux, j'ai connu . . . peu importe. Après Spéleïeff, j'étais dégoûtée de tant d'argent mal dépensé. Tandis qu'après Chéri, j'ai . . . j'ai cinquante ans, et j'ai commis l'imprudence de le garder six ans."

Elle fronça le front, s'enlaidit par une moue maussade.

"C'est bien fait pour moi, on ne garde pas un amant six ans à mon âge. Six ans! Il m'a gâché ce qui restait de moi. De ces six ans-là, je pouvais tirer deux ou trois petits bonheurs si commodes, au lieu d'un grand regret. . . . Une liaison de six ans, c'est comme de suivre un mari aux colonies: quand on en revient, personne ne vous reconnaît et on ne sait plus porter la toilette."

Pour ménager ses forces, elle sonna Rose et rangea avec elle la petite armoire aux dentelles. La nuit vint, qui fit éclore les lampes et rappela Rose aux soins de la maison.

"Demain, se dit Léa, je demande l'auto et je file visiter le haras normand de Spéleïeff. J'emmène la mère La Berche si elle veut, ça lui évoquera ses anciens équipages. Et, ma foi, si le cadet Spéleïeff me fait de l'œil, je ne dis pas que. . . ."

Elle se donna la peine de sourire d'un air mystérieux et tentateur, pour abuser les fantômes qui pouvaient errer autour de la coiffeuse et

"Come now, come now . . . let's try to take stock. It isn't now, when that boy doesn't mean anything to me anymore, that I'm going to let myself lose heart. I've been living alone for six months. In the South I got along quite well. For one thing, I kept moving around. And those acquaintances I made on the Riviera or in the Pyrenees were good for me; I had such a comfortable feeling whenever they left . . . Like starch poultices on a burn: they don't cure you, but they give you relief, provided that you keep changing them. My six months of moving from place to place remind me of the story of that homely Sarah Cohen who married a monster: 'Every time I look at him,' she said, 'I think that I'm pretty.'

"But even before those six months, I knew what it was like to live alone. For example, how did I live after I left Speleyev? Oh, yes, I kept going to bars and bistros with Patron, then Chéri came along right away. But even before Speleyev, young Lequellec was snatched away from me by his family, who married him off . . . poor boy, his pretty eyes full of tears . . . After him, I remained alone for four months, I remember. The first month, I cried, and how! Oh, no, it was over Bacciocchi that I cried so much. But when my crying was over, no one could hold me down, I was so happy to be alone. Yes! But at the time of Bacciocchi I was twenty-eight, and I was thirty after Lequellec, and in between the two of them, I was with . . . never mind. After Speleyev I became disgusted about squandering so much money. Whereas, after Chéri, I'm . . . I'm fifty, and I was imprudent enough to hold onto him for six years."

She wrinkled her brow, and her peevish pout made her look ugly.

"I deserve what I get, a woman my age doesn't hold onto a lover for six years. Six years! He ruined whatever I had left. In those six years I could have derived two or three smaller bits of happiness, so conveniently, instead of one big regret . . . A six-year relationship is like following your husband to the colonies: when you get back, no one knows you and you don't know how to dress anymore."

To conserve her strength she rang for Rose, and together they rearranged the little armoire where the lace was kept. Night came, lighting the lamps and recalling Rose to her household duties.

"Tomorrow," Léa said to herself, "I'll request the car and I'll make a flying visit to Speleyev's stud farm in Normandy. I'll take along old lady La Berche if she likes; it'll remind her of her old carriage teams. And, you know, if the younger Speleyev makes eyes at me, I may very well not . . ."

She took the trouble to smile in a mysterious, provocative way, in order to delude the ghosts that might be straying around the vanity

du lit formidable qui brillait dans l'ombre. Mais elle se sentait toute froide, et pleine de mépris pour la volupté d'autrui.

Son dîner de poisson fin et de pâtisseries fut une récréation. Elle remplaça le bordeaux par un champagne sec et fredonna en quittant la table. Onze heures la surprirent comme elle mesurait, avec une canne, la largeur des panneaux entre-fenêtres de sa chambre, où elle projetait de remplacer tous les grands miroirs par des toiles anciennes, peintes de fleurs et de balustres. Elle bâilla, se gratta la tête et sonna pour sa toilette de nuit. Pendant que Rose lui enlevait ses longs bas de soie, Léa considérait sa journée vaincue, effeuillée dans le passé, et qui lui plaisait comme un pensum achevé. Abritée, pour la nuit, du péril de l'oisiveté, elle escomptait les heures de sommeil et celles de l'insomnie, car l'inquiet recouvre, avec la nuit, le droit de bâiller haut, de soupirer, de maudire la voiture du laitier, les boueux et les passereaux.

Durant sa toilette de nuit, elle agita des projets inoffensifs qu'elle ne réaliserait pas.

"Aline Mesmacker a pris un bar-restaurant et elle y fait de l'or. . . . Évidemment, c'est une occupation, en même temps qu'un placement. . . . Mais je ne me vois pas à la caisse, et si on prend une gérante, ce n'est plus la peine. Dora et la grosse Fifi tiennent ensemble une boîte de nuit, m'a dit la mère La Berche. C'est tout à fait la mode. Et elles mettent des faux cols et des jaquettes-smoking pour attirer une clientèle spéciale. La grosse Fifi a trois enfants à élever, c'est une excuse. . . . Il y a aussi Kühn qui s'ennuie et qui prendrait bien mes capitaux pour fonder une nouvelle maison de couture. . . ."

Toute nue et teintée de rose brique par les reflets de sa salle de bains pompéienne, elle vaporisait sur elle son parfum de santal, et dépliait avec un plaisir inconscient une longue chemise de soie.

"Tout ça, c'est des phrases. Je sais parfaitement que je n'aime pas travailler. Au lit, Madame! Vous n'aurez jamais d'autre comptoir, et les clients sont partis."

Elle s'enveloppa dans une gandoura blanche que sa doublure colorée imprégnait d'une lumière rose insaisissable et retourna à sa coiffeuse. Ses deux bras levés peignèrent et soutinrent ses cheveux durcis par la teinture, et encadrèrent son visage fatigué. Ils demeuraient si beaux, ses bras, de l'aisselle pleine et musclée jusqu'au poignet rond, qu'elle les contempla un moment.

"Belles anses, pour un si vieux vase!"

Elle planta d'une main négligente un peigne blond sur sa nuque et

table and the enormous bed gleaming in the shadows. But she felt
aloof and full of scorn for other people's sensuality.

Her dinner of fine fish and pastries restored her spirits. Instead of
bordeaux, she had a dry champagne, and she was humming when she
left the table. The hour of eleven overtook her as she was using a walking-stick to measure the width of the panels between her bedroom
windows; she was planning to replace all the tall mirrors with antique
canvases painted with flowers and balusters. She yawned, scratched
her head, and rang for her night clothes. While Rose was taking off her
long silk stockings, Léa thought back on the day she had gotten
through successfully; moment after moment, it now lay in the past, and
this satisfied her like a chore she had accomplished. Sheltered for the
night from the perils of idleness, she was looking forward to the hours
of sleep and even to those of sleeplessness, because at night a restless
person regains the right to yawn out loud, to sigh, and to curse the
milkman's wagon, the street cleaners, and the awakening sparrows.

While dressing for the night she let her mind form a number of innocuous plans that she'd never carry out.

"Aline Mesmacker has taken over a restaurant and bar, where she's
coining money . . . Obviously, it gives you something to do, besides being
an investment . . . But I can't see myself as a cashier, and if I took on
some woman as a manager, it wouldn't be worth it anymore. Dora and
big Fifi are running a night spot together, old lady La Berche tells me.
That's all the rage right now. And they wear men's detachable collars and
dinner jackets to attract a special clientele. Big Fifi has three children to
bring up, that's an excuse . . . And then there's Kühn, who's getting bored,
and who'd gladly accept capital from me to start a new fashion house . . ."

Naked, and tinged brick-red by the reflections from her Pompeian
bathroom, she was spraying on her sandalwood perfume and unfold-
ing a long silk nightgown with unconscious pleasure.

"All that is just talk. I know perfectly well that I don't like working.
To bed, madame! You'll never have another sales counter, and your
customers have left."

She wrapped herself in a white North African tunic which was
bathed in a barely perceptible pink light by its colored lining, and she
went back to her vanity table. Her two raised arms combed and held
up her hair, which the dye made stiff; her arms framed her weary face.
Those arms were still so beautiful, from the full, muscular armpit
down to the round wrist, that she paused for a minute to study them.

"Lovely handles for such an old vase!"

She nonchalantly stuck a pale yellow comb in the hair on her nape,

choisit sans grand espoir un roman policier sur un rayon, dans un cabinet obscur. Elle n'avait pas le goût des reliures et ne s'était jamais déshabituée de reléguer ses livres au fond des placards, avec les cartons vides et les boîtes de pharmacie.

Comme elle lissait, penchée, la batiste fine et froide de son grand lit ouvert, le gros timbre de la cour retentit. Ce son grave, rond, insolite, offensa l'heure de minuit.

"Ça, par exemple . . ." dit-elle tout haut.

Elle l'écoutait, la bouche entrouverte, en retenant son souffle. Un second coup parut plus ample encore que le premier et Léa courut, dans un geste instinctif de préservation et de pudeur, se poudrer le visage. Elle allait sonner Rose quand elle entendit la porte du perron claquer, un bruit de pas dans le vestibule et dans l'escalier, deux voix mêlées, celle de la femme de chambre et une autre voix. Elle n'eut pas le temps de prendre une résolution, la porte s'ouvrit sous une main brutale: Chéri était devant elle, en pardessus ouvert sur son smoking, le chapeau sur la tête, pâle et l'air mauvais.

Il s'adossa à la porte refermée et ne bougea pas. Il ne regardait pas particulièrement Léa mais toute la chambre, d'une manière errante et comme un homme que l'on va attaquer.

Léa, qui avait pourtant tremblé le matin pour une silhouette devinée dans le brouillard, ne ressentait pas encore d'autre trouble que le déplaisir d'une femme surprise à sa toilette. Elle croisa son peignoir, assujettit son peigne, chercha du pied une pantoufle tombée. Elle rougit, mais quand le sang quitta ses joues, elle avait déjà repris l'apparence du calme. Elle releva la tête et parut plus grande que ce jeune homme accoté, tout noir, à la porte blanche.

"En voilà une manière d'entrer, dit-elle assez haut. Tu pourrais ôter ton chapeau, et dire bonjour.

— Bonjour", dit Chéri d'une voix rogue.

Le son de la voix sembla l'étonner, il regarda plus humainement autour de lui, une sorte de sourire descendit de ses yeux à sa bouche et il répéta avec douceur:

"Bonjour. . . ."

Il ôta son chapeau et fit deux ou trois pas.

"Je peux m'asseoir?

— Si tu veux", dit Léa.

Il s'assit sur un pouf et vit qu'elle restait debout.

"Tu t'habillais? Tu ne sors pas?"

Elle fit signe que non, s'assit loin de lui, prit un polissoir et ne parla

and, without expecting too much, she chose a detective story from a shelf in a dark closet. She wasn't a collector of fine bindings, and had never gotten out of the habit of consigning her books to the back of closets, along with empty cardboard boxes and medicine bottles.

While she was bent over, smoothing out the delicate, cool cambric of her large bed, turned down for the night, the loud outside bell rang. That deep, full, unusual sound was an affront to the midnight hour.

"Well, I'll be . . . ," she said aloud.

She listened to it, her mouth slightly open, holding her breath. A second ring seemed even louder than the first, and, with an instinctive urge for preservation of modesty, Léa ran over to powder her face. She was about to ring for Rose when she heard the slamming of the house door and the sound of steps in the vestibule and on the stairs; she heard two voices mingling, her maid's and someone else's. She didn't have the time to face the situation; her bedroom door was opened by a heavy hand: Chéri stood before her, his unbuttoned overcoat revealing his dinner jacket, his hat on his head. He was pale and looked mean.

Shutting the door, he leaned his back against it and remained motionless. He wasn't looking especially at Léa, but at the room in its entirety, with the roving gaze of a man about to be attacked.

Though Léa had trembled that morning because of a man's form in the fog that she had thought was his, now all that troubled her so far was the annoyance a woman feels when caught by surprise at her toilette. She closed her peignoir, adjusted her comb, and groped with one foot for a fallen slipper. She blushed, but by the time the blood had left her cheeks, she had already taken on a semblance of calm again. She raised her head and looked taller than that young man darkly silhouetted against the white door on which he was leaning.

"That's some way to make an entrance," she said, fairly loudly. "You might take off your hat and say hello."

"Hello," said Chéri in an arrogant tone.

The sound of his voice seemed to surprise him; he looked around in a more human way; a sort of smile descended from his eyes to his lips, and he repeated more gently:

"Hello . . ."

He took off his hat and walked two or three paces into the room.

"May I sit down?"

"If you like," Léa said.

He sat down on an ottoman and saw that she had remained standing.

"Were you dressing? Were you on your way out?"

She shook her head, sat down at a distance from him, picked up a

pas. Il alluma une cigarette et demanda la permission de fumer après qu'elle fut allumée.

"Si tu veux", répéta Léa indifférente.

Il se tut et baissa les yeux. La main qui tenait sa cigarette tremblait légèrement, il s'en aperçut et reposa cette main sur le bord d'une table. Léa soignait ses ongles avec des mouvements lents et jetait de temps en temps un bref regard sur le visage de Chéri, surtout sur les paupières abaissées et la frange sombre des cils.

"C'est toujours Ernest qui m'a ouvert la porte, dit enfin Chéri.

— Pourquoi ne serait-il pas Ernest? Est-ce qu'il fallait changer mon personnel parce que tu te mariais?

— Non. . . . N'est-ce pas, je disais ça. . . ."

Le silence retomba. Léa le rompit.

"Puis-je savoir si tu as l'intention de rester longtemps sur ce pouf? Je ne te demande même pas pourquoi tu te permets d'entrer chez moi à minuit. . . .

— Tu peux me le demander", dit-il vivement.

Elle secoua la tête:

"Ça ne m'intéresse pas."

Il se leva avec force, faisant rouler le pouf derrière lui et marcha sur Léa. Elle le sentit penché sur elle comme s'il allait la battre, mais elle ne recula pas. Elle pensait: "De quoi pourrais-je bien avoir peur, en ce monde?"

"Ah! tu ne sais pas ce que je viens faire ici? Tu ne veux pas savoir ce que je viens faire ici?"

Il arracha son manteau, le lança à la volée sur la chaise longue et se croisa les bras, en criant de tout près dans la figure de Léa, sur un ton étouffé et triomphant:

"Je rentre!"

Elle maniait une petite pince délicate qu'elle ferma posément avant de s'essuyer les doigts. Chéri retomba assis, comme s'il venait de dépenser toute sa force.

"Bon, dit Léa. Tu rentres. C'est très joli. Qui as-tu consulté pour ça?

— Moi", dit Chéri.

Elle se leva à son tour pour le dominer mieux. Les battements de son cœur calmé la laissaient respirer à l'aise et elle voulait jouer sans faute.

"Pourquoi ne m'as-tu pas demandé mon avis? Je suis une vieille camarade qui connaît tes façons de petit rustre. Comment n'as-tu pas pensé qu'en entrant ici tu pouvais gêner . . . quelqu'un?"

nail polisher, and said nothing. He lit a cigarette and asked permission to smoke after it was lit.

"If you like," Léa said again, with indifference.

He was quiet, his eyes lowered. The hand holding his cigarette was trembling slightly; he became aware of it and rested that hand on the edge of a table. Léa was doing her nails with slow movements, occasionally casting a brief glance at Chéri's face, especially his lowered eyelids and the dark fringe of his lashes.

"It was still Ernest who opened the door," Chéri finally said.

"Why shouldn't it be Ernest? Did I have to change my staff because you got married?"

"No . . . You know, I was saying that . . ."

Silence fell again. It was broken by Léa.

"May I know whether you intend sitting on that ottoman for very long? I'm not even asking you why you take the liberty of coming to see me at midnight . . ."

"You can ask me," he said eagerly.

She shook her head:

"I'm not interested."

He got up brusquely, making the ottoman roll away behind him, and he walked over to Léa. She felt him leaning over her as if he were going to hit her, but she didn't recoil. She was thinking: "What should I be afraid of in this world?"

"Oh, you don't know why I've come here? You refuse to hear why I've come here?"

He tore off his coat, flung it across the room onto the chaise longue, and crossed his arms, yelling right into Léa's face in a muffled but triumphant tone:

"I'm back to stay!"

She was handling small, delicate tweezers, which she closed calmly before wiping her fingers. Chéri dropped onto a seat again, as if he had just used up all his strength.

"Good," said Léa. "You're back. That's very nice. Whose advice did you ask on the subject?"

"My own," said Chéri.

It was she who got up this time, in order to dominate him more easily. The beating of her heart, now calm, allowed her to breathe easily, and she wanted to play her part faultlessly.

"Why didn't you ask *my* advice? I'm an old pal, and I know your bumpkin-like ways. Why didn't it enter your mind that, by barging in, you might embarrass . . . someone?"

La tête baissée, il inspecta horizontalement la chambre, ses portes closes, le lit cuirassé de métal et son talus d'oreillers luxueux. Il ne vit rien d'insolite, rien de nouveau et haussa les épaules. Léa attendait mieux et insista:

"Tu comprends ce que je veux dire?

— Très bien, répondit-il. "Monsieur" n'est pas rentré? "Monsieur" découche?

— Ce ne sont pas tes affaires, petit", dit-elle tranquillement.

Il mordit sa lèvre et secoua nerveusement la cendre de sa cigarette dans une coupe à bijoux.

"Pas là-dedans, je te le dis toujours! cria Léa. Combien de fois faudra-t-il que . . . ?"

Elle s'interrompit en se reprochant d'avoir repris malgré elle le ton des disputes familières. Mais il n'avait pas paru l'entendre et examinait une bague, une émeraude achetée par Léa pendant son voyage.

"Qu'est-ce . . . qu'est-ce que c'est que ça? bredouilla-t-il.

— Ça? c'est une émeraude.

— Je ne suis pas aveugle! Je veux dire: qui est-ce qui te l'a donnée?

— Tu ne connais pas.

— Charmant!" dit Chéri, amer.

L'accent rendit à Léa toute son autorité et elle se permit le plaisir d'égarer un peu plus celui qui lui laissait l'avantage.

"N'est-ce pas qu'elle est charmante? On m'en fait partout compliment. Et la monture, tu as vu, cette poussière de brillants qui. . . .

— Assez!" gueula Chéri avec fureur, en abattant son poing sur la table fragile.

Des roses s'effeuillèrent au choc, une coupe de porcelaine glissa sans se briser sur l'épais tapis. Léa étendit vers le téléphone une main que Chéri arrêta d'un bras rude:

"Qu'est-ce que tu veux à ce téléphone?

— Téléphoner au commissariat", dit Léa.

Il lui prit les deux bras, feignit la gaminerie en la poussant loin de l'appareil.

"Allez, allez, ça va bien, pas de blagues! On ne peut rien dire sans que tout de suite tu fasses du drame. . . ."

Elle s'assit et lui tourna le dos. Il restait debout, les mains vides, et sa bouche entrouverte et gonflée était celle d'un enfant boudeur. Une mèche noire couvrait son sourcil. Dans un miroir, à la dérobée, Léa

His head lowered, he inspected the room from side to side, its closed doors, the metal-armored bed with its sloping stack of luxurious pillows. He didn't see anything out of the way, or anything new, and he shrugged his shoulders. Léa was waiting for something more than that, and she persisted:

"Do you understand what I mean?"

"Very well," he replied. "The gentleman hasn't come home? The gentleman is sleeping elsewhere?"

"That's none of your business, my boy," she said calmly.

He bit his lip and nervously flicked his cigarette ash into a bowl containing jewelry.

"Not in there! I keep telling you!" Léa shouted. "How many times do I have to . . . ?"

She broke off, reproaching herself for having assumed the tone of their everyday arguments, against her will. But he didn't seem to have heard her; he was examining a ring, an emerald that Léa had bought during her trip.

"What's . . . what's this?" he stammered.

"That? It's an emerald."

"I'm not blind! I mean: who gave it to you?"

"Someone you don't know."

"Delightful!" said Chéri, with bitterness in his voice.

That tone of voice gave Léa back all her authority over him, and she allowed herself the pleasure of leading him a little further astray, since he had left himself open to it.

"Isn't it charming? I get complimented on it all over. Did you notice the setting, that powdering of brilliants which . . ."

"Enough!" Chéri roared in a frenzy, slamming his fist down on the fragile table.

At the shock, some roses lost their petals and a porcelain bowl rolled onto the thick carpet without breaking. Léa reached for the phone, but Chéri intercepted her hand roughly:

"What do you want with that phone?"

"To call the police," Léa said.

He seized her two arms, pretending to be acting boyishly as he shoved her far away from the phone.

"Come on, come on, it's all right, don't do anything foolish! A person can't say a thing without you dramatizing it right away . . ."

She sat down, turning her back to him. He remained standing with empty hands, and his puffy, half-open mouth was like a sulky child's. A dark lock of hair covered one eyebrow. Léa was secretly observing

l'épiait; mais il s'assit et son visage disparut du miroir. A son tour, Léa
sentit, gênée, qu'il la voyait de dos, élargie par la gandoura flottante.
Elle revint à sa coiffeuse, lissa ses cheveux, replanta son peigne, ouvrit
comme par distraction un flacon de parfum. Chéri tourna la tête vers
l'odeur.

"Nounoune!" appela-t-il.

Elle ne répondit pas.

"Nounoune!"

— Demande pardon", commanda-t-elle sans se retourner.

Il ricana:

"Penses-tu!

— Je ne te force pas. Mais tu vas t'en aller. Et tout de suite. . . .

— Pardon! dit-il promptement, hargneux.

— Mieux que ça!

— Pardon, répéta-t-il, tout bas.

— A la bonne heure!"

Elle revint à lui, passa sur la tête inclinée une main légère:

"Allons, raconte."

Il tressaillit et secoua la caresse:

"Qu'est-ce que tu veux que je te raconte? Ce n'est pas compliqué.
Je rentre ici, voilà.

— Raconte, va, raconte."

Il se balançait sur son siège en serrant ses mains entre ses genoux,
et levait la tête vers Léa mais sans la regarder. Elle voyait battre les
narines blanches de Chéri, elle entendait une respiration rapide qui
essayait de se discipliner. Elle n'eut qu'à dire encore une fois: "Allons,
raconte . . ." et à le pousser du doigt comme pour le faire tomber. Il
appela:

"Nounoune chérie! Nounoune chérie!" et se jeta contre elle de
toutes ses forces, étreignant les hautes jambes qui plièrent. Assise, elle
le laissa glisser à terre et se rouler sur elle avec des larmes, des paroles
désordonnées, des mains tâtonnantes qui s'accrochaient à ses dentelles, à son collier, cherchaient sous la robe la forme de son épaule et
la place de son oreille sous les cheveux.

"Nounoune chérie! je te retrouve! ma Nounoune! ô ma Nounoune,
ton épaule, et puis ton même parfum, et ton collier, ma Nounoune,
ah! c'est épatant. . . . Et ton petit goût de brûlé dans les cheveux, ah!
c'est . . . c'est épatant. . . ."

Il exhala, renversé, ce mot stupide comme le dernier souffle de sa
poitrine. A genoux, il serrait Léa dans ses bras, et lui offrait son front
ombragé de cheveux, sa tremblante bouche mouillée de larmes, et ses

him in a mirror; but he sat down and his face was no longer visible in the mirror. Now it was Léa's turn to sense, with annoyance, that he was looking at her from behind, at her figure made broader by the loosely fitting tunic. She returned to her vanity table, smoothed her hair, put her comb in place again, and opened a perfume bottle as if absentmindedly. Chéri turned his head toward the fragrance.

"Nursie!" he called.

She made no reply.

"Nursie!"

"Apologize," she ordered, without turning around.

He sniggered:

"That's what you think!"

"I'm not forcing you. But you're going to leave. And this minute . . ."

"I apologize," he said promptly, in a surly way.

"Say it better!"

"I apologize," he repeated, very quietly.

"Good!"

She came back over to him and passed one hand lightly over his bowed head.

"All right, tell me the story."

He gave a start and shook off her caress:

"What do you want me to tell you? It's not complicated. I'm back here, that's all."

"Tell me, come on, tell me."

He was rocking back and forth on his seat, with his hands squeezed between his knees; he had his head raised in Léa's direction but he wasn't looking at her. She could see Chéri's white nostrils flaring, she could hear his quick breathing, which he was trying to control. She merely needed to say once more "Come, tell me" and to push him with her finger as if to make him fall. He called out:

"Dear Nursie! Dear Nursie!" And he flung himself at her with all his might, hugging her tall legs, which buckled. She sat down and let him slip to the floor and roll against her with tears, broken phrases, and groping hands that clutched her lace and her necklace and reached under her gown to find the shape of her shoulder, and under her hair to feel her ear.

"Dear Nursie! It's you again! My Nursie, oh, my Nursie! It's your shoulder, your own perfume, and your necklace, my Nursie! Oh, it's terrific! . . . And that little burnt smell in your hair! Oh, it's . . . it's terrific . . ."

Leaning back, he breathed out that silly word as if it were the last breath to issue from his chest. On his knees, he hugged Léa in his arms, offering her his hair-shaded forehead, his trembling, tear-soaked lips, and his eyes,

yeux d'où la joie coulait en pleurs lumineux. Elle le contempla si profondément, avec un oubli si parfait de tout ce qui n'était pas lui,
qu'elle ne songea pas à lui donner un baiser. Elle noua ses bras autour
du cou de Chéri, et elle le pressa sans rigueur, sur le rythme des mots
qu'elle murmurait:

"Mon petit . . . mon méchant. . . . Te voilà . . . Te voilà revenu. . . .
Qu'as-tu fait encore? Tu es si méchant . . . ma beauté. . . ."

Il se plaignait doucement à bouche fermée, et ne parlait plus guère:
il écoutait Léa et appuyait sa joue sur son sein. Il supplia: "Encore!"
lorsqu'elle suspendit sa litanie tendre, et Léa, qui craignait de pleurer
aussi, le gronda sur le même ton:

"Mauvaise bête. . . . Petit satan sans cœur. . . . Grande rosse, va. . . ."

Il leva vers elle un regard de gratitude:

"C'est ça, engueule-moi! Ah! Nounoune. . . ."

Elle l'écarta d'elle pour le mieux voir:

"Tu m'aimais donc?"

Il baissa les yeux avec un trouble enfantin:

"Oui, Nounoune."

Un petit éclat de rire étranglé, qu'elle ne put retenir avertit Léa
qu'elle était bien près de s'abandonner à la plus terrible joie de sa vie.
Une étreinte, la chute, le lit ouvert, deux corps qui se soudent comme
les deux tronçons vivants d'une même bête coupée. . . . "Non, non, se
dit-elle, pas encore, oh! pas encore. . . ."

"J'ai soif, soupira Chéri. Nounoune, j'ai soif. . . ."

Elle se leva vite, tâta de la main la carafe tiédie et sortit pour
revenir aussitôt. Chéri, pelotonné à terre, avait posé sa tête sur le
pouf.

"On t'apporte de la citronnade, dit Léa. Ne reste pas là. Viens sur
la chaise longue. Cette lampe te gêne?"

Elle frémissait du plaisir de servir et d'ordonner. Elle s'assit au fond
de la chaise longue et Chéri s'y étendit à demi contre elle.

"Tu vas me dire un peu, maintenant. . . ."

L'entrée de Rose l'interrompit. Chéri, sans se lever, tourna languis-
samment la tête vers Rose:

". . . 'jour, Rose.

— Bonjour, Monsieur, dit Rose discrètement.

— Rose, je voudrais pour demain matin neuf heures. . . .

— Des brioches et du chocolat", acheva Rose.

Chéri referma les yeux avec un soupir de bien-être:

"Extra-lucide! . . . Rose, où est-ce que je m'habille demain
matin?

from which joy was flowing in the form of bright tears. She looked at him so fixedly, so totally forgetful of everything else in the world, that it didn't occur to her to kiss him. She threw her arms around Chéri's neck and hugged him gently to the rhythm of the words she was murmuring:

"My little boy . . . my bad boy . . . here you are . . . here you are back again . . . What have you done this time? You're so bad . . . my beauty . . ."

He was lamenting softly, his lips closed, and was scarcely talking anymore: he was listening to Léa as he rested his cheek on her breast. He begged "More!" when she interrupted her amorous litany, and Léa, who was afraid she'd start crying, too, scolded him in the same tone of voice:

"Evil creature . . . little heartless devil . . . Big scoundrel that you are . . ."

He raised his eyes toward her in gratitude:

"That's right, bawl me out! Oh, Nursie . . ."

She pushed him away, so she could see him better:

"So you still loved me?"

He lowered his eyes in childish confusion:

"Yes, Nursie."

A little burst of stifled laughter that she couldn't hold back warned Léa that she was very close to surrendering to the most awesome joy in her life. An embrace, a tumble, the turned-down bed, two bodies clinging together like the two living halves of a single severed animal . . . "No, no," she said to herself, "not yet, oh, not yet . . ."

"I'm thirsty," Chéri sighed. "Nursie, I'm thirsty . . ."

She got up quickly, groped for the carafe, which had become lukewarm, and went out, returning immediately. Chéri, curled up on the floor, was resting his head on the ottoman.

"I'm having lemonade brought for you," said Léa. "Don't stay there. Come onto the chaise longue. Does this lamp bother you?"

She was trembling with the pleasure of serving him and giving him orders. She sat far back on the chaise longue, and Chéri stretched out on it, half-leaning on her.

"Now you're going to tell me a little . . ."

Rose's arrival interrupted her. Without getting up, Chéri languidly turned his head toward Rose:

"Hi, Rose."

"Hello, sir," Rose said discreetly.

"Rose, for tomorrow morning at nine I'd like . . ."

"Brioches and hot chocolate," Rose finished his sentence.

Chéri closed his eyes again with a sigh of comfort:

"Sharp as a tack! . . . Rose, where should I get dressed tomorrow morning?"

"— Dans le boudoir, répondit Rose complaisante. Seulement il faudra sans doute que je fasse retirer le canapé et qu'on remette le nécessaire de toilette comme avant? . . ."

Elle consultait de l'œil Léa, orgueilleusement étalée et qui soutenait, tandis qu'il buvait, le torse de son "nourrisson méchant".

"Si tu veux, dit Léa. On verra. Remonte, Rose."

Rose s'en alla et pendant le moment de silence qui suivit, on n'entendit qu'un confus murmure de brise, et le cri d'un oiseau que trompait le clair de lune.

"Chéri, tu dors?"

Il fit son grand soupir de chien de chasse.

"Oh! non, Nounoune, je suis trop bien pour dormir.

— Dis-moi, petit. . . . Tu n'as pas fait de mal, là-bas?

— Chez moi? Non, Nounoune. Pas du tout, je te jure.

— Une scène?"

Il la regardait d'en bas, sans relever sa tête confiante.

"Mais non, Nounoune. Je suis parti parce que je suis parti. La petite est très gentille, il n'y a rien eu.

— Ah!

— Je ne mettrais pas ma main au feu qu'elle n'a pas eu une idée, par exemple. Elle avait ce soir ce que j'appelle sa tête d'orpheline, tu sais, des yeux si sombres sous ses beaux cheveux. . . . Tu sais comme elle a de beaux cheveux?

— Oui. . . ."

Elle ne jetait que des monosyllabes, à mi-voix, comme si elle eût écouté un dormeur parler en songe.

"Je crois même, continua Chéri, qu'elle a dû me voir traverser le jardin.

— Ah?

— Oui. Elle était au balcon, dans sa robe en jais blanc, un blanc tellement gelé, oh! je n'aime pas cette robe. . . . Cette robe me donnait envie de fiche le camp depuis le dîner. . . .

— Non?

— Mais oui, Nounoune. Je ne sais pas si elle m'a vu. La lune n'était pas levée. Elle s'est levée pendant que j'attendais.

— Où attendais-tu?"

Chéri étendit vaguement la main vers l'avenue.

"Là. J'attendais, tu comprends. Je voulais voir. J'ai attendu longtemps.

— Mais quoi?"

"In the boudoir," Rose answered obligingly. "Only, I'm sure you'll want me to have the sofa-bed taken out and your shaving kit brought back, like before . . . ?"

She was looking at Léa for guidance, Léa, who was reclining proudly and supporting the torso of her "nasty infant" while he drank.

"If you like," Léa said. "We'll see. Go back upstairs, Rose."

Rose left, and during the moment of silence that followed, all that could be heard was the confused murmur of the wind and the call of a bird that had been fooled by the moonlight.

"Are you asleep, Chéri?"

He uttered his loud hunting-dog's sigh.

"Oh, no, Nursie, I'm too comfortable to sleep."

"Tell me, boy . . . You didn't create an uproar at your place?"

"At home? No, Nursie. Not at all, I swear."

"No scene?"

He looked up at her without raising his trusting head.

"No, Nursie. I left because I left. The girl is very nice, and nothing happened."

"Ah!"

"I wouldn't swear to it that she had no idea of what was coming, I must say. This evening her face had what I call her orphan look, you know: eyes so dark beneath her beautiful hair . . . You know how beautiful her hair is?"

"Yes . . ."

She was uttering only monosyllables, sotto voce, as if she were listening to a man talking in his sleep.

"I even think," Chéri continued, "that she must have seen me crossing the garden."

"Oh?"

"Yes. She was on the balcony in her white sequin dress, such a cold white! Oh, I don't like that dress . . . Ever since dinnertime that dress had made me feel like running away . . ."

"Really?"

"Yes, Nursie. I don't know whether she saw me. The moon hadn't risen yet. It rose while I was waiting."

"Where were you waiting?"

Chéri vaguely stretched out a hand in the direction of the avenue.

"There. I was waiting, you understand. I wanted to see. I waited a long time."

"For what?"

Il la quitta brusquement, s'assit plus loin. Il reprit son expression de méfiance barbare:

"Tiens, je voulais être sûr qu'il n'y avait personne ici.

— Ah! oui. . . . Tu pensais à. . . ."

Elle ne put se défendre d'un rire plein de mépris. Un amant chez elle? Un amant, tant que Chéri vivait? C'était grotesque: "Qu'il est bête!" pensa-t-elle avec enthousiasme.

"Tu ris?"

Il se mit debout devant elle et lui renversa la tête, d'une main qu'il lui posa sur le front.

"Tu ris? Tu te moques de moi? Tu as. . . . Tu as un amant, toi? Tu as quelqu'un?"

Il se penchait à mesure qu'il parlait et lui collait la nuque sur le dossier de la chaise longue. Elle sentit sur ses paupières le souffle d'une bouche injurieuse, et ne fit pas d'effort pour se délivrer de la main qui froissait son front et ses cheveux.

"Ose donc le dire, que tu as un amant!"

Elle battit des paupières, éblouie par l'approche du visage éclatant qui descendait sur elle, et dit enfin d'une voix sourde:

"Non. Je n'ai pas d'amant. Je t'aime. . . ."

Il la lâcha et commença de retirer son smoking, son gilet; sa cravate siffla dans l'air et s'enroula au cou d'un buste de Léa sur la cheminée. Cependant il ne s'écartait pas d'elle et la maintenait, genoux contre genoux, assise sur la chaise longue. Lorsqu'elle le vit demi-nu, elle lui demanda, presque tristement:

"Tu veux donc? . . . Oui? . . ."

Il ne répondit pas, absorbé par l'idée de son plaisir proche et le désir qu'il avait de la reprendre. Elle se soumit et servit son jeune amant en bonne maîtresse, attentive et grave. Cependant elle voyait avec une sorte de terreur approcher l'instant de sa propre défaite, elle endurait Chéri comme un supplice, le repoussait de ses mains sans force et le retenait entre ses genoux puissants. Enfin elle le saisit au bras, cria faiblement, et sombra dans cet abîme d'où l'amour remonte pâle, taciturne et plein du regret de la mort.

Ils ne se délièrent pas, et nulle parole ne troubla le long silence où ils reprenaient vie. Le torse de Chéri avait glissé sur le flanc de Léa, et sa tête pendante reposait, les yeux clos, sur le drap, comme si on l'eût poignardé sur sa maîtresse. Elle, un peu détournée vers l'autre côté, portait presque tout le poids de ce corps qui ne la ménageait pas. Elle haletait tout bas, son bras gauche, écrasé, lui faisait mal, et Chéri sentait s'engourdir sa nuque, mais ils attendaient l'un et l'autre, dans

He brusquely left her and sat down a distance away. His expression was once again one of savage distrust:

"Well, I wanted to be sure that no one else was here."

"Oh, yes . . . You were thinking about . . ."

She couldn't keep from giving a laugh that was full of contempt. A lover in her house? Another lover, while Chéri was still alive? It was grotesque. "How silly he is!" she thought fervidly.

"You're laughing?"

He stood up in front of her and pushed her head back, placing a hand against her forehead.

"You're laughing? You're making fun of me? You have . . . You have a lover? You have somebody?"

As he spoke, he was leaning forward and pressing her nape against the back of the chaise longue. She felt on her eyelids the breath of a mouth that was insulting her, but she made no effort to free herself from the hand that was wrinkling her forehead and rumpling her hair.

"Have the courage to say that you have a lover!"

She fluttered her eyelids, dazzled by the nearness of the shining face that was approaching hers; she finally said in a muffled voice:

"No. I have no lover. I love you . . ."

He released her and started to take off his dinner jacket and his vest; his tie whizzed through the air and wrapped itself around the neck of a bust of Léa on the mantelpiece. Meanwhile, he didn't move away from her; he kept her sitting on the chaise longue, his knees against hers. When she saw him half-naked, she asked him, almost sadly:

"So you want to? . . . Do you? . . ."

He didn't answer; he was absorbed by the thought of his imminent pleasure and his desire to take her again. She submitted and served her young lover as a good mistress should, attentively and seriously. Meanwhile, with a sort of terror she saw the moment of her own defeat approaching; she endured Chéri like a torture, pushing him back with her strengthless hands while grasping him between her powerful knees. Finally she grabbed him by an arm, gave a feeble cry, and sank into that abyss from which love reascends pale, mute, and filled with a longing for death.

They didn't slacken their embrace, and no word troubled the long silence during which they came back to life. Chéri's torso had slipped down onto Léa's side, and his pendent head was resting on the sheet, eyes closed, as if he had been stabbed while on his mistress' body. She, slightly turned in the other direction, was supporting nearly all the weight of his body, which was showing her no mercy. She was panting very quietly; her left arm, crushed beneath him, hurt; and Chéri felt

une immobilité respectueuse, que la foudre décroissante du plaisir se fût éloignée d'eux.

"Il dort", pensa Léa. Sa main libre tenait encore le poignet de Chéri, qu'elle serra doucement. Un genou, dont elle connaissait la forme rare, meurtrissait son genou. A la hauteur de son propre cœur, elle percevait le battement égal et étouffé d'un cœur. Tenace, actif, mélange de fleurs grasses et de bois exotiques, le parfum préféré de Chéri errait. "Il est là", se dit Léa. Et une sécurité aveugle la baigna toute. "Il est là pour toujours", s'écria-t-elle intérieurement. Sa prudence avisée, le bon sens souriant qui avaient guidé sa vie, les hésitations humiliées de son âge mûr, puis ses renoncements, tout recula et s'évanouit devant la brutalité présomptueuse de l'amour. "Il est là! Laissant sa maison, sa petite femme niaise et jolie, il est revenu, il m'est revenu! Qui pourrait me l'enlever? Maintenant, maintenant je vais organiser notre existence. . . . Il ne sait pas toujours ce qu'il veut, mais moi je le sais. Un départ sera sans doute nécessaire. Nous ne nous cachons pas, mois nous cherchons la tranquillité. . . . Et puis il me faut le loisir de le regarder. Je n'ai pas dû le bien regarder, au temps où je ne savais pas que je l'aimais. Il me faut un pays où nous aurons assez de place pour ses caprices et mes volontés. . . . Moi, je penserai pour nous deux, — à lui le sommeil. . . ."

Comme elle dégageait avec précaution son bras gauche fourmillant et douloureux et son épaule que l'immobilité ankylosait, elle regarda le visage détourné de Chéri, et elle vit qu'il ne dormait pas. Le blanc de son œil brillait, et la petite aile noire de ses cils battait irrégulièrement.

"Comment, tu ne dors pas?"

Elle le sentit tressaillir contre elle, et il se retourna tout entier d'un seul mouvement.

"Mais toi non plus tu ne dormais pas, Nounoune?"

Il étendit la main vers la table de chevet et atteignit la lampe; une nappe de lumière rose couvrit le grand lit, accusant les reliefs des dentelles, creusant des vallons d'ombre entre les capitons dodus d'un couvre-pieds gonflé de duvet. Chéri, étendu, reconnaissait le champ de son repos et de ses jeux voluptueux. Léa, accoudée près de lui, caressait de la main les longs sourcils qu'elle aimait et rejetait en arrière les cheveux de Chéri. Ainsi couché et les cheveux dispersés autour de son front, il sembla renversé par un vent furieux.

La pendule d'émail sonna. Chéri se dressa brusquement et s'assit.

"Quelle heure est-il?

the back of his neck getting numb; but they both waited, immobile out of respect, until the lightning of their pleasure subsided and left them.

"He's asleep," Léa thought. Her free hand was still holding Chéri's wrist, which she squeezed gently. One of his knees, the exceptional form of which was familiar to her, was bruising her knee. At the level of her own heart, she could perceive the even, muffled beating of his. Clinging and forceful, a mixture of heady flowers and exotic species of wood, Chéri's favorite scent hovered about. "He's here," Léa said to herself. And she was immersed in a blind feeling of security. "He's here for good!" she exclaimed to herself. The prudence, caution, and cheerful good sense that had guided her life, the hesitations and humiliations of her mature years, and her acts of renunciation—they all receded and disappeared in the face of love's brutality and arrogance. "He's here! He's left his home and his pretty little ninny of a wife, and he's come back, he's come back to me! Who can take him away from me? Now, now, I'm going to organize our life . . . He doesn't always know what he wants, but I do. We'll probably have to go away. We're not hiding, but we're looking for peace and quiet . . . Besides, I need time in which to look at him. I probably never took a good look at him in the days when I didn't realize that I loved him. I need someplace where we'll have enough room for his whims and for my firm wishes . . . I'll do the thinking for both of us—he can sleep . . ."

While carefully freeing her left arm, which ached with pins and needles, and her shoulder, which was paralyzed by immobility, she looked at Chéri's face, which was turned away from her, and she saw that he wasn't asleep. The whites of his eyes were shining, and the little black wings of his lashes were beating irregularly.

"What, you're not asleep?"

She felt him give a start, up against her, and he turned completely over in a single motion.

"But weren't you sleeping, either, Nursie?"

He reached out for the night table and found the lamp; a patch of pink light covered the big bed, throwing its lace into relief and hollowing out valleys of darkness between the plump bulges of the down-filled comforter. Chéri, stretched out there, recognized the playing field of his repose and of his amorous games. Léa, leaning on an elbow next to him, caressed the tapering eyebrows that she loved, and pushed Chéri's hair back. As he lay that way, his hair tangled on his forehead, he looked as if he had been bowled over by a furious wind.

The enamel wall clock chimed. Chéri brusquely rose to a sitting position.

"What time is it?"

— Je ne sais pas. Qu'est-ce que ça peut bien nous faire?

— Oh! je disais ça. . . ."

Il rit brièvement et ne se recoucha pas tout de suite. La première voiture de laitier secoua au-dehors un carillon de verrerie, et il eut un mouvement imperceptible vers l'avenue. Entre les rideaux couleur de fraise, une lame froide de jour naissant s'insinuait. Chéri ramena son regard sur Léa, et la contempla avec cette force et cette fixité qui rend redoutables l'attention de l'enfant perplexe et du chien incrédule. Une pensée illisible se levait au fond de ses yeux dont la forme, la nuance de giroflée très sombre, l'éclat sévère ou langoureux ne lui avaient servi qu'à vaincre et non à révéler. Son torse nu, large aux épaules, mince à la ceinture, émergeait des draps froissés comme d'une houle, et tout son être respirait la mélancolie des œuvres parfaites.

"Ah! toi . . ." soupira Léa avec ivresse.

Il ne sourit pas, habitué à recevoir simplement les hommages.

"Dis-moi, Nounoune. . . .

— Ma beauté?"

Il hésita, battit des paupières en frissonnant:

"Je suis fatigué. . . . Et puis demain, comment vas-tu pouvoir. . . ."

D'une poussée tendre Léa rabattit sur l'oreiller le torse nu et la tête alourdie.

"Ne t'occupe pas. Couche-toi. Est-ce que Nounoune n'est pas là? Ne pense à rien. Dors. Tu as froid, je parierais. . . . Tiens, prends ça, c'est chaud. . . ."

Elle le roula dans la soie et la laine d'un petit vêtement féminin ramassé sur le lit et éteignit la lumière. Dans l'ombre, elle prêta son épaule, creusa son flanc heureux, écouta le souffle qui doublait le sien. Aucun désir ne la troublait, mais elle ne souhaitait pas le sommeil. "A lui de dormir, à moi de penser", se répéta-t-elle. "Notre départ, je l'organiserai très chic, très discret; mon principe est de causer le minimum de bruit et de chagrin. . . . C'est encore le Midi qui au printemps nous plaira le mieux. Si je ne consultais que moi, j'aimerais mieux rester ici, tout tranquillement. Mais la mère Peloux, mais madame Peloux fils. . . ." L'image d'une jeune femme en costume de nuit, anxieuse et debout près d'une fenêtre, ne retint Léa que le temps de hausser l'épaule avec une froide équité: "Ça, je n'y peux rien. Ce qui fait le bonheur des uns. . . ."

La tête soyeuse et noire bougea sur son sein, et l'amant endormi se plaignit en rêve. D'un bras farouche Léa le protégea contre le mau-

"I don't know. What's that to us?"

"Oh, I was just making talk . . ."

He gave a short laugh, but didn't lie down again right away. The first milk wagon created a carillon of tinkling bottles outside, and he turned imperceptibly in the direction of the avenue. Between the strawberry-colored curtains a cold sliver of early daylight was making its way inside. Chéri turned his eyes toward Léa and examined her with that kind of strength and fixity which makes the gaze of a confused child or a distrustful dog so terrifying. An unfathomable thought arose in the depths of his eyes, whose shape, whose very dark gillyflower hue, and whose glint, either stern or languorous, had only helped him make conquests, but had never helped him show his feelings. His naked torso, broad in the shoulders, slim at the waist, emerged from the crumpled sheets as if from raging surf, and his whole being breathed the melancholy that goes with perfect works of art.

"Oh, you . . . ," Léa sighed in rapture.

He didn't smile, accustomed as he was to receive homage unceremoniously.

"Tell me, Nursie . . ."

"Yes, beauty?"

He hesitated, fluttering his eyelids and shivering:

"I'm tired . . . Besides, tomorrow how will you be able . . ."

With a tender shove Léa brought the naked torso and the heavy head back down on the pillow.

"Don't worry. Lie down. Isn't Nursie here? Don't think about a thing. Sleep. You feel cold, I bet . . . Here, take this, it's warm . . ."

She rolled him up in the silk and wool of a small feminine garment that she took from the bed, and she turned out the light. In the dark she offered him her shoulder, happily made a place for him at her side, and listened to the breathing that matched her own. No desire was troubling her, but she didn't feel like sleeping. "It's for him to sleep and for me to think," she repeated to herself. "As for our departure, I'll arrange it very skillfully and discreetly; I believe in creating the least amount of noise and unhappiness . . . The South will still be the most pleasant place for us in the spring. If I had only myself to think about, I'd prefer to stay here in peace and quiet. But there's old lady Peloux and the younger Madame Peloux to consider . . ." The image of a young woman in night attire, standing anxiously by a window, only occupied Léa long enough to make her shrug her shoulders with a cool sense of justice: "I can't do anything about it. One man's meat . . ."

Chéri's silky dark head stirred on her breast, and her slumbering lover lamented in his sleep. With a fierce arm Léa defended him

vais songe, et le berça afin qu'il demeurât longtemps — sans yeux, sans souvenirs et sans desseins, — ressemblant au "nourrisson méchant" qu'elle n'avait pu enfanter.

ÉVEILLÉ depuis un long moment, il se gardait de bouger. La joue sur son bras plié, il tâchait de deviner l'heure. Un ciel pur devait verser sur l'avenue une précoce chaleur, car nulle ombre de nuage ne passait sur le rose ardent des rideaux. "Peut-être dix heures? . . ." La faim le tourmentait, il avait peu dîné la veille. L'an dernier, il eût bondi, bousculé le repos de Léa, poussé des appels féroces pour réclamer le chocolat crémeux et le beurre glacé. . . . Il ne bougea pas. Il craignait, en remuant, d'émietter un reste de joie, un plaisir optique qu'il goûtait au rose de braise des rideaux, aux volutes, acier et cuivre, du lit étincelant dans l'air coloré de la chambre. Son grand bonheur de la veille lui semblait réfugié, fondu et tout petit, dans un reflet, dans l'arc-en-ciel qui dansait au flanc d'un cristal empli d'eau.

Le pas circonspect de Rose frôla le tapis du palier. Un balai prudent nettoyait la cour. Chéri perçut un lointain tintement de porcelaine dans l'office. . . . "Comme c'est long, cette matinée . . . se dit-il. Je vais me lever!" Mais il demeura tout à fait immobile, car Léa derrière lui bâilla, étira ses jambes. Une main douce se posa sur les reins de Chéri, mais il referma les yeux et tout son corps se mit à mentir sans savoir pourquoi, en feignant la mollesse du sommeil. Il sentit que Léa quittait le lit, et la vit passer en silhouette noire devant les rideaux qu'elle écarta à demi. Elle se tourna vers lui, le regarda et hocha la tête, avec un sourire qui n'était point victorieux mais résolu, et qui acceptait tous les périls. Elle ne se pressait pas de quitter la chambre, et Chéri, laissant un fil de lumière entrouvrir ses cils, l'épiait. Il vit qu'elle ouvrait un indicateur des chemins de fer et suivait du doigt des colonnes de chiffres. Puis elle sembla calculer, le visage levé vers le ciel et les sourcils froncés. Pas encore poudrée, une maigre torsade de cheveux sur la nuque, le menton double et le cou dévasté, elle s'offrait imprudemment au regard invisible.

Elle s'éloigna de la fenêtre, prit dans un tiroir son carnet de chèques, libella et détacha plusieurs feuillets. Puis elle disposa sur le pied du lit un pyjama blanc et sortit sans bruit.

against the bad dream, rocking him, so that for a long time—unseeing, void of both memories and purpose—he would remain the "nasty infant" she had been unable to give birth to herself.

AWAKE for some time now, he refrained from moving. His cheek on his folded arm, he was trying to guess the time. A clear sky must have been pouring an unseasonable heat onto the avenue, because not the shadow of a cloud passed over the blazing pink of the curtains. "Ten o'clock, maybe? . . ." He was famished, since he hadn't eaten much at dinner the evening before. A year earlier, he would have leaped up, ruining Léa's sleep and uttering ferocious cries for his foaming hot chocolate and chilled butter . . . Now, he didn't budge. He was afraid that, if he moved around, he might fritter away any remaining joy and the visual pleasure he took in the glowing pink of the curtains and in the steel and copper volutes of the bed that sparkled in the colorful atmosphere of the bedroom. His great happiness of the night before seemed to him to have taken refuge—now shrunken to a tiny size—in a reflection, in the rainbow that was dancing on the side of a water-filled pitcher.

Rose's cautious tread brushed the carpet on the landing. A circumspect broom was cleaning the courtyard. Chéri discerned a faraway tinkling of porcelain in the butler's pantry . . . "How long this morning is . . . ," he said to himself. "I'm going to get up!" But he remained completely motionless, because behind him Léa yawned and stretched out her legs. A soft hand was placed on Chéri's back, but he shut his eyes again, and his whole body started to live a lie, though he didn't know why, feigning the lifelessness of sleep. He felt Léa get out of bed, and saw her walking like a dark silhouette over to the curtains, which she opened halfway. She turned in his direction, looked at him, and shook her head with smile that was not at all victorious, but determined, fully accepting any risk. She wasn't in a hurry to leave the bedroom, and Chéri, his eyes opened a crack between his lashes, was following her every movement. He saw her open a railroad timetable and run her finger down its columns of figures. Then she seemed to be making a calculation, her face raised skyward and her brow knitted. Not yet powdered, a thin twist of hair on the back of her neck, with a double chin and a ravaged throat, she was unwisely exposing herself to those unseen eyes.

She left the window, took her checkbook out of a drawer, wrote a few checks, and detached them. Then she laid out a pair of white pajamas on the foot of the bed, and went out noiselessly.

Seul, Chéri, en respirant longuement, s'aperçut qu'il avait retenu sa respiration depuis le lever de Léa. Il se leva, revêtit le pyjama et ouvrit une fenêtre. "On étouffe", souffla-t-il. Il gardait l'impression vague et le malaise d'avoir commis une action assez laide.

"Parce que j'ai fait semblant de dormir? Mais je l'ai vue cent fois, Léa, au saut du lit. Seulement j'ai fait semblant de dormir, cette fois-ci. . . ."

Le jour éclatant restituait à la chambre son rose de fleur, les tendres nuances du Chaplin blond et argenté riaient au mur. Chéri inclina la tête et ferma les yeux afin que sa mémoire lui rendît la chambre de la veille, mystérieuse et colorée comme l'intérieur d'une pastèque, le dôme féerique de la lampe, et surtout l'exaltation dont il avait supporté, chancelant, les délices. . . .

"Tu es debout! Le chocolat me suit."

Il constata avec gratitude qu'en quelques minutes Léa s'était coiffée, délicatement fardée, imprégnée du parfum familier. Le son de la bonne voix cordiale se répandit dans la pièce en même temps qu'un arôme de tartines grillées et de cacao. Chéri s'assit près des deux tasses fumantes, reçut des mains de Léa le pain grassement beurré. Il cherchait quelque chose à dire et Léa ne s'en doutait pas, car elle l'avait connu taciturne à l'ordinaire, et recueilli devant la nourriture. Elle mangea de bon appétit, avec la hâte et la gaieté préocupée d'une femme qui déjeune, ses malles bouclées, avant le train.

"Ta seconde tartine, Chéri. . . .

— Non, merci, Nounoune.

— Plus faim?

— Plus faim."

Elle le menaça du doigt en riant:

"Toi, tu vas te faire coller deux pastilles de rhubarbe, ça te pend au nez!"

Il fronça le nez, choqué:

"Écoute, Nounoune, tu as la rage de t'occuper de . . .

— Ta ta ta! Ça me regarde. Tire la langue? Tu ne veux pas tirer la langue? Alors essuie tes moustaches de chocolat et parlons peu, mais parlons bien. Les sujets ennuyeux, il faut les traiter vite."

Elle prit une main de Chéri par-dessus la table et l'enferma dans les siennes.

"Tu es revenu. C'était notre destin. Te fies-tu à moi? Je te prends à ma charge."

Elle s'interrompit malgré elle, et ferma les yeux, comme pliant sous

Left alone, Chéri took deep breaths, realizing that he had been holding his breath ever since Léa got up. He arose, put on the pajamas, and opened a window. "It's stifling," he puffed. He couldn't shake off the vague, uneasy impression that he had done a rather ugly thing.

"Why did I pretend to be asleep? After all, I've seen Léa get out of bed a hundred times. But this time I pretended to be asleep . . ."

The bright daylight gave the room back its flowery pinkness; the pastel hues of the blond and silvery Chaplin portrait were smiling on the wall. Chéri tilted his head and shut his eyes so that his memory could bring the room back to the way it had been the night before, mysterious, with a color like the inside of a watermelon, the magical dome of the lamp, and, above all, the excitement and delight he had staggered under . . .

"You're up! The chocolate is on its way."

He noted gratefully that in the last few minutes Léa had done her hair, put on delicate makeup, and doused herself with the perfume he knew so well. The sound of her kindly, cordial voice permeated the room, along with a good smell of toast and cocoa. Chéri sat down next to the two steaming cups, and took the heavily buttered bread from Léa's hands. He was looking for something to say, though Léa didn't suspect it, because she had usually found him taciturn and meditative when food was served. She ate with a hearty appetite, with the haste and preoccupied cheerfulness of a woman who has packed her trunks and is having lunch before catching a train.

"Another slice of toast, Chéri . . ."

"No, thanks, Nursie."

"Not hungry anymore?"

"No."

She shook a finger at him, laughing:

"You're just asking for two laxative pastilles, I can see it coming!"

He wrinkled his nose, very upset:

"Listen, Nursie, you're much too concerned with . . ."

"Ta ta ta! That's my business. Stick out your tongue. You don't want to stick out your tongue? Then, wipe off your cocoa mustache, and let's talk, briefly but seriously. Unpleasant subjects should be discussed rapidly."

She reached across the table for one of Chéri's hands and held it in both of hers.

"You're back. It was our destiny. Do you trust me? I'll look after you."

Unwillingly she interrupted her speech, closing her eyes as if she

sa victoire; Chéri vit le sang fougueux illuminer le visage de sa maîtresse.

"Ah! reprit-elle plus bas, quand je pense à tout ce que je ne t'ai pas donné, à tout ce que je ne t'ai pas dit. . . . Quand je pense que je t'ai cru un petit passant comme les autres, un peu plus précieux que les autres. . . . Que j'étais bête, de ne pas comprendre que tu étais mon amour, l'amour, l'amour qu'on n'a qu'une fois. . . ."

Elle rouvrit ses yeux qui parurent plus bleus, d'un bleu retrempé à l'ombre des paupières, et respira par saccades.

"Oh! supplia Chéri en lui-même, qu'elle ne me pose pas une question, qu'elle ne me demande pas une réponse maintenant, je suis incapable d'une seule parole. . . ."

Elle lui secoua la main.

"Allons, allons, soyons sérieux. Donc, je disais: on part, on est partis. Qu'est-ce que tu fais, pour *là-bas*? Fais régler la question d'argent par Charlotte, c'est le plus sage, et largement, je t'en prie. Tu préviens *là-bas*, comment? par lettre, j'imagine. Pas commode, mais on s'en tire quand on fait peu de phrases. Nous verrons ça ensemble. Il y a aussi la question de tes bagages, — je n'ai plus rien à toi, ici. . . . Ces petites choses-là c'est plus agaçant qu'une grande décision, mais n'y songe pas trop. . . . Veux-tu bien ne pas arracher toujours tes petites peaux, au bord de l'ongle de ton orteil? C'est avec ces manies-là qu'on attrape un ongle incarné!"

Il laissa retomber son pied machinalement. Son propre mutisme l'écrasait et il était obligé de déployer une attention harassante pour écouter Léa. Il scrutait le visage animé, joyeux, impérieux de son amie, et se demandait vaguement: "Pourquoi a-t-elle l'air si contente?"

Son hébétement devint si évident que Léa, qui maintenant monologuait sur l'opportunité de racheter le yacht du vieux Berthellemy, s'arrêta court:

"Croyez-vous qu'il me donnerait seulement un avis? Ah! tu as bien toujours douze ans, toi!"

Chéri, délié de sa stupeur, passa la main sur son front et enveloppa Léa d'un regard mélancolique.

"Avec toi, Nounoune, il y a des chances pour que j'aie douze ans pendant un demi-siècle."

Elle cligna des yeux à plusieurs reprises comme s'il lui eût soufflé sur les paupières, et laissa le silence tomber entre eux.

"Qu'est-ce que tu veux dire? demanda-t-elle enfin.

were buckling beneath the weight of her victory; Chéri saw his mistress's impetuous blood mantling her cheeks.

"Oh," she resumed in a lower tone, "when I think of all I never gave you, all I never said to you . . . When I think that you seemed to be just a little temporary lover like the rest, though a bit more precious than the rest . . . How stupid I was not to understand that you were the love of my life, my love, the love that comes only once . . ."

She opened her eyes again, and they looked bluer, of a deeper blue in the shadow of her eyelids; she breathed jerkily.

"Oh," said Chéri beseechingly to himself, "let her not ask me a single question, let her not call for a single answer right now; I couldn't say even one word . . ."

She shook the hand she was holding.

"Come on, come on, let's be serious. So, I was saying: we're leaving, we're already gone. What will you do to settle things in that other place? Have Charlotte make the financial arrangements, it's the wisest thing, and generously, please. How will you let the people in that other place know? By letter, I imagine. It's not easy, but you can manage it if you don't make any fancy declarations. We'll work it out together. Then there's the matter of your belongings—I don't have anything of yours here anymore . . . These little things are more annoying than a major decision is, but don't worry about them too much . . . And please don't always be pulling off the little bits of skin around the nail of your big toe! That's the kind of tic that leads to an ingrown toenail!"

He let his foot fall mechanically. His own silence was weighing on him, and he had to muster an exhausting attention to listen to Léa. He was scrutinizing his mistress's animated, joyful, imperious face, and he was wondering vaguely: "Why does she look so happy?"

His dullness of mind became so obvious that Léa, who was now delivering a monologue on the advisability of buying old Berthellemy's yacht, stopped short:

"Would anyone expect him to give me even an opinion? Oh, you're always just twelve years old!"

Chéri, freed from his stupor, passed his hand over his forehead, and gave Léa a melancholy glance.

"With you, Nursie, I have every chance of staying twelve years old for half a century."

She blinked her eyes several times as if he had breathed on her eyelids, and she let a silence fall between them.

"What do you mean?" she asked finally.

— Rien que ce que je dis, Nounoune. Rien que la vérité. Peux-tu la nier, toi qui es un honnête homme?"

Elle prit le parti de rire, avec une désinvolture qui cachait déjà une grande crainte.

"Mais c'est la moitié de ton charme, petite bête, que cet enfantil-lage! Ce sera plus tard le secret de ta jeunesse sans fin. Et tu t'en plains! . . . Et tu as le toupet de venir t'en plaindre à moi!

— Oui, Nounoune. A qui veux-tu que je m'en plaigne?"

Il lui reprit la main qu'elle avait retirée.

"Ma Nounoune chérie, ma grande Nounoune, je ne fais pas que me plaindre, je t'accuse."

Elle sentait sa main serrée dans une main ferme. Et les grands yeux sombres aux cils lustrés, au lieu de fuir les siens, s'attachaient à eux misérablement. Elle ne voulut pas trembler encore.

"C'est peu de chose, peu de chose. . . . Il ne faut que deux ou trois paroles bien sèches auxquelles il répondra par quelque grosse injure, puis il boudera et je lui pardonnerai. . . . Ce n'est que cela. . . ." Mais elle ne trouva pas la semonce urgente, qui eût changé l'expression de ce regard.

"Allons, allons, petit. . . . Tu sais qu'il y a certaines plaisanteries que je ne tolère pas longtemps."

En même temps elle jugeait mou et faux le son de sa voix: "Que c'est mal dit. . . . C'est dit en mauvais théâtre. . . ." Le soleil de dix heures et demie atteignit la table qui les séparait, et les ongles polis de Léa brillèrent. Mais le rayon éclaira aussi ses grandes mains bien faites et cisela dans la peau relâchée et douce, sur le dos de la main, autour du poignet, des lacis compliqués, des sillons concentriques, des parallélogrammes minuscules comme ceux que la sécheresse grave, après les pluies, dans la terre argileuse. Léa se frotta les mains d'un air distrait, en tournant la tête pour attirer vers la rue l'attention de Chéri; mais il persista dans sa contemplation canine et misérable. Brusquement il conquit les deux mains honteuses qui faisaient sem-blant de jouer avec un pan de ceinture, les baisa et les rebaisa, puis y coucha sa joue en murmurant:

"Ma Nounoune . . . ô ma pauvre Nounoune. . . .

— Laisse-moi!" cria-t-elle avec une colère inexplicable, en lui ar-rachant ses mains.

Elle mit un moment à se dompter, et s'épouvanta de sa faiblesse, car elle avait failli éclater en sanglots. Dès qu'elle le put, elle parla et sourit:

"Just what I say, Nursie. Just the truth. Can you deny it, honest fellow that you are?"

She decided it was best to laugh, but her nonchalance already concealed a great fear.

"But that childishness is half of your charm, silly boy! Later on, it'll be the secret of your eternal youth. And you complain about it! . . . And you have the nerve to come complaining about it to me!"

"Yes, who else should I complain to?"

He took back the hand she had drawn away.

"Darling Nursie, big Nursie, I'm not only complaining, I'm accusing you."

She felt her hand held tightly in his firm hand. And his large dark eyes with their shiny lashes were no longer avoiding hers, but were staring at them unhappily. She tried not to begin trembling.

"It's nothing much, nothing much . . . I just have to say two or three words very curtly; he'll answer with some coarse insult; then he'll sulk and I'll forgive him . . . There's no more to it than that . . ." But she couldn't come up with the urgent reprimand that would change the expression in his eyes.

"Come now, come now, my boy . . . You know that there are certain jokes I won't put up with for very long."

But, at the same time, she found the sound of her voice flabby and false: "What a bad line . . . It's like a line from a bad play . . ." The ten-thirty sunshine reached the table that was separating them, and Léa's polished nails shone. But the sunbeam also illuminated her large, shapely hands, and on the soft loose skin on the back of the hand, and around the wrist, it engraved complicated networks, concentric furrows, and tiny parallelograms like those that dry weather engraves on clayey soil after a period of rain. Léa rubbed her hands together absentmindedly, turning her head to divert Chéri's attention to the street; but he maintained his doglike, unhappy scrutiny. Brusquely he seized the two shameful hands that had been pretending to play with one end of a belt; he kissed them once, twice, then laid his cheek on them, murmuring:

"My Nursie . . . oh, my poor Nursie . . ."

"Let me go!" she shouted in unexplainable anger, pulling away her hands.

It took her a minute to get control of herself, and she was frightened at her weakness, because she had almost burst out sobbing. As soon as she was able, she said with a smile:

"Alors, tu me plains, maintenant? Pourquoi m'accusais-tu tout à l'heure?

— J'avais tort, dit-il humblement. Toi, tu as été pour moi. . . ."

Il fit un geste qui exprimait son impuissance à trouver des mots dignes d'elle.

"*Tu as été!* souligna-t-elle d'un ton mordant. En voilà un style d'oraison funèbre, mon petit garçon!

— Tu vois . . ." reprocha-t-il.

Il secoua la tête, et elle vit bien qu'elle ne le fâcherait pas. Elle tendait tous ses muscles, et bridait ses pensées à l'aide de deux ou trois mots toujours les mêmes, répétés au fond d'elle: "Il est là, devant moi. . . . Voyons, il est toujours là. . . . Il n'est pas hors d'atteinte. . . . Mais est-il encore là, devant moi, véritablement? . . ."

Sa pensée échappa à cette discipline rythmique et une grande lamentation intérieure remplaça les mots conjuratoires: "Oh! que l'on me rende, que l'on me rende seulement l'instant où je lui ai dit: "Ta seconde tartine, Chéri?" Cet instant-là est encore si près de nous, il n'est pas perdu à jamais, il n'est pas encore dans le passé! Reprenons notre vie à cet instant-là, le peu qui a eu lieu depuis ne comptera pas, je l'efface, je l'efface. . . . Je vais lui parler tout à fait comme si nous étions quelques minutes plus tôt, je vais lui parler, voyons, du départ, des bagages. . . ."

Elle parla en effet, et dit:

"Je vois. . . . Je vois que je ne peux pas traiter en homme un être qui est capable, par veulerie, de mettre le désarroi chez deux femmes. Croix-tu que je ne comprenne pas? En fait de voyage, tu les aimes courts, hein? Hier à Neuilly, aujourd'hui ici, mais demain. . . . Où donc, demain? Ici? Non, non, mon petit, pas la peine de mentir, cette figure de condamné ne tromperait même pas une plus bête que moi, s'il y en a une par là. . . ."

Son geste violent, qui désignait la direction de Neuilly, renversa une jatte à gâteaux que Chéri redressa. A mesure qu'elle parlait, elle accroissait son mal, le changeait en un chagrin cuisant, agressif et jaloux, un chagrin bavard de jeune femme. Le fard, sur ses joues, devenait lie-de-vin, une mèche de cheveux, tordue par le fer, descendit sur sa nuque comme un petit serpent sec.

"Même celle de par là, même ta femme, tu ne la retrouveras pas toutes les fois chez toi, quand il te plaira de rentrer! Une femme, mon petit, on ne sait pas bien comment ça se prend, mais on sait encore moins comment ça se déprend! . . . Tu la feras garder par Charlotte, la tienne, hein? C'est une idée, ça! Ah! je rirai bien, le jour où. . . ."

"So now you're pitying me? Why were you accusing me a little while ago?"

"I was wrong," he said humbly. "For me, you were . . ."

A gesture of his expressed his inability to find words worthy of her.

"'You were!'" she said caustically and with emphasis. "There's an expression out of a funeral eulogy for you, youngster!"

"See!" he said reproachfully.

He shook his head, and she saw clearly that she wasn't going to make him angry. She tensed all her muscles and curbed her thoughts by repeating the same few phrases again and again in her mind: "He's here in front of me . . . See, he's still here . . . He isn't out of reach . . . But is he really here in front of me? . . ."

Her thoughts escaped from that rhythmically imposed discipline, and a great inner lamentation replaced the words she had been pronouncing like a charm: "Oh, if I could return, if I could only return to the moment when I said to him, 'Another slice of toast, Chéri?' That moment is still so close to us, it isn't lost forever, it's not yet in the past! Let's continue our life as it was at that moment, the little bit that has elapsed since then won't count; I erase it, I erase it . . . I'll speak to him exactly as if it were a few minutes ago; let's see, I'll talk to him about our departure, his belongings . . ."

In fact, she did speak:

"I see . . . I see that I can't treat like a man a being who is capable, out of inertia, of disrupting the lives of two women. Do you think I don't understand? When it comes to trips, you like short ones, right? Yesterday in Neuilly, today here, but tomorrow . . . Where will it be tomorrow? Here? No, no, my boy, don't bother to lie; that condemned-man's expression on your face wouldn't even fool a stupider woman than I am, if there is one in those parts . . ."

Her violent gesture, which indicated the direction of Neuilly, knocked over a cake dish, which Chéri set right again. While she spoke, she was aggravating her sorrow, transforming it into a burning, aggressive, jealous chagrin, a chagrin as voluble as a young woman's. The rouge on her cheeks was turning purple, and a lock of her hair that had been curled with the iron fell down onto the back of her neck like a little wiry snake.

"Even the woman over there, even your wife—you won't always find her home any time you feel like returning! My boy, no one knows how a wife is won, but they know even less how she's lost! . . . Are you going to have yours guarded by Charlotte—are you? There's an idea for you! Oh, what a laugh I'll have on the day when . . ."

Chéri se leva, pâle et sérieux:

"Nounoune! . . .

— Quoi, Nounoune? quoi, Nounoune? Penses-tu que tu vas me faire peur? Ah! tu veux marcher tout seul? Marche! Tu es sûr de voir du pays, avec une fille de Marie-Laure! Elle n'a pas de bras, et le derrière plat, mais ça ne l'empêchera guère. . . .

— Je te défends, Nounoune! . . ."

Il lui saisit les deux bras, mais elle se leva, se dégagea avec vigueur, et éclata d'un rire enroué:

"Mais bien sûr! "Je te défends de dire un mot contre ma femme!" N'est-ce pas?"

Il fit le tour de la table et vint tout près d'elle, tremblant d'indignation:

"Non! Je te défends, m'entends-tu bien, je te défends de m'abîmer ma Nounoune!"

Elle recula vers le fond de la chambre en balbutiant:

"Comment ça? . . . Comment ça? . . ."

Il la suivait, comme prêt à la châtier:

"Oui! Est-ce que c'est ainsi que Nounoune doit parler? Qu'est-ce que c'est que ces manières? Des sales petites injures genre madame Peloux, maintenant? Et ça sort de toi, toi Nounoune! . . ."

Il rejeta la tête en arrière orgueilleusement:

"Moi, je sais comment doit parler Nounoune! Je sais comment elle doit penser! J'ai eu le temps de l'apprendre. Je n'ai pas oublié le jour où tu me disais, un peu avant que je n'épouse cette petite: "Au moins ne sois pas méchant. . . . Essaie de ne pas faire souffrir. . . . J'ai un peu l'impression qu'on laisse une biche à un lévrier. . . ." Voilà des paroles! Ça, c'est toi! Et la veille de mon mariage, quand je me suis échappé pour venir te voir, je me rappelle, tu m'as dit. . . ."

La voix lui manqua, tous ses traits s'éclairèrent au feu d'un souvenir:

"Chérie, va. . . ."

Il posa ses mains sur les épaules de Léa:

"Et cette nuit encore, reprit-il, est-ce qu'un de tes premiers soucis n'a pas été pour me demander si je n'avais pas fait trop de mal *là-bas*? Ma Nounoune, chic type je t'ai connue, chic type je t'ai aimée, quand nous avons commencé. S'il nous faut finir, vas-tu pour cela ressembler aux autres femmes? . . ."

Elle sentit confusément la ruse sous l'hommage, et s'assit en cachant son visage entre ses mains:

Chéri stood up, pale and serious:

"Nursie! . . ."

"What's with 'Nursie'? What's with 'Nursie'? Do you expect to frighten me? Oh, you want to strike out on your own? Go! You're sure to see a lot of action, with a daughter of Marie-Laure as your wife! Her arms are flimsy and her behind is flat, but that will hardly stop her from . . ."

"I forbid you, Nursie! . . ."

He gripped both of her arms, but she stood up, tore herself loose vigorously, and burst into hoarse laughter:

"Naturally! 'I forbid you to say one word against my wife!' Isn't that it?"

He walked around the table and came right up to her, trembling with indignation:

"No! I forbid you—do you hear me?—I forbid you to spoil my Nursie for me!"

She stepped backward far into the room, stammering:

"How's that? . . . How's that? . . ."

He was following her, as if ready to deal out physical punishment:

"Yes! Is that the way Nursie should talk? What kind of manners are these? Nasty little insults in Madame Peloux's style now? Coming from you, from you, Nursie? . . ."

He threw back his head proudly:

"*I* know how Nursie should talk! I know how she should think! I've had the time to learn. I haven't forgotten the day when you told me, shortly before I married the girl: 'At least don't be cruel . . . Try not to make her suffer . . . I have the impression to some extent that a doe is being handed over to a greyhound . . .' That's talking! That's you! And the night before my wedding, when I ran away to visit you, I recall you told me . . ."

His voice failed him; all his features were brightened by the flame of a recollection:

"Come, darling . . ."

He placed his hands on Léa's shoulders.

"And even last night," he continued, "wasn't one of your first concerns to ask me whether I hadn't done too much damage 'in the other place'? My Nursie, I've known you all along to be a wonderful person, I loved you as a wonderful person when we took up together. If we have to break up, is that any reason for you to act like other women? . . ."

She had a vague sense that there was a ruse concealed in his compliments, and she sat down, hiding her face in her hands:

"Que tu es dur, que tu es dur . . . bégaya-t-elle. Pourquoi es-tu revenu? . . . J'étais si calme, si seule, si habituée à. . . ."

Elle s'entendit mentir, et s'interrompit.

"Pas moi! riposta Chéri. Je suis revenu parce que . . . parce que. . . ."

Il écarta les bras, les laissa retomber, les rouvrit:

"Parce que je ne pouvais plus me passer de toi, ce n'est pas la peine de chercher autre chose."

Ils demeurèrent silencieux un instant.

Elle contemplait, affaissée, ce jeune homme impatient, blanc comme une mouette, dont les pieds légers et les bras ouverts semblaient prêts pour l'essor. . . .

Les yeux sombres de Chéri erraient au-dessus d'elle.

"Ah! tu peux te vanter, dit-il soudain, tu peux te vanter de m'avoir, depuis trois mois surtout, fait mener une vie . . . une vie. . . .

— Moi? . . .

— Et qui donc, sinon toi? Une porte qui s'ouvre, c'était Nounoune; le téléphone, c'était Nounoune; une lettre dans la boîte du jardin: peut-être Nounoune. . . . Jusque dans le vin que je buvais, je te cherchais, et je ne trouvais jamais le Pommery de chez toi. . . . Et la nuit, donc. . . . Ah! là là! . . ."

Il marchait très vite et sans aucun bruit, de long en large, sur le tapis.

"Je peux le dire, que je sais ce que c'est que de souffrir pour une femme, oui! Je les attends, à présent, celles d'après toi . . . poussières! Ah! que tu m'avais bien empoisonné! . . ."

Elle se redressait lentement, suivait, d'un balancement du buste, le va-et-vient de Chéri. Elle avait les pommettes sèches et luisantes, d'un rouge fiévreux qui rendait le bleu de ses yeux presque insoutenable. Il marchait, la tête penchée, et ne cessait de parler.

"Tu penses, Neuilly sans toi, les premiers temps de mon retour! D'ailleurs, tout sans toi. . . . Je serais devenu fou. Un soir, la petite était malade, je ne sais plus quoi, des douleurs, des névralgies. . . . Elle me faisait peine, mais je suis sorti de la chambre parce que rien au monde ne m'aurait empêché de lui dire: "Attends, ne pleure pas, je vais aller chercher Nounoune qui te guérira. . . ." D'ailleurs tu serais venue, n'est-ce pas, Nounoune? . . . Oh! là là, cette vie. . . . A l'Hôtel Morris, j'avais embauché Desmond, bien payé, et je lui en racontais, quelquefois, la nuit. . . . Je lui disais, comme s'il ne te connaissait pas: "Mon vieux, une peau comme la sienne, ça n'existe pas. . . . Et tu vois ton cabochon de saphir, eh bien, mon vieux, cache-le, parce que le bleu de ses yeux, à elle, il ne tourne pas au gris aux lu-

"How unkind you are, how unkind you are . . . ," she stammered. "Why did you come back? . . . I was so calm, so self-sufficient, so used to . . ."

She realized she was lying, and she broke off.

"Not me!" Chéri replied. "I came back because . . . because . . ."

He opened his arms wide, let them drop, then opened them again:

"Because I couldn't do without you anymore. There's no use in my trying to come up with anything else."

They remained silent for a moment.

Sunk in depression, she was observing the impatient young man, who was as white as a sea gull, his light feet and open arms seemingly ready to take off in flight . . .

Chéri's dark eyes were wandering somewhere over her head.

"Oh, you can boast," he suddenly said, "you can boast that, for the last three months especially, you've made me lead a life . . . a life . . ."

"I?"

"Who else if not you? A door opened—it was Nursie. The phone rang—it was Nursie. There was a letter in the garden mailbox—maybe from Nursie . . . I looked for you even in the wine I drank, and I never found the Pommery that I got at your place . . . And at night . . . Oh, my! . . ."

He was walking very fast and noiselessly, to and fro, on the carpet.

"Believe me, I know what it is to suffer for a woman, I do! Now I'm waiting for the ones who'll come after you . . . they'll be ciphers! Oh, you really poisoned me! . . ."

She was slowly straightening up and following Chéri's comings and goings with a swinging of her body. Her cheeks were dry and shiny, their feverish red making the blue of her eyes nearly unbearable to look at. He was walking with his head bowed, and talking continuously.

"Imagine what Neuilly was like without you, the first days after I returned! Besides, everything was without you . . . I nearly went crazy. One night, my wife was ill, I don't remember what was wrong, aches, neuralgia . . . I felt sorry for her, but I walked out of the bedroom because nothing in the world could have prevented me from telling her: 'Wait, don't cry, I'll go fetch Nursie and she'll make you well . . .' And you would have come, too, wouldn't you, Nursie? . . . Oh, my, that life . . . At the Hotel Morris I had hired Desmond, at a good salary, and sometimes at night I used to tell him about you . . . I'd say to him, as if he didn't know you: 'My friend, a skin like hers is to be found nowhere else . . . And you see your cabochon sapphire? Well, my friend, hide it away, because the blue of her eyes doesn't take on a

mières!" Et je lui disais comme tu étais rossarde quand tu voulais, et que personne n'avait le dernier avec toi, pas plus moi que les autres. . . . Je lui disais: "Cette femme-là, mon vieux, quand elle a le chapeau qu'il lui faut" — ton bleu marine avec des ailes, Nounoune, de l'autre été — "et la manière de s'habiller qu'elle a, tu peux mettre n'importe quelle femme à côté, tout fout le camp!" Et puis tes manières épatantes de parler, de marcher, ton sourire, ta démarche qui fait chic, je lui disais, à Desmond: "Ah! ce n'est pas rien, qu'une femme comme Léa! . . ."

Il claqua des doigts, avec une fierté de propriétaire, et s'arrêta, essoufflé, de parler et de marcher.

"Je n'ai jamais dit tout ça à Desmond, songea-t-il. Et pourtant ce n'est pas un mensonge que je fais là. Desmond a compris tout de même." Il voulut reprendre et regarda Léa. Elle l'écoutait encore. Assise très droite à présent, elle lui montrait en pleine lumière son visage noble et défait, ciré par de cuisantes larmes séchées. Un poids invisible tirait en bas le menton et les joues, attristait les coins tremblants de la bouche. Dans ce naufrage de la beauté, Chéri retrouvait, intacts, le joli nez dominateur, les prunelles d'un bleu de fleur bleue. . . .

"Alors, n'est-ce pas, Nounoune, après des mois de cette vie-là, j'arrive ici, et. . . ."

Il s'arrêta, effrayé de ce qu'il avait failli dire.

"Tu arrives ici, et tu trouves une vieille femme, dit Léa d'une voix faible et tranquille.

— Nounoune! Écoute, Nounoune! . . ."

Il se jeta à genoux contre elle, laissant voir sur son visage la lâcheté d'un enfant qui ne trouve plus de mots pour cacher une faute.

"Et tu trouves une vieille femme, répéta Léa. De quoi donc as-tu peur, petit?"

Elle entoura de son bras les épaules de Chéri, sentit le raidissement, la défense de ce corps qui souffrait parce qu'elle était blessée.

"Viens donc, mon Chéri. . . . De quoi as-tu peur? De m'avoir fait de la peine? Ne pleure pas, ma beauté. . . . Comme je te remercie, au contraire. . . ."

Il fit un gémissement de protestation et se débattit sans force. Elle inclina sa joue sur les cheveux noirs emmêlés.

"Tu as dit tout cela, tu as pensé tout cela de moi? J'étais donc si belle à tes yeux, dis? Si bonne? A l'âge où tant de femmes ont fini de vivre, j'étais pour toi la plus belle, la meilleure des femmes, et tu

gray cast in strong light!' And I used to tell him how bitchy you could be when you wanted to, and how no one could get the last word with you, not me or anyone else . . . I'd tell him: 'My friend, when that woman is wearing the hat that's just right for her'—your navy blue with a brim, Nursie, from last summer—'with her way of carrying clothes, you can put any other woman next to her, and she'll make them all disappear!' And then your terrific way of talking and walking, your smile, your stylish way of holding yourself . . . I'd say to Desmond: 'Oh, a woman like Léa is really something! . . .'"

He snapped his fingers with proprietary pride, and, out of breath, he stopped both walking and talking.

"I never said all that to Desmond," he thought to himself. "But I'm not lying right now. Desmond understood, anyway." He intended to continue, and he looked at Léa. She was still paying attention. Seated very erectly now, she was showing him in direct light her noble but ravaged face, on which the dry trace of hot tears shone. An unseen weight was pulling down her chin and her cheeks, and was making the trembling corners of her mouth look sad. In that wreckage of beauty Chéri rediscovered intact her pretty, domineering nose and her irises, as blue as a blue flower . . .

"Well, you see, Nursie, after months of a life like that, I get here, and . . ."

He stopped, frightened at what he had almost said.

"You get here, and you find an old woman," Léa said in a weak but calm voice.

"Nursie! Listen, Nursie! . . ."

He fell on his knees, leaning against her, revealing on his face the cowardice of a child that can no longer find the words to cover up a wrongdoing.

"And you find an old woman," Léa repeated. "So what are you afraid of, child?"

She put an arm around Chéri's shoulders, feeling the defensive stiffening of his body, which was suffering because she was hurt.

"Come now, my Chéri . . . what are you afraid of? Of having wounded me? Don't cry, beauty . . . On the contrary, I'm so grateful to you . . ."

He uttered a moan in protest, and struggled weakly. She rested her cheek on his tangled black hair.

"You said all that, and thought all that, about me? And I was so beautiful in your eyes, yes? So kind? At the age when so many women's lives are over, I was for you the most beautiful and the best

m'aimais? Comme je te remercie, mon chéri. . . . La plus chic, tu as dit? . . . Pauvre petit. . . ."

Il s'abandonnait et elle le soutenait entre ses bras.

"Si j'avais été la plus chic, j'aurais fait de toi un homme, au lieu de ne penser qu'au plaisir de ton corps, et au mien. La plus chic, non, non, je ne l'étais pas, mon chéri, puisque je te gardais. Et c'est bien tard. . . ."

Il semblait dormir dans les bras de Léa, mais ses paupières obstinément jointes tressaillaient sans cesse et il s'accrochait, d'une main immobile et fermée, au peignoir qui se déchirait lentement.

"C'est bien tard, c'est bien tard. . . . Tout de même. . . ."

Elle se pencha sur lui.

"Mon chéri, écoute-moi. Éveille-toi, ma beauté. Écoute-moi les yeux ouverts. N'aie pas peur de me voir. Je suis tout de même cette femme que tu as aimée, tu sais, la plus chic des femmes. . . ."

Il ouvrit les yeux, et son premier regard mouillé était déjà plein d'un espoir égoïste et suppliant. Léa détourna la tête: "Ses yeux. . . . Ah! faisons vite. . . ." Elle reposa sa joue sur le front de Chéri.

"C'était moi, petit, c'était bien moi cette femme qui t'a dit: "Ne fais pas de mal inutilement, épargne la biche. . . ." Je ne m'en souvenais plus. Heureusement tu y as pensé. Tu te détaches bien tard de moi, mon nourrisson méchant, je t'ai porté trop longtemps contre moi, et voilà que tu en as lourd à porter à ton tour: une jeune femme, peut-être un enfant. . . . Je suis responsable de tout ce qui te manque. . . . Oui, oui, ma beauté, te voilà, grâce à moi, à vingt-cinq ans, si léger, si gâté et si sombre à la fois. . . . J'en ai beaucoup de souci. Tu vas souffrir, — tu vas faire souffrir. Toi qui m'as aimée. . . ."

La main qui déchirait lentement son peignoir se crispa et Léa sentit sur son sein les griffes du nourrisson méchant.

". . . Toi qui m'as aimée, reprit-elle après une pause, pourras-tu. . . . Je ne sais comment me faire comprendre. . . ."

Il s'écarta d'elle pour l'écouter; et elle faillit lui crier: "Remets cette main sur ma poitrine et tes ongles dans leur marque, ma force me quitte dès que ta chair s'éloigne de moi!" Elle s'appuya à son tour sur lui qui s'était agenouillé devant elle, et continua.

"Toi qui m'as aimée, toi qui me regretteras. . . ."

Elle lui sourit et le regarda dans les yeux.

"Hein, quelle vanité! . . . Toi qui me regretteras, je voudrais que, quand tu te sentiras près d'épouvanter la biche qui est ton bien, qui est ta charge, tu te retiennes, et que tu inventes à ces

of women, and you loved me? How grateful I am to you, darling . . .
The most wonderful person, you said? . . . Poor boy . . ."

He grew limp and she supported him in her arms.

"If I had been such a wonderful person, I would have made a man
of you, instead of merely thinking about the pleasure of your body and
mine. The most wonderful woman, no, no, I wasn't, darling, because
I held onto you. And now it's too late . . ."

He seemed to be asleep in Léa's arms, but his stubbornly shut eyelids were constantly quivering, and with one motionless closed hand
he was gripping her peignoir, which was slowly tearing.

"It's too late, it's too late . . . Even so . . ."

She bent over him.

"Darling, listen. Wake up, beauty. Listen to me with your eyes
open. Don't be afraid to look at me. I'm still the woman you loved, you
know, the most wonderful person . . ."

He opened his eyes, and his first tearful glance was already filled with
a selfish, beseeching hope. Léa turned away her head: "His eyes . . . Oh,
let's get this over with fast . . ." She rested her cheek on Chéri's forehead.

"It was I, child, really I, that woman who told you: 'Don't be need-
lessly cruel, show mercy to the doe . . .' I had forgotten my own advice.
Fortunately you remembered. You're being weaned from me very belatedly, my nasty infant, I've carried you on my breast far too long, and
now in your turn you've got a lot to carry: a young wife, perhaps a child
. . . I'm to blame for all that you lack . . . Yes, yes, beauty: because of
me, here you are at twenty-five, so lightweight, so spoiled, and so
somber all at the same time . . . I feel very sorry about it. You're going
to suffer—you're going to make others suffer. You who loved me . . ."

The hand that was slowly tearing her peignoir clenched tightly, and
Léa felt on her breast the claws of the nasty infant.

"You who loved me," she went on after a pause, "will you be able
. . . I don't know how to make you understand me . . ."

He moved away from her to listen, and she came close to shouting
to him: "Put your hand back on my breast and your nails back in their
traces! My strength deserts me the moment your flesh pulls away
from me!" Now it was she who was leaning on him, as he knelt down
in front of her; she went on:

"You who loved me, you who will miss me . . ."

She smiled at him and looked into his eyes.

"Ah, what vanity! . . . You who will miss me, whenever you feel that
you're coming close to frightening that doe who is yours to own, yours
to protect, I want you to restrain yourself. At moments like that I want

instants-là tout ce que je ne t'ai pas appris. . . . Je ne t'ai jamais parlé de l'avenir. Pardonne-moi, Chéri: je t'ai aimé comme si nous devions, l'un et l'autre, mourir l'heure d'après. Parce que je suis née vingt-quatre ans avant toi, j'étais condamnée, et je t'entraînais avec moi. . . ."

Il l'écoutait avec une attention qui lui donnait l'air dur. Elle passa sa main sur le front inquiet, pour en effacer le pli.

"Tu nous vois, Chéri, allant déjeuner ensemble, à Armenonville? . . . Tu nous vois invitant Madame et Monsieur Lili? . . ."

Elle rit tristement et frissonna.

"Ah! Je suis aussi finie que cette vieille. . . . Vite, vite, petit, va chercher ta jeunesse, elle n'est qu'écornée par les dames mûres, il t'en reste, il lui en reste à cette enfant qui t'attend. Tu y as goûté, à la jeunesse! Tu sais qu'elle ne contente pas, mais qu'on y retourne. . . . Eh! ce n'est pas de cette nuit que tu as commencé à comparer. . . . Et qu'est-ce que je fais là, moi, à donner des conseils et à montrer ma grandeur d'âme? Qu'est-ce que je sais de vous deux? Elle t'aime: c'est son tour de trembler, elle souffrira comme une amoureuse et non pas comme une maman dévoyée. Tu lui parleras en maître, mais pas en gigolo capricieux. . . . Va, va vite. . . ."

Elle parlait sur un ton de supplication précipitée. Il l'écoutait debout, campé devant elle, la poitrine nue, les cheveux en tempête, si tentant qu'elle noua l'une à l'autre ses mains qui allaient le saisir. Il la devina peut-être et ne se déroba pas. Un espoir, imbécile comme celui qui peut atteindre, pendant leur chute, les gens qui tombent d'une tour, brilla entre eux et s'évanouit.

"Va, dit-elle à voix basse. Je t'aime. C'est trop tard. Va-t'en. Mais va-t'en tout de suite. Habille-toi."

Elle se leva et lui apporta ses chaussures, disposa la chemise froissée, les chaussettes. Il tournait sur place et remuait gauchement les doigts comme s'il avait l'onglée, et elle dut trouver elle-même les bretelles, la cravate; mais elle évita de s'approcher de lui et ne l'aida pas. Pendant qu'il s'habillait, elle regarda fréquemment dans la cour comme si elle attendait une voiture.

Vêtu, il parut plus pâle, avec des yeux qu'élargissait un halo de fatigue.

"Tu ne te sens pas malade?" lui demanda-t-elle. Et elle ajouta timidement, les yeux bas: "Tu pourrais . . . te reposer. . . ." Mais tout de suite elle se reprit et revint à lui comme s'il était dans un grand péril: "Non, non, tu seras mieux chez toi. . . . Rentre vite, il n'est pas midi, un bon bain chaud te remettra, et puis le grand air. . . . Tiens tes

you to discover for yourself all that I failed to teach you . . . I've never spoken to you about the future. Forgive me, Chéri: I loved you as if we were both going to die immediately afterward. Because I was born twenty-four years before you, I was a condemned woman, and I was dragging you down with me . . ."

He was listening so attentively that he looked cruel. She passed her hand over his worried forehead to rub away the crease in it.

"Can you picture us, Chéri, going for lunch together to Armenonville? . . . Can you picture us inviting over Madame and Monsieur Lili? . . ."

He laughed sadly and shivered.

"Oh, I'm as done for as that old woman is . . . Quickly, boy, quickly, go and look for your youth, which has only been slightly damaged by older women. There's much more of it left for you and for that girl who's waiting for you. You've had a taste of her youth! You know that it isn't completely satisfying, but that one keeps coming back to it . . . Well, it wasn't just last night that you began to make the comparison . . . And what am *I* doing here, giving advice and showing how noble I am? What do I know about you two? She loves you: it's her turn to tremble; she'll suffer like a woman in love, not like a perverted mother. Speak to her as a master, but not as a capricious gigolo . . . Go, go quickly . . ."

She was speaking in a tone of hasty supplication. He was listening on his feet, planted in front of her, his chest bare, his hair tousled, looking so tempting that she clasped her hands, which were about to take hold of him. He may have guessed her feelings, and he didn't flinch. A ray of hope, as mindless as the hope that may be felt by people in mid-air as they fall from a tower, flashed between them and vanished.

"Go," she said quietly. "I love you. It's too late. Leave. But leave right away. Get dressed."

She got up, brought him his shoes, and laid out his wrinkled shirt and his socks. He was turning around in circles, clumsily wiggling his fingers as if they were numb with cold, and she had to find his suspenders and tie herself; but she took care not to go near him, and she didn't help him. While he was dressing, she frequently looked down at the courtyard, as if she were expecting a carriage to arrive.

Once dressed, he looked paler; his eyes were widened by an aura of fatigue.

"You don't feel ill?" she asked. And she added timidly, her eyes downcast: "You could . . . rest . . ." But immediately she got hold of herself, and addressed him as if he were in great danger: "No, no, you'll be better off at home . . . Go home quickly, it isn't noon yet; a good bath will set you up, and then the fresh air . . . Take your gloves

gants. . . . Ah! oui, ton chapeau par terre. . . . Passe ton pardessus, l'air te surprendrait. Au revoir, mon Chéri, au revoir. . . . C'est ça. . . . Tu diras à Charlotte. . . ." Elle referma sur lui la porte et le silence mit fin à ses vaines paroles désespérées. Elle entendit que Chéri butait dans l'escalier, et elle courut à la fenêtre. Il descendait le perron et s'arrêta au milieu de la cour.

"Il remonte! il remonte!" cria-t-elle en levant les bras.

Une vieille femme haletante répéta, dans le miroir oblong, son geste, et Léa se demanda ce qu'elle pouvait avoir de commun avec cette folle.

Chéri reprit son chemin vers la rue, ouvrit la grille et sortit. Sur le trottoir il boutonna son pardessus pour cacher son linge de la veille. Léa laissa retomber le rideau. Mais elle eut encore le temps de voir que Chéri levait la tête vers le ciel printanier et les marronniers chargés de fleurs, et qu'en marchant il gonflait d'air sa poitrine, comme un évadé.

. . . Oh, yes, your hat's on the floor . . . Put on your overcoat, you might catch a sudden chill. So long, Chéri, so long . . . Right . . . Tell Charlotte . . ." She shut the door behind him, and the silence cut short her vain, despairing words. She heard Chéri stumble on the staircase, and she ran to the window. He was walking down the front steps, and he stopped in the middle of the courtyard.

"He's coming back up! He's coming back up!" she cried, raising her arms.

In the tall mirror a panting old woman made the same gesture, and Léa wondered what she could have in common with that wild creature.

Chéri resumed his walk to the street, opened the gate, and went out. On the sidewalk he buttoned his overcoat to conceal his day-old linens. Léa let the curtain fall again. But she still had enough time to see that Chéri was raising his head to the spring sky and the blossom-laden chestnut trees, and that, as he walked, he was filling his lungs with air, like an escaped prisoner.

A CATALOG OF SELECTED DOVER BOOKS IN ALL FIELDS OF INTEREST

100 BEST-LOVED POEMS, Edited by Philip Smith. "The Passionate Shepherd to His Love," "Shall I compare thee to a summer's day?" "Death, be not proud," "The Raven," "The Road Not Taken," plus works by Blake, Wordsworth, Byron, Shelley, Keats, many others. 96pp. 5$\frac{3}{16}$ x 8¼. 0-486-28553-7

100 SMALL HOUSES OF THE THIRTIES, Brown-Blodgett Company. Exterior photographs and floor plans for 100 charming structures. Illustrations of models accompanied by descriptions of interiors, color schemes, closet space, and other amenities. 200 illustrations. 112pp. 8⅜ x 11. 0-486-44131-8

1000 TURN-OF-THE-CENTURY HOUSES: With Illustrations and Floor Plans, Herbert C. Chivers. Reproduced from a rare edition, this showcase of homes ranges from cottages and bungalows to sprawling mansions. Each house is meticulously illustrated and accompanied by complete floor plans. 256pp. 9⅜ x 12¼. 0-486-45596-3

101 GREAT AMERICAN POEMS, Edited by The American Poetry & Literacy Project. Rich treasury of verse from the 19th and 20th centuries includes works by Edgar Allan Poe, Robert Frost, Walt Whitman, Langston Hughes, Emily Dickinson, T. S. Eliot, other notables. 96pp. 5$\frac{3}{16}$ x 8¼. 0-486-40158-8

101 GREAT SAMURAI PRINTS, Utagawa Kuniyoshi. Kuniyoshi was a master of the warrior woodblock print — and these 18th-century illustrations represent the pinnacle of his craft. Full-color portraits of renowned Japanese samurais pulse with movement, passion, and remarkably fine detail. 112pp. 8⅜ x 11. 0-486-46523-3

ABC OF BALLET, Janet Grosser. Clearly worded, abundantly illustrated little guide defines basic ballet-related terms: arabesque, battement, pas de chat, relevé, sissonne, many others. Pronunciation guide included. Excellent primer. 48pp. 4$\frac{3}{16}$ x 5¾. 0-486-40871-X

ACCESSORIES OF DRESS: An Illustrated Encyclopedia, Katherine Lester and Bess Viola Oerke. Illustrations of hats, veils, wigs, cravats, shawls, shoes, gloves, and other accessories enhance an engaging commentary that reveals the humor and charm of the many-sided story of accessorized apparel. 644 figures and 59 plates. 608pp. 6 ⅛ x 9¼. 0-486-43378-1

ADVENTURES OF HUCKLEBERRY FINN, Mark Twain. Join Huck and Jim as their boyhood adventures along the Mississippi River lead them into a world of excitement, danger, and self-discovery. Humorous narrative, lyrical descriptions of the Mississippi valley, and memorable characters. 224pp. 5$\frac{3}{16}$ x 8¼. 0-486-28061-6

ALICE STARMORE'S BOOK OF FAIR ISLE KNITTING, Alice Starmore. A noted designer from the region of Scotland's Fair Isle explores the history and techniques of this distinctive, stranded-color knitting style and provides copious illustrated instructions for 14 original knitwear designs. 208pp. 8⅜ x 10⅞. 0-486-47218-3

Browse over 9,000 books at www.doverpublications.com

CATALOG OF DOVER BOOKS

ALICE'S ADVENTURES IN WONDERLAND, Lewis Carroll. Beloved classic about a little girl lost in a topsy-turvy land and her encounters with the White Rabbit, March Hare, Mad Hatter, Cheshire Cat, and other delightfully improbable characters. 42 illustrations by Sir John Tenniel. 96pp. 5³⁄₁₆ x 8¼. 0-486-27543-4

AMERICA'S LIGHTHOUSES: An Illustrated History, Francis Ross Holland. Profusely illustrated fact-filled survey of American lighthouses since 1716. Over 200 stations — East, Gulf, and West coasts, Great Lakes, Hawaii, Alaska, Puerto Rico, the Virgin Islands, and the Mississippi and St. Lawrence Rivers. 240pp. 8 x 10¾.
0-486-25576-X

AN ENCYCLOPEDIA OF THE VIOLIN, Alberto Bachmann. Translated by Frederick H. Martens. Introduction by Eugene Ysaye. First published in 1925, this renowned reference remains unsurpassed as a source of essential information, from construction and evolution to repertoire and technique. Includes a glossary and 73 illustrations. 496pp. 6⅛ x 9¼. 0-486-46618-3

ANIMALS: 1,419 Copyright-Free Illustrations of Mammals, Birds, Fish, Insects, etc., Selected by Jim Harter. Selected for its visual impact and ease of use, this outstanding collection of wood engravings presents over 1,000 species of animals in extremely lifelike poses. Includes mammals, birds, reptiles, amphibians, fish, insects, and other invertebrates. 284pp. 9 x 12. 0-486-23766-4

THE ANNALS, Tacitus. Translated by Alfred John Church and William Jackson Brodribb. This vital chronicle of Imperial Rome, written by the era's great historian, spans A.D. 14-68 and paints incisive psychological portraits of major figures, from Tiberius to Nero. 416pp. 5³⁄₁₆ x 8¼. 0-486-45236-0

ANTIGONE, Sophocles. Filled with passionate speeches and sensitive probing of moral and philosophical issues, this powerful and often-performed Greek drama reveals the grim fate that befalls the children of Oedipus. Footnotes. 64pp. 5³⁄₁₆ x 8 ¼. 0-486-27804-2

ART DECO DECORATIVE PATTERNS IN FULL COLOR, Christian Stoll. Reprinted from a rare 1910 portfolio, 160 sensuous and exotic images depict a breathtaking array of florals, geometrics, and abstracts — all elegant in their stark simplicity. 64pp. 8⅜ x 11. 0-486-44862-2

THE ARTHUR RACKHAM TREASURY: 86 Full-Color Illustrations, Arthur Rackham. Selected and Edited by Jeff A. Menges. A stunning treasury of 86 full-page plates span the famed English artist's career, from *Rip Van Winkle* (1905) to masterworks such as *Undine, A Midsummer Night's Dream,* and *Wind in the Willows* (1939). 96pp. 8⅜ x 11.
0-486-44685-9

THE AUTHENTIC GILBERT & SULLIVAN SONGBOOK, W. S. Gilbert and A. S. Sullivan. The most comprehensive collection available, this songbook includes selections from every one of Gilbert and Sullivan's light operas. Ninety-two numbers are presented uncut and unedited, and in their original keys. 410pp. 9 x 12.
0-486-23482-7

THE AWAKENING, Kate Chopin. First published in 1899, this controversial novel of a New Orleans wife's search for love outside a stifling marriage shocked readers. Today, it remains a first-rate narrative with superb characterization. New introductory Note. 128pp. 5³⁄₁₆ x 8¼. 0-486-27786-0

BASIC DRAWING, Louis Priscilla. Beginning with perspective, this commonsense manual progresses to the figure in movement, light and shade, anatomy, drapery, composition, trees and landscape, and outdoor sketching. Black-and-white illustrations throughout. 128pp. 8⅜ x 11. 0-486-45815-6

Browse over 9,000 books at www.doverpublications.com